Lightning Rod

Richard Koehn

Published by Saor Publishing, 2025
Concordia, Kansas

Published by Saor Publishing

PO Box 7, Concordia, KS 66901

www.saorpublishing.com[1]

Library of Congress Control Number: 2024952512

Publisher's Cataloging-in-Publication Data

Koehn, Richard.

Lightning Rod / Richard Koehn.

—First edition.

382 pages ; 23 cm.

ISBN 979-8-9921978-1-5 (hardcover)

ISBN 979-8-9921978-0-8 (softcover)

ISBN 979-8-9921978-2-2 (digital)

1. Fiction—Family Drama. 2. Fiction—Psychological Fiction. 3. Fiction—Suspense.

I. Title.

Printed in the United States of America

10 9 8 7 6 5 4 3 2 1

1.　http://www.saorpublishing.com

Acknowledgments

Among these pages is evidence of a particular form of telepathy. A careful effort was made to communicate by sending the pictures to the reader's mind with clear descriptions, tried and true phrases, and vague suggestions. These are the joints and seams of the product. But the true value of the communication is reflected in the magic by which the final stroke was accomplished. It was the creative power induced by the support of my giving wife. The first to bring my failings in the work to my attention and set me on a more productive path. Loyal friends also supported my efforts along the way. It is they for whom I am thankful.

I also want to give special thanks to my son and daughter. Without them, the computer's relentless counterattack would have conquered me.

Prologue

Clad in his overalls and Mennonite beard, Sam Danziger strode down the path with purpose, his boots crunching on the gravel. He moved steadily from the expansive clearing where his mobile farm equipment was parked, winding past the side of the barn. As he rounded the corner, he approached the massive roll-away door, its imposing bulk marking the entrance to the barn's shadowy depths. He pushed on the edge of the heavy, wooden door with all his strength. He slowly and painfully put the stubborn structure in motion. He told himself the time to grease the rollers again was long overdue. He pushed on the door just long enough to provide an opening to squeeze his lean, thirty-four-year-old body.

The sunshine behind him sliced through the opening into the huge room. As he stepped forward onto that golden path, sunlit dust particles and tiny bits of straw appeared in its beam before him. They floated down from the cracks of the floorboards of the hayloft above. Sam looked up at the cracks between the boards and imagined rats or a coon busy doing something up there. He stopped and listened. With his head tilted back and his goatee jutting toward the far wall, he squinted at the widest crack, where dust and stray bits of hay trickled through. He listened for the sounds the intruder in his imagination would make but heard nothing. Maybe the sound of his movement had frozen the creature doing mischief in his hayloft. He clapped his hands twice and waited motionless. Everything up there was very quiet.

All he heard were the joyful sounds of his three oldest children playing on the tire swing hanging on a cottonwood behind the tool shed.

His other two children, eight-year-old Andrew and Lena, the youngest at five, were last seen by him an hour earlier. He supposed they were still playing with the four one-week-old puppies by the back porch and trying to name them.

The next moment, he was aware of the feeling of dust on his face and its throat-tickling smell. He realized that he had walked into a dust-fall. He rubbed his hand across his face and stroked his goatee to brush the dust away. He removed his straw hat and whacked it twice against the leg of his overalls. He pulled a ragged blue bandana from a back pocket and wiped the sweatband in his hat. The air felt good with free access to his thinly covered head. He wiped his forehead, replaced his hat, and continued toward the back of the room. The shovel he was after was in the corner of the back wall.

Someone sneezed. It was a dainty sneeze, which gave him the first impression that it came from outside. On second thought, there was much more to sneeze about in the loft than out in the yard. He reasoned it could be a child's sneeze.

He turned and stared again at the spot in the ceiling. His pulse rate quickened, and dread furrowed his brow. In his experiences, haylofts were near the top of his list of prime locations for the devil's workshop. He frowned at the thought that some children's misbehavior could be taking place up there right now. He walked to the ladder that took you up to the opening through which you entered the loft.

As he climbed the ladder, he realized he hadn't seen Andrew or Lena around for the last hour. He hoped it wasn't those two who were hiding from him after his noisy struggle with the barn door, but he wouldn't be surprised if it were.

My goodness! What if they were up there being naughty? What would he do, and what would he say to them? Looking up through the opening, he stopped climbing. He felt very uncomfortable with the possibility he imagined was before him. He turned his head and looked down the ladder to the floor below. He wished there was someone there of greater authority who could advise him. Or give him permission to climb back down and ignore what he imagined he was about to find.

He looked back up. No, they would need to be punished. It was his God-assigned responsibility. It was for the good of their development into God-fearing Christian adults. From early on, children need to be shown what they get for being naughty. You give the devil the slightest chance, and he'll have you from then on.

Convinced of his duty to his God, he continued up the ladder and poked himself up to his waist through the opening in the loft floor. He stopped and looked around the raftered room for any sign of life.

Neatly stacked bales of hay filled two-thirds of the room. Each stack of six bails was arranged to create walkways between them. It provided small, dark places to hide. He remained standing on the ladder for several seconds, looking and listening. "Is anyone up here?"

His voice, though at a volume only a little above his normal speaking voice, slapped the silence like a clap of thunder. The heavy silence stuffed the room and absorbed his words. He stood a moment longer, speaking to the dread in his heart. He told himself that he needn't be so alarmed. There was no one up there. The sneeze must have come from outside in the yard. He let a few more seconds pass.

Relieved, he started climbing back down to the ground floor. He had descended two steps when he heard her small voice. "Daddy, I'm scared."

His heart jumped. Dread came up into his throat. He swallowed hard. His worst fear took his breath, then quickened it. He quickly re-climbed the top few rungs of the ladder, stepped onto the loft floor, and called out, "Lena, where are you?"

She appeared from between stacks of hay bales and, head down, walked toward him. There were a few strands of straw stuck in her Dutch-yellow braided hair. Her bare feet, brown and chapped from exposure to the months of summer, stuck out from the hem of her flower-printed, homemade dress. Her steps made no sound as they carried her to her father across the smooth wooden loft floor. Her expression was wide-eyed, and she wore a serious frown.

He squatted down on the ball of one foot, resting a forearm on his thigh. She came to him quickly and put her arms around his neck. He held her close, saying, "Why are you scared, Lena?"

She spoke into his shoulder, making it hard to hear what she said, "I can't hear you with your face down there. Look at me and tell me what scared you."

She lifted her face to him. There were tears in her eyes, and her lower lip trembled. She whined, "Andrew said we had to hide cuz you was gonna kill us!"

All right, that's it, he told himself. *I know what they been doin'.* He hollered at the niche in the stacked hay from which Lena had emerged, "Andrew, get out here right now!"

Lena began to cry. He took her by the arm, whirled her away from him without letting go, and stood up. His tone was threatening. "I'm not gonna kill you because God will for what you've been doing," he spat.

Lena's crying became louder, and she tried to pull away from him. There was no sign of Andrew. "Don't make me come in there after you, Andrew. It will be a lot worse if I do!" He bent down to Lena. "And you be quiet, or I promise you a whippin' you'll never forget."

He stepped toward the opening between the hay bales where Lena had appeared, pulling her with him. As he got closer to the stack of bales, Lena began to cry harder and pulled back, nearly escaping his hold on her. Sam stopped to give her attempted escape his full attention.

That was when Andrew chose to bolt from his hiding place in the hay. He made it past his dad to the ladder easily. His dad hollered his name. He took four or five hurried steps down the ladder, lost his footing, and fell the rest of the way. It was a twelve-foot drop. He lay motionless on the concrete floor.

Andrew had disappeared from Sam's view, and he was unaware of Andrew's fall. He yelled at Andrew, "Get back here, Andrew! Don't you run from me!"

He started for the ladder, pulling Lena along. She was crying and struggling against her eventual confrontation with the Almighty and punisher of every sin, God. She knew He waited outside way up in the sky to reach down and strike her dead because her daddy said so. *Today, tomorrow, someday when you least expect it.* She heard of it happening to lots of sinners.

Suddenly, her father, who had reached the ladder, looked down, yelled Andrew's name, and released his hold on her wrist. The sudden release and lack of resistance caused her to fall backward onto the smooth, wooden loft floor and land on her butt, bumping her tailbone. Surprise and pain brought a scream from her throat. She saw her father disappearing through the opening to the room below, yelling, "Andrew? Andrew!"

She sat up and, still crying from the pain in her tailbone, crawled, hands and knees, to the ladder opening and looked down. Andrew lay on his back. Her father was kneeling beside him, trying to pick Andrew up, crying, "Andrew... oh Andrew! Dear God!"

Lena stopped crying as if she had never cried in her life. She got to her feet and ran back between the hay bales to the furthest dim corner. She scrunched up into a ball, hugging her legs with her forehead pressed to her knees. God had killed Andrew for what they did, and she was next.

Sarah Danziger was out on the back porch knocking the caked mud off Andrew's Sunday shoes with a table knife. She pounded on the heels and soles with the handle of the knife. Then she scraped the knife vigorously, in a whittling fashion, against the edge of the sole. The motion shook her head, dislodging strands of her long dark hair from its bobby-pinned black Mennonite head cover.

She didn't know how many times she had told Andrew to change out of his church clothes and shoes as soon as he got home from church.

Last Sunday, when he heard the rain start beating on the roof of the little Mennonite country church, he was beside himself with worry. He could hardly sit still, in a tizzy over the miniature pioneer settlement of roads, bridges, and dirt houses he had created the day before. He had spent all day Saturday on the "excavating," as he called it.

When they got home after church, he jumped out of the car and made a furious run through the muddy yard to see if he could save his creation.

A few minutes later, he had come to the house looking guilty. There was mud from his knees down. He was "so terribly sorry" and was "ready to take the lickin' I deserve."

"It doesn't matter no more anyway," he had said, standing before her, head bowed, hands in his pockets. He was resigned to his punishment for getting in the mud. He had lost his creation despite sacrificing obedience to his mother to save it. "Nothin' matters, not even life itself. The whole world turned to mud, just piles of mud." She couldn't bring herself to punish him after that.

Later, Sam expressed his displeasure with her in the dispensing of "constructive punishment." "You shouldna let him get away with it, Sarah. A good spankin' woulda let him know he must learn to obey those greater than he. When he's an adult, obeying God will be a lot easier. Besides, just plain ol' sinful pride made him disobey in the first place."

Sarah was convinced that since Andrew had endured so many spankings with the leather strap and still hadn't learned the consequences of disobedience, another one wouldn't make much difference. She had only thought that, though. To say that aloud to Sam Danziger would have been one of the more foolish things she'd done since her fifteen-year marriage to him.

She thought she heard some yelling by the barn but let its familiar presence in their rowdy family of three boys and two girls slip past her concern.

Then, she heard Sam yelling her name. The tone of his voice caused goose bumps to rise on her arms. Something was wrong! She dropped the shoe and table knife, moved quickly down the porch steps to the corner of the house, and looked toward the barn. Sam was carrying Andrew in his arms, running toward the pickup parked in the driveway. He hollered at her.

"Get in the pickup and drive. We need to get Andrew to the hospital!"

Sarah ran for the pickup. "What's wrong with him?" she cried. "What happened?

"He fell out of the loft!"

"Oh my God!"

Her words made Sam glance at her and frown.

They each reached the pickup at the same time, Sam at the passenger's door and she at the driver's door. She grabbed the door handle and jerked it open.

From the other side of the pickup, Sam yelled at her. "Sarah! What are you doing? You need to open the door for me! Hurry!"

She ran around the front of the pickup to the passenger's side. Sam stood waiting, holding Andrew. With wide stricken eyes, she saw her lifeless son's arms dangling limp, straight down toward the ground. Those eyes, those mother's eyes, were transfixed as she groaned at the sight of her precious son's death-pale face. She jerked the door open.

Sam struggled to get into the seat.

"Oh my God, Sam, his lips are turning blue! He's not breathing!" Her hand still gripped the door handle, and she began to jump up and down, screaming. "He's not breathing! Oh, my God, Sam, he's not breathing, he's not breathing! Oh my God! Andrew, Andrew!"

Sam saw her losing control. "Sarah!" he yelled. "Sarah! Control your tongue; you're using His name. Just get around in the pickup and drive! We gotta get to the hospital!"

Then, a sob broke out, twisting his face into anguish. "Please, Sarah! We have to hurry! Please! You have to drive!"

She heard the pain and the fear in the man who was her shelter, her footing, the sign pointing the way of her life. The sound slapped her back into the urgency of the moment. She slammed the door shut, ran around the front of the pickup to the driver's side, and threw herself into the seat behind the wheel. With a twist of the key, the engine responded immediately. She stomped the clutch, jerked the gear-shift lever into first gear, and accelerated into the yard. Turning in a wide circle, tires spinning, sand and dirt flying, the door slammed shut from the force of motion. The pickup sailed out onto the highway with no regard for the possibility of oncoming traffic. There simply was no time to have another accident. The hospital was twenty-five miles away in the neighboring town.

Neither was there any room in their alarmed minds for Lena, who had been forgotten. Left in a dark corner of the hayloft, she became someone else. Someone who would need to be better suited to deal with God's wrath.

Part 1

CHAPTER 1

Lena Danziger did not remember her brother's funeral, though it had been only nine years. What she remembered of that tragic time in her childhood was the night, and most of the next morning she had spent huddled and trembling in the total darkness of a corner of the hay loft. It was the one place on their farm she hadn't been to since and could not be made to go.

There had been all kinds of scary sounds in the darkness that night. They had made her squeeze her eyes shut tight and press her shaking hands against her mouth. She didn't dare move or make a sound so no one would know she was there, especially God. It didn't work.

She remembered a giant, hairy old man with gold teeth and a big silver key on a long clanking chain around his neck. Him she remembered well, for he still threatened her to this day in her nightmares. He had a sparkling golden axe in one hand and kept reaching down for her with the other. His long, skinny fingers curled like a chicken claw, getting ready to clamp her arm. She wanted to run but couldn't get up. She tried and tried, then saw her father's face. He shook his head and scowled and held her down for God to chop her head off. Then God spread His great white wings and began to flap them against heaven's rafters.

The flapping ruckus of a bird of some kind, trying to find a place to roost in the loft, had woken her from one nightmare into a real one.

She had bitten her hand to keep from screaming, neither feeling the pain nor tasting the blood. Sometime during the night, she had wet her pants.

Her two older brothers, Harley and Daniel, and her older sister Katy learned around nine thirty that morning that Lena was not at the hospital with their parents, as they had assumed. They frantically ran out of the house to look for her, going straight to the barn first.

Lena remembered hearing them out in the yard calling her name. She had hoped they wouldn't come to the barn but knew they would sooner or later. They would take her out of the barn, and that's when God would reach down from the sky and kill her, the same as Andrew.

Even now, at the age of fourteen, she had a feeling that when some good little thing came along and chose to knock on *her* door, she was being set up. She was being tricked into feeling good just before that moment God had been waiting for to finally inflict His punishment on her. "When you least expect it."

The expectation of that lightning bolt striking her at any moment had gone with her from the barn into the light of her first day as a five-year-old girl who only looked like Lena. She had been pushed into the strangling grip of perpetual fear and had changed forever.

She screamed and kicked her big sister Katy, who had carried her from the barn to the house. Pressing Lena's squirming body against her chest, Katy held tight to the little sister she thought she knew to save her from hurting herself. She hadn't known it wasn't the Lena of the day before, and it was too late to save her.

But with the help of Lena's father praying for her and the church's persistent prescription of "God's will," after two years, she finally acquired a taste for fear. She was cured by tolerance. That's what finally worked. But that's not what the Mennonite preachers said. Keeping to the obedience of God's will, "that's what saved Lena," they said: "Sam's obedience to God."

They didn't know about her dog Butch, his loyalty to her, his obedience to her need for someone to accept her as she is. Now, her security blanket, Butch, was as much a part of her as the sweat that woke her in the middle of the night. Saved? By Butch, maybe.

She lay on her back panting. The covers were kicked to the foot of the bed, and her soft cotton homemade nightgown was soaked from her armpits up. She rose to a sitting position, deftly removed the sweaty garment, and tossed it to the floor.

The cold of the November night that had crept into her bedroom felt good on her hot, damp skin. She sat like that for a moment, lifting her arms away from her body to air out her armpits.

She turned her face toward the small ticking alarm clock that stood on a stand beside her bed. She could barely see the face of the clock in the dark, but not the numbers. She really hadn't needed to look at the clock to know what time it was. It was the same time that the sweats woke her up every night; well, almost every night.

She lowered her arms and flopped back against the mattress, landing too high on the pillow. She scooted down to settle her long, blonde hair into the hollow that made it *her* pillow. She lay flat and straight, her long gangly legs together, her hands on her stomach, one on top of the other. All she had to do now was to wait until she fell asleep again. Sometimes, it happened, and sometimes, it didn't. She had a feeling it wasn't going to this time.

That would be okay. Tomorrow was Saturday. No school. She frowned at the sudden train of thought that those two words had provoked. No school: maybe no school *at all* after this weekend. That depended on how she would handle her father. He had already told her it was time to "get to doin' what God had intended for a woman to do, and that didn't include more arithmetic than a woman needed." She loved to learn things, especially English and literature. She wanted to be a writer, which meant attending school and maybe even college.

She sat up, struggled with the covers, and flopped back, pulling them over the goosebumps that began decorating her body. She snuggled down into her nest, wishing she could stay like that, suspended in time forever. The coming moment that faced her this morning, however, was frightening. She intended to have it out with her father about school. Standing up against his will was the last thing she wanted to do.

Obedience that was his thing; that was the banner he carried for God: *obedience, obedience!* "*You have to be obedient, Lena. God does not tolerate a sinful child, and disobedience is a sin. Disobey your parents, and you're disobeying God.*"

How many times had she heard that? It wasn't that she didn't believe it. The problem was that he was wasting his breath on her. It was too late. *And he knows it. He remembers the hayloft. So, give it a rest why dontcha.* It was out of his hands. She had God to answer to, not him.

Waiting for God to strike you dead has a way of lining up your priorities. Worrying about that was at the top of her list. Telling her father she was not quitting school in the eighth grade was right under that.

However, now, she didn't know for sure which she was losing sleep over, the ever-occurring nightmare of God sneaking up on her or her plans to tell her father that she was going to keep right on going to school and for him to get over it. *Wouldn't that shake the rafters of heaven, talking like that to God's little helper?*

Wouldn't work. She didn't know what would work. Why does he have to always be in the way? Why can't he just leave her alone and let her be happy in her last days?

Maybe she would just take off and go live with Katy and Lewis. Her dad wouldn't be around to watch every move she made, and she could keep going to school. Her sister wouldn't mind her moving in with them. They got another bedroom down in the basement. She could babysit little Jacob whenever needed and help Katy in all kindsa ways.

Lena flopped and twisted into a position on her side, closed her eyes, and wished she could go to sleep. Frustration spun her mind; she pressed her mouth against the index finger curled up in her fist. But then, on second thought, her moving in with her sister might do more harm than good.

The last time Lena checked the clock before falling asleep, she saw it was barely six o'clock.

CHAPTER 2

There she was, in some *park!* She'd never been there before. It was strange. There were no trees or shrubbery. The only thing in this park was a merry-go-round. Her father was pushing some puppies on it, round and round, way too fast. They were sliding off the whirling platform one by one, sailing out into the air to... she couldn't see where. *Why is he doing that? Poor puppies.* She knew that her dad was going to see her any second now. Suddenly, he stopped pushing on the merry-go-round and turned toward her.

"Lena? Is that you? Lena?" He didn't recognize her! She was struck with despair. *He can't see me, the real Lena.* Then he turned away, walking toward the barn and calling her name. "Lena?... Lena?"

Suddenly, she was awake. Her mother was calling her name and shaking her by the shoulder.

"Lena, get up! You need to go help your dad." Then, she saw Lena's nightgown lying on the floor beside the bed. "Well, for heaven's sake, Lena, whatever possessed you to take your gown off?" She picked up the gown, stood holding it, and frowned at Lena. Lena pulled the covers over her head. Her mother tossed the gown onto the foot of the bed, then grabbed the top edge of the covers and jerked. "Get out of that bed and put some clothes on right now; shame on you!"

Lena waited for her mother to leave or at least turn away. She didn't.

"Get out of bed now, Lena."

She scrambled out of bed and grabbed her underwear off an old wooden chair next to the closet door. She was very uncomfortable with her mother there. She glanced at her mother. She was looking at the bed. At least she wasn't watching her put her panties and slip on.

"Your bed looks like a tornado struck it. What in the world were you doing?"

That's it, thought Lena. *I'm sick and tired of being accused. Every time something's not exactly how it usually is, and I'm close by, that means I did it! It's like I'm a flaw in the machinery of this family's life.* She reached for her dress, lifting it from the back of the chair. *I'm not a hitch in your get-along,* she thought.

Sarah became stuck in mid-motion as if she had been instantly frozen. Eyes wide and focused on Lena, she stared. She held her breath. *Did she say something? I think I heard her say something!* She let her breath go and quietly asked, "Did you say I'm not a hitch in your get-along?"

Lena was awestruck. That's exactly what she *thought,* but she didn't say it out loud. *What is going on? Am I going crazy?*

Sarah was ecstatic. Her senses were reeling. Was this the moment she'd been waiting for all these years? She waited again for an answer. Lena remained silent as she stared at her mother in disbelief. She wanted to run to her for reassurance. She wanted to hug her and ask her if she was insane. The words were on the tip of her tongue.

Sarah saw the fear in Lena's face and knew she wasn't going to answer. The disappointment was staggering. The lack of her daughter's progress, which she lived with daily, was overwhelming. Was it her fault? Was it she who wasn't smart enough to help her child? She put her face in her hands, and the coming tears blurred her vision. "Why, oh why," she whispered. She lowered her hands and looked at Lena. "I'm sorry," she softly said.

Lena heard it. *Why, oh why, what? She* asked herself. *Now, what did I do?* She must have spoken her thoughts out loud.

Her father's familiar warning slapped her memory. "Remember your place, Lena, and keep it. God claims an obedient child." Then she heard the apology. She blinked and, frowning, shook her head. *Sorry for what?* She was confused. She should be the one apologizing. *So, say something dummy.* But she didn't know how. She hated herself for not knowing how to express her feelings.

She rose from the chair and went to the small dresser, which held all the clothes not hanging in the closet. Her black head cover lay on top of the dresser, reminding her of the decision she had to make about whether she would wear it that day.

Sarah was struck again by disappointment. Lena acted like she hadn't heard her apology. As usual, she made no sound. As usual, Sarah waited for an answer. Ever since Andrew's death, Sarah had waited for an answer. Lena and Andrew had been close. Lena had run away from the cemetery during

Andrew's funeral. When she was found hiding in the driveway culvert, everyone said it would take a while for her to stop grieving for Andrew.

"One of these days, she'll stop hiding and start talking again, too. Just give her time."

She was well into her third-grade year when she quit hiding while she was at school. She figured God wouldn't get her in front of all the other kids. But no one could coax her into talking normally again, not even her dad, especially her dad.

Sarah thought Lena was afraid of her dad during those early grade school years. Not that she ran from him, but she never went out of her way to be near him. She avoided him most of the time, circling him, keeping a wary eye out, and always hesitating at his beck and call. Of course, anyone Sarah was "silly" enough to mention it to would say she was imagining things, "looking for the worst." She had mentioned it to only a few and, after being shushed by each one of those, learned to keep it to herself. However, she never quit believing it. Lena hadn't been like that with her dad before "the accident."

Now, looking at her dress, she wondered what could have been. What was in this beautiful young woman, her most precious child, that may never be brought to its God-intended fullness?

Once again, as she has done a million times before, she would ask her daughter to try to speak in a normal voice, ever hopeful that this would be the time.

"My lands, Lena, speak up. I know you have a bigger voice than that." She moved closer to Lena, got behind her, and began tying the sash to her homemade dress. "You were much louder even when you were a baby. I've heard you bawl from clear across the house. Lena was silent.

Sarah went on. "I can only wait so long, and then, I'll have a nervous breakdown. You'll have to explain to the church why I'm rolling around on the floor, kicking the furniture, and foaming at the mouth. Not to mention all the cuss words the preacher will hear."

Lena laughed at her mother's words, not loud like her sister Katy, but louder than ever before. Sarah was taken by her heart, feeling enormous pleasure.

Lena wanted to hug her mother, but she couldn't. Lordy, lordy! How silly can you get? She sat in the old wooden chair, looked at the floor, and put her hands between her knees.

Sarah watched Lena fiddling with the head cover. "So, to satisfy my curiosity, why were you not wearing your nightgown?" Sarah got nothing from Lena but that so-familiar look that made you think she was wondering why you asked. After a moment, Sarah did not expect an answer. If she didn't answer in four or five seconds, she wasn't going to and never would. Sarah pointed at the head cover.

"Do you want to wear that thing today, or would you rather I put your hair in braids? I don't think we're going to town until this afternoon. Daniel and Harley are fixing that fence on the south end of the pasture, so your dad wants you to help him with something in the barn. You won't want to wear the head cover in the dust and dirt."

Lena returned the cover to the dresser, picked up a pink rat-tail comb instead, and nodded. She thought her mother didn't really want an answer; she hardly ever did. Why didn't she wait for an answer? She wanted to tell her about the sweats and the nightmares. If she could just tell her mother about her worry for her sanity... *So, tell her! Start talking! Careful, Lena, know your place.* Nothing came out.

She handed the comb to her mother, but when her mother took hold of it, Lena couldn't let go. She ached to hold her mother's hand and to feel her skin. Not like in the act of braiding her hair, washing her face, or putting her arms into her coat. She had done that dutifully when Lena was little. Lena wanted a spontaneous touch of friendship. An unspoken acknowledgment of the female connection that's supposed to exist between a young lady and her mother.

How silly! She let go of the comb and jerked her hand back. *Respect is not free, Lena. You must earn it.* She had heard that a couple of million times, too. *Obedience will get you God's respect. But if God, in all his wisdom, cannot find anything in you to respect, then how can a mere person?* It made sense. It also made it impossible for her to expect respect from anyone, especially someone as close to royalty as her mother.

She was damaged goods. *Know your place, Lena, and keep it.* There were times like this when she appreciated her father. In the rare moments when she was right on the verge of stepping out of her place, her dad's words would yank her back. She had to admit that she would be a real hell-raiser if it weren't for him.

She had moved back to the chair and turned it to face the closet door. She sat down in it with her back to her mother, ready to have her hair braided. The trembling inside had almost gone.

Sarah had not moved when Lena jerked back her hand. The comb in Sarah's hand had remained stuck in mid-air where Lena had left it. Her disappointed eyes were on Lena, her heart still pounding. She stood transfixed in the rare moment, powerless to keep it from slipping away.

She let the hand holding the comb fall to her thigh. She stood another moment, then moved to the back of the chair. She lifted a handful of Lena's luxurious, long, blond hair and ran the comb through it in slow, smooth strokes.

So beautiful, she thought. Her heart ached in her throat. She didn't allow the tears to fall, waiting for a moment when she could be alone. *Oh, Lena, where have you gone that you can't return to us? What could you have done at so young an age to have angered God so much? Maybe not you... who then?* She continued her long, smooth strokes. *Probably no one,* she thought.

CHAPTER 3

From the bottom of the stairs in the living room, Sam's loud, impatient voice burst up the stairs and into Lena's bedroom. "Lena, are you up there?" It struck her as sharply as it had that day in the hayloft. Lena jumped as if she'd been stuck with a pin, jerking an uncompleted braid out of her mother's hands. "Lena!" His voice, almost the same as that day, hurled her senses into the loft. She felt a frantic impulse to fall to the floor and crawl somewhere to hide. Her mind was filled with the sight of hay bales around her, the feel of the loft's wooden floor, and the smell of hay dust. She was about to sneeze but only rose from the chair and looked at her mother with wild, frightened eyes.

Sarah saw the look on Lena's face. She felt instant anger at her husband. *He did it again! He knew she wouldn't answer; even if she did, he couldn't hear her from down there. So why yell? He does it over and over. It's like he just moved in yesterday.*

"Damit," she muttered, then mentally covered her mouth in regret, too late to close the cage of the flying cuss word. She saw Lena sneeze, then again, and again, and a fourth time. She had never seen that happen before.

She turned from Lena and stomped into the hallway, stopping at the top of the stairs. Sam had reached the third step on his way up. He stopped when he saw her, made sure she saw his impatience, then went back down. He was already wearing his hat and coat, so she knew he was on his way out and expected Lena to follow soon. After he disappeared into the kitchen, she waited for the slam of the back door before returning to Lena's bedroom.

He knows what he's done. She wondered if it had been on purpose; *surely not.*

When she reentered the bedroom, Lena had returned to the chair and sat rigid as a marble statue facing the closet door. The abandoned, mistreated braid had come undone.

As Sarah approached, she saw Lena trembling and thought she must be crying. She laid her hand on Lena's shoulder and bent over her to see her face. "Oh, Lena, are you alright?"

She was not crying but shaking uncontrollably. Sarah moved to a position directly in front of her and knelt on one knee to look into her face. Lena bowed her head and looked down at her lap, where her clenched fists pressed her fingernails into the palms of her hands.

Lena was scared. The terror she was experiencing had happened only in her nightmares before. She would wake up, and reality would pull her out of the old man's grip. But now, there was no hairy old man, only the terror. *Oh God!* What can save her this time?

Suddenly, she realized that her mother was kneeling on the floor in front of her. She raised her face to her. There were words in her mind she was anxious to blurt out to her, but she couldn't squeeze them past the responsibility to stay in her place. The responsibility her father had instilled in her.

She stared at her mother. *Why won't she help me? What have I done to her that's so terrible? God has good reason, but she doesn't know about that. Does she?*

Sarah saw a look in her daughter's expression that she had never seen on another human being. It startled her and raised goose bumps on her arms. With a jerk, Lena rose and, in a whisper, said, "Sam told you, didn't he?" She pushed past Sarah, knocking her on her butt, and rushed from the room.

Sarah got up from the floor and hurried to catch Lena. She heard her bare feet already pounding on the stairs. Lena was out the back door before Sarah reached the kitchen.

The door was wide open, and the cold November breeze blustered right in. It sent a chill through Sarah as she ran through the kitchen and onto the back porch. She saw Lena running barefoot toward the highway with no coat on. Her long dress danced in the wind, and her hair flew madly around her head. She screamed her name! "Lena," then began to trot after her. "You get back here and put some shoes on and a coat. It's too cold to be outside with no coat on. Lena, I mean right now, dammit!"

Lena began to slow down and looked back at her mother. She stopped and turned to face her. They stood panting, each staring at the other.

Lena couldn't believe what she was doing. She was too cold to be concerned about anything else. *Good lord!* She was out here in the dead of winter without a coat. Her mother called her. "Lena? Are you coming in or not? C'mon, it's cold!"

Looking down at her bare feet, amazed, Lena approached her mother. She was fully aware of the events that had sent her out here, but the reaction that she had experienced didn't seem nearly as logical now as it had been then. Her mother, also without a coat, was still standing watching her. Her arms folded across her chest, shivering in the cold wind, she waited for her!

The cuss word! She heard it out of her good mother's own mouth. The glowing persona that made her mother the model of proper behavior had become smudged. Her light dimmed enough that Lena could see a real person. In an instant, she had become a citizen in Lena's world. Lena heard the cuss word. Like a noise in the night, it was just enough reality to save her from the loft.

Mother and daughter hurried to the house in silence. Lena was busy avoiding possible injury to her bare feet, and Sarah was focused on getting into the house to warm up. She saw the open kitchen door. *Now, just how warm is that gonna be?*

They got inside, and Lena slammed the door behind them. The kitchen wasn't much better than outside. They headed for the living room to stand close to the gas heater. Sarah squatted down to turn the fire up. She moved to stand beside Lena to join her in holding their stiff, red hands in the warm rays of heat that rose from the heater.

Lena's hair looked strange. One braid was hanging down neatly on one side of the part, and the other was in complete tangled disarray. "As soon as my hands warm up, I'll finish braiding your hair," Sarah said. Lena did not respond. "Did you hurt your feet?"

Lena stuck one foot out in front of her, letting the heel rest on the linoleum floor. They both examined it briefly. Lena shook her head.

"You need to put some socks on and leave your shoes off until the puffiness from the cold goes down."

They fell silent again. The hiss of the heater seemed to fill the house, amplifying the silence. Sarah had questions zooming around in her head that she was anxious to ask. One pushed its way to the forefront. Her lack of confidence in Lena's willingness to answer made her hold back.

Lena moved toward the stairs. *To get some socks,* Sarah thought. "Bring the comb back with you," she said.

As Lena climbed the stairs, Sarah heard the kitchen door open and close. *Sam!* She quickly squatted and turned the heater down to its original setting: Sam's setting.

Sam entered the room, his forehead wrinkled in disgust as he walked toward Sarah.

"Where's Lena? Did you tell her I needed her in the barn?"

"Yes, I told her, and she'll be down soon. She's just not quite ready yet."

"What, for Pete's sake, could be takin' her so long? I needed her over thirty minutes ago."

Sarah felt an urge in her spirit to tell him what had happened. Lena had just taken off barefoot down the driveway for no sane reason. But those words didn't fit. There *was* a sane reason. So, those words wouldn't be exactly true. Sam had scared her somehow. She wasn't going to put the reason on Lena this time. She wouldn't take the easy way out.

Not this time. It's just a stupid habit, a bad one at that, and I'm breakin' it. Lena is not a hitch in my get-along.

Sarah stepped out of her husband's domineering control with no small amount of apprehension. Ignoring the churning in her stomach, she turned and boldly faced him.

"Sam, you're just gonna hafta wait. She's not feeling like herself this morning and hasn't had breakfast yet. She needs a little more time to make herself ready for the day. Whatever you need help with can surely wait a little bit longer. It won't be the end of the world."

Sam's stare made her feel she had forgotten her place. However, the roof had not caved in, nothing had blown up, and low and behold, the world was still going around the sun. Sarah was encouraged and even congratulated herself. She had stood up to Sam.

They heard Lena on the stairs, her steps quick. She navigated the steps as carelessly as only the young and nimble could, then stopped. Sam and Sarah saw her standing, one foot forward on the lower step and the other still resting on the step behind.

The sight of her father had stopped her in mid-stride. She saw them looking at her and continued down the stairs cautiously.

Sam had seen her shy away from him every time she came in sight of him for the past nine years. Once, when she was seven, he was working on a one-way. He had hoisted one end off the ground with a chain and tackle to re-weld a cracked factory seam. While he was in a position on the ground with one leg under the one-way, the chain slipped and let the heavy machinery pin his leg. It broke just below the knee. Lena was with him for some rare reason, and when she heard him cry out in pain, she ran away and hid. She didn't tell anyone what had happened. He had been able to holler for help loud enough and long enough to get Katy's attention away from the clothes she was hanging on the line. His leg mended just fine, but the hurt in his heart never went away.

The weeks it had taken to recover were spent searching the pages of his bible for God's explanation of the punishment being laid upon him. Not the broken leg but the loss of his youngest and favorite child. He would also hobble about alone on his crutches in the barn. He would lean on the rubber pads pressed into his armpits and stare up the ladder to the loft, trying to imagine even a hint of wisdom in his actions up there that day.

For the first three or four years, he tried everything God allowed to win her back. Then, he finally agreed with the church that God had "given her a path," and she would go that way regardless of Sam's wishes. It was the way God intended.

"Treat her the same way you do your other children, with the same love and authority," preacher Reimer had told him. "And if it's God's will, she'll grow out of her affliction and become stronger because of it."

Sam had obeyed the church and was therefore aligned with God, but his estrangement from his child was a heavy cross to bear. He carried it along. God's will ruled the church; therefore, it ruled Sam's house.

When he saw her hesitation on the stairs, he was struck again with the pain of his loss. The feeling it gave him added to his agitation. As she descended the stairs, he saw her shoes in her hand and her hair all undone. Had she just gotten out of bed? He was out of patience.

"Well, it's about time you got up! Half an hour ago, I called you out of bed; I've been waiting, Lena!"

He turned to face Sarah. "You knew I was waiting for her help, and you let her lay in bed?" He started toward the kitchen, anger pushing him along. He stopped and turned to her.

"You're letting her rule you, Sarah. You baby her, and she's just as capable as any fourteen-year-old. From here on, I expect you'll treat her just like anyone with two hands, two legs, and a sound mind.

He warned Lena, "You get your shoes on and eat some breakfast, then come out to the barn; we have work to do."

Sarah took a bold step toward him with brave words in her mouth, but he disappeared into the kitchen. She would never have yelled after him.

The back door opened and closed like the final ching of the chisel on the stone tablets of the Ten Commandments. Sarah stood looking at the vacant kitchen doorway, arms straight down at her sides, tight fists at their ends. She pictured her single-minded husband marching hell-bent for the barn as if on a mission, determined to avoid some wrong he might do his God. She couldn't imagine. She pulled a chair away from the dining table and carried it to a place closer to the heater. Lena sat on the bottom step of the stairs and was putting on her shoes. Sarah tapped the back of the chair.

Come here, Lena, and I'll finish your hair.

CHAPTER 4

Lena finished tying her black oxfords. She retrieved the pink rattail comb from the step she sat on and went to sit in the chair. She handed the comb to her mother.

She dreaded being with her father this morning for who-knows-how long. But it would be a good time to tell him she would not quit school... no matter what. He could beat her, commit her to the loony bin, or even make her spend the night in the hay loft; she didn't care. He couldn't make her quit school.

She felt her mother's strong hands tugging her hair as she deftly braided it. She wanted to ask her mother to be with her when she and her dad would get into it over school. She wanted her help with what to say when he proclaimed his "final word on the matter." But the more she thought about it, the more she admitted that her mother had no more influence over her husband than Lena had over her father. What could a mere mother-slash-wife say to change the instructed mind of God's little helper? *We count, too, not only God. Whoa, we'd go to hell twice and three times on Sunday for that kinda talk!*

Sarah had finished combing the tangles of the cold winter wind out of Lena's hair. She then began the repetitive motions that would quickly produce a long blond braid. There was hesitation in her voice. "Lena, what were you talking about... when we were upstairs, just before you ran out... you asked if your dad told me... told me what?"

Lena was sure her mother was asking the question because of something she heard her say, but she couldn't recall saying anything like that. She thought back and tried to recall what she had heard. In her memory, she heard her father at the bottom of the stairs. She remembered how she longed for help from her mother and her despair when she wondered why her mother never offered it.

Suddenly, there it was. She heard herself say, "*Sam told you, didn't he?*" She heard it as if someone else had said it.

Lena's shoulders stiffened, and her head jerked. Sarah saw the motion, and her hands stopped winding the rubber band around the end of the braid. She stood motionless, focused on Lena, ready to grab her if she took off running again. Lena was still.

Sarah wound the band twice more, then let the braid fall to Lena's back. She put her hands on Lena's shoulders and bent to see her face. She gently asked, "Can you tell me what you meant?" Lena shook her head. Sarah remained bent over and continued to look at Lena. If she could just see some sign of Lena's intentions. Was that her answer? Did she not want to say, or did she even know the answer? She surely knows *why* she said it! It seems it had come from some deep secret, so deep that she would run away barefoot into the dead of winter to keep it. Sarah stood up straight. *She knows why she said it!* "Tell me, Lena. What do you think your dad told me? Is it some secret between you two?"

Lena rose from the chair and faced her mother. She felt a little frightened. The words had come from... she didn't know where. The strange sound of her own voice in her mind was all a little too weird. The word insane entered her mind and gave her goosebumps. She hugged herself and shivered. "I don't know why I said it," she whispered.

When Sarah heard the whisper, it seemed a little clearer this time. Maybe a little louder. The possibility strengthened her hope, and she wanted to encourage Lena.

Her hug surprised Lena and caused her to stiffen, but only for a moment. Then she let herself be guided into her mother's hug. It felt strange and awkward. Her arms hung at her sides, and she didn't know what to do with them.

Her mother released her and stepped back, beaming.

"I knew you were improving the minute you spoke upstairs a while ago. Now you must keep trying and practicing so your voice gets louder."

Now, Lena felt like some kind of project. Her mother hadn't really wanted to know *why* she said those words. She had just been scared that Lena might be insane. If you are sane, you will always know why you say things. Maybe her mother needed to take her to the doctor.

Lena was shaky inside, and she knew that soon, she would be shaking all over the place. She needed to find something to do to stop the shaking. She quickly walked to the coat closet and put on her heaviest coat. She would rather face her dad than go through the shakes.

Sarah stood silent, dumbfounded, watching her daughter put her coat on and disappear into the kitchen. She heard the back door open and close and was reminded of the sounds she imagined ghosts making.

Lena ran the fifty yards to the barn. Compared to the bright morning, it was dark inside. Before her eyes adjusted, she could hear her dad moving things around in a storage room at the back of the barn.

She had always felt alarmed in the barn; at least, she couldn't remember when she hadn't. It wasn't that there was anything in there to be afraid of; she just had this feeling that she should be ducking, and she kept wanting to look behind her.

She was halfway to the storage room when her dad stepped out. He saw her, stopped, and spoke in a perturbed tone. "Girl, it's about time you got here! I was on my way to get you and run you out here like a six-year-old brat." He turned back toward the storage room. "Now take your coat off, get in here, and help me with this tarp."

He disappeared into the small room, and Lena's first impulse was to flip him the finger and walk back to the house. She told herself she needed to get her 'talk' with him about school over with. She could never have boldly disobeyed "Sam Danziger," not to his face anyway. She could at least flip him the finger behind his back, though. So, she did and walked to the doorway, hanging her coat on a hook.

She saw that he had nailed two 2x4s up, so they stuck out from the wall, creating supports for a shelf that wasn't there yet. On the floor, there was a large ten-foot, rolled-up, wheat-truck tarp. He pointed to the tarp.

"We need to lay this tarp across those 2x4s on the wall there." He was standing at the end of the tarp nearest her.

I'm gonna lift this end so you can get your arms under it, then I'll get under the other end, and we'll lift it to the 2x4s."

It was a good plan and would have worked well for someone stronger than Lena. She couldn't lift her end that high. Sam got his end up onto the protruding 2x4 nearest him, then hurried over and helped her with hers. They were finally successful, but during Lena's struggle, she had scratched the inside of her upper arm on a sharp piece of wire that protruded from one of the tie-down eyelets along the edge of the tarp.

Sam saw her twisting her arm with one hand to examine the wound; it was bleeding.

What's wrong with your arm," he asked. He was surprised to see that she had been hurt on something made of canvas. How unlikely was that? What else could go wrong this morning? He moved closer to her for a better look and took her arm.

She stiffened as if shocked, and a wild impulse swelled her eyes for an instant. She stood still, staring at the wall, anxious for him to let go of her.

You're bleeding. What cut you?"

When she was little, trying to find the perfect words to answer him had been a terrifying experience. She had avoided it at all costs and stayed away from him. Years later, her reluctance to answer him was a force of habit. Her apparent disinterested silence usually provoked a sermon-flavored lecture. She had heard it all, over and over; she knew every "Thou shalt not" and "God will" this and "God won't" that, by heart. She wanted him to let go of her.

Not expecting an answer, Sam let go of her arm and moved closer to the tarp to see if he could tell what had scratched her. It would probably be rusty if it were metal and cause more than just a scratch. He saw the wire twisted around the metal edge of the tie-down eyelet. It had been rusty for a long time, and there was blood on it.

He turned to Lena. "You need to go clean that scratch with some rubbing alcohol so you don't get lockjaw or infection. Then put some iodine on it."

She stood still, assessing the situation. She could not leave now; it was time to tell him she *would* be going to school on Monday. She moved toward the doorway, stopped, and looked back at her dad. His eyes were on her, his face telling her the final word had been spoken. Her instinctive inclination to duck was overwhelming. She ran from the room, grabbed her coat, and didn't stop until she reached the kitchen door. She did not hear him tell her to come right back.

CHAPTER 5

There was a large window above the kitchen sink. As Sarah washed the breakfast dishes, she had a clear view of the backyard. It was where the clothes-line posts stood, extending to the edge of their north wheat field.

A grey ribbon of asphalt highway cut across miles of new winter wheat on its way to the small farming town of Garland. Every time she gazed out of the window toward the highway, it reminded her of that day she drove down that highway to the hospital. She could still feel God's name on her lips and hear Sam's sobbing prayers in her heart. The feeling of terror in her mind was gone now; in the same way, the pain of a severed arm or leg goes away but leaves the feeling of its presence.

There is little memory of the days between Doctor Jackman shaking his head and saying, "I'm sorry," and the moment she discovered Lena missing at Andrew's funeral. The words "Lena's run off" had shocked her. Sarah remembered feeling panic as she ran to save her child. When she found Lena in a dark, dirty culvert, she felt purpose come back to life inside her. She had found Lena *and* herself.

Sarah could also see the barn from the window. She turned her attention to it as the barn's door popped open, and Lena burst into the yard, running toward the house. Struck with instant panic, Sarah dropped a dinner plate back into the water and hurried to the door. She jerked the door open and nearly leaped out onto the porch. Lena came running up the porch steps, head down, past Sarah, and into the house.

Sarah yelled after her. "Lena! What's wrong?"

Now in the living room, Lena moved quickly toward the stairs, throwing her coat towards the closet and ignoring her mother. Sarah yelled again, anger mixed in with fear ringing loud and clear. "Lena, stop! Tell me what's happened... now!"

Lena whirled at the bottom of the stairs and furiously yelled back at her mother. "Nothing happened! Everything is just hunky dory! Sam, the man, is still right in there holding my head down!"

Then she was up the stairs and out of sight before Sarah could believe her ears. She stood astonished, peering at the stairs. She heard splashing in the kitchen. The water! "Ooh!"

Irked, she ran into the kitchen to find the sink overflowing onto the linoleum floor. "My lands!" she exclaimed, quickly turning the water off. She stood in the water, looking down at it without seeing it. Stuck in her vision was Lena's face, yelling at her.

Her yelling was loud!

She wiped her hands dry on the white apron she wore. Exciting thoughts scrambled around in her mind, and she didn't know what to do first. Lena, it seemed, was getting her voice back. "Thank you, God," danced quietly on her lips.

Disregarding the wet floor, she left the kitchen and climbed the stairs to Lena's room. She stood at the closed door momentarily, savoring the feeling of standing in the presence of a true miracle. It was a real honest-to-goodness answered prayer. She tapped lightly and went in.

Lena stood in her open closet, staring at her neatly hung clothes. On her way to packing her clothes, she hadn't stopped to think that her mother would follow her to her room. She should have known after yelling out that way. *Mercy. Musta shocked Mom's socks off. It surprised me, too. Where'd that come from?*

She couldn't do any packing now. She moved away from the closet to flop down across the bed. On her stomach, propped up on her elbows, chin in her hands, she stared out the window at the side of her bed. It would be better to get hold of Katy first anyway. How was she gonna do that? No telephone. *Can't walk three miles to her place.*

Since the day she became aware of the lack of modern conveniences in their way of life compared to the English kids at school, she had always wondered why they were not allowed to have a radio or a telephone. Maybe it was a way for the church to keep the Mennonite kids from seeing how green the grass was on the other side of the fence. *Keep us from wandering off into the "ever-so-sinful world,"* she thought."

She waited for her mother to say whatever she came to say. She would figure out how to contact Katy later. She heard her mother move to the bed and felt it quake as she sat on it. There was a clear difference in the tone of her mother's voice: excitement, Lena guessed.

"I'm sorry I yelled at you," Sarah said. "You scared me. I thought something terrible mighta happened." She fell silent; Lena didn't respond. Sarah could hardly contain herself. She wanted desperately to know what to say that would cause Lena to speak again.

Lena turned on her back and stared at the ceiling. Then Sarah saw the mark on her underarm. She leaned closer to see better, and concern made her frown.

"What's that on your arm?"

Now that her mother had brought it to her attention, Lena noticed the scratch was stinging. She needed to take care of it. She rose to a sitting position and lifted her arm to show the scratch to her mother.

Sarah saw it had bled only a little, and the blood was now dry.

"Did you scratch it in the barn?" Lena nodded.

"On what," Sarah asked. She had to listen closely to hear Lena.

"Wire."

"You said wire?" Lena nodded. Sarah heaved a heavy sigh; disappointed Lena had stopped speaking.

She rose from the bed. "C'mon, let's clean it up and put some iodine on it. It could get infected."

As they descended the stairs toward the bathroom, Lena began to form her plan to move in with her sister. On their way to town this afternoon, she would ask to be let out at the turn-off to Katy's and walk the rest of the way. It was only a mile from the highway. Then, she would talk her sister into letting her live with her so she could go to school. Katy could bring her back to the house and help pack her things. They could be back at Katy's with all her stuff before Mom and Sam got back from town.

She hated to put Katy on Sam's bad side, but it was the only way. Katy would understand, especially since she herself had tried to go against Sam and continue school so she could graduate. Katy would have been the first of the relatives to have graduated. It didn't work; "that's not God's will" had been the reason. Katy never said so, but Lena knew that's why she married at sixteen and left. *That* must have been God's will *cause Sam Danziger gave it his thumbs-up, and God's little helper sure knows God's will.*

She wondered if God kept him informed of His will: *maybe in a memo on little pure white-as-the-driven-snow sheets of cloud, written in embossed zillion-carat gold lettering.* Or was it the church?

Her mother had the alcohol out of the medicine cabinet and was soaking a ball of cotton with it. She took Lena's arm and began wiping away the dried blood.

For her, getting married wouldn't be the way. Fourteen is way too young. Then she got honest with herself. She wouldn't get married at any age. She wouldn't get married if it was the only way to breathe or stay outta hell.

Sarah finished cleaning the scratch and got the bottle of iodine from the medicine cabinet. She talked pleasantly as she got another cotton ball, held it on the open top of the iodine, and tipped the bottle.

"What were you and your dad doing in the barn?" The dark liquid soaked into the cotton ball, and she applied the stinging medicine to the scratch. Lena winced a little but was taken more by her mother's words. She knew her mother was only trying to get her to talk and didn't give a dead fly what she and Sam were doing in the barn. She wanted to accommodate her mother. She really did, but ... it was like a dream she had once.

She was way up on a tall wooden fence, standing on the edge of the top board. There was bubbling lava and a white-hot fire at the bottom of one side of the fence and a dark, bottomless pit on the other. She was holding onto a rope that hung from so high up in the blue sky that she couldn't see what it was tied to. She would fall off the fence if she let go of the rope. She could easily avoid falling into the fiery lava by dropping off the dark side. But she couldn't let go because she didn't know what was down there.

Her mother stopped daubing the scratch. Looking straight ahead at the wall, Lena wondered if she was looking at her. She couldn't help but glance at her mother's face.

Yes, she is.

Her eyes were fixed on Lena, and Lena saw the intense focus there as if she were working on the answer to a very profound problem. As their eyes stared into each other, Lena felt the impulse to hug her mother for the second time that morning. But what if her mother stepped back, held her off, or resisted her hug? Then, all her suspicions would become valid facts. The possibility that she could be wrong about being of no value to her mother would be gone. What would she be left with? No! It was better not to take the chance. Now, at least, she still had the "problem" between them, which was better than nothing.

Sam's voice shattered the silence from the bathroom doorway. "What must I do, Lena, to get you to help me?"

Sarah and Lena both jerked, startled to the heart. Sarah nearly dropped the bottle of iodine as she turned to Sam. Her tone was filled with anger.

"My goodness, Sam, you scared us to death! You could have warned us!" Sam took his glare off Lena and shot it at Sarah. A glance was all she got. He was not a calm man, and his focus was on Lena.

"I told you to come back. Aren't you done yet?"

Sarah was beside herself. Sam had interrupted something she had felt between her and Lena. Maybe it was a call in the distance from her long-lost daughter. Then, like a clap of thunder in bad weather, Sam had crashed the fragile moment as surely as a sparrow in a hurricane. She took a step toward him and spoke precisely and with calm conviction.

"You need to leave us alone, Sam... for the rest of the day."

Sam did *not* say, *Sarah, Sarah, you're only making things worse. You're letting her use you like any other fourteen-year-old would get what she wants. You've babied her all her life. She needs to be pushed harder than other kids, and you're doing the opposite*. Instead, he was silent... this time. Lena was getting out of hand, and he would soon need to do something about it. *The older they get, the harder it is*. His stomach churned; his fists squeezed. *Why can't she just do as she's told?* He turned and burst from the doorway. He stomped down the stairs, and a moment later, he hollered from the kitchen.

"There's water in here that needs mopping up!" The final word forever holds its stature. The back door opened and closed, leaving the house in lifeless silence. The walls held their breath.

Sarah had not moved. She stood exposed like the final wall of a demolition project, still waiting for the wrecking ball to swing. It had not swung. She inhaled victory and exhaled relief in a great sigh. She turned to the medicine cabinet and put away the iodine, cotton, and alcohol. She saw Lena staring at her.

"C'mon," she said, "Let's go mop up the kitchen floor and fix you some breakfast."

Lena followed her mother to the kitchen. She had been astonished by her mother's resistance to Sam.

Mercy me, will wonders never cease?

Now, her excitement toward her mother brought up unexplored longings that made her tremble at the thought.

They entered the kitchen, Sarah going to the broom closet for a mop and Lena to the brim-full sink. Her hand went into the warm dishwater, pushing a small amount of water up and over the lip of the sink to splash on the floor. She twisted her hands through the dishes to pull the rubber stopper. Her heart was thumping against the inside of her chest as she stood, letting the water drain to a useful level.

At an assembly in school, the speaker said that doctors have determined that hugging is good for you. *What could it hurt?* Her mother had hugged her only a while ago, the first time she could remember. That was her fault. The few times it could have happened, she had always run away. *What if not this time?*

Sarah had gotten a mop and bucket and was soaking up the water that had run over the sink. Her eyes were on the floor, and she noticed the hem of Lena's dress shaking. She looked up at Lena and saw that she was trembling uncontrollably. She stopped mopping and stood up straight.

"Lena? Are you alright?"

Lena put the stopper back into the drain and pressed her shaking hand on the edge of the sink. Her heart was beating wildly now. She was going to do it, and the unknown frightened her. She let go of the edge of the sink and turned on her waist to face her mother.

What Sarah saw in Lena's face was extraordinary. There was warm affection in her eyes and a hint of an invitation in her small, scared smile. Sarah was mesmerized. She leaned the mop handle against the counter's edge and moved to Lena's side.

Their arms wrapped around each other; Sarah's cheek rested against her baby's soft golden hair. Lena's tear-wet face was buried in her mother's neck and shoulder.

Lena turned her face to her mother's ear and whispered, "Thank you." She felt her mother's hold tighten and her body quake with sobs. Lena had been afraid for nothing.

Chapter 6

The dishes were done, the floor was dry, and their heart-to-heart rang crisply in her mind. Lena sat on a tall bar stool at the kitchen counter, eating a bowl of Post Toasties. The cereal had never tasted so good. Though she was way too excited to eat, she gobbled it down.

She would forever cherish the twenty or thirty minutes she and her mother talked while they worked on the dishes.

She quickly polished off the Post Toasties, anxious to move about in the shiny new atmosphere that talking with her mother had created. She tossed the spoon into the sink and winced at its clatter against the porcelain. Tipping the bowl to her mouth, she gulped down the last bit of sugared milk. She sent the bowl after the spoon. She slipped from the stool and walked with light steps to the stairs. She bound up them two at a time.

Wow! What a day!

She wondered which bedroom her mother was in. She felt like she had overdosed on the medicine of well-being. Her confidence was a giant muscular arm brushing the world out of her way. She no longer had a reason to keep her plans to pack and leave a secret. She would tell her mother right now and bring her into the plan to disobey her father. Her mother would stand by her side on the battle line against him. The fact that her mother was the loyal wife of the enemy never entered her mind.

She burst into her brother Harley's bedroom, where her mother was making the bed. Sarah had her back to Lena and bent forward, reaching over the bed.

Sarah had heard Lena come rumbling up the stairs. Still fairly beaming from that magic moment in the kitchen with her precious daughter, she wondered if she would hear Lena's voice from the doorway. She longed to hear it sail through the room to her. After finishing the bed, she stood still, keeping her back to the doorway, and waited for it.

Lena came in but said nothing, flopping down on the bed. When Sarah saw the excitement in Lena's flushed face, she was consumed by pleasure.

Lena's words came the next moment, and Sarah was enthralled. The sound filled her heart with accelerating joy, but her excitement smeared the words in her mind. Then the words became clear. At first, they confused her, like being yelled at from across the yard on a windy day. She thought she heard right, but then she was sure she couldn't have. *"I'm gonna pack my clothes and all of my stuff and go live with Katy,"* Lena had said as plain as day.

Sarah's elation turned to shock. She stood staring at Lena, dumbfounded. She shook her head slightly and said, "What?" She frowned, and her expression begged Lena for confirmation or maybe correction. "Live with Katy?"

Lena had put on a beaming smile as she landed on the bed, but now the weight of her mother's response fell on her like a giant blob of lead. Her smile was now only a tight, thin disguise. A familiar, careful feeling was spreading its coldness inside her. She saw the disbelief in her mother's eyes.

Lena carefully placed both feet flat on the floor and sat up straight. Her rigid spine held her head perfectly level. She fastened her eyes on the doorway across the room, appearing as if she had been filled with cement.

Inside, the statue that held Lena's trembling heart mourned her mistake. This was the kind of mistake her watchful father had never let her make. Remember to keep your place, Lena.

The hugging and the talking with her mother had felt right. Had she stepped out of her place or been set up? *When you least expect it!*

She recognized the day as having been too good to be true. This had been a fine set-up. Stellar! Fate had outdone itself. Is the bolt of lightning on its way? Will the next moment be when God strikes her dead?

There was the loud flapping of giant wings. The turbulent air they set in motion brought hot tears to her staring eyes. It tangled her loose hair and sent barn dust and thin stems of hay into a choking swirl around her. She sneezed violently. The metallic smell of warm, thick blood and razor-sharp steel turned her stomach. This time, she couldn't show God a brave face; she was terrified!

Sarah was transfixed. She watched Lena transform before her very eyes. She saw her sneeze, then was startled into throwing her hands out to catch Lena as she fell off the bed. Without a sound, Lena folded into a lump, her legs under her, her face hidden in her hands down against her thighs. She began to tremble violently before Sarah bolted out of her shock.

"Lena!" She fell to her knees beside Lena, placing one hand on her round, tight back, and bent to put her face close to Lena's.

"What's wrong?" she shouted.

She couldn't see her face. She needed to see her face. "Lena, look at me!"

She tried to pull Lena's hands away from her face. Her arms were stiff, almost immovable. Lena's whole body jerked with Sarah's tugging.

A whimper slipped from Sarah's throat. "Please, Lena! Tell me what's wrong!" Then she shouted again and shook Lena roughly. "Lena... Lena! What are you doing? Answer me!"

A voice unfamiliar to this place of Lena's terror in the dark hayloft came rushing from far off into Lena's senses, calling her name. The desperate calling saved her again. It was as if God recognized that voice as worthy, her mother!

Lena was amazed! She moved her hands and turned to look into her mother's face. In her mother's dark brown eyes, she saw fear, regret, and the demands made by serious questions. In those eyes... that's where her place was! There, with the love of a mother for her child.

Damn you, Sam. All this time, you tricked me.

He had hidden it from her and made her think "her place" was by herself where she wouldn't be in the way of others. She stared; her mother stared back.

My mother has brown eyes, beautiful brown eyes.

Mother and daughter rose together. Their movements brought them to a position up-right on their knees. They came together for the second time to hold each other. Lena entered her real "place," and her mother held her there.

Sarah: "Are you alright?"

Lena: "You have brown eyes."

Sarah was mystified and wondered why she said that. She relaxed her hold to move back and ask, but Lena tightened her hug. Sarah hugged back and asked Lena why she said such a thing.

"I didn't know." were the soft-spoken words against her shoulder

Sarah's surprise shut her mouth for several seconds. The silence was loud but not uncomfortable. Sarah finally spoke. "You didn't know my eyes are brown?"

Lena shook her head against the front of her mother's shoulder as best she could. "I never saw 'em before."

The statement was more of a revelation to Lena than it was to Sarah. They lived in the same house, day after day, year after year, for fourteen years. How was it possible that she hadn't ever seen the color of her mother's eyes? Maybe it isn't the house you live in that teaches you about those with you in that house. But your *world* shows you your family.

She had always been the only one in her world. Her family lived *around* her, in the living room, at the breakfast table, in the back seat of their car on the road to church. They had never been with her in her world and stood where she stood in the ferocious wind of God's wings. They had never run blindly with her from the lightning that crackled from God's gold-toothed smile. They had never had to duck the gleaming axe she knew was on its way to her neck as their father's God-helping hands held her down on the chopping block. She didn't know the color of their eyes either.

That's amazing!

Lena eased herself from her mother's arms and sat back on her heels, letting her hands lie in her lap. Her mother relaxed that way as well. For a grace-filled moment, they faced each other. Mother and daughter were each really seeing the other for only the second time.

Her mother asked, hopefully, "What just now happened, Lena? Can you tell me?" She then gave Lena's knees a quick look. "Did you hurt yourself?"

As Lena pulled up the hem of her dress, bared her knees, and said nothing, Sarah's inner caution warned her that Lena wouldn't answer. But Lena examined her knees and spoke normally.

"No skins or burns. Feels ok."

Sarah's heavy sigh was an unconscious reaction to her inner relief. "I'll bet you'll have bruises tomorrow, though. You landed on the floor *terribly* hard!" However, the injury to Lena's knees was not as concerning as the fear that squeezed Sarah's stomach. She didn't know much about seizures, but she'd heard accounts by those who she knew suffered from epilepsy. The sad stories of the fits suffered by the insane were what had her worried.

"Can you tell me what happened? Did you... did you... blackout or something like that?"

"Blackout?" Lena shook her head. "No. You mean pass out, fainted?"

"Yeah, did you?"

"No, I was just scared. I just wanted to hide."

"Scared of what, Lena, hide from... what?" Sarah gestured around the room. "There's nothing here to be afraid of."

Lena stood up and went to the bed to sit on it. Of course, there was nothing to be afraid of in the house. But she hadn't been there in the house. She didn't want to tell her mother that she hadn't been there with her, safe and sound in Harley's room. She'd been in the barn, diving behind hay bales to hide from God. There was God to be afraid of. He would finally punish her, chop her head off, or strike her dead with a bolt of lightning. He wouldn't do it in the house but in the barn's hayloft. That was the scene of the crime; that's where she had been sent to be afraid. If she told her mother that... *I'd be on my way to the crazy house before noon.* Of course, she knew she wasn't crazy. *But all crazy people think that.*

There had been times when she was pretty sure that she *was* crazy. When she was little, and something went wrong, she would travel back in time to the hayloft. She would try to hide from the same old guy that her dad had held her down for that night. Then, without knowing how, she would find herself hiding in the weeds or under the combine and think she had gotten away from the old guy. She knew the old guy was really God. But it had been a long time since that had happened. Years!

Until today, when it happened twice on the same day, maybe I am crazy.

Gripping anxiety caused her breathing to come in short, erratic gasps. She told herself that if she were crazy, the thought that she might be would not have entered her mind. That made her feel a little more comfortable again. She felt comfortable with her mother now, but she could not tell her about God in the hayloft. Not now anyway, maybe never.

Sarah watched her daughter sitting still while her hands fidgeted at the waistband of her dress. She knew Lena was deep in thought. It made her wonder what, if anything, might happen next, and that made her feel careful. Then she remembered the moment before Lena had pitched forward off the bed. It brought back the words in the treasured sound of Lena's full voice that had shaken her to stunned disbelief. She was going to pack and leave. Move in with Katy? Sarah felt the same startled jerk again in her insides. Her mouth came open to protest, but an inner warning to be cautious held her voice. Her spirit screamed to find out why Lena wanted to move out. Yet she was afraid her demand to know would antagonize that sleeping thing that hid inside Lena and compelled her to unholy behavior.

Since the accident in the barn, she had always believed that there was something foreign living in Lena. Not a monstrous creature or some ugly growth but some power of a spirit that took her over at certain times and drove her to strange behavior. It wasn't anything like fear, shame, or anything as common as that. Those were the feelings that it *caused*. Everyone has that ordinary stuff in them. It was as if there was an irritating stone rubbing against her soul. The secret of it haunted the barn and raged between Lena and her father.

The uneasy silence between mother and daughter had been there for quite a while. Sarah could see that Lena was a little nervous but acting normal again. She feared Lena might leave the room without saying what was on her mind. She scooted across the floor and sat next to Lena. She took a chance and spoke in a pleasant tone with caution.

"So, are you ok? You're not afraid now, are you?"

Lena lifted her face to her mother, saw her brown eyes, and was awe-struck again. She was still for a moment, consumed by those eyes.

Then she shook her head and said, "No, I'm not scared here... with you."

Sarah frowned, a little puzzled. "But you were here with me a little while ago when you said you were scared."

Lena felt startled inside her again, but it was only a jerk, come and gone. It wouldn't possess her this time. She need not be concerned about stepping out of her place, the place that "Sam the man" had made for her. Her mother had shown her where she truly belonged. The feeling it gave her made goose bumps burst up her arms and fizz on her scalp. She was in wonderland! But she didn't dare tell her mother things that would make her wonder if she might be a lunatic. So, how would she explain being in the hayloft, scared out of her wits, when she had never left the room?

Sarah saw a sudden storm of panic in Lena's expression, and her hands balled up into tight fists. She reached over and laid a hand on Lena's arm.

"Please, Lena, tell me why you're so jumpy. What are you afraid of?"

Lena was silent, tossing things about in her mind. She searched for something to tell her mother, only making a mess of her mind. She dropped her head toward her fists in her lap, shrugged her small shoulders, and lied.

"I guess... I don't know, mom."

Donning a mask of helplessness, she looked at her mother and shrugged again. She felt awful about her lie but didn't know what else to do. She had to protect herself.

From my own mother?

The beautiful word "mom" from Lena's mouth had not slipped by Sarah. It warmed her heart and gave her goosebumps. The second thing was the lie. She had never known Lena to tell a lie; well, no, she wouldn't have. Lena had hardly said anything her whole life. Now, the lie began to turn from an ugly transgression to a sweet treasure. It had danced so freely from her daughter's once silent lips. Sarah became thankful for the lie; yes, even a lie.

Sam would have punished Lena for the lie and ignored the beautiful sound of her voice. He would also not have been concerned about why his daughter needed to lie. Sarah wondered about that need but decided to give Lena time to work out that problem. Sarah smiled at Lena and shook herself. "My," she said, "it gave me goosebumps when you called me mom!" Lena squirmed, ill at ease and a little embarrassed.

I don't think you ever called me mom! It was "mama" when you were little, until the..." She caught herself. It was too late; Lena was looking at her knowingly.

Lena finished the sentence for her. "The accident in the barn?"

Lena's voice gave Sarah goosebumps again. She nodded, and they were silent. Then she said, "After that, you quit talking. When you were the age when children started calling their parents, mom, and dad, you weren't saying anything."

She turned her face away from Lena and stared down at the floor.

"I'm sorry I missed that. Seeing you turn inside yourself and be so alone broke my heart."

Lena was amazed! She sat motionless, afraid to move. She didn't want to change the atmosphere. This is where she belonged, in this air! She sure didn't need to protect herself from her mother!

Not hardly! Maybe from Sam... Sam, for sure!

Sarah noticed a change in Lena's demeanor. She had quit picking at her dress and turned to face Sarah. She could tell that Lena was listening to her.

She, regretfully, began to let the pleasure of this miracle fade into the background. It was time to address Lena's intentions to pack up and move out of her house.

CHAPTER 7

"You said you want to go live with Katy. Do you mean that?" Sarah asked.

The flash of her mother's face minutes earlier when she had blurted out her intentions to move to Katy's house came to Lena's mind. She realized her mistake in thinking her mother would go against her father. She would need to talk her mother into helping her.

There was a hint of pleading in her tone. "I just wanna finish school! And you know he ain't gonna let me. At Katy's, he won't be there to stop me, and Katy will help me because he wouldn't let her go to school either."

"So that's what all this has been about, your dad not letting you go to school."

"Well, what's wrong with going to school? All the English kids go till they graduate, and some of em even go to college. The freshman English teacher, Mrs. Arnold, says one of these days, you won't even be able to get a job without a high school diploma."

Sarah knew there were other kinds of Mennonite churches where the men didn't wear a beard, and the women didn't wear a head cover. They even made *their* children go to high school. As far as she knew, the Holderman Mennonites were the only ones who discouraged higher education. She had no idea how that all came about.

Sarah rose from the bed and began picking up Harley's clothing from the floor as she talked.

"You wanna be like the English kids? Go dancin', go to the beer joint and get drunk, run around till all hours of the night? A girl can get herself in a lotta trouble runnin' around like that with boys late at night."

She opened the closet and tossed the armload of dirty clothes onto a pile of the same lying on the closet floor. She closed the door and turned to Lena, who still sat on the bed, considering her mother's words.

"Is that what you want, Lena? Is that the kind of girl you wanna be?"

"No! Not a bit!" Her skin crawled at the thought. She wrapped her arms around herself and shook her head. "You know I would never do that!"

Sarah saw the scowl and disgust in Lena's expression. She had unintentionally hit a raw nerve. She was seeing something in her that she had never imagined. She had witnessed her daughter's physical growth without ever getting to know her. But then, how could she have? Lena was a closed book. Sarah had never seen anything but the cover. Today was the turning of the first page.

She went to the bed and sat next to Lena. "Yes, I believe you wouldn't be like that. But I've heard what goes on with those kids, and I'm just saying that being around them in school is just asking for trouble. It can happen without you wanting it to."

Lena had never considered that possibility, and it made her sit still, her mind hard at work. She remembered when one of the senior girls, Linda Gibson, had disappeared from school not long after she became the subject of dark rumors.

"Did you know she's not even in town anymore?"
"Somewhere in Colorado having her baby..."
"Raped? Naw, not Linda. She'd beatcha to the back seat."

When Lena first heard the older high school kids talking, she felt sick and was afraid she would throw up. The memory of the disgust and panic that had come over her caused her to recognize a vast, deep chasm that separated her from "those kids." She knew her mother had nothing to worry about.

Frustration strained her voice. "Now you're saying that you don't trust me to do the right thing when I choose between right and wrong. Do you think I would do what other kids do? Wouldn't that mean I musta been brought up the same as them?"

"Of course not!" Sarah was defensive. "You were not brought up like they were."

"Then how can you think I would do what they do? How can just bein' in the same school make me like them? Doesn't how you were raised at home make you what you are?"

Sarah was both in awe and pleased by her fourteen-year-old daughter's good sense. Her little girl had just made an observation that had never occurred to her. She put her arm around Lena's shoulders. Glowing pride would have burst forth in her heart, but it was overshadowed by the possibilities that Lena's words had brought her.

She recalled the sad stories of some of the families of the Mennonite community. There had been several runaways, alcoholics, and even illegitimate pregnancies in the children of those good church-member families. Those awful things had happened despite the strict rules of the church and its claim to be "the true church where even God himself comes to church." My goodness! Considering the sinful things that went on in their own families, how could they make such a claim?

Now, she was getting confused. The gospel truth the church claimed to preach concerning such matters seemed a little slippery, and it wasn't easy for her to hold on to her beliefs.

Her beliefs? Maybe not, she thought. She had been brought up on the thou shalt-nots her parents taught her. Her father had instructed his family at the supper table by way of gossip. Come to think of it, she had never seen her father reading the bible. The instructions he had passed down to her and her siblings were the ones learned and hashed over by word of mouth. Sarah realized her beliefs were created by group discussions among aunts and uncles at Sunday dinner tables. The entire Mennonite community's beliefs were the results of "the gospel according to John Holderman. She had claimed them all her life. They were as stuck to her as her ears, but were they hers? She suddenly felt guilty for her thoughts, and she admonished herself for thinking that she might be brain-washed. *It's just a thought. No one can read your mind, silly! The church will never know what you think!*

Now, she did not know how to answer her daughter. She wasn't sure that the answer she would give her now would be the same as the one she had given her other children years before. In fact, she wasn't comfortable with the realization that the beliefs that she had helped to instill into her older children were, in her opinion, hand-me-downs of hearsay. She had always taken for granted that the bible in the hands of others was her guide. Now, she felt apprehension rising in her. The fact that she herself had never opened the bible soaked into her brain. Whose interpretation of the scriptures led her through right and wrong and oversaw the passing of it on to her children... Sam's? Sam had surely been there to preach to her and the children. He instigated many little spur-of-the-moment sermons. She imagined the layers of wallpaper in this house were soaked and petrified with his forceful rantings. But she couldn't help thinking that he used the same attitudes and opinions to interpret his bible as the ones she was born with. He had grown up with her in the same church, dependent on the same preachers for feeding the word. She saw now that he hadn't led her anywhere. No, it's not Sam who she's been following!

For heaven's sake, we've been following the church and being herded by them! Lena was looking down at her hands in her lap, and Sarah bent her head down and around to see Lena's face; she spoke earnestly.

"I'm not sure what to say to you, Lena. But I trust you to do what is right when the time comes."

Lena was not shocked this time. In the last few hours of this day, a new and wonderful feeling spread through the air of her world. Her mother's words inflated her confidence. "The English kids aren't as bad as everybody thinks they are. They ain't any worse than Karl and Danny Dierkson, that's for sure!"

"Well, I've heard about some of the things those Dierkson boys have done, and if the English kids are as bad as that, then you shouldn't be around them. No girl should be around them."

"But Karl and Danny aren't the only ones! And I'm around those kids more than the English kids! Nobody says anything about that! Nobody says I gotta quit going to their house to visit, or I gotta quit going to church cuz being around them might turn me into a slut or something."

"Here!" Sarah's tone was scolding. "You don't need to use that kinda language, Lena!"

Lena hung her head, thinking, *I should have said harlot. That's in the bible. Or even "bad girl."* Sorry," she said.

Sarah looked across the bed out the window; "But you're right," she said.

Her eyes were on the upper branches of the elm trees that stood behind the house, but she saw faces and heard the voices of her childhood. She remembered things that now came to her, bearing questions without answers. She began sorting through things she had learned years ago that she could now use to justify her defiant thoughts against the church.

"I don't know Lena. It's like all Mennonite parents have been taught that it's not safe to go out and live in worldly ways, so we have to stay in the shelter of the church. Nobody has even considered that maybe how we teach our children is so good that they won't fall into the traps of worldly ways. It's like the church doesn't think we can raise our children well enough. I've never thought of it before, but that almost makes me mad."

"Well then, don't you think finishing school ain't gonna do no harm?" The hope in Lena was sticking out all over.

Sarah saw it and was very pleased that Lena was there with her in body and, more wonderfully, in spirit. She had been gone for so long. Having her attention was strange and caused blank spaces in Sarah's responses to her. She spoke carefully as if she were exchanging information with a stranger at the scene of a car accident.

"I suppose there is no harm in going to school, but is it necessary? Will you need a diploma to get you through life? What would you do after you graduate from high school? You'll get married, have kids, and raise a family. I don't know of any Mennonite woman who needed to go to school to do that. Just didn't need to." Lena nearly blurted out her desire to become a writer, but that would be a little too bold. Even her mother would scoff at that fairytale.

"But Mom, that was years ago! Nowadays, there's more to life than raisin' kids, cleanin' house and... an, an," she flung her arms into the air, "goin' to church and fixin' Sunday dinner!" She was silent for a moment and then quietly added, "Ain't never gettin' married anyway." Her mom barely heard that and let it slip away.

Sarah was surprised by Lena's outburst. Wow! This was amazing. This person, this young lady, this lively, rambunctious stranger getting emotional just like everyone else, is Lena, her Lena! She wanted to jump up and down and clap her hands; the joy was overwhelming!

Then, with the flash of Lena's fleeing image going off in her mind, caution grabbed her. She wondered what Lena might do next. She held her breath and stared. Lena flopped back onto the bed, agitated, like a normal teenager. A normal teenager! Sarah let her breath out and smiled to herself.

Lena yanked herself back into a sitting position, seriously composed, determined to persuade her mother.

"I have got to get away from Sam," she said. She saw her mother frown and quickly retracted the slip of the tongue. "Sorry…I mean, father!" *Father? I guess. Daddy? Never!*

Her tone became sing-songy, almost funny. "He's gonna keep me from bein' what I wanna be, and I have to graduate from high school so I can go to college. And that's all there is to it." Any questions? She sat quietly, studying her sweaty hands. *What are you doing, numbskull? Sounding like an idiot!*

She began bouncing slightly on the bed and rubbing her hands together. "I'm sorry, Mom. I don't mean to be disrespectful. I guess I'm just so nervous!" She looked her mother in the face with "please" coming out of every pore. "I really need you to help me talk to Sam!" She hadn't noticed that she slipped again. Sarah let it go, paying more attention to Lena's actions. She reached over and touched Lena's shoulder.

"Lena, stop bouncing. It's okay. You need to relax and calm down, and you'll feel better."

She let her hand drop from Lena's shoulder. Sarah was tense, ready to grab Lena if she suddenly took off again. Lena squeezed her hands together. After a few moments of Lena staring expectantly at her, Sarah was reassured that she would not do anything rash.

"I don't want you to move out, Lena. You just got here. Do you see what I mean?"

Lena was still for a moment, then hung her head and nodded.

Sarah continued speaking. "We have a lot of catching up to do! I'm not sure I know you. You are so full of surprises. It's gonna take a while to get used to you the way you are now, and I want to get used to you." Sarah was silent and waited for Lena to argue her case, but Lena did not respond. Apprehension quickened Sarah's heart again as her memory of Lena's earlier behavior made her wary. How long does it take to be sure that a miracle has happened? Should she keep talking about this? She felt like she was taking a chance that Lena might go into a spell again. She could shut up and start again later, give Lena some time to… Lena's voice, loud and clear, interrupted her.

"I'm not leaving cuz I don't want to live here; I just want to go to school, and yesterday was my last day.

Sarah heaved a great sigh, relieved. Lena had just passed the test of a trying moment. Sarah could finally feel some confidence in Lena's new behavior. Lena was going to be alright, which made it impossible to allow her to move out. Sarah had longed for this day all these years; she couldn't let her leave now.

"I don't want you to go, Lena, but I'll talk to your dad. You know it isn't gonna change anything. To him, everything will be better in the long run if you quit school."

Lena turned sullen and gave up. It was plain to see that her mother would do no good with Sam and that she wanted her to stay here with her. That left her no choice but to sneak off. She wasn't looking forward to walking the three miles to Katy's, let alone running out on her mother.

CHAPTER 8

Sarah wanted to do her Saturday grocery shopping and return to the house as soon as possible. The eight miles to Garland seemed longer than usual. It was taking forever!

She hadn't laid eyes on Lena since she and Lena had gotten the dinner dishes done. Lena hadn't spoken at the dinner table, and Sarah had left her alone. As far as Sam knew, everything was the same as usual.

But Sarah was worried about Lena. She had walked all over the place calling for her while Sam waited in the pickup, anxious to get to town.

"Come on, Sarah, let's go," Sam had hollered from the pickup. "She's probably hiding someplace, playing her silly game. She'll be alright. She's just being hard to get along with. I can't see why you're any more worried about the way she's acting today than you are any other day."

Sarah hadn't told him that it wasn't likely that Lena was hiding. Sarah feared Lena had gotten it into her head to walk to Katy's.

Now, as they drove down the highway to Garland, she kept her eyes focused on the ditch on her side of the highway. She didn't expect to see Lena walking in plain sight but could not entirely give up on the possibility. As they approached the turn-off to Katy's, she peered down the flat, straight ribbon of gravel road but saw no one. Her first feeling was relief that she wasn't there. Then, it was replaced by a nagging dread that Lena would be gone from the house when she and Sam got back from town. What would Sam do?

He will hit the ceiling and then some.

All he would see is her disobedience. Now might be the best time to tell him about the change in Lena. Maybe he would see her as a normal girl with real reasons for her actions. Maybe he would deal with those reasons sensibly. Not just order her to be obedient without giving her a chance to explain.

It occurred to Sarah that Lena might not talk to her father. She may fall back into her silent way toward him. She had to make sure that her husband and daughter talked, face to face, about Lena attending school. She turned her face to Sam and spoke.

"Sam, I've been waiting for a time away from Lena to tell you what happened this morning."

Sam looked at Sarah and then turned his attention back to the highway.

"What happened?" he asked, and when Sarah did not answer immediately, he continued to speak.

"I knew something was afoot the way you two were acting. What happened?"

"You won't believe it. It's a miracle, Sam." He could hear the excitement in his wife's voice. A miracle? He didn't think so.

"Miracles don't happen anymore, Sarah. God performed miracles in biblical times to show the people that Jesus was his son. He blesses us with things we need. We don't need miracles. We need only God. God takes care of us without our asking. We should spend our time and words thanking God instead of wishing for a miracle."

Sarah felt deflated. Dread smothered most of her excitement. *There he goes again, pushing me down.*

She stirred a little, disgust sounding in her voice. "Well, I don't know what else to call it when someone who hasn't talked for nine years suddenly starts talking!"

Sam jerked his head to face her and then quickly back to the highway. "Lena started talking. You mean out loud?"

"Yes, out loud! We talked while doing the breakfast dishes and, for quite a while, as I straightened up Harley's room. She talked as normal as you can get."

Sarah saw no reaction in Sam's expression as he stared down the highway. Her husband of twenty-four years did not need to show her what he was feeling. Despite his expression, she knew he was as excited as she was.

Without taking his eyes off the highway, Sam asked, "What brought all this on? What did she say?"

"Well, not a lot at first. Up in Harley's room, she went through one of her episodes. Sam, she fell off the bed awful hard and hid her face on the floor, scared to death! After I finally got her to calm down and up off the floor, she wouldn't tell me why she did that. I tried to get it out of her, but..."

Sam broke in. "She wouldn't talk?"

"She talked just fine but wouldn't tell me what happened." She frowned and gave Sam an anxious look. "Do you think she could have had one of those epileptic... fits?" Associating her daughter with the word "fits" was dreadful to her.

Sam shook his head. "If she just acted scared, it wasn't epilepsy." Sarah was silent, her mind busy hoping for her little girl's health and welfare. Sam interrupted her thoughts. He said, "So, tell me what her first words were."

Sarah realized she hadn't told Sam about the first episode when Lena ran barefoot down the driveway. Now, she remembered that Lena's first words had been anger at him when she returned from helping him in the barn. She didn't know what to say. She was silent, struggling with the decision.

Then she just said it. "She was mad at you, Sam! So mad! She came from the barn and ran up the stairs. It scared me because I thought something bad might have happened in the barn. I yelled at her and told her to tell me what happened. She yelled back and called you Sam, the man. She said you were still holding her head down."

Sam was scowling when Sarah finished, and his insides were churning. He felt fallen upon by some overwhelming weight. He wanted to cry out and tell the world his disappointment and anguish. But he had no right. He must endure God's chastisement, as all of God's children must. The world could do nothing for him, so why look to them with his pain? Only God can redeem a man of sin.

She just... won't... get over it! Holding her head down? What does that mean? What does she think he had done to her? That question! It had grown in his brain like an ugly weed. No answer would get rid of it. He continued to stare out through the windshield. He absently shook his head.

She just won't get over Andrew's death! She blames me.

Sarah watched her husband and saw the hurt in his expression.

He spoke in a quiet tone. "I just don't know..." He shook his head again, "What have I done to cause God to keep my daughter away from me?"

Sarah's heart ached for her husband. She reached out and touched his arm. There were no words in her to comfort him. What could she say? Every expression of support she knew had passed from her heart to him more than once. Any offering from her would only be repetition. But she couldn't just sit there quietly and watch.

"Please, Sam, you mustn't blame yourself. Things happen without rhyme or reason." She knew, of course, that saying that would get an argument.

"No, I don't believe that. God is in control, and He has a reason for everything."

Sarah felt an unfamiliar, bold confidence in her own opinion. She spoke up, opposing Sam's attitude.

"Yes, I believe that too. But it doesn't make sense that He would keep His reason a secret if it's something you've done wrong, and He expects you to make it right."

Sam Danziger was impressed by his wife's bright reply. Surprise showed on his face as he looked at her with new appreciation. Sarah saw the look and was offended. Sarcasm permeated her thoughts. *Well, my goodness, look who can think, Sarah! Does he think I'm brainless?* She kept her feelings to herself but remained perturbed.

Sam turned his eyes to the highway, but this unfamiliar side of his wife captured his attention.

"That makes a lot of sense," he said. "Maybe I've been looking at my problem with Lena all wrong."

Sarah was stunned. *Did I hear that right? My goodness!* Now she was elated! Encouraged, she pushed her opinion forward.

"Maybe you have. And now that Lena is talking, I think you should try to talk to her about some things, school especially."

"School? What about school?"

"She wants to keep going and finish. She wants to go so bad and has just about convinced me that it can't hurt." She turned her face back toward the windshield. She saw Garland's tall white grain elevator standing in the distance, high above the roofs of the small town. They would soon be in town, and the time she was utilizing on Lena's behalf would be gone in a few minutes. She spoke as if to herself.

"What could it possibly hurt?"

Sam did not hesitate with his response. "For one thing, it will teach her some worldly habits unacceptable to our church. I will not expose any of my children to Satan's teaching and let him persuade their young minds to his way of behaving. All my children, including Lena, can read, write and do arithmetic. That is all they need to live in this world as God intended. Daniel, Harley, and Katy never went to high school, and they're doing just fine." He was silent for a moment. In a quieter tone, he added, "Lena has already gone three months longer than she needed to. She is not returning to school Monday, and that's all there is to it."

Sarah heard the familiar slamming of the door with Sam's order and knew there would be no point in knocking again. Dread crept quietly into her spirit. She was sure Lena would not be home when they got back to the house. She spoke the final words in a flat, matter-of-fact way.

"Don't be surprised if she's packed and gone when we get home."

Because of Sam's lack of reaction, she couldn't tell if he had heard her or not. *Surely, he heard.*

CHAPTER 9

Lena left the house after dinner to walk the three miles to Katy's. She knew she couldn't make it there before Sam and her mother passed the turn-off to Katy's. A couple of giant cottonwoods stood at the turn-off that she could hide behind until she saw the pickup go by.

She reached the trees when her mother was walking to the pickup in the yard after searching for her.

Lena sat in the weeds on the cold, hard ground behind the trees, her bright blue, heavy coat zipped up to her chin. She hugged her long cotton dress to her cold legs, pulling them tightly against her chest.

The temperature of the sunny November afternoon had dropped a couple of degrees. Although an occasional shiver caused her arms to squeeze tighter, she was more aware of the discomfort in her spirit. She had not felt good about going against her mother's wishes. But she felt new strength and determination after making the decision. Nobody could stop her from doing what she was sure she needed to do. They didn't have the right to, especially Sam.

However, her excitement had waned after the difficult half-hour walk across the wheat field. She began to think rationally. She was still sure she needed to escape from under Sam's thumb. She just didn't feel as good about doing it as she had earlier. There were some regrets. She had just discovered a new joy in her mother's attitude toward her. It was wonderful. She wanted to have the pleasure of it always. Surely, her moving to Katy's wouldn't change *that,* would it?

She heard a far-away humming of a vehicle out on the highway coming from the direction of the house. She peered cautiously around the trunk of the tree toward the highway. It was a light-colored car that she didn't recognize. She watched it for a moment, then turned back into her hideaway. She listened to it swish past the turn-off and continued toward town. Then she heard the familiar noise of an old wheat truck. Without looking, she knew it was either old man Spiker or one of his sons, Benny or Chris, heading for town.

Chris was her age and nastier than nasty itself, always saying bad things to her. It made her want to *slap a hair lip on em*. She stuck her head out from behind her cover to give the truck a drop-dead look. She saw her father's white pickup close behind the truck as it slipped past her. She jerked back out of sight.

Lordy lordy! It's a good thing I looked!

If she had missed seeing them, there was no telling how long she would have sat there in the cold, waiting for them to pass. She sat momentarily, then quickly crawled through the weeds to the other end of her hideout to see better. She watched their pickup follow Spiker's truck around a curve and out of sight.

She got to her feet and stomped to the gravel road through the dead, brittle weeds in the ditch. She started walking down the road, hoping Katy would be home. The shopping her mom and Sam-the-man did in town on Saturdays normally took a couple of hours. She wouldn't have time to sit around waiting for Katy. The thought roused her into a trot. Her shoes and swishing coat were the only sounds of life in this flat, vacant piece of the world.

She didn't have a watch and wondered what time it was as she walked up the driveway to Katy's house. Casey, the black and white border collie, pounced off the porch with several barks. His butt-end squirmed around, trying to pass him like the trailer on a jack-knifed semi. She smiled at the thought and bent down to pat him on his side.

"Hey Casey, how you doin' boy?" The dog's ears stiffened and pointed up as if he heard a strange noise. He looked up at her face with great interest. He tried to put his front paws on her, and she pushed him away. "No," she ordered, wondering if he was surprised to hear her voice. *Do dogs experience surprise?* She looked toward the house. "Is your boss home?" she asked the dog.

Inside the house, Katy was trying to rock her fussy ten-month-old son to sleep.

Sam Danziger's oldest child, Katy, was a very attractive young woman. Well, as attractive as the Mennonite church would allow a healthy, twenty-year-old woman to be. Her dress had to be plain, home-made and calf-length. She wore not a drop of make-up. Her brown hair was uncut and parted in the middle. It was partially covered by a small, black scarf tied in a knot under her chin. She wore the traditional black shoe-string-tied oxfords. There was no way to tell if she had a good figure because the dress was straight, loose, and buttoned to her throat. Even her arms were covered with loosely fitted sleeves that buttoned snuggly around the wrists. Her face, however, was easily seen as beautiful.

She saw her little sister coming up the driveway through the front window, and the surprise stopped her rocking. What in the world was Lena doing there? Jacob, the baby, began to squirm in her arms, and she restarted her rocking.

The dog on the porch barked and ran to Lena. She raised her face and looked at the house. Katy watched closely through the window. She stopped rocking abruptly. *Lena's mouth moved!* She appeared to be talking to the dog.

Careful not to awaken her baby, she rose from the rocking chair and moved to the door. Then, realizing the inconvenience of having her arms full of a sleeping child, she turned and carried Jacob to her bedroom and laid him in his crib. She watched Jacob for a moment to be sure he was indeed asleep, and then she ran to the front door and flung it open. Lena was just coming up the steps onto the porch.

"Lena, what are you doing here? Did you walk from home?"

Lena stopped in front of Katy, who stood in the doorway staring in wonder.

"Yes," Lena frowned. "Every lousy inch of the way and my butt is draggin." Then, with a grin, she asked, "Would you mind, dear sister, if I came in and sprawled out somewhere soft for a couple of years?"

Katy was astonished. With her eyes wide open and mouth a gawk, she stood transfixed, speechless. Lena raised her hand and snapped her fingers in Katy's face.

"Hello in there. Is anybody home?"

Katy stepped aside as Lena squeezed past her into the living room. Katy watched as Lena walked to the couch and flopped down on it with a loud expression of relief.

Then, forgetting the cold November air breezing through the open door, Katy rushed to the couch. "Lena! Is that you? It can't be you!" Her face was made even more beautiful by her beaming smile. "Who is this stranger in my house?"

Lena laughed. "Katy, you're as crazy as I am, crazier!" She sat up, and Katy, laughing, plopped down onto the couch beside her newly emerged little sister. She sat amazed, grinning, and staring. Lena stared back for a moment, then became embarrassed. Her grin turned a little stiffer. She said, "You act like you never saw me before."

"My land Lena I... I'm speechless! It's such a surprise, a wonderful, big surprise. You have a beautiful voice." She took Lena's hand and managed to keep her grin even as the tears welled up. "The most beautiful voice I have ever heard."

Her arms reached for Lena, and she hugged her, holding her tight for a long time. *This hugging is okay, I guess,* Lena thought, *but that's plenty.* She was very uncomfortable. Then, she felt ashamed for wanting to push away from the hug. You're supposed to love a hug... if you're normal. Still, she began to pull away from Katy gently.

She tossed out a laugh with, "Oh my gosh, you're crushing me to death!" Katy released her tight embrace and wiped tears from her cheeks.

"What in the world has happened? Does Mom and Dad know?" Then she flung up her arms and rolled her eyes. "Of course, they know! When did this happen?"

"This morning. I don't know why, but it just came out. I yelled at Mom. I didn't mean to, but I was so mad at Sam I wanted to just bust wide open!"

"Sam? You mean Dad... Sam! You call Dad by his name?" Lena shrugged as though she were helpless in the matter and nodded. "But I..." She started to explain, but Katy, still grinning, interrupted. "Surely not to his face, do you?" Lena quickly shook her head.

"Oh no... no, no! I'm crazy but not stupid!"

Katy laughed, delighted. She nodded, acknowledging the implication.

"No, you wouldn't get away with that one, that's for sure."

Then Lena saw Katy do something she had seen her do only rarely. She untied the knot under her chin that held her head cover on. She took it off and tossed it onto an end table next to the couch. She shook her head to let her long, brown, luxurious hair fall free to her shoulders. Her big sister was truly beautiful.

Katy faced Lena with a mischievous glint in her eyes and spoke enthusiastically. "So, what did "Sam" do to piss you off so bad?"

Well, I'll be! Her big sister was a sailor in disguise. If Sam ever heard her talk like that, her head would be on the chopping block so fast... Lena now wondered about her brothers. What big sins are they hiding from God's little helper? Lena felt more comfortable in her family than ever before. Katy was impatient to hear the rest of the story. "Come on, Lena, tell me what happened."

"Oh..., he won't let me finish school! The same thing he did to you."

Katy's expression turned somber. "Harley and Daniel too."

Lena showed surprise. "I didn't know he made them quit." A picture of her father holding an axe while standing on a cloud at the schoolhouse door flashed in her mind.

"Daniel wanted to take business in college and open an accounting firm someday."

"What about Harley," Lena asked.

"Harley? You know Harley! He just wanted to chase the girls."

The implication gave Lena a shock! She felt the surge in her chest begin, and she sprang to her feet, ready to run. The familiar panic was rising in her. But she was determined to stand fast this time. She would not duck and hide as she had always done. It was different now. Then she realized she was on the front porch, rushing toward the steps. She stopped and looked out across the yard, her eyes open wide and frightened. She looked back at the open front door, which she could not remember going through. Katy came up to the doorway, both hands covering her mouth. Her expression was a tight frown over frightened eyes. She dropped her hands and took a step forward.

"Lena? What are you doing?"

"Nothing! I just..." It had happened again. Her nightmare had come to life. She had been wide awake. But this time, it was only a quick flash. Her newly found connection with her family was her ground to stand on. The connection had brought her back quickly. She would cling to it with all her might.

"Everything is fine," she said. "I... I just felt like I needed some fresh air."

"You sure?" Katy put a hand on her shoulder. "You scared the livin' daylights out of me, jumpin' up and takin' off like that."

"Sorry. I guess I'm just nervous. I need to get back home and pack my stuff before Mom gets home.

"Pack your stuff? What are you talking about? Where are you going?"

Suddenly, Lena realized she had yet to discuss her desire to move in with Katy.

"Oh, damn," she groaned. "I'm getting way ahead of myself!" She took Katy's hand and continued talking as she led her back into the house.

"Let's go back in and sit down and talk. I gotta ask you something."

Katy, mystified and curious, let Lena pull her to the couch to sit. She was still steeped in wonder over Lena's sudden return to normal. Lena's voice, soft but firm and easily heard, was as if it had never been any other way. She wondered at what age she had started saying cuss words to herself. Judging from the ease with which they flowed, she had been doing it for a while.

Lena sat silently, looking out the window, formulating her speech. She was in a hurry and blurted, "I want to come live with you!"

Katy didn't know what to say.

Lena rushed on. "I need to get away from Sam. He will keep me from going to school if I'm in his house. Living here, he can't stop me."

Katy's mind began to scramble for a nice way to say no. She had a bad feeling about this but didn't know why exactly. Nor did she have the words to answer Lena if she asked why. She knew she would.

Katy's pause gave Lena a rush of anxiety. *She's gonna say no! Please, please, please! Don't say it!* This was a shocker! It had not occurred to her that her big sister would refuse her. She turned away from Katy and flopped back against the couch.

Katy said, "I'm not sure you should do this." Her words twisted Lena's stomach.

Lena whined, "Why? You got plenty of room, doncha? I would be down in the basement, out of the way. And I could help out! You would have a built-in babysitter! Free!"

The "I would be down in the basement" part of her appeal is what did it. Katy was suddenly aware of the cause of her reluctance to say yes. It was Lena being in the basement, directly under their bedroom. She had become next to addicted to the freedom their privacy provided since the first day of their marriage. The arrival of the baby had already tightened their space. Lena was a teenager, and teenagers have big ears and inquisitive imaginations. The situation would be uncomfortable. Lewis would be against it for sure.

"Do you really believe Dad is gonna let you just move out and come over here to live like you want to?" She shook her head. "Hardly. He'll be dragging your butt back to the house so fast you won't know what happened."

Lena knew Katy was right but could not give herself up to the enemy. Her whole childhood, beset with ducking, running, and hiding from a thing much bigger than her, had created a hardened warrior. She had determination and tenacity beyond her years. "I don't care, Katy! I am not gonna quit school no matter what he does." She rose to her feet and started toward the door.

"Where are you goin'?" Katy asked.

"I don't know, but it won't be where Sam can find me."

"That's silly, Lena! And besides, every time you go to the schoolhouse, he'll come and get you."

Lena stopped halfway to the door and hollered, "Then I won't go to the schoolhouse." She stood panting, her frustration overriding logic. Katy flinched at Lena's outburst. Her quiet little sister's loud, angry voice was so strange.

Katy measured her words carefully. "But I thought this was about *going* to the schoolhouse."

Lena whirled around to face Katy. She stood glaring at Katy. Tears sprang into her eyes, and her chin quivered. She turned away from Katy, and no matter how many times she swallowed, she could not squeeze back the crying. When it came, she lowered her head, covered her face with her hands, and quaked. Katy gawked, astonished. It had been nine years since she had seen Lena shed a single tear.

Chapter 10

Lena ran out of Katy's house, and Katy called to her to come back. She didn't stop but ran down the road toward the highway a mile ahead. She had no picture in her mind of a destination; she just knew she couldn't stay there.

She was approaching the highway when the sound of a vehicle coming down from the north made her heart jump. That was the direction her parents would be coming from town. She stopped and squatted on the green carpet of newly planted wheat. She felt stupid for going through the motions of hiding in that wide-open space. But she was stuck. Hugging her knees, she peered anxiously in the direction of the sound. She couldn't make herself just stand up. *In front of the pope and everybody. Probly look like a blue bolder. Just what you'd expect to see in a field of new green wheat.* Then she saw that the vehicle was a brown car, not Sam's white pickup. She stood up and walked to the ditch along the highway.

As she got closer to her house, the tool shed came into view, and she could see her brother Harley with her dog Butch in front of it. It appeared that Butch was attempting to socialize with Harley. Harley ignored him and went inside the shed. Butch saw Lena's familiar figure walking along the ditch, and it sent him hell-bent toward her.

She saw him appear on the other side of the highway at the ditch's far edge. When he descended into the ditch, she realized he intended to cross over to be with her. Out of the corner of her eye, she saw a red car fast approaching. It was much too close and going too fast to stop for a dog on the road. She screamed at the top of her voice. "Butch, get back!" Then with a stern tone, "No, Butch, no!" The dog halted on the edge of the asphalt. His ears perked tightly as if to identify a noise, a stranger. But his eyes told him it was not a stranger. He bound out onto the highway, alert only to the mystery of the familiar figure who sounded like a stranger. She screamed again, "No, Butch, no!"

She heard the red car's tires squeal just before its metal hulk swallowed Butch from her sight and then continued on its way as if nothing happened. She was consumed with horror. Her eyes, wide with astonishment, pierced the edge of the highway. Butch was gone, snatched off the face of the earth. She ran across the highway into the ditch of weeds, screaming his name. She could not see him. She twisted, jerked her head around, and pivoted on her feet to face every direction. Suddenly, he burst out of the weeds at the bottom of the ditch, several feet from her. He ran toward the house, turning his head back at his right shoulder. With a silent snarl, he turned again as if something had a hold on him there. She saw blood slinging out from that side of his mouth. She ran after him and watched him disappear under the porch.

Her brother Harley, who was just leaving the tool shed, heard her screams. Seeing her run from the other side of the highway confused him. He saw someone he thought was Lena, but it was also someone who had a voice. She was chasing Butch, who was running toward the house. He remembered hearing the squeal of tires before leaving the shed and suspected what might have happened.

Lena reached the porch before Harley and was down on hands and knees, looking under the porch. She was trying to get Butch to come to her. Harley dropped to the ground beside her and looked under the porch. Butch lay on his side, his tail end nearest Lena's outstretched hand. She patted the ground, softly calling his name. "Here, Butch, c'mon boy, c'mon." She patted the ground again. "Here, Butch." The dog did not respond.

Then Harley's attention was drawn from the motionless dog he feared was dead to his little sister. He was awe-struck. He did not recognize the voice of the person beside him. She spoke again as clearly as he had ever imagined she could.

"C'mon, big boy, come to Lena." There were the makings of tears in her voice. She crawled on her stomach to her dog under the porch, pleading as she strained to reach him. Harley watched and listened to her broken heart.

"Please, Butch! C'mon. Come to Lena, don't go off somewhere now. Please don't be dead." The weeping started as her hand touched the dog's hip. Harley saw her outstretched body quake there on the cold, dark floor of that tomb. His eyes filled with tears as he listened to her grief. He was amazed at her voice and the crying he had never heard before. He raised himself upright with his legs folded under him and sat back on his heels. He cleared his eyes of the tears, his spirit suffering with his little sister.

He called her. "Lena, come out and let me get him out from under there." He waited. It took a while for her to stop crying. Pressed to the ground, she began to push herself backward from under the porch. When her head cleared the edge of the porch, she sat up and stared, unseeing, at the side of the porch in front of her.

"Maybe he's not dead," Harley said.

Without moving, she spoke to him, God, or herself. Whoever she spoke to, Harley heard her every word.

"It's my fault," she murmured. She did not see Harley's silent examination of her. He could not take his eyes off her. The sound of her voice was so normal. And yet he dared not mention it lest it vanish like the splendor of a perfect dream.

"If I woulda kept my mouth shut, he woulda paid more attention to the traffic and woulda never ran out in front of the car." Harley sat quietly, absorbing the reality of a talking Lena. He knew he would have to wait until later to figure it out. Right now, he needed to help her.

He ducked under the porch to his stomach and pulled himself as close as possible to the dog. He lay still, watching for any movement, but saw nothing that would indicate life. Not even a faint, desperate struggle for a single breath. The dog was on its side, and Harley took hold, with one hand, of both its hind feet and backed out of the small space.

Lena watched Harley pull Butch from under the porch. She began to cry again, silently, knowing her dog must be dead.

When Harley was out, he carefully pulled carefully pulled the lifeless animal out into view. She whispered through her tears, "Oh, Butch, I'm so sorry."

Then she just sat there on her folded legs, her hands limp in her lap, and wept.

Harley sat on his heels, watching her. He felt guilty for not feeling the same grief that she suffered for the dog. His emotions were of wonder and gratitude for the return of his little sister. Out of respect, he said nothing.

He wanted to talk with her. How had she managed to find her voice? Had it come to her as a reflex to save ol' Butch? Would she still have it when she got over Butch? He waited, and she finally stopped crying.

He spoke in a quiet tone. "Sorry, Lena, I know how much ol' Butch meant to you." Drained of tears, she shrugged and remained silent.

He said, "There's always been the chance that this would happen sooner or later, bein' this close to the highway." He looked out at the highway as a car went humming by, headed toward town.

"When I heard you scream, I didn't know who it was or who it could be. Even when I saw you out in the field, I didn't imagine it was you at first." He turned his stare away from the highway and looked at her. She continued looking at the dog's still body.

"I never heard you scream before, he said."

She looked at him silently and then noticed movement in the distance. Looking down the highway, she said, "Here come Mom and Sam."

Harley saw the pickup come into plain view from behind the trees. He followed it with his eye to the driveway as he mused over Lena's calling their dad by his first name. What other surprises was she gonna come up with? He didn't have to wait for one.

"I guess I'll be catchin' hell here in a minute," she said.

Harley jerked his head around to look at her. He was shocked and then started laughing.

"Don't laugh, Harley. I killed my dog, and I deserve to be punished."

Harley was apologetic. "I was laughing at your cussing... and you didn't kill Butch. It was an accident."

"Well, accidents don't just happen. If I wouldna been doin' something I shouldn't, it wouldna happened."

It occurred to him that he hadn't wondered why she had been out in Spiker's wheat field.

"What were you doin' that you weren't supposed to?"

She wasn't sure she wanted to tell Harley, but she couldn't come up with a reason not to. She felt compelled to talk to somebody about it. That feeling was new to her. Only yesterday, she wouldn't have needed a specific reason to keep silent. She answered him.

"I was at Katy's house asking if I could move in with her."

"Move in with her?"

Yeah, you know... change my address, live there, be part..."

"Yeah, yeah, I know, I got it. But why is what I wanna know." Lena was slow to answer. Then they heard the pickup doors slam, and their mother called to them from the other side of the house. "Harley, Lena! Help get the groceries in!"

Harley rose and started for the other side of the house. He reached the corner and turned to look at Lena, who hadn't moved.

"Are you comin'?" She was looking at her dead dog and shook her head, then jerked to look at him.

"Don't you tell Sam about this!" Her expression was threatening. "You do, and I'll be pissed at you forever." He stared at her, shaking his head.

"I just can't believe it," he said.

"Harley, I mean it! You keep your mouth shut, or I'll whomp on your head till the hair flies! I'm serious!"

"Ok, ok! I won't say a word!" He wasn't sure what exactly he wasn't supposed to tell their father about, Butch getting hit by a car or her trip to Katy's. Then he smiled at her and said, "Man, you're mean," and disappeared around the corner.

Lena sat close to her dead companion with her legs folded under her, one hand gently stroking his head. Then she rose to her knees and slid her hand under his head and the other under his haunches and lifted him to her chest. When she saw his limp neck let his head flop over her arm, a sob of utter grief groaned from her throat. She sat that way for a few seconds, feeling the weight of her regret holding her down, crushing her soul. It pressed the tears from her broken heart. "Oh, Butch," she moaned. "It's all my fault! I'm so, so sorry!" She shuddered and touched the top of his head with her lips. Holding her dead dog, sobbing, she struggled under the weight to stand and slowly trudged around to the back of the house.

She walked behind the barn, over to behind the tool shed, and headed toward the south end of the pasture. It took a while to reach the grove of cottonwoods.

She went deeper into the trees and found a clear spot at the foot of a large cottonwood. She went to her knees, laid Butch there on his side, and sobbed even more.

After a while, she found a branch she thought was stout enough to dig a hole in the sandy pastureland. It didn't work. It took nearly half an hour of stabbing, then scooping by hand to make a hole barely deep enough to notice. She decided she needed a shovel. She went back to the tool shed and got one.

She seemed to be out of tears but felt defeat take over her whole existence. All that was left for her to do was to bury Butch and go back to shutting up and staying out of the way. She wouldn't be able to go through being the cause of harm to another loved one. Her new voice had caused nothing but trouble and grief.

She returned to the grave site, head bowed, shovel in hand, dragging her shame and regret along with her. She tossed the shovel to the ground and sat beside her fallen buddy. She gently pulled Butch to her and up on her lap, the moister in her eyes blurring the world around her. She cried out of control for a long time. She killed the best friend she'd ever had.

Chapter 11

Harley saw the tail end of the pickup bed sticking out from behind the side of the house where the kitchen door was set.

When he got to the pickup, he saw his father enter the kitchen with both arms loaded with groceries. His mother had already gone inside. Five more sacks of groceries were in the pickup bed. His father exited the house as he got a sack into each arm. "Where's Lena?" Sam asked.

Harley kept moving toward the house as he answered, "Round on the other side of the porch."

"What's she doin'? Is she gonna help?"

"I don't know."

Harley entered the house and set the groceries on the kitchen table. As his mother put the groceries away, she asked, "Has Lena been home all the time we were gone?" Harley hesitated. He didn't know if the people to whom he had promised Lena to be silent included his mother or not. He chose to be cautious.

"Why? What's wrong?"

"Nothing, yet. I want to know if she went to Katy's." Harley headed for the door without answering and sidestepped his father as Sam entered the kitchen. He went out, and his father set the groceries on the table. Sarah, her back to Sam, listened for him to say something indicating that he had heard her and Harley talking.

"I'll go get Lena to help you put away those groceries," he said and walked out. She was relieved.

When Harley came in with the last sack of groceries, she asked again, "Did Lena go to Katy's?"

Harley had had time to figure out how to keep from lying to his mother. "I can't imagine Lena walking to Katy's house. What makes you think she did?" Sarah heard it in his voice and stopped unpacking to look at his face. He was studying the pattern of the linoleum flooring at her feet.

"Harley, look at me." He raised his face and met her eyes for an instant, then found something on his hand to study

"What?" he asked.

A small glint of amusement shone in her eyes. "Don't what me! You're slick, but not that slick. You never could get one by me. I know you wouldn't lie to me, but you were gonna try to fake me out. Well, it didn't work when you were a squirt, and it won't work now. You might as well tell me what I want to know." He leaned against the table, resting his butt against the edge, and folded his arms across his chest.

"Ok, she got back about fifteen minutes before you got here." Sarah went back to putting groceries away.

"Has she talked to you?" he asked. "Do you know she's talking… I mean, out loud?" Sarah looked at him. She saw excitement in him and his raised eyebrows accenting his question.

"It's true, Mom, Lena's back!"

Sarah was pleased. "Yes, I know, we talked nearly all morning. Her talking to you, too, means she might be back for good. I've been hoping all day that it's not just temporary. And knowing that she surely talked to Katy, and now you, makes me feel sure about it."

Harley let his excitement move him about the room. "Isn't it great," he exclaimed. "Isn't it damned amazing?"

He stopped pacing and glanced at his mom. She was at the cabinet, putting away canned goods, with her back to him.

"Yes, it is," she said. "And that's for sure!" He was surprised that she hadn't heard the cuss word.

She turned and faced him. "Did she say anything about wanting to move in with Lewis and Katy?"

"Yeah."

"Did she say if Katy said she could or not?"

"Didn't get a chance. That's when you called us to help with the groceries."

The door popped open then, and Sam stepped into the room, speaking to Harley. "Didn't you say Lena was around the other side of the porch?"

"Yes."

"Well, she's not there. Go find her and tell her to get in here to help her mother." Sarah spoke up. "It's okay, Sam. I really don't need any help now." Though she was anxious to talk to Lena, now wasn't the time.

"No, you probably don't need help, but Lena needs to be helping." He went back out, leaving the door open for Harley.

Harley moved to the door and heard his mother say, "You better hope your dad doesn't ever catch you cussing like that." He went out, letting the door slam behind him, in a hurry to find out where Lena had taken her dead dog.

After walking around to search in all of Lena's hiding places, Harley still hadn't found her. Hollering her name might have helped, but he doubted it. Besides, their dad was out and about somewhere. Harley didn't want him to know where he was if he decided to come and help find Lena.

He had given up and was walking back to the house when he realized that her hiding places would not make good places in which to bury a dog. As he walked past the old model T, he turned and looked out across the flat expanse of the west pasture. He tried to imagine a secluded spot in that area that she would pick. He thought of the small grove of elms that were huddled at the edge of the north wheat field. When he looked toward the wheat field, he could see the top half of the elms above a small hill. He made up his mind to go there and, walking at a fast pace, got to the top of the hill a few minutes later. He couldn't see her anywhere, so he continued down the hill.

He saw her kneeling behind the largest elm tree. Suddenly, she disappeared behind the tree. He called her. "Lena, it's me."

She poked her face out from behind the tree, saw him, and resumed her prior position. As he approached her place next to the tree, he saw a shovel in the weeds and a shallow hole she had dug. The dead dog was in the hole. She was sitting in the weeds beside the hole that she had dug. With her hands in her lap, she stared at the open grave.

Harley's quiet voice was a harsh intrusion on the silence there in that somber air. The sad elm trees stood like stiff sentries, paying their respects to the dead.

"The hole's not deep enough, Lena. The coyotes will dig it up." She did not move when he spoke. A fresh trace of tears stained her voice. She was irritated. "Damn the stupid coyotes! We're having a funeral here. And it's not just a hole. It's a grave, the final resting place of a dear departed loved one." As she gazed into the grave, her hand went to the pile of dirt, gathered a little of it, and tossed it on the dead dog.

Harley stood in awe of this familiar figure who was a complete stranger. How much of her had he missed? What mysterious power had denied him this precious sister?

She sat on her legs scrunched against the earth, mourning the first casualty of her return to the world in which her loved ones lived. She was convinced that the new sound of her voice had killed Butch. She leaned over sideways, reached for the shovel, and stood up, looking at the dead dog in the shallow hole. She turned to look behind her at Harley.

Harley moved to her side. "You want me to dig the hole... the grave, deeper?" She handed Harley the shovel.

"Thanks," she said, then dropped back down on her knees and began to lift the dead weight from the hole. She struggled. Harley dropped the shovel and got down to help.

After removing Butch from the hole, Harley began the task of digging a deeper grave in the sandy earth.

Lena sat as she had before and watched.

Harley tossed a shovel full of dirt. "Well, you didn't tell me what Katy said about you movin' in with her."

"She said no."

Harley continued to dig. "She just said no? She give a reason?"

Lena raised her shoulders and gave a don't-ask-me-look to Harley. "I don't know fer sure. She kinda said it wouldn't do any good. I didn't argue much cuz I didn't wanna get her on Sam's list. And maybe she's right."

"Why do you want to move out?" The "do" came out in a grunt as he stabbed the earth for another scoop full of sandy dirt.

"You should know why. He did the same thing to you and Daniel... and Katy. Did you know Katy got married to get out of the house? He made all of you quit school." Harley didn't mention that he had quit voluntarily. Lena continued. "And now it's my turn; only I'm not quittin." They grew silent. Lena got another handful of dirt and absently tossed it into the hole. Harley stopped and looked at her.

He said, "You keep puttin' the dirt back in, it's gonna take longer."

"Oh, sorry; I wasn't thinkin.'"

Harley was knee-deep in the hole, had quit digging, and stood looking at the bottom of it. With the shovel in one hand, he began stabbing it into the earth at his feet. The word "married" had brought his thoughts back to Linda Gibson.

"Lena."

Lena looked at him. "What?"

With his head down, he continued to stab the shovel. "Can I tell you something, and you won't tell anyone?"

"Who, me? You know what a blabbermouth I am."

He looked up at her and almost smiled. The shovel stood still.

"You know Linda Gibson."

"Yeah. Somebody said she..." Lena felt that little twist of panic in her stomach. She ignored it this time. "Got...you know, in trouble and went to Colorado." Her heart upped its beat, and her breath came quicker. She sat still, her eyes locked to Harley's, feeling the early tremors of panic.

Harley said, "She's staying with her grandparents till she has the baby." He looked back down at the shovel. "Our baby."

Lena was struck dumb and, for a moment, was as still as stone. Then, that little twist of panic that had trembled in her stomach burst into her chest and arms. The dust of the hayloft grabbed her breath, and she struggled for air. Then she realized that she was holding her breath. She let it out, then sat very still and waited.

What Harley saw was Lena stiffen. Her upper body rose into a rigid posture. It startled him. He moved on hands and knees to be at her side but halted. She dropped her hands to her lap, slumped to her previous relaxed posture, and sat with her eyes closed. He sat back, his butt on his heels. He noticed the tremble in her, and her hands shook in her lap. "You ok?" He reached over and laid his hand on her shoulder.

"Gimme a minute," she whispered. After a moment, she heaved a great sigh and opened her eyes. She could not look at Harley. He had actually...! She couldn't even think it. She shook her head, scrambled to her feet, and, brushing the dirt from her dress, nodded her head toward the grave.

"How long you gonna make the poor dog wait? Till he gets cold and leaves?"

Harley was astonished at the sudden change in her manner. Her first reaction was shock as he had expected. But then, to immediately pretend she hadn't heard what he said made him stare in wonder. Then, her apparent indifference irritated him.

"Lena, did you hear what I said? I got Linda Gibson pregnant and..."

Lena clapped her hands over her ears and hollered, "No, no, no, I don't want to hear it. Shut up, Harley, just... shut up or so help me...!" She stood with her head down, her hands pressed against her ears.

Harley sat very still with his mouth open and stared.

She stomped her foot and begged, "Please, Harley, please! Bury poor ol' Butch, and we'll go."

Seeing that she was more distressed than he was angry, Harley made short work of dragging the dead dog into the hole and covering it without ceremony.

The fact that Lena made no protest made him think that his problem had taken precedence over the loss of her beloved dog. She didn't even mention marking the grave.

They silently walked back toward the house, and as they approached the old Model T, Harley's attention was drawn to it. His question about whether he could get it running again returned to him. He stopped beside it. Lena took a few steps farther, then stopped and turned to look back at him, wondering.

He continued toward her, and as he passed by, he said, "I'm goin' to Colorado."

At that moment, their father, who was in the tool shed, saw them and became anxious about talking to Lena. He wanted to hear her voice. He suspected that Sarah, in her excitement, had exaggerated Lena's sudden recovery. He did not want his suspicions to be a fact. He wanted to hear Lena talk with a voice as clearly and normal as God had first given her. Then he would know that her trouble had been Satan's doing. It would prove that his hard-earned position with God had always been intact. For nine years, he had questioned his worthiness of God's blessings.

He waited until they approached the shed, then walked out to meet them. "Lena, I was looking for you by the porch a while ago." She stopped, looked at her father, and waited for the rest. Harley also stopped and directed his attention to Lena. He wondered if she would be as forthcoming with her new voice to their father as she had been to him and their mother. She said nothing.

The moment was awkward for Sam, but he didn't know why. This was his daughter, who was as familiar to him as daylight, but he didn't know how to start a conversation with her. God's marvelous creation, she had been left with him to be led through childhood to God's service. He knew his responsibility to God regarding his children and had confidence in his instruction to them. However, this child had never responded or spoken her mind to him. He had never fully known the effects of his efforts with her. Sarah claims she has talked to her. If she can talk, what are the words to say to her to cause her to talk to him?

She was like a stranger whose first words might offend him in some way and start them off on the wrong foot. But she was not a stranger. She was subject to his instruction and command. He should guide her along as usual for her own good: God's intended purpose. There was no other purpose to consider. Even though he was at a loss for words, he finally spoke.

"You were needed to help with the groceries, but you ran off again." He waited for her to answer. She was silent as usual. This was the time to test her and verify Sarah's account of her recovery.

"What do you have to say for yourself?"

Lena was cautious. Now, unlike many times before, her voice presented a problem for her. She had always just stood quietly and listened to her father. Knowing she wouldn't speak, he would soon leave her alone. She had never had to decide what to say to him. Now, however, he waited for an answer. He pressed her further.

"Your mother said you talked to her; talk to me, Lena. Tell me why you ran away. Maybe you had a good reason. I wanna know." At first, he made her want to run away again. She became very uncomfortable, and she clutched the skirt of her dress in tightly clenched hands. Then she heard, "Maybe you had a good reason." *Maybe?* She looked at Harley, not for support but to convey to him that it was okay to tell "the reason." She saw that he did not understand. Then she looked Sam squarely in the face and defiantly said, "I had to bury Butch."

Her words could not have been clearer. Sam was startled. The sound of her voice was profound, jerking his attention and letting her obvious air of defiance slip by him. He felt the goosebumps raise the hair on his scalp. He was slow to adjust and was silent, oblivious to the context of her words. Lena and Harley waited for their father's reaction to Lena's "good reason." That information had only collided with Sam's brain and had yet to penetrate. He spoke his feelings about Lena's voice instead. "I'm glad to hear you talking." He stood looking at her, his expression revealing nothing of his pleasure, then walked off toward the house. Lena and Harley stood in relief, watching their father's brisk, steady stride. But Lena was struck with a sense of disappointment, too.

Well, I'll be! He's just walkin' off? Now there's a puzzle for yuh. Did he not hear what she said? She thought he had always liked Butch, *so it can't be that he doesn't care if the dog is dead or not.*

She followed Harley, who walked toward the house, aware of the time being close to supper. Harley said, "He didn't say a word about Butch."

Lena: "You noticed.

CHAPTER 12

Sam entered the house into the kitchen. The table was set for supper, and Sarah was taking off her apron.

Sam pulled his arms from his coat sleeves, struggling with the snug fit of flannel against flannel.

Sarah was anxious about Lena. "Did Harley find Lena?"

"Yeah, they're coming."

"Where was she?"

Sam had his coat off, holding it in both hands, heading for the coat closet. "I saw them coming from that grove of trees over by that dried-up water hole."

Sarah stood facing Sam, her apron in her hands. "What in the world was she doing out there? Did she say? Did she talk to you?"

At that moment, Lena's words soaked into Sam's brain. "Well, isn't that something? I just now realized what she said." He stared at Sarah, his eyes on her, but seeing Lena as she had spoken.

Sarah stared back, waiting. "Well? What did she say?"

"She said she had to bury Butch!"

Sarah frowned. "Bury Butch?"

Sam headed for the closet, wondering. Sarah remained still, watching Sam as he left the kitchen to put his coat away. "What happened to Butch?" she asked the empty doorway. The kitchen door, coming open, startled her.

Lena and Harley entered and saw their mother staring at them, specifically at Lena. "Are you okay?" she asked.

Lena unzipped her coat and began to pull herself from it. She wondered why her mother was asking if she was okay. "Yeah, I'm okay. Why?"

"You must feel terrible about Butch. What happened?"

Lena took her coat off and tossed it on a chair beside the door. Harley held his coat by the collar, watching Lena. Sarah saw Lena's manner become apprehensive.

Lena lowered her eyes to the floor, examining her options in this serious matter of Butch's death. *What a strange deal. After all these years, I finally*

79

start talking, and that's what kills my dog. She spoke as if she were alone. Her disgust showed in her words. "Everybody duck... I'm gonna say something."

Sarah wasn't close enough to hear, but Harley was. He said, "It wasn't your fault, Lena."

Sarah was suddenly drawn to her daughter by a mother's instinct to protect her children. She moved to her side, took one of Lean's hands into both of hers and bent her head over to look at Lena's lowered face. She spoke kindly. "I didn't hear what you said, sweetheart."

"It doesn't matter, Mom, I killed poor Butch."

"You killed him? How did you do that?"

"It was my fault he ran out on the highway."

Sarah patted her daughter's hand. "Don't be so hard on yourself. You didn't call him out to the highway, did you?" Lena shook her head. Her mother added, "No, of course you didn't. It was not your intention that Butch be killed."

"But if I wouldna been on the other side of the highway it wouldna happened. You don't always have to have intentions to be the blame."

"And you're right about that, but that's what accidents are."

Lena raised her head and looked at her mother. "Accidents don't just happen; something must cause it. People cause accidents."

"But it's what's in your heart that counts." Then, a notion occurred to Sarah that had never entered her mind. She passed it on to her daughter, and the amazement of its discovery was clearly in her voice. "I don't think the things people do are as important as why they do them."

Sam entered the room, and his shirt sleeves were rolled up to the elbows where he had left them after washing up for supper. Sarah stood up straight and spoke final words of comfort to Lena. "Chin up. Losing Butch is one of those accidents you can't blame yourself for."

Harley left the room to hang his coat in the closet and Sam pulled his chair away from the table. Its scraping on the linoleum floor filled the gap in the conversation. "Supper's getting cold," he said and sat, then scooted his chair closer to the table.

Sarah said, "Daniel's not back from the church, but there's no sense waiting." Then, she also took her place at the table. "Get washed up, Lena."

Lena entered the bathroom where Harley was washing his hands and waited her turn. "I guess I'm not gonna catch it after all unless Sam the man is waitin' till everyone's gathered round for optimum effect."

Harley pulled the hand towel from the rack and began drying his hands. "Whaddya mean by that? Optimum? Whereja get that word? And why are you callin' Dad Sam, the man? You're just askin' for trouble."

Lena went to the sink, turned the water on, and swiped her hands through the faucet's stream. "No worse than you sneaking to Colorado." She turned the water off. Harley tossed her the towel. "I'll be there before anyone knows it... unless you tell."

"I'm not telling. You going to Colorado might come in handy for me, too." She had dried her hands and now tossed the towel back to Harley. She reached the doorway before Harley could find the implication in her words and left him talking to himself.

"Oh no, you don't, Lena. I don't think so." He rushed to catch up with her before she got to the kitchen but failed.

Their parents were waiting for them, so they quickly took their places at the table. Sam said grace, and after everyone said amen, he pulled the bowl of fried potatoes to himself. Thus began the spooning and the passing. Lena's joining in the collective "amen" did not go unnoticed by Sam. He spoke to Lena without looking at her. "Well, Lena, it's a wonderful blessing that God has given you back your voice. You would do well to thank Him. We would all do well to thank Him. I know I'm very thankful."

No one said anything. The bowls, platter, and busy silverware made their clattering sounds as they do, regardless of the occasion: celebration or survival. Sam broke the silence with little evidence of which occasion was now confronting Lena. He lifted his face toward her and, conveying his authority, said, "I would like to hear you tell us what exactly happened to poor ol' Butch."

Survival would be the occasion, she decided. Her first impulse was to ignore him as she had always done before. There was no getting away this time. She became uncomfortable in her unfamiliar position as one of those who were required to answer their father's questions. She knew all eyes were on her. She had stopped filling her plate at the sound of his voice and now raised her head to cautiously examine his demeanor.

He sat leaning forward toward her as if to press into her his demand for an answer. His eyes burned with tense purpose.

Her face grew hot. She began to feel the weight of his hands on her shoulders. Dread punched her in the stomach, and she began to feel the panic that would take her to the hayloft. She whispered inaudibly to her assailant, *Please God!* The hayloft loomed in her mind.

Her hands flew up to the height of her shoulders, and she flung herself against the back of her chair. The spoon for the green beans sailed from her hand, dinged against the wall behind her, and clattered to the floor.

Harley exclaimed, "What the hell!" His startled voice slapped the air, and Lena gasped at its reality, sucking it in. She had started rising, got halfway up, returned from the hayloft to the kitchen, and sat back down. "*Hell.*" The cuss word echoed in her mind, sent there from Harley's startled mouth. It had jerked her from her trip to the hayloft. She looked sharply at Harley, who had instantly realized what he had said and was staring at his father.

Sam had jerked in surprise at Lena's behavior but gave it second place in his attention to Harley's outburst of profanity. He saw Lena return to her sitting position, but his full attention was on Harley. He sat staring at him for a moment, then leveled an expression of contempt at Harley. He frowned at the filth he perceived as the devil at work in his son.

Then suddenly, his face became like stone, set in what he must do. He slowly raised himself to a straight and rigid posture. Silence fell around them and hissed its warning. The father's voice, like a rumbling out of a distant approaching storm, brought Harley down to less than nothing.

"Leave my table," he growled. "And take the devil with you!"

There was no hesitation in Harley. He pushed his chair back and rose in one motion. Lena watched him quickly leave the room.

Sarah frowned at her husband, this stiff, relentless, self-appointed keeper of God's will with no give. *Worse than a stuck drawer.* "Sam! Do you have to always...?"

The look he gave her shut the words off in her throat. She sat looking at him. She wanted to stand up to him and ask questions that would provoke answers from him that he would examine and wonder if she might have the right one. She has never dared. She needn't take sides. *Give it time, and it will work itself out. It always has before. No harm done yet. Children seem to always come through it. Katy and Daniel did.* She turned back to her plate.

Lena saw her mother's retreat and understood her position, which was every bit as suppressed by Sam as her own. She wasn't the only one being held down by the neck. Of course not! Sam had the whole family rounded up for judgment day, like a sacrifice.

So, what is God's little helper trying to pay for?

Sam resumed eating, as did Sarah. Lena made a move to rise and leave the table.

Sam said, "Where are you going?" He pointed to her plate of food. "Eat your supper. You're not getting out of telling me what happened to your dog, so you might as well make up your mind to stay here till you do."

Lena's tone was flat and matter-of-fact. "I was on the other side of the highway, and Butch saw me and came running across. He didn't see this car coming and ran out in front of it."

Sam had stopped attending to his plate to listen and now he cut a piece from his chicken-fried steak. He left it stuck to his fork and returned his attention to Lena. He let her see his puzzlement. "What were you doing on the other side of the highway?"

She did not hesitate. "I was coming back from Katy's."

Sam could see her defiance. In fact, he could see that she was sticking it in his face. That perturbed him to the point of sending him into a potential fit of scolding, but he held himself. He heaved a heavy sigh to compensate.

Lena's newfound careless bravery did not allow Sam to continue the interrogation. His next question never left his mouth. She would control the proceedings.

"I went to Katy's to ask her if I could live with her and Lewis. And the reason for that is because I am gonna keep on going to school, and if I stay here, it would be nothing but trouble." She had not taken her eyes off Sam while she spoke, and her stare remained fixed in place.

She was challenging him! He was taken aback, suddenly astonished by her aggression. It was just yesterday that she was quiet, little Lena. It had been hardly any problem, just a trying test of his faith in God's willingness to bless his family. His faith had won out. He had met the task with gladness for every sacrifice and heartbreak. He had kept his eye on the reward for the war he waged and had won against the evils of sin. And God had, at last, blessed him mightily. His blessing sat across the kitchen table from him, the child he loved the most. He would not fall now from his responsibility to his God. Not now.

"Lena, Lena, you are not in charge here. You will not move to Katy's, and you will not go to school. You have more than enough schooling in order to do what God created you to do. We were put here on this earth to serve God, to do His will, not our own. To know His will, we must study His word, not your math book, geography, or English book. Even the man, who is head of the family, need not have the knowledge of the world's books, only the bible. So, the woman God put under the man to be his helpmate needs schooling even less. She needs only to follow her man and what he teaches her of the bible.

Lena's heartbeat quickened. She could feel it thumping against the walls of her chest like when she had once felt a baby sparrow's heartbeat against the palm of her hand. She wanted to jump up from her chair and holler her words while pacing and flinging her arms in the air.

But she sat quietly, staring at her plate and panting. There was only a slight dusty smell of hay in her nose. She sat up straight, set the heels of her hands against the edge of the table, and pushed herself away. The chair scraped against the floor, and she rose to her feet. There was nothing more to say. She had no desire to discuss school with Sam, *"the steel sponge."* It would be a waste of words. Her eyes were on her mother as she moved toward the doorway to the living room.

Her mother was staring at Sam, and then she turned to Lena. Lena saw the helplessness and regret in her mother's face, the apology in her soft brown eyes. Lena went through the doorway, her back to the kitchen. She heard the scrape of the chair and Sam's warning voice, "Sarah!" and nothing more. Not her mother calling her name or a single footstep behind her. She climbed the stairs two steps at a time, walked quickly down the hall, and stood at Harley's closed door. She would not be denied her right to go to school. She had decided. She would need to talk Harley into helping her.

CHAPTER 13

After church services, Daniel parked his old Ford in the driveway next to his father's pickup. He walked, bible in hand, to the house and entered by the front door. There was no one in sight. No sounds of life were to be heard anywhere in the big old house. He had expected to see Lena in the living room since she had not gone to church. He climbed the stairs, went to his room, and changed out of his church clothes. No telling where Harley was. He hadn't gone to church either. He changed into overalls, a blue long-sleeved denim shirt, and high-top laced work shoes. He then headed for the barn to look for Harley.

As he approached the barn, he heard a single clang of metal against metal. He stopped and listened. Then he heard a voice, irritated in tone and distinctly male. "Damit, you just can't go!" He had found Harley and someone he was talking to. Probably Lena. *Go where?* He continued toward the back of the barn. The closer he got, the clearer the voices became. He heard a girl say, "C'mon Harley, you can't leave me here with Sam!" At first, he was surprised, then confused. It wasn't Lena, after all, since Lena doesn't talk. Harley must have some friend of his here. But how had she gotten here? He hadn't seen a strange vehicle anywhere. *Sam? Did she say, Sam?* Why would Harley be leaving a girlfriend with his dad? It grew quiet, and as he was about to turn the corner, he heard the clatter of metal again, like a dropped wrench, then Harley's "Damit!"

He turned the corner, and he saw the girl standing with her back to him. She was wearing a sky-blue dress with little yellow flowers printed all over it. It was a homemade dress, the hem of which hung below her calves. She wore white anklets, the tops folded into cuffs, and her blonde braids hung to the middle of her back. Very Mennonite and very familiar. *Lena?* There wasn't another girl there, just her and Harley. Harley was lying across the fender of the old Model T, messing around under the hood.

Daniel was astonished and stood unnoticed behind the two for several seconds. Absorbed by questions about the unfamiliar voice he had heard, he was silently grappling with his confusion. It was Lena, the only girl there, at least the only girl he could see. So where was the girl he had heard talking? Then, an explanation began to gleam dimly in his imagination. But he couldn't say it. It was too... unlikely, a foolish association with hopeless wishing. Instead, he asked, "Where's your girlfriend Harley?"

Lena jumped, startled. "What?" Whirling around and seeing Daniel, she scolded, "Lordy, you scared me to death!" Daniel was shocked at the sound of her voice. The dim possibility that had been a product of his imagination suddenly burst into brilliant reality.

"Lena! That was you I heard talking!" He walked to her and stared, his pleasure pushing aside any words that he could have said. He was half smiling, half gawking, fully displaying his surprise and joy. Lena smiled back, a little embarrassed by the attention.

Harley slid off the fender to his feet and saw their awkward shyness as they each searched for words. Then, what happened next amazed him. Daniel moved in and took astonished Lena into his arms, and for a moment, exactly as long as God would allow, he hugged her. Harley grinned. *Whoa, Danziger kids hugging? The Devil's in the driveway; watch out now! Dad would have a nervous breakdown!*

Lena let go. She stepped back, red-faced and ill at ease. Looking at the ground, she moved to the Model T, feeling uncomfortable and unsure of what else to do. Her pleasure was soaring to invisible heights. *Lordy, lordy,* she moved to the Model T. *What's this family comin' to? All this hugging and showing some caring. On purpose, yet. Sam, the man, would just pop and disappear into thin air. Surely!*

Daniel was excited out of his usual serious demeanor. He felt silly and couldn't help laughing. He raised his arms to the pale winter sky and hollered, "Hal-le-lu-ja, Lena is back!"

Watching the joy of his older brother, Harley chuckled and leaned back on the Model T's front fender. This was something! Lena was also taken by her beloved brother's unfamiliar manner. Her laughter was surprising to Daniel. He went to her, pulled her again into his arms, and hugged her clear off the ground, saying, "Holy cow! Wow!" Then, dropping her back to Earth, he stepped back and held her at arm's length. He shook his head and grew serious, still smiling. "Welcome back, little sister." I missed you a lot, kiddo."

Lena was thrilled to pieces and blushing. She should look him in the eyes and say something, even if it's stupid. She had a voice now. It was her responsibility.

"It's been a while," she said, looking only as high as his smile. *Good crap, what was that? It's been a while. So stupid!* Embarrassed, her face felt hot.

Daniel beamed. "Say it again. Let me hear your beautiful voice again!"

She looked away and down again. "Daniel! You're making me embarrassed. It's just talking."

"Oh no, it's not just talking. It's *your* voice, my sister Lena's voice, the missing voice of all my days." Then, letting his amazement hush his tone, he said, "I am having a conversation with my little sister Lena! When did this happen? How did it happen?"

Lena shrugged.

Harley picked up a grease rag off the Model T's radiator and moved away from the fender, wiping his hands. "Mom said she hollered at her from the stairs yesterday morning, loud and clear. She was mad at Dad about school."

Daniel was not aware of the conflict over school. "What about school?" However, the sound of that question stirred an old feeling in him, making him frown. Now, his attention averted from his elation for Lena. He stared at her with some concern. "He's doing it again, isn't he? He's taking you out of school, too."

"I ain't gonna quit," she said, her tone flat and determined.

"How are you going to get away with that? None of the rest of us could." She gave Harley a long, deliberate look.

Harley was suddenly aware of what she was about to say about going to Colorado. He couldn't let that happen. He shook his head at her and tried to threaten her with his eyes. Daniel saw their attempt to hide the exchange between them.

"Uh oh, what are you two up to now? I saw that look and sneaky shake of your head, Harley."

"I wasn't shaking my head at Lena. I was just thinking about this stubborn old bucket uh bolts here."

He turned to the Model T. "It doesn't wanna start."

Daniel saw the look of disgust on Lena's face in response to Harley's words. He didn't believe Harley one little bit.

"So, why are you trying to get it runnin? You going someplace?"

"No, not really, just thought I'd see if I could get it runnin' for something to do. Just for the heck of it, that's all."

Lena stepped quickly to Harley's side and spoke to him quietly.

"You should tell him. You can't do this by yourself."

Daniel barely heard the sound, but not the words at all. Harley became angry with Lena. "Well, hell, you sure know how to talk now." Lena backed away, astonished. Harley grabbed a ratchet wrench and furiously began turning the bolts that fastened the carburetor on top of the engine. She returned to Daniel's side, silently staring at Harley's backside draped over the Model T's fender. The extent of Harley's effort to keep his secret hadn't occurred to her. She felt stupid and regretful. She couldn't remember Harley ever being mad at her. It was a bad feeling. She hadn't realized it before, but navigating life's seas was a lot different for those with voices than those who only talked to themselves.

Daniel could see in Lena's expression the hurt that Harley's burst of anger had caused. He stepped toward Harley as he talked.

"C'mon, Harley, it looked like Lena was just trying to help. I don't know what you're trying to do, but maybe she has a better perspective of your situation from where she stands than you do. Maybe what you're gonna do, whatever it is, shouldn't be a secret. Maybe telling me what's goin' on might make things easier." Harley just kept working on those bolts.

Lena stood by in silence. She had learned her lesson and would keep her mouth shut. It was Harley's deal, but she hoped he would ask Daniel to take them to Colorado. That old Model T had been sitting in the weeds long before she was born. It wasn't gonna get them past town, let alone to Colorado Springs. Maybe it wouldn't matter for her at all. She hadn't yet talked Harley into letting her go with him.

Daniel stood beside Harley, watching him remove the carburetor from the engine.

"C'mon Harley, tell me what's goin' on." It was as if Harley hadn't heard. "You're going try to drive this pile of antique parts someplace, aren't you?" Harley was paying no attention. He slid to the ground, bent down to a toolbox next to the front wheel, and dug around in it till he came up with a stiff putty knife. He flopped over the fender and began to wedge the putty knife between the carburetor and the surface of the engine to free it from the gasket. The gasket had been there many years and was stuck good. He struggled with it and knew that if he became impatient and careless, there was a good chance he would slip and ruin the cork gasket. That would make re-using it impossible, and finding one for a Model-T Ford to replace it would require a miracle.

That ain't the only miracle I need. Just let me get this thing runnin' and on the road! That's all I ask.

Daniel was out of patience and agitated at Harley's decision to ignore him. He felt an urge to grab him and wrestle him to the ground. He would sit on him and give him the Dutch-rub until he told all, the way he did when they were kids.

But Harley didn't seem to be a kid anymore. It would be like wrestling Uncle John. He had gotten serious the past few months. Daniel had seen him standing alone on the edge of the yard, looking off to the west like a man waiting for a late shipment of answered prayers. Something was nagging at his little brother, and it was changing his appearance. His grin was not as explosive as it had always been, the flash not as bright, and his eyes spoke of purpose rather than mischievous invention. Something sinister was remodeling the irresponsible, come-what-may kind of kid he'd always been. Eighteen was still too young to be an adult. Daniel wished Harley would ask him for help, no matter what he was getting into.

He stalked off over to where Lena stood watching. "You know what's goin' on, so tell your rock-headed brother if he doesn't speak up, you will."

Lena was uncomfortable and felt a passing notion that her previous role as a post with legs and ears had its advantages. For a second, she supposed she could still get away with shuttin' up and staying out of it. But she couldn't possibly have deprived herself of the new-found pleasure of being a working part of her precious family. She spoke to Daniel. "Hey," she said, "Harley's the one with the plan. If it works, he did it; if it fails, he did it. I'm not his daddy. I'm all for letting him make his own mistakes." Silence poured from her last words and soaked the atmosphere.

Daniel stood stone still, staring at this person who was once his silent little sister. Harley had stopped scraping and could have passed for a sack of seed thrown across the Model T's fender.

Lena spoke again. "Just between you, me, and the Model T, I think the plan stinks but may be necessary."

Without looking back at Lena, Harley went back to his scraping. Daniel was so mesmerized that he no longer had space in his brain to fuss with Harley. He said to Lena and smiled, "Harley's right, you do know how to talk." She looked away, unable to muster enough boldness to openly bask in the words she took as a compliment.

Daniel studied her blushing face for a moment, pleased that he could have that effect on her. Pleased that she acknowledged his praise of her. "So, you're not gonna tell me?"

She continued to look at the ground and shook her head.

He spoke softly, hoping Harley couldn't hear. "Okay," he said. "Maybe later," and walked off toward the house. He heard his parents' car coming up the driveway and became anxious to talk to his father.

CHAPTER 14

Harley was irate. Lena had all but told Daniel what he was going to do. Now, Daniel would go to Dad and tell him that Harley was trying to get the old Model T to run, and maybe he better find out why. Harley would then have to reveal his intentions, and that would be the end of that. He stood looking at the car, disgusted and discouraged. There would be no sense in continuing to try to get it to run if Daniel told him.

Lena stood nearby feeling terrible. *What's the good in talking if you keep saying the wrong thing?* She quietly walked over to Harley, leaned against the fender, and peered in at the engine, trying to appear interested in Harley's efforts. "So, what do you think is wrong with this ol' thing?" she asked with as much light-heartedness as she could muster. She risked a glance at Harley's face. She could see that he was unhappy and that her act wasn't working.

"I'm sooo sorry," she moaned. "I didn't have the right to let Daniel know, but I didn't think he would say anything to Sam, and I still don't. I think he's on our side. I think he would help us if we explained the situation."

Harley turned to Lena, exasperation honing his voice to a sharp edge. "What do you mean us? When I hit the road, there won't be no us! You're not going, Lena! Can't you get that through your thick head?"

Lena stepped away from Harley and stared, resisting the urge to run.

Harley moved away from the engine, holding the carburetor and examining it closely. The cork gasket was still clinging to the base but was damaged. It was probably beyond use. He hadn't been able to save it.

"Damit to hell," he said aloud to himself. He turned and looked at Lena, who stood a few feet behind him, arms folded across her chest. At least she hadn't gotten mad and stomped away in a huff. He began to feel bad about blowing up at her. "I'm sorry I hollered at you."

"It's okay, you're just pissed at the car."

He stared at her. He couldn't get used to her cussing. He set the carburetor on the fender, pulled a piece of old t-shirt from his hip pocket, and, wiping his hands, said, "You're right, but I shouldn't be taking it out on you. Sorry."

She pointed at the carburetor. "Can you fix that thing-a-ma-jig there?"

"I don't even know if there's anything wrong with it yet. The gasket that seals it to the engine is shot. If I can't come up with a gasket to replace it, there ain't no sense fixing anything cuz the gas would run all over the motor and probably catch on fire or blow up."

"So, what can you do?"

At that moment, they heard the plap of the screen door slamming. Harley hurried to lay the carburetor on the engine and quietly closed the hood. He hurried around like a crazy man, gathering up all the tools. He stuffed them into the toolbox and tossed it into the front seat. He grabbed the door handle, twisting it to the open position so it would latch without slamming it. He carefully swung the squeaky car door closed. He and Lena gave the area a quick visual once over to make sure he hadn't left any evidence of his work and started for the house. Lena saw the piece of t-shirt in his hip pocket, jerked it out, ran back to the Model T, and tossed the rag under it. As she caught up with Harley, they saw their father climb into his pickup to drive down the driveway. He turned out onto the highway and headed toward the church.

They had stopped beside the tool shed at the first sight of Sam, hoping he wouldn't see them. He hadn't looked their way. They watched his pickup disappear on the other side of the house where the highway lay. They continued toward the house, assuming dinner would soon be ready.

Harley said, "I wonder where he's going without dinner."

Lena was sarcastic. "Back to the church to hold somebody down for God."

Harley frowned at her. "Whaddya mean by that?"

She was silent, then after a few steps, she shook her head and said, "Never mind, I'm just being mean."

This sounded strange to Harley, coming from his little sister. But it wasn't strange. He realized that just because she hadn't said anything mean all these years didn't mean she hadn't thought it. He was sure she had always talked to herself like everyone else. So, why shouldn't she talk aloud the same way? As they walked together, stride for stride, it made him feel great to have her there.

They entered the house through the *kitchen door. Their mother was alone in the kitchen doing the final preparations for dinner.*

"Dinners ready," she said. "Get washed up." Carrying a large plate of fried chicken and walking toward the dining room, her gaze fell on Harley's jeans. "My lands, Harley, you're grease from head to toe! What have you been doing?" Harley looked down at himself.

"Nothin', just messin' around with some stuff."

"Messing is for sure," came from his mother as she passed through the doorway into the dining room. "Change your clothes before you come to the table."

He headed for the stairs, got there, and turned to his mother. "Where's Daniel?"

"Upstairs, I guess."

He bounded up the stairs two steps at a time.

Lena had gone to the bathroom to wash her hands. She was sure Sam had gone back to the church and was doing what the church does. He would be gone for a while. She dried her hands and stood looking into the mirror for a moment. She pulled out the bobby pins that held the head cover, removed it, and laid it on the vanity. She shook her hair loose, letting it fall below her shoulders. *Sam isn't here; I don't need to wear that thing.* She quickly ran a brush through her hair a few times, then went into the dining room. She went to her place at the table and sat. There was no place set for Sam.

Sarah came from the kitchen into the dining room and stood behind the chair at her place at the table. She noticed the absence of Lena's head cover but said nothing. *No matter, Sam's not here.* "Where is everyone?" she asked no one in particular, then walked to the bottom of the stairs and hollered up. "Hey, you guys, we're ready to eat!"

Upstairs, Daniel heard his mother as he came out of his room on his way to Harley's room. Instead, he turned back toward the stairs, obeying his mother's calling. He would talk to Harley after dinner. He needed to find out just exactly what he was up to. He wouldn't have given a second thought to Harley working on the Model T if Lena hadn't said what she said about not being able to do it by himself. Do what by himself? That's what he had to find out. Knowing Harley, it would be something wrong, impossible, or forbidden. Then he heard Harley in the hallway behind him.

"Daniel!" He stopped, turned to him, and waited.

As Harley approached Daniel, he saw in his expression that his big brother wasn't going to quit poking his nose in his business. He felt the urge to tell Daniel his plans and to ask him for help. But Lena, being the only one who knew what he was going to do, was already one too many. Besides that, if, for some reason, their dad ever asked Daniel why he was working on that old car, he knew Daniel would not be able to lie to his father. Truth and honesty live like a king in Daniel. The only way that he could be sure he would get away with sneaking off to be by the side of his child's mother was to be there before anyone knew. And to be by Linda's side when she gave birth to their child was the one thing he would do no matter what it took. He spoke to Daniel.

"You gotta believe me, nothing is goin' on with the Model T. I'm not takin' off anywhere. And Lena doesn't know what she's talkin' about."

Daniel was skeptical. "Then what did she mean when she said you couldn't do it by yourself."

"I don't know. You'll have to ask her."

That answer surprised Daniel. He expected at least an attempt at a believable story from Harley. He knew he could lie and had gotten quite good at it. Growing up under their father's high expectations and the no-excuses method of grading his children's efforts had taught him well. Had he caught Harley in a lie he couldn't lie his way out of?

Daniel asked, "Well, if you didn't know what she was talking about, why did it make you so mad at her?"

Harley stomped past him to the stairs and took them down into the dining room. Daniel watched him retreat and felt the satisfaction of real progress. He was sure he could eventually get Harley to tell him his secret. Following Harley, he reached the Sunday dinner table as the others were settling around in their places.

Harley was glad that his father wasn't there. Who knows what Daniel might say that would bring questions out of his father that he did not want to answer. His only option would be to lie, and he hated that, especially to his father. He had never lied to his mother, never had to. It was easy to get a word of praise or a little pat on the back from her. She never insisted that he try, with the last ounce of will, to be blameless in God's eyes.

They ate in silence for a time, then Daniel, determined as he was, did exactly what Harley half expected but hoped he wouldn't. Without looking up from his plate, he asked, "So, how's the work on that old Model T coming along?"

Harley stopped shoveling it in and stared at Daniel with disgust. He laid his fork down and flopped back against his chair. He sat staring at his plate in complete dejection, waiting for the response from his mother that he knew would come and that Daniel was counting on. Their mother raised her face to Daniel and noticed Harley's demeanor.

"Who are you talking to," she asked Daniel. He looked at his mother with nonchalant innocence, hiding his cunning.

"Oh, I was just wondering if Harley got the old jalopy running yet."

Sarah felt some amusement as she recognized the rivalry between her sons. It was much the same as when they were little boys, one manipulating the other into a position of surrender. She smiled and spoke to Harley, who seemed to be the one on the defensive and losing ground. "Do you actually think you can get that bucket of bolts started and running?"

Harley sat up straight again and resumed eating. He had no idea how he was going to get this conversation off the road it was going down without lying to his mother. Daniel persisted, working his maneuvers. "So, what are you going to do with it if you get it running?"

Harley shrugged. "I don't know." He gave Daniel his best expression of utter contempt. "Maybe I'll drive you somewhere you can't walk back from and dump you."

Sarah was shocked. She realized there was more than just competitive sparring going on between her sons. "Here," she scolded, "Don't talk that way to your brother. What are you two fighting about now?"

Daniel gave Harley a sharp look and frowned, feeling his brother's anger. Harley got up from the table and started to walk away.

Their mother was quick to stop him. "Harley! Don't you walk away from me! You just sit yourself back down and tell me what is going on." Harley returned to his chair and sat, showing great disgust. His mouth was shut tight, and his jaw clamped stubbornly. His mother stared at him, searching for the words to use on these two nearly grown men who were acting like spoiled brats.

"Don't be so silly, Harley. You're older than you're acting." She turned her attention to Daniel. "Daniel, what are you doing to your brother? "

He shook his head. "I'm not doing anything to him. I think he is up to something he's not supposed to be doing, and I'm trying to find out what it is... for his own good."

Lena had finished her fried chicken dinner and spooned canned peach slices from a large bowl into her dessert dish. She glanced at Daniel. *Boy, if you only knew, and I think you should!*

Sarah continued her questioning. "Okay, Harley, out with it. Why are you trying to get the Model T to run? I know you're not going anywhere down the highway with it because you would have to buy tags for it. To do that, you would have to have a title for it, and that doesn't exist." She looked at Daniel. "My guess is that he just wants to see if he can do it, and if it does start, he'll just drive it around here at the house." Her attention went back to Harley. "Isn't that right, Harley?"

Looking down at his half-eaten food, Harley was suddenly struck by his mother's revelation. The fact that he would need a title had never entered his mind. His plan, the answer to his greatest problem, had been made impossible by the utterance of a few words of fact.

Stupid, stupid, stupid was all he could think. He burst from his chair and was in the kitchen and out the back door before his mother could stop him. The three remaining at the table looked at each other.

Sarah frowned, wondering what was wrong with her youngest son. Daniel saw a situation more serious than he had thought.

Lena, feeling an overwhelming desire to save someone other than herself, rose to follow Harley.

Her mother stopped her. "Please, Lena, tell me what is going on with Harley. I can see that something has him worried."

Uh oh, now what do I do? Lena was frustrated. Panic was creeping up. What could she say? She couldn't betray her trusting brother again. She would not lie to her mother. She wished she couldn't talk! Living had been a lot easier then. It was Sam and his stupid idea that education makes you a lost sinner. She wouldn't have had a reason to say anything if he hadn't made her quit school. It's him again, messing things up. Well, she didn't have to say anything now. She could just shut up and be done with it. She stood facing her mother.

"I can't say, mom! Harley trusted me not to say when he told me, so I'm not. You will have to ask him."

Her mother sat looking up at her, and Lena saw the surprise in her beautiful brown eyes. "Don't be mad at me," she said. "Please!" She ran into the kitchen and out the back door. The screen door slammed; Sarah flinched.

CHAPTER 15

The slap of the kitchen screen door against frozen, dark, silent walls of electric-lit windows echoed against the brittle winter air. It announced to barnyard and beast Sam Danziger's assault on the workday was about to commence. Early morning chores needed doing, and he would lead his children into the fray. They each had their assignment. Each knew the routine that would accomplish their tasks and were now engaged, all but one. Lena, bless her heart, was getting ready for school as usual.

Sarah was in the kitchen clearing breakfast dishes off the table.

Lena's plate and glass of milk remained untouched, awaiting her appearance for breakfast. Sarah needed to get Lena to eat her breakfast. As she started up the stairs, she hollered. "Lena!"

Lena's response was immediate. "I'll be down in a minute!"

For an instant, Sarah was jolted by the unfamiliar voice that came down the stairs. She was accustomed to calling her name, waiting a few seconds for the sounds that would let her know Lena was on her way. In all those years, she had never heard Lena answer her call. It caused goosebumps on her arms. Her face still pointing up the stairs, she closed her eyes, and a whisper barely moved her lips. "Thank you."

Then Lena's voice came down the stairs again: "Where are my blue socks? Are they in the dirty clothes box?"

"I don't know Lena. Come and eat your breakfast. It's already cold."

Sarah returned to the kitchen, wondering why Lena wanted her blue socks. She wore them only with her dark blue dress with the tiny white flowers. Those were school clothes! The realization stopped her in her tracks and whirled her around for a return trip to the stairs. She spoke aloud in her distress.

"Oh, Lena!"

She reached the stairs, quickly climbed them, and hurried down the hall to Lena's room. She pushed the door and nearly collided with Lena, "Oops! Sorry!"

Lena staggered backward, "I'm coming, I'm coming!"

She was wearing a blue dress with socks in hand. Her hair was done in two braids, and she held schoolbooks in the crook of her arm against her chest.

Sarah stared at her, not knowing what to say, wishing she didn't have to say anything. She admired her daughter's determination and wished she could keep going to school, if for no other reason than to make her happy. It made her heart heavy to think she would have to discourage her dreams for the future. Did she, Sarah, really believe that there was no need for an education and that it would cause Lena to become lost in worldly ways? Or was she just taking the easy way out, giving in to avoid the fight with Sam that would be sure to come if she supported Lena? She looked sadly at Lena and shook her head. "It won't work, Lena; you know it won't."

Her mother's words struck Lena like a punch in the stomach. Suddenly, she couldn't move. Every impulse in her was pushing and pulling at her body to duck and dive under cover in the corner of the hayloft. But she was stuck, protruding up toward open space like a lone condemned weed in heaven's garden to be pulled up and flung away by God himself. She hugged the schoolbooks against her chest so tight it hurt. Squeezing her eyes shut, she gritted her teeth and waited, her whole head quivering under the strain.

Sarah sucked in her breath and held it when she saw Lena's reaction. She was startled and couldn't move for a second, but then she grabbed for her like she would if she were a falling baby. She wrapped her in both arms and held her tightly against her. "Lena, it's okay. I'll help you!"

Lena's eyes flew open at the sound of her mother's voice. She saw her open bedroom door, not a wall of baled hay that made up her hideaway in the loft. Her mother was squeezing her to death. "I'm okay, Mom."

Sarah released her immediately and stepped back. Her look of concern pleased Lena and led her to reassure her mother.

"Don't worry, I'm fine."

"Well, I'm not. I am worried to death about you."

Lena stood looking at her mother as if the episode had not happened. She had a strange feeling of being out of sync. As if she had known a moment in time that no other soul had experienced. She wondered, again, how it felt to be insane. Then she wondered why God had not struck her dead. Was it because He saw her gritting her teeth, expecting it, and He wanted it to be a surprise?

Sarah saw her daughter staring at her, knowing very well that she no more saw her than you could see a ghost. Some other vision or memory took up her mind.

"Lena, what can I do to help you? What is so terrible that you can't tell your mother? Please let me help you."

"I don't know what you mean. You know Dad won't let me go to school. That's the problem." She started to walk around her mother. "But I am going to school," she said.

Sarah took her by the arm and stopped her. She began to feel a little perturbed at Lena's stubbornness. Her rebellion was getting to even her.

"Don't you talk to me that way, Lena! You are still the child here, and I am the adult."

That shocked Lena. Not the words but her mother's threatening tone. She stared at her for a moment, took a backward step toward the bed behind her, and then waited for her mother to let go of her arm. Sarah let her go. She got to the bed, tossed her books onto it, and plopped down beside them.

Sarah continued. "You cannot go to school. Not against your dad's will. He won't allow it, and if you do get there, he will just come get you."

Lena searched her mother's expression for a sign of apology but saw a grave warning instead. She started whining. "But can't you talk to him, make him understand there's nothing wrong with going to school? School would be good for me. It's good for everybody; you know that."

"Lena, I don't know any such thing. I know your dad said no more school, and what he says goes. He has his reasons, and you should be thankful that you have a father who is here to do what he thinks is best for his children."

Best for his children? You mean best for "God's little helper." No one could make her believe that Sam Danziger did anything for any other reason than to keep in good with his God. Why do you think he held her down that day for God to chop her head off?

The suddenness with which it happened stunned Lena. *That's silly*, her mind said. It was like cold water dashed in her face. What she had known in her heart all her life was silly! The cold splash was overwhelming. The idea that God would chop off her head and her ducking around waiting for it to happen was even sillier. She was embarrassed by the childlike thinking that had led her this far. *How ridiculous can you get?* She was glad no one could read her mind!

She remained sitting on the bed but had strayed from the situation with her mother. She was now staring at the floor, browbeating herself for being stupid. Her mother's scolding voice pulled her back to the situation.

"Lena, are you listening to me?"

She jerked her face up to see her mother's stern focus on her. "Yes, I'm listening!"

"Then take those clothes off and put on something that you can work in. Your dad wants you to help Harley today." Then, on second thought, she spoke again but with a calmer tone. "Go eat your breakfast first."

Lena rose from the bed and wasted no time exiting the room and clomping down the stairs. Sarah, frowning, watched her leave. Deep in thought about her concerns for her daughter, she began making Lena's bed.

Lena, alone in the kitchen, had not finished her breakfast when she heard the school bus out on the highway. She jumped up from her chair, dropped her fork into her plate, and ran to the coat closet. She grabbed her coat. She had to get outside where the bus driver could see her coming before he honked his horn to announce his arrival as he always did.

Not taking the time to put her coat on, she ran out the door and into the yard to the place where he turned the bus around. She struggled into her coat as the bus rolled up and stopped. The folding door scraped open, and Lena was on the bus before anyone on the farm knew the bus had driven up.

That is, anyone but Sarah. From Lena's bedroom window, she saw the bus turn from the driveway onto the highway, heading north toward town. She felt sorry for Lena. Telling the bus driver he no longer needed to stop there must have been hard for her.

She left the room after making the bed and picking up discarded clothes. As she descended the stairs, she wondered what she could say to Lena to make her feel better.

The cold air coming up the stairs escaped her attention until she was just a few steps from the bottom. *Where in the world is the cold air coming from?* she thought as she reached the dining room floor and started for the kitchen. *The kitchen door must be open.*

She entered the kitchen and saw that the door was indeed open. When she reached it, she looked out into the yard to see if Lena had gone out. She saw no one and pulled the door shut.

Inside, she saw the door of the coat closet standing open. She moved toward it intending to close it, when her eyes fell upon Lena's unfinished breakfast. She was surprised she had left a bite or two of the eggs and toast. The glass of milk had only a swallow left in it, which was not like Lena at all. She really liked milk. She would not have deprived herself of the last swallow to hurry to go help Harley.

She went to the closet to close the door. Lena never left doors open, which made Sarah wonder. Then she saw that Lena's coat was gone and closed the door.

The picture of the big yellow school bus out on the highway flashed into Sarah's mind, and she realized that she had not heard its honking arrival. Had Lena rushed out into the yard where the driver could see her coming, thus eliminating his need to honk? There was more than one reason for her to be running to the bus before it honked, and one of them was to get on it before anyone knew it was there.

Anger rose in her as she yanked the closet open, jerked her coat on, and headed for the kitchen door. She hollered as she went. "Lena, are you in the house? Leeenaaa!" She stopped and stood still to listen for an answer. The silence was heartbreaking. She left the house, slamming the kitchen door behind her.

CHAPTER 16

It seemed even colder in the early daylight than it did in the dark. She hugged herself as she hurried along the slick, trodden path in the snow to the barn. She entered the barn through the walk-in door and saw Sam sitting on a milking stool at the side of one of the four milk cows he milked every morning.

She said, "Is Lena in here?"

Without looking up from milking, he said, "No, I haven't seen her."

The squirts of fresh milk, from the udder to the half-filled bucket, splooshed in rhythm with Sam's squeezing hands. It was the only sound in the large spacious room as Sarah stood still, her arms folded across the front of her heavy coat. She didn't know what would happen when she told Sam that Lena might have gotten on the school bus. She dreaded saying it. She would rather be someplace else when he reacted to it. She should go look for her.

Sam said, "She's supposed to be helping Harley, and at the moment, he's out at the horse tank, breaking the ice on it."

That sounded wonderful to Sarah. It was the excuse she needed to put off telling Sam where she thought Lena was. And who knows, the horse tank may be right where Lena is, after all. She turned back toward the door, and listening to the sploosh, sploosh of Sam milking, she quickly left the barn.

Sam stopped milking the cow to give his aching hands a break from the squeezing. He sat staring into the half-filled bucket of foaming fresh milk. His thoughts were being tossed around by the rough waters upon which his struggle with Lena had always sailed. He was sure that Sarah was out making a special effort to find where Lena was because she suspected Lena of some wrongdoing. It wouldn't surprise him if Lena had gotten on the school bus when he heard it in the driveway.

He didn't know what he would do or could do about it if she had. He was at his wits end with that girl. Sometimes, when he was alone, he longed to have her on his lap, hugging his arm like she used to.

He raised his hands from where they hung between his spread knees and flexed his fingers. Then, the routine of squeezing and pulling continued. He wondered if God himself had given up on Lena. The thought covered him like a gray sky and weighed down his spirit with self-appointed responsibility. He was tired of it. It seemed that the older she got, the less he cared.

Sarah walked in Harley's footprints in the snow to the windmill, where he was swinging an ax into the full, frozen-over watering tank. There was no one else around.

"Harley!" He stopped swinging the ax and turned to her. "Do you know where Lena is?"

He stood with his feet apart in a wide stance, holding the ax in both hands across the front of him, looking at his mother undecided. He had always tried hard not to lie to her. A few seconds ticked by. He turned back to the ice chopping and swung the ax into the ice. The sound cracked the frigid air but had little effect on the thick ice. Leaving the ax stuck there, he finally answered with his back to her.

"I saw her get on the bus."

Sarah was surprised. "You saw her get on the bus and didn't stop her?"

He jerked the ax out of the ice and planted it again in the same spot. This time, the ice broke there. The force of the blow tipped the broken edge into the water, causing a small splash. Harley flinched and nearly lost his hold on the ax handle but pulled the ax out of the water. Sarah was losing her patience.

"Harley, answer me! You knew she wasn't supposed to go to school!" He turned to his mother again, ax in hand as before.

"Mom, believe me, you don't want to hear what I have to say about it."

"I take it that you must think she should finish school."

"Yeah, the same as I think all of us should have finished school." He gave the barn, where he knew his father was, a quick look and lowered his voice. "Dad is wrong. School never hurt nobody. I hope Lena can be stubborn enough to get her way this time. The rest of us couldn't."

The notion to agree with her son came over Sarah, but she caught herself. To make that known would not be a good idea. She would not undermine her husband's authority or his efforts to raise their children as he saw fit. Harley didn't need to know that she had come to disagree with his father and the church where education was concerned. Besides, a Mennonite child's education wasn't so important that it should cause trouble between man and wife. Sam was with the church, and the church wasn't doing that bad a job on anything.

"Well, you could have saved her some trouble cause you know your dad is just gonna go get her when he finds out, and Lena is gonna be in a lotta trouble."

Harley had returned to his work on the ice and swung the ax again. It had occurred to him that when all the facts were in, he would be in deep trouble for not trying to keep Lena off the bus. He turned again to his mother.

"Dad wouldn't find out if you went to get her. That would solve the problem."

Sarah was surprised. Her youngest son had some dishonesty about him that she hadn't known about. Where had he learned to be that deceitful? Certainly not in his father's house. Then, a surprising afterthought raised her eyebrows slightly.

But not in high school with the English kids, either. He for sure learned more in his father's house than he did in a high school that he never went to.

Now, she felt the discomfort of guilt. She knew she had also deceived her husband many times to avoid his powerful control over her comings and goings. Could it be that her own hidden inner dishonesty, like an inherited affliction, was passed on to her son? Or had Harley been forced to use the same tactics that made it possible to live with his father as she had? She realized that she seemed to have that in common with Harley.

Maybe that was why she had always been on Harley's side when everyone else was yelling at him.

She began to feel a partnership with Harley in his idea to solve the problem: that she go to the school to get Lena. It didn't seem that awful. All she had to do was walk to the car, get in, and drive away. Sam would be in the barn for a while, so she could go and get back without him knowing it. She looked at the barn and was glad she had closed the door completely when she had gone out.

Without a word to Harley, she turned and retraced the footprints in the snow to the barn door. She stopped to listen for the sound of fresh milk splooshing into the milk bucket that Sam would be holding between his knees. He was still at it.

Then she started across the undisturbed snow, plowing a new path to their car parked in the driveway. She got into the car and closed the door as quietly as possible. With her eyes on the barn, she started the engine and turned the car down the driveway toward the highway to town.

As she turned onto the highway, she looked back at the farmyard and could barely see Harley standing beside the windmill, watching her leave. There were no other signs of life.

CHAPTER 17

Lena had not intended to board the bus when she ran out of the house.

The bus pulled up and stopped where she stood. The folding doors squeaked and clattered open like always. There was Mr. Sloan, whose familiar figure sat on the driver's seat. It felt so wrong not to do, at that moment, what she had always done at that moment in all those years before. She stepped up onto the first step in the doorway, but this time, she hesitated.

Mr. Sloan looked slightly puzzled but spoke kindly to her.

"Well, come on, Lena, you're holding up the works. No one's in your favorite seat." It was as if he had taken her by the hand and led her to the seat in which she always sat by herself.

She couldn't just blurt out, "*I'm not going to school anymore, Mr. Sloan, so you can go on down the road and forget about me.*"

"Did you forget your schoolbooks, Lena?"

She flopped back into the seat and shook her head.

In the next moment, they were moving back up the driveway and onto the highway, heading for Garland Junior High.

Lena's heart was pounding. *Lordy, lordy, what a boo boo!* What had she just done? What was she going to do now? *There it is again,* she thought. She had thought at the time that God was messing with her. He was making sure she would be in trouble with His little helper Sam. But low and behold, He had apparently changed His mind. A couple of first graders in the back of the bus had gotten into a squabble over a pocketknife. Mr. Sloan had pulled off the highway to take the knife out of the fight.

It was easy for Lena to simply sneak off the bus and run across the corner of Spiker's wheat field to the road going to Katy's.

She trotted down the snow-topped gravel road, keeping her step in a fresh tire track a car had made that morning. She frequently looked back toward the big yellow bus. It got smaller and smaller as it moved down the highway toward town.

It wasn't very much further to Lewis and Katy's.

She hated sneaking off like that, but knowing Mr. Sloan, he wouldn't have let her get off the bus no matter what. And she sure couldn't go to the schoolhouse. Sam would come after her, and there would have been hell to pay. Now, she could say she walked to Katy's, and all she would catch it for was not helping Harley. He probably wasn't doing much anyway.

The house was just up ahead, and Lena saw the dog, Casey, jump off the front porch. He came plowing through unbroken snow to meet her. She also saw that Lewis and Katy's green Chevy wasn't in the drive. Lewis must be gone to town. Then, a touch of anxiety rubbed her nerves. Maybe Katy was the one gone. She stopped trotting and stood still for a moment. Her eyes searched the farmyard for any movement, a sign of Lewis being there. She started walking toward the driveway. The dog came to her, wagging its tail. He jumped up to put his front paws on her. Without taking her eyes off her search of the yard, she caught the dog and pushed him away. She admonished the dog quietly. "No, Casey, down," she ordered.

She turned into the driveway, keeping her attention focused on the house and the barnyard beyond. Maybe no one was at home. The dog was beginning to irritate her. Its exuberance, dancing around in front of her, almost caused her to stumble.

"Quit, get away," she scolded. The dog got the hint and trotted off ahead of her to the porch. He climbed the four steps and sat at the top facing her. As Lena approached the steps, the dog began to bark at her, to welcome her, she imagined.

That should bring somebody out if there's anybody here.

She hoped it would be Katy. She stopped at the bottom of the steps, listening. Her imagination nudged her about this or that happening and whispered a little fear into her spirit. *What if Lewis is the only one here?* What if she showed up just when he had that stuff on his mind like men do? She began to tremble.

Rape was the most awful thing that could ever happen to a girl, and it happened all the time. Maybe this is supposed to happen. What if it was God who took over her mind and body and made her get on the bus so she would wind up here to get raped and who knows what. Now she was shaking so badly she could hardly stand up. Maybe this is the day God gets her.

When you least expect it.

She became yanked from the reality around her. She couldn't get away! Her cheek was pressed hard against the rough, dusty boards of the hayloft floor. She was trapped again under her daddy's grasp on her head, her straining child's neck displayed in sacrifice to God's raised axe. She would pay today!

Lewis Rhymer heard Casey barking out on the front porch. He hadn't heard a car drive up, so he wondered what had excited the dog but hadn't lured him off the porch.

Too curious to ignore the question, he walked into the living room to look through the door window. What he saw was the dog barking at Lena. She was squatting at the bottom of the steps, her face buried against her knees and her hands covering her head. She was apparently scared to death of Casey, which didn't make sense. She and the dog were old friends.

He instinctively jerked the door open, punched the screen door with both hands and yelled at the dog.

"HEY...! CASEY, NO...! GET OUTA HERE!"

He was out on the porch now, and the bang of his stomped foot on the wooden floor, the "GIT!" from his harsh mouth, and the violent wave of his arm sent the dog off the porch to the back of the house.

As for Lena, a voice was enough proof of reality to enable it to reach in for her and pull her back to the moment. She was not in the hayloft with her head against the floor. She raised her face to Lewis's voice, but the voice in her head cried rape.

Her scream was horrifying. Its startling force brought goose bumps up on Lewis's upper body and made him nauseous. He saw her kick her heels against the wet sidewalk and scoot on her butt backward in the snow. She screamed again. Lewis was shocked into dumb silence. He could only stare at Lena scooting on her butt backward away from him.

After waking from the shock, his first impulse was to help her, and he took steps in her direction. Her third scream stopped him cold. She was terrified of him! He was the problem! He stood for a moment, not knowing what to do, and then he turned and quickly went into the house. He slammed the door and looked through the window to watch Lena, bewildered at her lunacy. Lena had stopped scooting and sat leaning back, her knees up, her hands hidden in the snow behind her, holding her up. She stared at the window.

Lewis stepped back into the dimness of the house's interior, out of her vision, but kept her in view. He saw her scramble to her feet, run across the snow-covered yard, and down into the ditch. She fell to her hands and knees, then jumped up and made it onto the road. He watched her run down the road toward the highway, slipping and falling more than once. He was too confused and at a loss for words in his own mind to form an explanation for her behavior. What had he done?

Katy turned her car off the highway onto the road home. Under a fresh, crispy blue sky, the sun-lit snow glared at her from the flat land before her, blinding her to the detail in the distance. She squinted at the blank wall she was driving toward and noticed a blue blob at the side of the road. She realized it was a person. *Lena!* She was almost past Lena, squatting in the snow by the ditch before her reaction brought the car to a sliding halt. *What in the world...?* She jerked the car into park and scrambled from it. Leaving the car door stuck open, she hurried back to Lena, slipping and sliding on the snow-covered weeds along the ditch.

"Lena? What's wrong?" Lena stood as Katy reached her side. She was sobbing out of control, her face in her hands. There was no understanding her words in the wailing. Katy wrapped her arms around Lena and held her quaking body with Lena's face against her chest. "Oh, Lena! What happened? Can you tell me?"

They stood on the side of the road that way for a while. Lena continued to cry, and Katy felt the sting of her little sister's anguish in her own eyes. The crying began to subside, and Katy took Lena's face into her hands. She felt the wetness of her cheeks in her palms. She spoke softly, "Tell me what happened. Why are you crying?"

Lena spoke into Katy's shoulder. "I was so scared! I just knew I was gonna...! The last two words caught in her throat. They were there in her mind, raking against the serenity of the country roadside. She was appalled at the sound. *Get raped! Katy can't ever know. No one!* She had never felt so ashamed.

Thinking Lena had a catch in her voice from the sobbing, Katy waited for the end of the unfinished sentence that she had barely understood. But Lena remained silent.

Finally, Katy asked, "You just knew you were gonna what, Lena? What scared you?"

Lena didn't know what to say. Her mind scurried about, looking for a lie to tell her big sister. The scene at Katy's front porch, Lewis's loud voice. Then Casey running to the end of the porch and jumping down flashed into her mind. *Lewis musta thought I was scared of the dog.* "Casey," she said, barely audible.

Katy was surprised. Maybe she hadn't heard right. "Did you say, Casey?" She took Lena by the shoulders, took a step back from her, and examined her face. Lena looked down.

"The dog scared you?" Lena only nodded. Katy became alarmed. "Did he go after you?"

Lena shook her head. "He just barked. I thought I was gonna... wet my pants." She lied. Katy's laughter conveyed her relief. Lena also felt some relief, but only from Katy's probing. Her lie was heavy. She wanted to get away from her trusting sister. "I gotta go home," she said.

Katy was too concerned to let Lena walk away just like that. Lena couldn't leave without explaining some things. "Why did you come to the house? Did you want me for something?" Now, this Lena wouldn't have to lie about.

"For some dumb reason, I got on the bus this morning. Then I knew I had to get off, but I didn't want to go back to the house, so I came here." Lena saw the puzzled frown on Katy's face and knew the questions were on the way. She made motions to indicate that she was starting for home.

"I gotta go. I'll see you later." She began walking away down the road. Katy was disappointed but even more suspicious.

"Wait a minute, Lena. Can't you at least talk to me for a minute?" Lena stopped and turned to Katy, uncertain as to what to do. Katy continued to try to talk her into staying.

"Come to the house for a little while, and I'll take you home later. That way, you won't have to walk across Spiker's field. It's probably awful deep snow." Lena's heart began to beat faster. She could not go to Katy's house now! Not with Lewis there! She began to feel some panic.

No, no, no! Just calm down! You don't hafta go! You can always say no! She heaved a big sigh, keeping the panic at bay.

"I think I better go. Sam's gonna be rantin' and ravin' 'cause I'm supposed to be helping Harley." Katy stepped closer to her and became very serious.

"Look, Lena, I don't mean to be pushy, but there's something you're not telling me. You say you were on the school bus and then got off. For one thing, why were you on the bus? And another thing, I know as well as you do, that old man Sloan does not let kids just get off of the bus out in the middle of the country whenever they feel like it. I think, for your own good, you need to tell me what's goin' on. Why were you at my house? Why did you come all this way then leave before I got here? I'm sure Lewis probably made the dog stop barking at you and told you I would be right back from town. So why did you leave?"

Lena became miserable. She wanted to run again, and her overwhelming reaction to duck pushed her. She stood stooped and hung her head, unable to say anything. Katy took her by the arm.

"C'mon, Lena, get in the car, and you can tell me what's going on the way to the house."

Lena pulled away from Katy.

"I can't, don't you understand? I just can't!" She began walking backward away from her sister, emotion distorting the muscles in her face, getting her ready to cry. She turned and ran down the road. Katy shouted after her.

"Lena! Lena?" Then softly, aloud in her confusion, she said, "Well, for cryin' out loud." She hurried back to her car to turn it around and catch Lena. She could at least take her home.

The snow on the road was deep and slick. She put the car in gear to begin maneuvering it into a turnaround. She realized she would probably slide into the snow-filled ditch if she continued. She sat perplexed, her hands on the steering wheel, looking in the rearview mirror. Lena had left the road and was cutting across the corner of Spiker's field, struggling in the snow. Katy, angry at herself for letting Lena escape, finally set her car in motion toward her house. Maybe Lewis could explain Lena's behavior.

CHAPTER 18

Sarah pulled her car into the large, paved lot behind the schoolhouse, where school buses were parked. The bell signaling the beginning of classes had not yet rung, and many children were moving about on the lot. She didn't see Lena anywhere.

One bus, the last to arrive, was still unloading its students. Sarah did not know which bus Lena would have taken. She watched the children get off the last bus, hoping to see Lena. She parked the car, turned off the engine, and watched until the last child stepped down from the last bus. She heard the bell ring, and the bus yard was suddenly empty.

She quickly got out of the car, walked to the first door she saw, and entered the building.

There was no one in the hall. The final bell rang, and she realized everyone would, by now, be in their classrooms. There was no one from which to get directions to the school office.

She began walking down the hall, the soles of her oxfords tapping a rhythm against the tile floor, echoing in the emptiness. Peering at the door of each room as she passed, she looked for a sign that would point her to the office. There was none. She thought she must be in the wrong part of the building. Of course, the office would be in the front part of the building, and she was in the back. She imagined where the front of the schoolhouse would be from where she was in the hall. She turned at the end of the hall in that direction. She saw up ahead glass-paned double doors that she knew were the front doors. The office door was there across the hall from those doors. She walked quickly to the open door that had a small rectangular plaque beside it on the wall that said OFFICE. She entered the room. A woman sat behind a desk facing her. Ray Sloan, whom she recognized as Lena's bus driver, stood beside the desk. He had his back to her, talking with the woman.

She heard him say, "So I'm sure she's okay, but how do we get hold of her parents? None of those people have a phone."

She stood quietly in front of the counter until the woman took her attention from the bus driver and saw her. The woman's face shone with surprise as she spoke with a smile.

"Oh, I'm sorry I didn't hear you come in. May I help you?"

"I'm Lena Danziger's mother, and I need to take her home."

Mr. Sloan spun around and spoke with exuberance. "Oh, my goodness! We are so glad you are here! We were just trying to figure out how to contact you."

Sarah realized that they had been talking about Lena when she came in. That started her heart beating rapidly and anxiety curling in her stomach. She was frantic. "What happened to Lena? Did she get hurt or something?"

Mr. Sloan was almost instantly around the end of the counter, coming to her side with a reassuring smile. He exclaimed, "No, no, no! Lena's fine!" He took her by the arm and guided her to a couple of chairs standing against the wall. "I'm sure she is safe and sound at her sister's house."

Sarah did not sit. "How in the world...?"

Mr. Sloan spoke in a calm, soft voice. His manner made Sarah suspicious. He may be softening the blow of terrible news. "Please, Mrs. Danziger, have a seat, and I'll explain why I know Lena is okay." Her insides shaking, she sat, and he sat in the chair next to her.

"Lena got off the bus near the road to her sister's house, and when I saw her last, she was running down that road toward the house."

Then he explained to Sarah what happened on the bus and how Lena got off, repeatedly apologizing for his negligence.

Sarah sat on the edge of her chair, clasping her hands tightly in her lap as she listened. Relieved, she stood on unsteady legs, took Mr. Sloan's hand, and shook it. "Thank you very much, Mr. Sloan. Now I have to go find out what has gotten into that girl." She moved toward the doorway and then turned to Mr. Sloan. Thank you, sir, for looking after my daughter. And I'm sorry for the trouble Lena caused." She was out the door and walking quickly down the hall.

On the way to Katy's house, Sarah was alone in her struggle to justify her attitude against high school education. The argument with herself that ensued boggled her mind. As she drove, her thoughts returned to Mr. Sloan and the woman at the schoolhouse. She had felt their attention on her and imagined what they must have thought of her. *They probably thought she was a terrible mother keeping her child from getting an education. It's really none of their business,* she told herself. *So why do I care what they think?* She frowned. *But my caring must mean that I might be on their side, and deep down, I would prefer that Lena continue school.* Now, a little guilt crept into her feelings. She was being unfaithful to her husband and the church.

She drove into Lewis and Katy's driveway, attracting Casey, the dog, off the porch. He barked, waging his tail and anything else that was jointed. She parked beside their car and got out. Before she could reach the porch steps, Katy came out of the front door and waited for her to start up the steps. Sarah could see that she was excited.

"Are you looking for Lena?" she asked, her voice high-pitched and strained.

"Yes, where is she?"

"She's already gone home. She was down there when I came up the road, coming home from town a while ago." She pointed in the westerly direction of the road. "She was scrunched down on the side of the road, crying her eyes out."

"Well, for heaven's sake, what was wrong?"

"She said the dog scared her, but Lewis told me there's more to it than that. He said she was scrunched down on the ground, hiding her face, when he came out to hush the dog. When she looked up and saw him, she screamed bloody murder and backed away from him like he was a monster or something. He said she was scared to death of him, so he went back into the house. Then she got up and ran down the road." Katy was out of breath. Her face flushed red, intense anxiety burning in her eyes. "Why do you spose she acted like that?"

"I don't know, but there's something hidden in Lena that maybe even she doesn't know about. A secret that's just too terrible for her to face."

Sarah started back down the steps. "I gotta get back to the house before your dad finishes the milking." Then she stopped and turned to Katy. "So, you drove her home, and she was okay?"

"No!" Katy shook her head. "She wouldn't let me and ran off across Spiker's field."

Sarah hurried down the steps, speaking to her despair. "Oh, Lena, what is wrong!"

Sarah drove out on the snowy gravel road to the highway, barely aware of the slippery conditions. Her mind was filled with dread at what may be waiting for her at home if Sam finished milking and discovered she and Lena were gone. What would she do? Would she lie? Would she make up a story that she and Lena had gone to town after something? Could she lie to Sam? It would be the first time. Maybe she could, for Lena's sake. It would be a good reason... if there is such a thing as a good reason to lie. Then, a thought bobbed up to the surface of her mind. Why was she put in a position that required her to decide whether or not to lie to her husband? She hoped and prayed Lena had gotten back without Sam knowing it.

CHAPTER 19

Lena ran across the highway into the elms and cottonwoods behind the house, trying to avoid being seen by anyone. She hoped Sam would still be in the barn, knowing he wouldn't be. Harley could be anywhere. She needed to find Harley, to be with him when Sam saw her. She moved carefully along the back side of the house. Reaching the corner, she peeked around it to see if Harley was anywhere visible. From here, she could see the front of the tool shed. The door was open. He might be in there. There was no sign of life anywhere; even Butch was nowhere to... she caught her breath, and her face flushed. *Butch!* It wasn't going to be easy to leave her friend out of her everyday life.

She turned back into her hiding place, leaned her head back against the house, and closed her eyes. She let the picture of Butch running to the cover of the front porch play in her mind for a regretful moment. Then she opened her eyes and got back to the business of deception.

She peered around the corner again. There was still no one in sight. She left the corner of the house and ran to the barn through six inches of unbroken snow.

She reached the barn and walked along its backside, her attention on the interior. Listening for any sound of Sam, she heard nothing. She made her way around the old Model-T, which brought her into view of the back left side of the tool shed. She stopped in front of the Model-T, hoping it was Harley who was in the shed.

She could see that the only vehicle in the driveway was the pickup. Her hope rose. *No car. Maybe Sam went somewhere. No! He would have taken the pickup.* So, the car was gone because her mother had it. Where would she have gone this early in the morning? Dread in its heaviest form fell on her spirit when she became aware of the obvious answer to her question.

She moved back to a position that put the Model T between her and exposure. She felt the familiar urge to hide and squat down on her own tracks in the snow, making herself as small as possible. Her mind pulled at her body, causing muscles to quiver against the strain. She needed to run. A favorite hiding place of hers was not far away.

But fear was not her tormentor. This time, it was shame and regret that she would run from if she lost control. She had brought the shame on herself so she would not run and hide.

You can't hide from yourself.

She could only kick herself for getting on the bus and causing a problem for her mother. She would make up for it somehow, but she would not run away from it.

She stood up and stared at the tool shed. There was lots of wide-open ground between where she stood and the door on the front of the shed, which was now out of her view. Anyone on the place would be able to see her run to the shed. All she could do was hope that Sam wasn't someplace where he would see her.

Well, here goes nothin'.

She took off, running as fast as she could through the snow. She rounded the corner, intending to duck through the doorway into the shed. She slipped on the snow, nearly falling, recovered her footing, and crashed head-on into the object of her efforts to hide... her father. The impact and the tangle of feet nearly knocked her down.

Sam grunted and grabbed her arm, catching her before she fell. She clutched the front of his shirt to right herself and stood up straight. The moment was startling for them both and devastating for Lena. The shock of being discovered crushed her, and coming into physical contact with the dreaded one stifled her breath. Jerking her hands from the front of his shirt, she jumped back from him and stared wide-eyed for an instant. Her eyes left his face and met her hands as they rose to the height of her waist. She held them in front of her, palms up as if to examine them for a moment, then returning her astonished stare to his puzzled face, she wiped them on her coat. She whirled around, burst from the doorway, and fled the way of a startled sparrow.

Sam stood motionless like an electronic toy that had just been unplugged. A sudden lack of all the electric power in the world would not have caused any more discomfort than the absence he felt at that moment. He watched his cherished child run from him as if he were a disease. It was the only physical contact with her in nine years, and it had repulsed her as surely as a leper would.

She disappeared into the house through the kitchen doorway, slamming the door behind her.

Shaking his head in defeat, Sam lowered his eyes to stare into the brilliant snow outside the shed's doorway. Seeing only the thoughts that told of his great loss, he felt hopeless longing. Loss. That was the right word, and it was time he admitted it. After what just happened, it was clear that Lena was no longer his.

So, what's the use anymore?

After a moment, he stepped out of the shed, pulled the door closed, and started for the barn where he had left Harley to turn the cows out. He had noticed the car was gone as he had walked from the barn to the tool shed earlier. He figured Sarah had probably gone to the schoolhouse to get Lena back home.

Having heard the bus come and go, he had been fairly sure Lena had gotten on the bus. But now, it was obvious that Lena had not gotten on the bus, so he wondered where Sarah might have gone.

That question occupied his mind for only a moment. The realization that he had been wrong about Lena disobeying him started to medicate the blow she had dealt him back at the tool shed.

He was amazed at how tiny the thoughts were that could instantaneously change a situation into a complete opposite. He had been so sure that Lena had defied his authority once again. Discouragement had fallen on him with a heaviness hard to bear. He now realized that assumption was the makings of his burden, not fact. He had neglected his faith and let it shrink. The consequence was a misunderstanding. He decided that maybe misunderstanding, rather than money, is the root of all evil.

New hope lightened his step, and he felt renewed confidence in his desire to save Lena. He turned from his path to the barn and walked briskly to the house. He would have a talk with his stubborn child and continue to steer her away from the worldly ways that school teaches.

CHAPTER 20

Lena, bound by anxiety and fleeing to free herself, entered the house with a flurry of bumping feet and an opening and slamming of doors. She grazed a chair by the kitchen table, nearly knocking it over, and ran full tilt to the stairs. She was up them, her feet barely touching the steps, down the hall and into her room with the final slam of a door. She flopped onto the bed and lay on her back, panting and trembling. An arm covered her squeezed eyes. Then she flipped to her side, curled up into a ball, and began to cry.

Sitting at a small beat-up desk in his room reading his bible, Daniel heard the clamor Lena made coming up the stairs. He heard her run into the hall and slam the door to her room. His eyes continued to collect the words in his bible, but they would not make the delivery to his brain. He wondered what was wrong with Lena. He raised his face from the bible, twisted on his seat, and stared at the open doorway behind him. He rose from his chair and made his way out of his room and down the hall. As he approached her door, he thought he heard her crying. He knocked on the door. No response. With one hand on the knob, he called to her, his mouth close to the door.

"Lena? Are you alright?" Still nothing. "Lena?" He counted to ten, opened the door, and said, "I'm coming in," and stuck his head into the room.

He saw her sitting on the edge of the bed, one leg under her, the other hanging over the edge. She sat with her hands in her lap, her face toward the floor, staring. "What's wrong," he asked. "I heard you crying." She raised her face to him and shrugged her shoulders. He saw her red, puffy eyes and entered the room to sit beside her. He wanted to comfort her and tell her it would be okay. He sat still. "So, what happened?"

Her eyes returned to the floor. "I bumped into Sam when he came out of the tool shed." She looked at him, and he saw her expression, asking for understanding. "He grabbed my arm." She made it sound tragic. His soft heart went out to her, his little sister, who had always been a victim in this otherwise blessed family. A victim of ... what? Everyone said that she had been traumatized by witnessing her brother's death, but Daniel wasn't so sure. What do the preachers know about the human brain? They are all farmers. They know about the seasons and reasons for planting the soil and reaping the harvest. They know about the soul of the human being. Which one of them has ever cracked open a book on the mind of the human being? Each one is either a preacher farming or a farmer preaching.

Their remedy for her affliction was to let nature take its course and let God's will be done. It's as if they knew that God didn't want Lena to be treated by a doctor. They figured He wanted to treat her Himself or leave her odd, silent, and sad. How did they know doing nothing was God's will? They prayed. That was doing something.

He prayed, too. Thousands of prayers for her had poured from his heart during all those years. Maybe they had all taken the easy way and just prayed.

But then, he was neither a preacher nor a doctor. He didn't know, one way or the other, what effect seeing your brother get killed has on a little girl. He didn't even know if she had seen Andrew fall or if she had seen him after; neither did they. No one knows... except maybe their father. He was there. Maybe something else happened in the hayloft.

Then something ugly wisped through his thoughts. It brought goosebumps to his scalp, and hot waves of regret flooded his spirit. Why was Lena so afraid of their father? The question brought up in his mind the notion that their father could be the cause of Lena's trouble. The thought lived for only a flash like the sting of a charged nerve, then vanished, cloaked into oblivion by the impossibility.

"You cried because Dad grabbed your arm?"

"I guess. I don't know. Sounds stupid, doesn't it?" They were silent for a moment.

"So why did that make you cry," he asked. She flopped down to the bed on her side, hiding her face in the bedspread. She was near tears again.

"I don't know!" She slapped the bed in disgust. "What is wrong with me, Daniel?"

Daniel twisted and bent one leg on the bed to look at her. "What do you mean? I don't think there is anything wrong with you. Listen to yourself. You are talking, carrying on a whole conversation, and crying. Not that I want you to cry, but I'm glad you can, like a normal person. You haven't done those things for years, since you were five. I think you're doing great."

"Great? Are you kiddin'? I got Butch killed. I hate my own father. I thought I was gonna get raped and..." She jerked her face from the bedspread and peered at Daniel with as much shock in her expression as Daniel's.

Oh, no! All of a sudden, I have a big mouth.

Daniel stared at Lena, his mouth gaping open in disbelief. Lena stared back. *I didn't just say that, did I?*

The word came out of Daniel like it was something caught in his throat. "Raped?" His eyes searched Lena's wide-eyed expression for confirmation that he had not heard right. He got the opposite. "What are you talking about?" He sat staring at her, dumbfounded.

She jerked up to a sitting position, scooted to the edge of the bed, and assumed the demeanor of a stone statue. Daniel couldn't find any words to say.

Then tears began to trickle down the statue's cheeks, the stone face contorted, and her words came out warped and strangled. "There is...something... wrong... with me!" She wailed pitifully. Daniel was astonished. He couldn't think what to do.

Utter dismay shook Lena, and she sank her head into her hands. "Oh God," she cried, "I'm sorry, so, so sorry! I didn't know! I didn't know!"

Daniel was crushed. He gained some presence of mind and scooted close to her. He put his arm around her. He was overwhelmed. Her word rape loomed in his mind blocking off all thought. He then asked the only question available to him.

"Someone tried to rape you?" The question from his lips was even more foreign and confusing. When she couldn't answer, he took his arm from her, rose from the bed, and went to the door to close it. He felt protective of her shame, her secret. As he reached for the door to push it shut, he heard the kitchen door slam. He listened and heard footsteps move into the dining room and then to the bottom of the stairs. His father's voice was clear.

"Lena," he called. Daniel glanced back at Lena. She had jerked her face from her hands and sat staring at the doorway. She didn't make a sound.

Suddenly, she slipped her shoes off and moved silently to the closet. She disappeared inside, closing the door after herself.

Daniel moved quickly through the doorway and closed the door carefully behind him. As he sneaked down the hallway on tiptoes toward his room, he heard his father start up the stairs. He was in his room with the door closed in seconds, his anxiety hiding with him. He hoped and prayed his dad wouldn't come to ask him where Lena was. What would he do? He didn't want to tell him, couldn't possibly tell him, but that would require a lie. He was sure that he wouldn't be able to lie to his father. Poor Lena.

Sam climbed the stairs confident that he should resume the administering of his responsibility. It was his duty to lead his daughter to her Christian maturity. Her returning to normal reassured him that he had been right to let God perform His will in His own time. He was with God, and he had proof. Lena was healed, and not yet lost. He was pleased with himself for following his faith in his God all these nine years, the outcome of which gave him cause to feel confident of God's approval. He was sure that it was time to bend Lena toward her future as a Mennonite woman. He could expect her to conform to God's will without pandering to her handicap. Her only handicap now was the distance she had fallen behind in learning her service to God. He would catch her up in no time.

He felt lifted toward a higher position in his relationship with God. His step was light on the stairs as he climbed toward the management of his precious daughter's salvation. From the top of the stairs, he could see that Lena's bedroom door was closed. He walked to the door and knocked.

"Lena?" He waited for an answer, got none, and thought, *Stubborn!*

He opened the door and entered the bedroom. He was surprised to see that Lena wasn't there. He saw her head cover on the bed. She had just been there. He took the head cover off the bed and left the room, taking it with him.

In the hallway, he noticed Daniel's door closed and wondered if he was in his room. He moved toward the closed door, thinking that Daniel might know where Lena might be. He reached the door, opened it a crack, and called into the room. "Daniel, you in there?"

Daniel sat at the desk as before, his back to the door, bible in hand. His heart had fallen to the pit of his stomach when he heard the door open.

At the sound of his father's voice, his spirit hit bottom as well, taking hope with it. He wished he could just vanish and reappear later after his father found Lena. But there Daniel was, caught between helping his little sister or lying to his father. What would Jesus do? He sure wouldn't lie! "Yeah, I'm here."

His father pushed the door open and looked in on Daniel. Without entering the room, he asked, "Do you know where Lena is?"

That question suddenly offered Daniel an alternative. He could answer his father truthfully and still avoid betraying Lena. It would require disobedience, the lesser of two evils. But even the benefit of compromise could not arm him with the courage to turn and face his father. He answered the question with his back to him, leaving his eyes on the bible in his hands. His voice was small. "Yes, I know where she is."

Sam heard the confession but paid closer attention to the reluctance ducking behind it. He came into the room and stood beside Daniel. He felt a rare discomfort between him and his son. He waited for him to finish the answer to the question. After all, he had asked it to find out where he should go to find her. Daniel's silence grew longer. Regret began to churn in Sam's insides. He stared at Daniel. A tight frown and pressed lips gave him the face of a man hurting somewhere or holding off an inner explosion. It was hurt that altered his voice. "You're not gonna tell me, are you?"

Daniel shook his head. "I can't."

"Can't or won't?"

Daniel looked into his father's face. He thought he would see the hurt and disappointment he had heard in his voice. But a stern master of the house stood over him with commands blazing in his eyes and hardening his expression.

"So, I see how it is," his father said. "You've taken sides, have you? You would help Satan himself lure your little sister into the pits of hell?"

Daniel felt the sting of a slap in his spirit's face. He shrank from his father's usual, aggressive assault. But he was no longer a child. He was now inclined to stand for who he was. "I am not between you on one side and Lena on the other," he said. "I'm with you and Lena on the same side. You, Lena, and I fight against the devil together. But your fight with Lena is between you two. I will not let the devil make me go against either one of you. I will not lie to you, and I don't want to expose Lena to the fear she has of you. If you ask me where she is, Satan knows I will have to tell you, and that will suit the devil just fine because it will destroy Lena's trust in me. You will get my obedience, but Lena will get a brother she can't trust. Don't you see? That's when the devil wins. So, it's up to you."

Sam was stunned! He peered at his son as if he were a stranger. "You have never talked to me this way, with such disrespect, Daniel. What has gotten into you?" Daniel said nothing. Sam went on. "I am still your father, your superior, and I'll not have you talk to me as if I'm your brother or a buddy."

"I didn't mean any disrespect, Dad. I only want you to see the position you put me in. I'm damned if I do and damned if I don't, which will tickle Satan pink."

Sam frowned at the cuss word but didn't interrupt. Daniel finished with, "If you don't ask me where Lena is, the devil loses."

"Loses? He didn't lose anything! He just gave you a way to disobey your father with a clear conscience. Sounds like you would rather have Lena's trust than obey me."

"No, that's not true. I want both, and the only way that can happen is if you leave me out of the fight between you and Lena. I'm not saying I won't tell you where Lena is if you ask. I'm asking you not to ask. Why are you willing to destroy the relationship between me and Lena just so you will be obeyed?" Daniel could see the anger that had fallen on his father, but he wasn't sorry he had spoken his mind. He wished his father weren't so stiff-necked.

"Whether you obey me or not is not the issue here," his father growled. "Lena has not been with us close enough to learn about her God. I need to start teaching her. The sooner, the better. That is my concern at the moment."

"But you don't have to make me betray my little sister to save her. Where is your faith in the Holy Spirit? Maybe if you give Him some time to do His job on Lena, you won't have to sacrifice one good to save another." They were silent, Sam fuming at his son's insolence and Daniel wondering if he should have been so bold. But Daniel spoke again. "Besides," he said, "she can't hide from you forever. You don't have to know where she is this instant."

Sam stood silent for a moment, staring down at his son's upturned face, looking him in the eye, unflinching. He couldn't believe what was happening. He and Daniel had always been on common ground. Daniel had never defied him. Something unusual must have happened. It was impossible for Sam to accept Daniel's behavior as legitimate. He told himself it would be different later, and without another word, he quickly left the room.

Walking down the hallway, he remembered Daniel saying, "She can't hide from you forever." He stopped at Lena's closed bedroom door. If she was making an effort to hide from him, she could be in her closet. He reached for the doorknob but, on second thought, dropped his hand to his side.

He felt again as he had that day at the bottom of the ladder to the hayloft. Uncertainty concerning the need for the action that he felt obliged to take. The results of the decision he had made that day were tragic. But he made all his decisions in line with the word of God. The accident was God's will, wasn't it?

He stared at the door for a moment. Then, suddenly remembering the head cover in his hand, he hung it on the doorknob and continued down the hall to the stairs.

As he walked through the house and out the back door, he thought again of Daniels's words about the Holy Spirit doing His job on Lena. *Where did he get a notion like that? It isn't the Holy Spirit's job to watch over you and lead you to righteousness. It is a reward. You need to ask in faith. Then, if you're worthy and have obeyed His commandments, and your request is in God's will, your prayer will be heard. And even then, it may or may not be answered. That's the way the Holy Spirit works. It's not His job to watch over you and make sure you get to heaven. We have free will. We gotta be responsible for our own choices.*

As Sam entered the barn, he felt better about his decision to get after Lena and ensure she would be taught to make the right choices. Now, he wished he had told Daniel to tell him where she was hiding, ordered him, for Lena's sake.

CHAPTER 21

They were all at the supper table quietly making the gentle sounds of people eating without speaking. Even Sam was silent.

Lena ate as quickly as was within her mother's no-gobbling rule and was the first to leave the table. She wasted no time getting to the sanctuary of her room and the comfortable arms of her bed. She couldn't believe she had gotten through supper without incident with Sam. She wondered how long it would take him to speak to her about getting on the bus. She was sure her mother knew what she had done and had probably told him. He would surely get after her about it sooner or later. She was disappointed that her mother had not sought her out to discuss why it had happened.

That was the part of the day she was trying to keep her mind on. The bad part of the day was suffocating her. She cried into her pillow, desperate for an explanation for what her crippled mind had imagined of Lewis. It was inconceivable that he was capable of ... She could not let the word come to her mind and certainly not her mouth. She dared not say it again. The one time that she had blurted it out to Daniel was one time too many. *What is wrong with me? Am I really crazy?* She cried harder.

Sarah ate her supper, hardly aware of the food. Lena had her worried more than usual. The way Lewis had said she acted at his house was a puzzle. It sounded like something had scared her to death. She seemed to be acting again like she had before, running away from something for no known reason. Sarah hoped not. She made up her mind to talk to her as soon as she was through eating.

Sam also realized that Lena's early escape had given him an opportunity to begin instructing her soon after he went out to lock things up for the night. He finished eating and left the house.

This gave Sarah the first chance to go to Lena's room. Standing at the door and raising her hand to knock, she heard Lena crying. Her hand went to the knob, and she quickly entered. "Lena, what's wrong?"

Startled, Lena jerked to a sitting position. She had tried to cry quietly so she wouldn't have to explain why to anyone. Now, she would have to lie to her mother... again. She had no story prepared and didn't know what to say.

Her mother sat on the edge of the bed, concerned. "It's okay, Lena," she said. Don't worry about your dad. He doesn't need to know you got on the bus this morning. Crying isn't going to help anyway. It's all over with, and it will be our secret."

Lena heaved a deep sigh of relief. She wouldn't have to make up a lie about why she was crying after all. Her mother thought she was crying over school, not over what had happened at Katy's. She would play along to keep it that way. "I don't know why I got on the bus, it just happened."

"I know you went to Katy's," her mother said.

Lena was surprised. "How did you know?"

"I went to the school, and your bus driver told me he saw you walking down Katy's road. But when I got to Katy's, you had already come back to the house." Sarah saw what she thought was fear in her daughter's expression. She became cautious. "Katy said that Lewis told her you were upset."

Choosing to lie or not was no longer an option for Lena. She never gave it another thought; she just lied. "No, I wasn't upset! Why would I be upset?"

Sarah was surprised at Lena's answer. Why would she deny the truth when the facts were undeniable? She frowned at Lena. "Then why did Lewis say" ...?

Suddenly, Sam interrupted at the open door. "Lena, you and I are gonna have a talk." He came to the bedside and stood over them as if he were calling them to a challenge.

Sarah was stunned at his behavior and became angry, but Sam gave her no time to confront him. His assault on Lena was overwhelming. It was like the sudden fury of a storm came over him, tossed their senses like leaves in a dirt devil.

"I want you to sit still and listen to me," he ordered. "You might as well make up your mind to forget about going to school ever again because that will never happen. As soon as you accept that and start doing what you are supposed to do, you and everybody else will be much happier. You have brought discord into our family with your behavior lately, and I'm putting a stop to it right now. You are no different than anyone else in this family, so you better start acting like it. And until you are of age to be on your own, I expect you to do as you're told, when you're told. Do you understand?"

The storm abated as quickly as it arose, leaving a hush of silence as roaring as the outburst itself. Lena just stared.

Sarah, however, had, moments before, replaced stunned with anger. "Sam Danziger, you don't have to talk like that to a person to be understood!"

Sam turned his face to Sarah. "Are you going to keep babying her the rest of her life? It won't be long before she'll be a grown woman! She has to learn her responsibilities!" He turned his attention to Lena, leaving his wife without a chance to respond. "God has blessed you, Lena. He has healed you and made you whole. You must be what He intends you to be: His servant. We must serve God and do his will in all things, in every way. You might as well get that through your head. I will not allow any of my children to be exposed to any more of Satan's work than I have to. And that leaves high school out."

For the first time since that day in the hayloft, Lena spoke to her father without being told to. "I don't get it," she said.

Even though this was the second time he heard her fourteen-year-old voice, it did not diminish Sam's surprise. His senses jerked, and finding his voice took him a moment. "What do you mean? You don't get what?"

"How do you know what God intends for me to be? And how did you figure out that God wants all his people to be uneducated? Did he tell you that? If He did, why didn't He tell all the teachers and the government guys? And how about all His preachers in other churches? How come He didn't tell them? Their kids are going to high school."

The defiance in her words was unmistakable. Sam felt the pain they brought him but mistook her words for an attack on his authority. Exasperated and discouraged, anger rose in him, and he let it push him. His red face was stiff, straining from the warning that he couldn't hold back.

"You're getting a little too smart for your pants, little girl! You keep talking to me like that, and you'll find out all about education! You're not too big to spank yet!" Sarah sat stiff and astonished, staring at her husband.

Lena smelled the hayloft dust and felt the panic begin to rise in her. But this time, her father would not hold her down; she wouldn't let him. She scrambled off the bed and, standing in front of him, growled her defense.

"If you ever touch me again, I hope God strikes me dead!" She turned and ran from the room. Sam stood very still. The anger he had felt moments before left his face. He closed his eyes in despair.

CHAPTER 22

Everyone but Lena was at the breakfast table the following morning, telling their day's events. Lena was halfway down the stairs when she heard Harley talking about a stalled red pickup on the bridge. The words that stopped her mid-step were, "The girl is broke and headed for Colorado Springs. She said that after paying for a motel room, she wouldn't have the money to buy gas, so I offered to fix her pickup and buy a tank of gas."

Lena rushed the rest of the way downstairs to join the others, anxious to hear what Harley had to say about the girl going to Colorado Springs.

As she settled in her chair, Harley said, "I'll need to go to town right after dinner and get started on that pickup. So, who can let me use their vehicle?"

Daniel spoke up. "I'll need my car all day, but I can take you to town and come get you sometime this evening.

Harley nodded in agreement and said, "That will work. Thanks."

Lena's stomach churned with excitement. She couldn't believe her luck. It was a chance to get outta here just when she needed it the most. Her scheming went into high gear, turning out one bold scenario after another. All she had to do was get to the motel in town and talk to the girl with the red pickup. The hardest part would be getting to town without her family knowing it.

Then, a sobering thought flipped a switch in her scheming mind. *Harley must be planning the same thing. If he talks to the girl before I do, and the girl agrees to let him go with her, he won't let me go with them.* She had to get to town somehow and fast. After everyone finished breakfast, she would sneak over to Katy's. Katy would take her to town.

Another thirty minutes passed in her room while she paced the floor, hugging her pillow tightly. She finally heard the slam of the outside door. That would be Daniel, she guessed.

She got her Sunday coat from her closet, wishing she didn't have to wear it, considering Spiker's muddy field. But her everyday coat was downstairs in the hall closet. Her mother would see her and want to know where she was going. She heard Sam and Harley's muffled voices and then the kitchen door slamming. She would have to sneak out the front door while her mother was busy with the dishes.

She donned the coat, left the room, and crept down the stairs. The clatter of dishes in the kitchen assured her of her mother's whereabouts. She made no noise, crossing the living room and exiting through the front door.

Outside, she was off the porch and running for the corner of the house toward the highway when she heard Sam call her name. It came from over by the tool shed.

"Lena, what are you doing?"

Her heart leaped, and her head jerked around when she heard his voice behind her. She saw him at the doorway of the tool shed and slowed for two steps. Then she resumed her running and turned the corner, nearly falling. She caught her balance, ran a few more steps, and then slowed down to a walk. She stopped, kicked a small dead elm tree branch, and then turned to face the corner of the house.

In her mind, she could see Sam on the other side of that corner. He was probably staring at the spot where she had disappeared. Did he expect her to re-appear from behind the house and stand bowing before his judgment? She was sure of it. Just days ago, she would have kept running for the nearest hiding place and would have avoided him for the rest of the day,

She started walking back to the front of the house. She turned the corner, and, as she had expected, he was walking her way with authority in his step and purpose in the muscles of his face. He was the embodiment of authority.

She trembled inside and felt sick to her stomach. She stopped, consumed by the look of him. She could not push herself toward him any further. She could not mount the steps of the hangman's scaffold.

As he approached, he began. "Well, young lady, I see you have quit running from me, and it's well that you have. It's time you learn to know me as your father and obey me as well as you do your mother. Your days of ignoring me are over. I will not allow you to treat me like some kind of disease another day." He stood in front of her. "Now, tell me what you are up to. Where were you going?"

She trembled so that she could hardly stand. The smell of the hayloft was suffocating her, and her neck ached from the weight of his pressing hand. And yet there he was, standing three feet in front of her, his hands at his sides, peering at her. She was stiff and holding her breath. This time, it wasn't the dread of him that made her run. This time, she ran toward him. It was contempt for what he represented: a God that would kill her as surely as He had her brother.

Sam grabbed her arm as she tried to pass by him, and their eyes locked on each other. She jerked free of his hold, tearing the sleeve of her coat at the shoulder seam. She continued running, leaving him standing looking after her, astonished.

Lena leaped upon the porch, pushed through the door, and flew up the stairs to her room, slamming the door behind her. She leaned her back against it, panting. Eyes closed, she fought the tears welling up and damned Sam for interfering with her plans. She looked at the torn coat sleeve and lost the fight against her tears.

CHAPTER 23

Lena, upstairs in her bedroom, heard the familiar squeak of car brakes turning into the driveway. She quickly slid off the bed and reached the window just in time to see Daniel pull into the yard. She was surprised that her afternoon reading had allowed the sun to slip down on the horizon. She grabbed her coat and slipped it on while flying out of the room. She ran down the stairs and out the front door before anyone in the house knew she was there and gone.

She approached the car on the run as Daniel and Harley climbed out.

As Harley got out, he said, "Hey, Lena." Then, "Whoa, slow down! What's your hurry?"

She stopped and heaved a sigh, trying to catch her breath. "Nothing. I was wondering if you got the girl's truck fixed."

He shook his head and slammed the car door shut. "No, not quite. Why?" She shrugged as nonchalantly as she could. "Just wondering," she murmured.

Harley sensed in Lena's demeanor a deeper interest in the story of the red pickup than she was letting on. He stood examining her, waiting for her to hint at her intentions.

In the meantime, Daniel had left the car and walked toward the house. Lena watched him and then turned to Harley. "Is the girl gonna be stuck in town long?"

Harley frowned. "Probably not long, why?"

"Well, I thought if it was gonna be more than another day or so, she might wanna come out here and visit instead of being stuck in the motel room with nothing to do. What's her name?"

Ah ha, Harley thought. "Her name is Julia." He was starting to get the picture now, and it was just what he thought. Lena wants to talk to Julia about going to Colorado with her.

Harley moved closer to Lena, glanced at the kitchen door, and spoke softly. "I don't think Julia will be willing to be hobbled with both of us," he said

Lena inhaled deeply. She stopped breathing for a few seconds and then let her breath out with exasperation. She spoke in a half-whisper. "So, you are going with her!"

Harley stood silent momentarily and then walked off toward the kitchen door. Lena shut up and followed.

Their mother was in the kitchen, standing in front of the sink. At the sight of Lena, Sarah was relieved. "Lena! So that's where you've been all afternoon with Harley."

Lena shook her head." No. I was in my room, reading, trying to stay away from Sam."

Those were the words that Sam heard as he entered the kitchen. Daniel was behind him, craning his neck to see over his father's shoulder.

Sam was shocked to hear his daughter speak his name. The lack of respect cut him deeply. She spoke with less respect than if he were a neighbor. The other three had also heard the contempt in Lena's tone. They were silent, knowing what was coming.

He walked to her and stood in front of her. Her coat was off, and she held it by the collar. At first, her head was down, looking at the floor. But before Sam could begin his attack, it came up. There was no fear on her face, only growing confidence. She would not turn and run.

Sam saw defiance, and it stood before him at his disposal. His tone was irritated. "Now, since when did my children call me by my first name like a next-door neighbor kid? Don't you have any respect?" She was silent. There passed a moment when all signs of life in the house were inanimate objects.

But Sam lived in force. "Well, I can tell you right now you are going to get some respect in you. You've been babied long enough. It's time you learn that the world does not revolve around you but how God expects you to act around others. I told you before you're not too old to spank, but you didn't pay any attention to me. If you want to act like a spoiled brat, then you're going to be treated like a spoiled brat." He took her by the arm and pulled a chair away from the table. He pointed at the chair.

"Now, bend over that chair." Lena was stunned as she realized that he intended to give her a spanking.

Sarah stared at Sam in blank disbelief. Harley and Daniel were equally stupefied. They could see the fury in Sam's movements. It was no longer a matter of disobedience. It was now Sam against Lena, or even Satan, perhaps.

Sam whirled Lena around, turning her back to him. He placed his hands on her shoulders and pushed her toward the chair. She resisted but was no match for Sam's advantage of surprise or his strength. His jaw was carved in stone. Her knees bashed into the edge of the chair seat, causing her to fall across it on her stomach.

Her bewildered mind was trying to figure out if this was really happening. When she felt her dress being lifted past her panties and knew she was exposed to her father's eyes, she screamed. She then twisted and felt the edge of the chair scrape her back. She landed with her butt against the cold linoleum floor. She kicked up and out with all her strength, hitting her father solidly in the lap. His body gave with the impact and sent him back a step, but it did not discourage his effort. He took a step to regain his position at her feet. She kicked him again, surprising him and getting better results. He stepped away and stared at her with a shocked expression for a moment. Then, slightly bent at the waist, he moved to the back door and went out into the dark.

In the meantime, Lena scrambled to her feet and ran upstairs to her room.

When Daniel realized what his father was about to do, he quickly retreated to his room. Harley, however, still stood between the table and the door, where he had frozen, stunned. Now, he looked at his mother as if to ask if what he had just seen really happened. The question was in his pale face. Sarah picked up Lena's coat from the floor, laid it on the table, and went upstairs.

She stopped at Lena's bedroom door to listen and, without knocking, opened the door and looked in. Lena sat stiffly on the edge of the bed, her hands in her lap. She glared past her mother at the wall beside the door. Sarah entered, softly closed the door, and went to the bed to sit beside Lena. Their eyes locked, and Sarah saw the hatred Lena held for her father. Sarah shook her head in disappointment, and her spirit flinched in pain.

Words were inadequate for the telling of the humiliation that Lena had experienced at the hands of her angry father. Neither would Sarah have been able to find words that would excuse a father for such an outrageous action against his fourteen-year-old daughter. She could only put her arm around her precious daughter, pull Lena's head against her chest, and let her feelings speak of her regret for Sam's unforgivable deed. Lena knew only the shame burning inside her and an overwhelming need to escape Sam. To get as far away as she could, for starting tonight

CHAPTER 24

The morning, still cloaked in its midnight cape, came and took its place outside her window. It watched her quietly scurry about her room.

She stuffed a cardboard box with two changes of clothes, a comb, a hairbrush, and a toothbrush. The head cover lying on top of the chest of drawers barely got a glance.

Five minutes after four a.m., she had dressed, combed her hair, and put on her coat. She carefully descended the creaking stairs into the dark rooms below with the cardboard box under her arm. The squeaks in the floorboards could not be ignored, but they were a long way from her parents' bedroom.

Navigating the living room furniture in the dark, without bumps or stumbles, was easy. They had been in their current positions for years.

She reached the front door and, taking hold of the knob, she hesitated. She couldn't remember if the door had a squeak in it or not. She turned the knob carefully. The click of the latch seemed to explode in the house's stillness. She squeezed her eyes shut and cringed. She stood frozen momentarily and focused on the bedroom down the hallway. Nothing stirred. No one made a sound. But then she wouldn't be able to hear them open their eyes, would she? *What if Sam's layin' there, eyes wide open, listening the same as I am!* Well, she couldn't just stand there until he went back to sleep, which may never happen.

Holding her breath, she stood there for a few more seconds, then quickly pulled the door open wide. She ignored the short squeak that filled the quiet darkness. She plunged through the doorway into the biting cold night.

She pulled the door through its squeak again and let it latch. Then she ran for the east side of the house, where she squatted down next to the opening under the porch. If Sam was awake and heard the door and came out of the house looking, she would crawl out of sight under the porch.

She crouched there, shivering in the cold for a couple of minutes. She kicked herself, all the while, for not running to Daniel's car instead. That's where she intended to be in the first place. She planned to hide there as a stowaway and go to town with Daniel and Harley. She wouldn't be freezing her butt off right now if she hadn't panicked.

She rose from her crouch, went to the corner of the house, and peered around it toward the front door. She saw nothing but darkness shrouding the front of the house. She heard nothing. Should she go to the car now? What if Sam was looking out the front window? She would have to cross the yard to get to the driveway where the car was parked.

In the house, Sam stirred in his bed. He slowly came out of his sleep, irritated by something. There had been a noise in his dream that hadn't belonged there. Then he realized the sound hadn't been in the dream but somewhere in the house. He opened his eyes and raised his head to listen. He heard nothing. He lowered his head back to his pillow and continued to listen to the house.

Usually, when this happened, he would walk around in the dark rooms in case something had happened that would cause a serious problem.

He got out of bed and walked sleepily down the hallway to the living room. He stopped and scanned the room. In the firelight of the coal-burning heater, he could see enough to know nothing was amiss. He headed for the kitchen.

Outside, Lena was getting colder and colder. She had no gloves on. One hand was in her coat pocket, but the other was holding the box under her arm and was starting to ache. Would it be any warmer in the car? A slight breeze was making it colder, and the car would protect her from that. But would it be warm enough to stay there for two or three more hours? It would be seven o'clock or so when Daniel and Harley would be ready to leave for town. She was shivering uncontrollably now and wondered if she had acted too early or if this was even a good idea. Then, she considered the alternative. She had no choice. She stepped out from behind the house and made a dash for the car.

In the house, Sam entered the kitchen and saw nothing to be concerned about. He returned to the living room, where the moonlight streaming through the window caught his attention. *Must be a full moon,* he thought. He shuffled over in that direction to look outside.

Lena reached the car, jerked open the door to the back seat, and dove in. She pulled the door closed quietly and made it latch. She quickly scrunched down on the floorboard and stayed that way for several seconds, listening for any sounds from the house.

At that moment, Sam peered out the window. He gazed at the bright neon moon sifting its beam through the naked branches of the giant cottonwoods and elms. He was taken by its beauty, and that was all he saw.

Lena felt the temperature difference immediately upon entering the car. She was encouraged and regained some confidence in her plan.

She leaned back against the door and tried to relax despite the shivering. But, after fifteen or twenty minutes and noticing no improvement in her shaking, she realized she would not get any warmer. The possibility that she might fall asleep and freeze to death also crossed her mind. Surely, the temperature was below freezing. She didn't know. She should have had the sense to bring a blanket with her.

Well, she couldn't go back inside and wait till later, that's for sure. She would have no chance to sneak out to the car after five-thirty. Sam was always up by then. She would just have to stay in the car and take her chances. So what if she did wind up frozen like an ice cube? *Anything's better than living with God's little helper.* She hugged herself tighter and stared at the window in the other door.

The night sky was filled to running-over with the brightness of the moon and the stars. Their crisp presence made the air seem even colder. It wouldn't be hard to stay awake, shivering her head off. But, an hour later, Lena was asleep, dreaming.

She was deep in the frigid waste of the arctic ice lands running across frozen waters. The ice crumbled beneath each frenzied step as she ran. She couldn't outrun the breaking ice that sunk beneath her feet.

Suddenly, the world of ice cracked wide open with an ear-splitting explosion of sound. She woke with a jerk and, for an instant, did not know where she was. Then, the whirr of the starter trying to turn over the cold, stiff engine brought her out of her confusion. The engine coughed, sputtered, and then roared its readiness in the dim seven o'clock morning. The person at the wheel, whom she imagined was Daniel, got out of the car and slammed the door again.

She remained motionless for a moment. Then, feeling pain in her neck and hips, she shifted her position to gain some comfort. It didn't help much. Her butt was numb too. Oh well, it didn't matter. It would be just a few more minutes until they would be going down the highway to town. She would get up out of hiding and get all the kinks out then.

Lordy, lordy, what will Daniel and Harley do when she pops up in the back seat? *Harley is going to hit the ceiling.* She didn't care. She was going with that girl in the red pickup wherever she went, and no one was going to stop her.

She could feel the interior of the car beginning to warm up. She couldn't believe that she had fallen asleep. But at least she hadn't frozen to death. She was lucky it wasn't as cold as she imagined.

The minutes dragged by, and the sky in the window got lighter and lighter. Suddenly, she heard the kitchen screen door slap shut, and her brothers' voices came toward the car. The rhythm of her heart picked up, and she could feel it pound in her chest. They stopped talking before they got close enough for her to hear what they were saying. She waited. They would make her get out if they spotted her when they got into the car. She would have to find another way to get to town. She ducked her head down and squeezed her eyes shut. "*Please, please, please,*" she begged silently.

The passenger door opened and shut first. Harley, she said to herself. As the driver's door came open, he spoke from the passenger's side. "That old thing should be running by sometime this afternoon."

Daniel slammed the driver's door shut. As he put the car in gear, he asked, "Did Dad say anything about our going to town so early?"

"No, I think he's pretty upset about what happened with Lena last night."

"Yeah, he hardly spoke a word this morning. I don't think he paid us much attention." He moved the car into the turn-around, down the driveway, and onto the highway, heading for Garland.

Lena was anxious to achieve a more comfortable position. At the same time, she dreaded the battle she imagined she would have with her brothers when she revealed herself and her intentions. They would be fit to be tied, and she didn't know what they would do. Maybe turn right around and take her back to the house. There was silence between the brothers for about a mile, and then Harley finally asked the question burning in both their minds.

"Is Dad losing his mind or what? What in the world was he trying to accomplish last night?" Daniel turned his face to Harley and then back to the highway. He spoke with a tone of high hope in his voice. "He was just frustrated. Lena's not been the easiest child to deal with, and he has been trying to get her to come back to him ever since the accident. Lena was very close to him before. You know she's always been his favorite."

Harley nodded. "He'll probably never get over her kicking him," he said.

Sitting on the floor with her forehead resting on her knees, Lena listened with growing interest in the conversation. She jerked her head up, astonished at the word "favorite."

Then, a rush of embarrassment came over her and burned her face. Harley had seen her nearly naked. Her father, having seen her with her dress up over her head, was almost more than she could bear. *But Harley?* She began to feel sick to her stomach.

Daniel showed sudden wonder. "Lena kicked him?"

"Twice!" Daniel looked at Harley in disbelief.

Harley was adamant. "Hey, I think he had it coming! Whatever reason he had for doing what he did would be no excuse for a man to pull up his grown daughter's dress to spank her."

Now Daniel was astonished. His eyes were big, and his tone was half-hushed. "Are you kidding me? Our dad did that? Sam Danziger? Unbelievable!"

"Believe it, brother," was Harley's response. Daniel shook his head again. "I left the room because I knew he was gonna try to spank her, but I never imagined he was gonna... go that far!"

Lena was struck with the feeling that she was suffocating. Panic was using all the air. Her stomach was curling into knots, and she thought she might vomit. She squeezed her eyes shut and held her hand over her mouth. She wanted to run worse than she ever had in her whole life. She sat very still and shook. Tears wet her eyes, but she didn't make a sound.

After a few moments of silence, Daniel wanted to know more. "So, what happened after Lena kicked him?"

"Well, I think she hurt him with the second kick, and he backed off and left the house. I don't know if he left because he was hurt or if he came to his senses and realized what he had done."

Daniel was silent for a moment, then gave his supporting opinion in favor of his father.

"You know he regretted it and was ashamed. I think he lost control for a minute. He probably wishes he could take it all back, and that's why he was so quiet this morning."

"You think he'll apologize to Lena?"

"Sure, he will. I'm positive he will."

Lena's cheeks were wet with tears, and she almost sniffled but caught herself before she made the noise. She used the hem of her dress to wipe the tears and the dribble from her nose. She tried to imagine Sam saying he was sorry. It didn't fit. Daniel must see a different man than she did. Or Daniel's just kind and good or ignorant. She was sure he wasn't ignorant. *Always been his favorite?' How did he get that? He doesn't know Sam like I know Sam. Maybe he is ignorant.*

Suddenly, the tires hummed a different pitch, and she realized they were on the bridge, crossing over into Garland's city limits.

The way to the Champlin filling station was short. Daniel turned into the alley behind it, navigating the potholes and slick, hard-packed snow. The ride was rough. The front seat conversation had turned to the work on the pickup, and as the car stopped, so did the words. Lena heard the car doors open and felt the car jiggle as the two boys got out and slammed the doors. She heard the snow crunching under their footsteps as they walked toward the back of the filling station.

She waited until she heard the door on the building slam, then raised herself to peek out the window. There was no one in sight. She settled back down, accidentally kicking over the cardboard box containing her belongings. Now would be the time to get out of the car and make a run for it. She quickly replaced her stuff, putting it back in the box.

There was a lot of open space to run across, and she might be seen from the filling station. She rose to peek again. They wouldn't be able to see her from inside. She could run to the south side of the building and hide until they came out. Then, she could go around to the front, cross the street, and get to the cafe. They would never see her if they stayed in the back of the filling station until she got inside the café. She gathered her box and quickly left the car.

CHAPTER 25

There were only a few people in the café, all engrossed in their breakfasts. They paid no attention to Lena as she stood inside the door. She scanned the large room to choose one of the many empty booths.

She chose one deep within the room that was as close to the bathrooms as possible. She was sure she would be in the café for a while, if not all day. The possibility was overwhelming, and it made her quiver inside with dread.

She saw the order window across the room and the waitress standing by. She turned to look in Lena's direction. She saw her and immediately moved toward her, order book in hand. Lena watched her as she stopped at a stack of plastic tumblers. She stuck one under a waterspout and filled it. She slipped a menu under her arm and headed for Lena.

Lena felt gentle pangs of panic surge in her stomach. Her escape had so consumed her that she had not considered coming up with a normal reason to go to a café.

The waitress stopped at her booth, set the water down, and cheerfully greeted Lena. "Hi, may I help you?" Lena almost got up and ran. Instead, she stammered, "Uh, ... I'm... uh, not... I'm waiting for someone." The waitress was hesitant but smiled. "Oh, okay. If you need anything, just let me know," she said and walked away.

Lena heaved a shaky sigh of relief and slumped back against her seat. She relaxed a little and settled into the long wait that she had anticipated. The big Pepsi clock above the order window said eight-ten.

A little over an hour passed when a stranger walked into the café. Lena noticed the girl, who looked around eighteen years old.

That's gotta be her, she thought. Harley had mentioned at the supper table last night that he guessed she was "eighteen and skinny."

Lena was anxious but skeptical about asking this stranger if her name was Julia. Was it okay to walk up to a stranger and ask them what their name was? She was very inexperienced with strangers. Even with people she knew, she was shy at best.

146

She sat watching the girl scan the room. When her eyes landed on Lena, she started walking toward her. The sudden surprise in Lena caused heat to rise in her face and squeeze the breath from her lungs. The girl was heading straight for her.

Panic-struck, Lena headed straight for the dusty hayloft. She started sneezing profoundly and dove behind the stacked hay bales to escape God's deadly lightning bolt.

Then, in the next instant, she found herself on the cold, tiled floor, scrunched into the corner of a public restroom stall. Her trembling lips were pressed hard against her shaky fist.

She was dumbfounded and confused for a moment. Then reality shook her senses, and she began to cry. She trembled out of control.

After a while, she rose to her feet and stood staring at the stall's door. *Oh crap!* Her mind pictured the girl walking toward her where she had sat in the booth. Had she walked away from the girl she was looking for? Maybe she wasn't the girl. She needed to get back to the main room. She pushed the stall door open and rushed to the exit door. She jerked it open as well. She poked only her head out to peer anxiously down the short hallway and into the main room. The girl was nowhere in sight.

No!... No, no, no! She's not gone, is she? Can't be! Lena slipped through the door, carefully walked the few steps to the end of the hall and stopped. Her eyes flew to the Pepsi clock. *Half an hour? I was in the restroom for half an hour. Impossible!* Then, as she looked around, she realized the number of people in the café had risen considerably. It was a crowd.

She had done it again. She had slipped and fallen off the world and got left behind. She scanned the room with desperate eyes and carefully examined every booth, table, nook, and cranny, searching for the girl. *Gone!* All she could do now was go find her.

She got out on the sidewalk and just stood there. *Now, what do I do?* She wasn't even sure it was the right girl. Disappointment pressed her to the concrete, squeezing hot, stinging tears from her eyes. She wiped her cheeks with the palms of her hands and suddenly remembered her box. *Oh, oh! Where do you suppose that is by now?* She turned her attention back to the café and went back inside.

The counter was three steps to the right of the door. The woman who took your money stood behind it and gave a man his change, talking and laughing. A young couple stood in line behind him, waiting to pay.

Lena moved to the left of the counter, watching for an opportunity to speak to the check-out lady. She waited, hoping no other customer would come to pay. After a few minutes, the couple took their change, said thank you, and left the café. The check-out lady turned her attention to Lena. "Hi," she said. "What can I do for you?"

Lena felt stuck out, like a rabbit in the headlights. She faltered, putting very little effort into the volume of her voice. "I... uh... gotta...I...uh...left my box." The lady leaned toward Lena. "I'm sorry. What did you say?"

Lena cleared her throat and increased her effort. She pointed to the booth in which she had sat. "I left a box of my stuff in that booth over there. Did you see it or know where it might be?" The lady nodded. "Oh yes. I have it right here," she said. She reached under the counter, pulled it out, and handed it to Lena. "There you go." Lena was in awe. She took her box and stared at the lady, wanting to say something that would fully express her appreciation. The lady's expression was puzzled. "Is there something else?" "Oh. No! I just... Thank you," was all she could say. She made her way back out onto the sidewalk.

She didn't know what to do next. Her attention went to the filling station across the street, where she knew Harley was busy trying to fix the pickup. She couldn't see what was going on back there and felt compelled to find out if that was where the girl had gone. She could walk over to the back corner of the building and sneak a peek around behind. She stepped off the curb and then stopped. So, *I find out she's there, then what? There's no tellin' what Harley will do when he sees me. Doesn't matter. I gotta get outta here, no buts or maybes about it.*

She barely stepped toward the station when Harley emerged from behind the building with another person beside him. They were walking briskly, straight for her. She immediately spun around and, like a pinball, was kicked back into the café by no will of her own.

There she was again, in the hayloft. Hay dust buzzed her nose. Her sneezing shook her to the bone.

Inside, she stood at the door hunched over. With her face in her hands, she waited for the sneezing to release her. Her precious box lay on the floor, where it had landed while she had dealt with the sneezing. After regaining her composure, she picked up her box of things and headed toward the restroom.

As she walked, she spotted a vacant booth on the other side of the room and reached it just as Harley and his companion entered the café.

She sat and immediately saw him scanning the room for a booth. The person with him was a girl but not the stranger over which she had agonized earlier. *That's gotta be her! That's gotta be the girl with the pickup.... Julia? Julia. Finally!*

She was elated. It looked like things were going her way after all. Maybe she was wrong about God being out to get her. She sat still, watching. Her insides curled around, twisting knots in her stomach. Should she wait until they got into a booth and then walk over to join them, or should she just stand up and wave to Harley? But then she suddenly had no say in the matter.

The pinball effect kicked Harley and the girl out the door, and Lena fell into one of the holes, slowly rolling into the belly of the "machine." She cussed under her breath. A profound *"Why?"* beat on her paralyzed mind. Was God setting her up for that final bolt of lightning? *Where will I be tomorrow, dead?*

Lena left the café and stood out on the sidewalk again. She was right back where she was ten minutes ago, ready to be pinballed again. She was no closer to Colorado than she was yesterday. Harley and the girl weren't anywhere in sight.

Her disappointment sent her attention across the street to the filling station. She knew the girl, Julia, her only hope, was right behind that building, waiting for Harley to make it possible for her to be on her way. All Lena had to do was to "sashay" over there and start talking. She started toward the station. *Harley will flip his lid, blow his top, hit the ceiling, or whatever. Who cares? I gotta get away. I gotta go someplace where Sam can't find me, and I gotta do it now!*

With no hesitation this time, she made it halfway across the street when she froze. There they were again, coming back. She stopped breathing.

While she stood there oblivious to the possibility of traffic, Harley took at least six steps before he realized it was her. He slowed his pace but continued toward her. As he approached, he quickly looked up and down the street for on-coming traffic. So far, so good. He spoke in a loud voice. "Hey, Lena!"

She didn't answer. He reached a position close in front of her and stopped. "What are you doing here?" She looked frightened. Harley asked, "Where are the folks?" Lena shrugged and, never taking her eyes from Harley's, quietly answered, "At home, I guess."

Harley was taken aback. Considering Lena's usual reluctance to talk, he assumed she was withholding the fact that Daniel had brought her to town. "So, where's Daniel?" At that moment, an oncoming car fifty yards down the street honked its horn. The three startled loiterers in the middle of the street made haste to get to the sidewalk in front of the café.

Harley repeated his question. "Where'd Daniel go?" Lena's expression made Harley realize she had somehow come to town by some other means and was there secretly. And he was sure he knew why. His tone was accusing. "How did you get here, Lena?"

Lena was silent, staring him in the face. She needed time to answer that question. She lowered her head and quickly entered the café. Harley, irritated, followed, with Julia close behind.

Inside, the girls scooted in on one side of the booth, Harley on the other. They sat silent and uncomfortable. Lena was scheming a defense against Harley's expected attack. Harley wrestled with what to say to Lena, "yes" or "no," when she asked to go with him and Julia.

Julia was intrigued by the apparent fuss between Harley and his little sister. She could only wonder what that was all about. Apparently, some disagreement. She kept silent, unconcerned.

At that moment, the waitress materialized at the side of their table with a well-rehearsed question behind her smile. "Hi, how may I help you?" Harley volunteered. "Just cokes, I think." The two girls nodded in agreement without speaking. The waitress spoke cheerfully. "Okay, three cokes coming right up," and left the three sitting in silence. Then Harley broke the silence. To Lena, he said, "I still want to know how you got here. You didn't hitch-hike, did you?"

There was her out. She was tempted to take it and say yes. She hesitated with her answer, telling herself there was a good chance she'd get away with it, but the lies were piling up. She winced and gently shook her head. "No," she whispered. "I hid in Daniel's car and came with you guys."

Shock! Harley sat very still and stared at Lena. It was as if he had instantly frozen. Julia noticed and watched, wondering.

When Harley "came around," his voice was calm. He asked, "Why.... why did you have to sneak to town with us?"

Lena felt the *whole world c*losing in on her. She needed to run! The hayloft was right there!

But Harley spoke, bringing her back to the booth. "Look, Lena, I know what you're going through with Dad. After what happened yesterday, I don't blame you for wanting to get away from him, so you don't have to hide why you're here from me. I wanna help you." Lena was astonished. *Help me? Wow!* She sat up straight. *Or...., uh oh. Is this a setup? Just when you least expect it.* Then, the other thing he said smacked into her mind. *"The reason you're here!"* She frowned and stared at Harley. "So, you think you know why I snuck out of the house, hid in the car, at 4 o'clock this morning in the freezing cold, to come to town without anybody knowing about it? Harley nodded. "Yeah, you wanted to sneak off and talk to Julia about going to Colorado with us. Right?" Julia snapped to attention.

Lena squirmed in her seat and gazed at the front plate glass window. "Like tuh froze my butt off," she mumbled, then poked her face at Harley. "Why do you think I'd do such a crazy thing as that?" Harley just stared at her. Lena wouldn't be denied. "Could it be cuz Sam lives here, dontcha think?"

Even though Julia was intrigued by the fuss that was transpiring before her eyes, her focus was on the last question Lena so sarcastically asked. She didn't know who "Sam" was, but it sounded like something she would have asked just a few days ago about her "pile-a-crap" stepfather.

Suddenly, Lena was more than Harley's little sister. If "Sam" was, say... Lena's father and she was running from him, then Lena was a "comrade in arms." A sister on the same road to freedom as she was.

The connection to Lena that she now felt was a new feeling with which she was unfamiliar. Strangely enough, the notion that Lena might be going with them was now not as remote as she might have first imagined. She politely interrupted. "Who, if I may ask, is Sam?"

Harley and Lena exchanged looks as if each wanted the other to answer. Harley stepped up. "He's our father," he said. Lena, sarcastically, quipped: "*Your* father... my *problem*!"

At that point, their cokes arrived, and they each became engrossed in unwrapping straws and sipping their drinks.

In her silence, Julia was especially thoughtful about Lena's "problem." She could relate. She felt drawn to Lena's situation. She had managed to escape her awful dilemma at home only days ago.

Harley glanced at Julia and wondered how Lena's words affected his deal with her. Would he still have a ride to Colorado? He was having his doubts.

At that moment, Lena chose to pitch Julia her solution to her horrific, personal problem. She sat straight, turned her face to Julia, and quietly said, "Julia, I know we are complete strangers. You don't know me from Adam. But from what Harley told us about you at the supper table yesterday, I know you are a very good person. He is very lucky to have you helping him go to Colorado to marry the girl he loves. I don't wanna be any trouble to you, but, as you probably already guessed, my dad and I don't get along. And the only way I know to make that better is to leave. I have no way to go anywhere, so I thought... was hoping you would let me catch a ride with you to where Harley's going."

Harley stared at Lena, somewhat amazed at her maturity. Since she had found her voice, she kept surprising him with the impressive quality of her character that her silence had hidden. Now, he was struck with a sense that their father could be, at least partially, responsible for all the years that Lena had hidden herself in obscurity. Maybe to be who she really is, she does need to get away from their father.

Julia sat staring at Lena, touched by this young girl. "How old are you?" she asked. Lena glanced at Harley as if expecting him to butt in and step on her part, then blurted, "Fourteen! I'm fourteen and old enough to take care of myself." Julia was feeling closer and closer to this young stranger who had the guts to do what she wished she had done when she was fourteen. "How ready to go with me are you?"

Lena patted the cardboard box she had set on the seat between her and Julia. "Everything I'm taking is right here. All I have left to do is get in your pickup. Whatever happens after that is up to you."

Julia turned to Harley. "You said the pickup is almost ready to go. How long?"

Harley nodded, staring at Lena. "I'm guessing maybe a couple of hours or so." Turning to Julia, he said, "I'm ready to go, too," then winked at Lena.

Her spirit soared. She now flew high above the threat of the hayloft. Her beaming smile lit the dark, dusty corner where she had hidden from the wrath of Sam's God. The freedom took her breath away. She could barely whisper, "Thank you, Harley."

Julia saw the pleasure in Lena's demeanor. It made her feel good. A feeling she had not experienced in a long time... maybe never. She looked at the big Pepsi clock above the order window. 9:30, maybe they could be gone before noon. She was suddenly reminded of something that had been bothering her all morning. She got Harley's attention. "Hey, aren't you gonna take clothes or anything with you?" "Yeah, I've got a big duffle bag full of things I'll need that I smuggled in the car last night. I snuck it into the back of your pick-up this morning when Daniel wasn't looking. I'm all set."

As he vacated the booth, he spoke with friendly urgency: "I'd better get back to the pickup. I want to leave before noon." He walked to the counter, paid the check, and left the café.

By two o'clock that afternoon, Daniel had spent an hour looking for Harley to tell him Lena was missing and that he needed to help look for her. He had at first noticed the red pickup was gone but never gave it a second thought. Then, after another hour of searching for both Harley and Lena, he finally realized that they were probably with that girl, Julia, on their way to Colorado.

Part 2

CHAPTER 26

Lena Danziger was fourteen years old when she changed her name. It was a simple change: add two letters in the middle, an (a) and an (n), and you have a new name. This she decided while she had ridden in thoughtful silence down the highway with Harley and Julia seven years ago.

The name she had written on her school enrollment was Leanna Danziger. That was the day she left "Lena" back on the farm five miles south of Garland, Kansas.

Soon, going to school had become as routine as it was supposed to. Harley and Linda had rented a house for themselves a few months later. Her routine included a home she could run to, take for granted, and call her own. The comfort that came with those circumstances was lifesaving for Lena, now Leanna. Even Harley was getting it right, mostly. Friendship, with even one classmate, was as elusive as it had always been back in Garland. She, at least, was at a very comfortable distance from Sam. Harley and Linda's baby was born that February. In April, they took their new baby girl to show her off to the Danziger family in Garland. Leanna did not go. Even though it was the weekend and would not have interfered with school, Harley could not persuade her. She could not persuade even herself. If Harley could have assured her that Sam would not be there, nothing could have kept her away. She had missed her mother so much, but that wasn't enough to make her crazy enough to get within visual range of Sam.

When they returned to Colorado, Harley told Leanna of their mother's disappointment that she had not returned home with him. But worse than that was the shock of Leanna changing her name, which her father had given her. Harley said that after that, their mother had remained unusually quiet and kept to herself most of the time they were there.

On the other hand, their father nearly lost control when Harley told of Leanna's rejection of her given name. He had ranted and raved while pacing about the living room. His face stuck in an angry scowl, and he asked the ceiling and the floor what he had done to make her hate him. And what was she called now... Jezebel?

"Mom looked like Dad had slapped her in the face when he said that," Harley told Leanna.

Ashamed wasn't the word that described how Leanna had felt about herself. Appalled, was closer, and even that hadn't quite described the disgust that had made her hurry to the bathroom to throw up. She hated Lena Danziger without mercy for two months afterward. Or maybe it was Leanna who deserved her disdain. It was hard to tell one from the other at this early point in her transformation. All she knew for sure was that Lena was gonna be gone, and Leanna was gonna be free of her father.

Harley had talked his head off, trying to make her change her mind instead of her name. He couldn't do it. And what was even more tragic was that Leanna couldn't do it either. Neither could she take Lena to see her mother. Lena didn't deserve it, and Leanna couldn't bear to look at the heart she had broken. She had become Leanna Danziger in more than name only.

She was now Leanna Danziger, the waitress at Leon's Café on Fifth Street. She's that good-lookin' blond that runs around with Julia Sparks. She's the one who lives alone in Queens apartments and drives that beat-up old Plymouth.

That's the Leanna Danzinger that now, at twenty-two, leaned back in the old, painted-white, wooden chair at her kitchen table and heaved a heavy sigh. She stared at the sheets of forms strewn across the table, wishing she were finished with them so she could go to bed.

The clock on the wall above the small, white, beat-up refrigerator hummed its announcement of the hour, minute, and second. As its red hand made its way in monotonous jerks around and around the perimeter of the clock's face, it seemed to taunt Leanna. She thought 1:17 and five seconds, six seconds, seven seconds... and one week. *And one month, and one year, and so on.*

She tossed the pencil onto the table and stared at it. Her mind was six hours down the road east to the home place south of Garland. She missed her mother. She missed her at the same degree that she had missed her that first night she got here seven years ago.

Her eyes fell on an empty beer bottle that stood at the edge of the table. The brown transparent bottle stared back at her.

She rose with an effort, feeling the fatigue *that twelve hours of running your ass off in a restaurant does for ya. Lordy, lordy, I'm tired.*

Reaching the refrigerator, she jerked open the door. She reached in and pulled out another bottle of Coors. The bottle opener was still lying on the cabinet counter where she had left it after opening the first bottle. And the two after that. As she picked it up, the ever-reoccurring flash of the mental picture of her lifting the very first beer she ever drank struck her mind again. It happened every time she opened a beer, ever since that night of the beer bust at Emma's and Julia's apartment.

She was only fifteen, and she had gotten drunk for the first time. She had been surprised that she liked the taste, but what she liked the most was how the beer made her feel.

Emma's twenty-first birthday party was attended by people older than her by five or six years, and no one paid any attention to her.

That was the condition as usual. The "condition" of her entire life was even more awful because of her new surroundings. Living with Harley and Linda during the four years of high school, she had remained a stranger here in Colorado Springs. But at the party, after three beers, the "condition" hadn't bothered her. She hadn't cared that she was invisible and had no part in the production. She was the only one aware of her there on life's stage. The beer had made her just as important as the other players. The relief that came over her had been astonishing.

That was what, seven years ago? Now, she only got tipsy on a six-pack, but it sure made her feel better. She popped the lid off the beer. It hissed, and the lid fell to the counter to join the others. The sound it made was only a thin metallic clatter, but it seemed amplified by the silence. It was like the slamming of a prison door.

She was aware of these rooms where her presence seemed to mysteriously occur every night and vanish every morning. There was no reason for her to be here in her apartment or even on this earth. She had been accidentally created and, with a painful contraction, spit out into this world. And now, no one knew exactly what to do with her.

She couldn't fathom God's reasoning. *He doesn't know what to do with me either. 'Everyone is put on this earth for a reason.'* That is what she has always heard. But she was unnecessary to the existence of these old rooms, the scarred and rickety furniture, and even her faded blue jeans. Leon's restaurant, where she worked, had always operated just fine before her and would after her. That was the extent of her world; none of those things needed her, yet here she was every morning and night. She was here to confirm the truth in another old saying: "Everyone makes mistakes." *And Sam said God doesn't make mistakes. Ha!*

She lifted the beer and took two big swallows. She turned her back to the counter and leaned against it. She felt the edge press into the soft flesh just at the top of her butt. She lifted the bottle to gaze at it, giving it her attention as if it had spoken some secret to her.

Why was she so close a friend to this brown, long-necked, inanimate object, and even more, its bitter nectar? It was true that she had only one actual friend, Julia. But having only one friend wasn't the "why" of her relationship with this long-necked buddy.

She took another draw from the bottle and walked across the room to a large, brown, dilapidated sofa. She plopped into its softness like a pig would a mud hole. She laid her legs bent beside her on the cushions, her side against the fat, raggedy, stuffed arm.

She was again alone, in the middle of the night, sitting with her other friend. She felt cozy with its presence and comfortable with its silence. But even better than that, she was satisfied with being unnecessary. *That's* why they were friends. Its way of making her comfortable with her lack of self-esteem was what made her long-necked buddy so friendly.

A few months ago, she had become aware of the important part the beer played in the routine of her life, and the realization had startled her. She immediately became alarmed, frightened of addiction. The last two bottles of a six-pack had remained in the fridge, forsaken.

Avoiding the beer had not made any difference in her life, and about a week later, she drank them both in about thirty minutes. That didn't make any difference either. They hadn't produced the usual results, and the following night, she made sure she had a full six-pack to start the night. She was relieved that she wasn't an alcoholic.

She peered at the bottom of the bottle. Two more good swallows, and it would be empty, and the bottom would be as unnecessary as she was. She tipped the bottle to its final significance, and it became litter on the bare hardwood floor beside the couch. From there, she would shamefully remove it first thing in the sober morning and bury it at the bottom of the trash can. It would be hidden along with its six-pack crew and the carton they "rode in on." She couldn't forget to do that in case Harley and Linda came over unannounced.

After a moment, she rose, went to the refrigerator, and enlisted a replacement. She popped the top and, this time, returned to the chair at the table. She scrutinized the mess of papers that were forms of an application for enrolment at the Colorado Springs Fine Arts Academy. The bottle came to her lips, and she guzzled without taking her eyes off the challenge on the table. She didn't need to fill these out right now, did she? She peered at the clock, 1:45, and she was tired. The time to rise for work would come soon.

She rose from the table and returned to the sofa. She continued to nurse the bottle of beer, and as the bottle emptied, her spirit filled. Her self-worth found its comfort mark. The beer-instilled attitude filled her with the right to be anything she chose to be. She would be a guzzler tonight if she wanted to. She would be here alone with her other friend and to hell with the girl from the hayloft. That girl insists that she right some wrong. Does she have to reconcile with God before He picks His moment to strike her dead in mid-stride? No. She was going to be just fine. She didn't need the "loving arms of God" to protect her, which she's never had anyway, just the opposite.

That was the part of Lena that remained in Leanna. Her self-imposed conviction for her part in the sin that killed her brother. It gave God a good and righteous reason to someday, any day He chose, to kill her as well. She would take her punishment as surely as eight-year-old Andrew had.

She unconsciously shook her head and took another swig of beer. *That wasn't right,* she thought. At twenty-two years old, she could honestly, and with much relief, tell herself that to hold this childish notion about God and herself was foolish. She had outgrown her ignorance.

But what about the shrapnel in her subconscious? It festered there and infected her judgment, causing her soul to perceive herself as unworthy. She consciously knew that she savored these moments of relief from her constant struggle to measure up, to be counted among the worthy. She could never quite make the grade and always fell short. But that's okay. *Have a few beers, and it won't matter.*

She took a long draw. She'd feel like standing shoulder to shoulder with the best. She would accept her position, low though it may be, and be comfortable.

Being friendly to that good-looking guy who comes into the restaurant every afternoon for a coffee break and teases her would be, at this moment, easy for her. The fact that she had yet to go out on a date with anyone didn't strike her as a handicap at all. Not like it does when she's sober and at the restaurant. It was amazing how the impossibilities that controlled her in his presence seemed to fade away with the beer.

She hardly knew his name. *Kyle? Kyle...Brunghardt.* She hardly spoke to him at the restaurant, afraid she would reveal her shortcomings and chase him away. If he were here now, she would have no problem with flirting right back.

But the problem was, he wasn't here. The power the beer gave her to ignore her low self-esteem was useless now. Then, she began to see the dilemma and the irony in her situation. The very thing that empowered her to be comfortable with people was the thing that kept her from *being* with people.

She felt a hint of panic rising in her chest, trapped like she was being held down again. The hot surge of anxiety that flushed over her body brought a terrible memory back. She felt the almost forgotten pressure of her father's rough hands on her neck.

She jumped to her feet, dropped the bottle of beer onto the cloth-covered sofa, and stood shaking, brushing her hand furiously against the back of her neck. She stood stock-still, head bent down, arms propped out away from her body.

She was frozen like that, as if anticipating some creepy insect suddenly crawling on some other part of her body. Nothing happened. The sensation on the back of her neck went away. Her eyes fell to the beer bottle spilling its foaming content on the sofa. She quickly stepped forward and grabbed the bottle.

The spilled beer had soaked quickly into the cloth of the sofa, making a large dark spot in the brown fabric. She held the bottle by its neck and stared at the ugly spot on the sofa without seeing it. She began to feel sick. She bent over and then sank to her knees. Hot tears burned her eyes, and finally, hopelessness pressed her chin to her chest. Maybe she *was* an alcoholic! The empty beer bottle was there in her hand. It was so familiar. It seemed to fit her.

She jerked it away from herself, and it clattered on the hard floor. Pitiful images of trashy alley people with bloated faces, dazed eyes, and slack mouths cluttered her mind. Grubby hands reaching out from ragged coat sleeves filled her with loathing. She began to sink sideways toward the floor.

She lay on her side in a fetal position, her tear-wet cheek against the hard, dusty floor, her spirit fallen upon and crushed. She wept loudly, out of control.

The blank, silent walls watched as the hours shuffled by like mourners at a casket viewing. She cried herself to sleep there on the hardwood floor. Her fitful sleep cast her into nightmares. She was running and hiding, struggling and falling, jerked to the edge of consciousness. Then, she was pushed back into her torment to start it all over again.

CHAPTER 27

A gigantic bass drum rolled toward her, threatening to smash her flat. Its deafening boom, boom, boom, bounced her out of her sleep. It was someone pounding on the door. Startled, she pushed herself up, rose franticly to her feet, and rushed in jerks to the door. Whoever it was, called her name from outside of the door. "Lena!" Then, "Leanna!"

It must be Harley.

As she reached for the deadbolt, the picture of the mess in her living room that she had just passed through flooded her mind and froze her for a second. She jerked around to confirm the trashy scene. The five empty beer bottles standing around on the floor caused a rush of dread in her. She scrambled to scrape away the evidence of her secret. She slid and rolled the bottles under the couch, saw the stain on the cushion, and felt a twinge of panic. She reached under the couch, pulled one bottle out, and set it on the floor. One beer wouldn't condemn her, but it would explain the stain on the couch.

She rushed to the door and turned to give the room a quick, last look. *Okay!* She twisted the deadbolt from its locked position and jerked the door open. It *was* Harley frowning at her, standing in early morning daylight.

"Are you alright? Julia called me and said you hadn't gotten to work yet. She thought you might be sick or something."

She stared at him. Her eyes went past him into the bright summer morning. She was alarmed at the disappearance of the night. She whirled around and pierced the clock above the refrigerator with sharp, anxious eyes. It was six-thirty!

She ran for the bedroom. She was thirty minutes late for work! She flew through the process of changing out of her blue jeans into her uniform. She doused cold water on her face, dried it, and ran through the apartment, grabbing a comb and her handbag as she flew. The lipstick and her hair would have to be done while she drove.

Harley had been left standing in the living room, expecting to get the chance to talk to Leanna. The beer bottle next to the couch had caught his attention. He was mildly surprised. His little sister wasn't so little anymore. He had never seen her indulge in any of the adult vices.

Having a beer probably wasn't the only thing she did that people did at the age of twenty-two. The notion that there could have been more than one empty bottle standing around never occurred to him. He had glanced around the room for any sign of cigarettes and saw none. He smoked himself and couldn't reprove anyone for the same habit or even having a beer now and then. He just couldn't see his little sister Lena with a beer bottle in her mouth. But then Leanna was not Lena. It was hard to get used to. He had moved toward the couch to pick the beer bottle up off the floor and saw the stained cushion.

Looks like she spilled a lot of it. Probably didn't drink enough to notice. Somehow, that had made him feel better.

He picked up the bottle as Leanna burst into the room, rushing for the front door.

"Hey, hey, slow down! You alright? Tell me what's going on!"

Leanna saw the bottle in his hand, and her speeding heart jumped even faster.

She didn't slow down going past him and didn't look him in the face. "What do you mean what's going on?" She reached for the door and turned to face him. "Nothin's going on."

"I mean, how come you overslept? Did you have any trouble? Were you sick?" Then he grinned and lifted the bottle to eye level. "Or were you up all night drinkin' and carousing?" She suddenly felt hot and shaky inside. She forced a hint of a smile.

"Not hardly," she said quietly. Then, quick to get out of answering any more questions with lies, she stepped out onto the tiny concrete porch. With the need to be polite, she turned again to say something, anything. Instead, tears lumped up in her throat and prevented her voice. She had no words anyway. She turned back to resume the dash to her old car. She missed-judged the edge of the porch, stepped off of it unprepared, and stumbled. She landed on one bare knee, scraping it against the narrow, concrete sidewalk. Her cry of pain barely escaped her lips.

From inside, through the open door, Harley saw her fall. He moved quickly to help her but got out only onto the porch before she got to her feet and limped to her car. Bewildered, he watched her drive away. The muffler on the old green Plymouth was rattling against the frame. The automatic transmission slipped as it changed gears. He turned back to the apartment door, closed it, and left. He worried that he, too, might be late for work.

Leanna's day at work was a disaster that had found a lot of places to happen... repeatedly. She couldn't keep her orders straight. She dropped things, like whole plates of food. Counting change back was a first-grader's trial and error process. Consequently, the till came up short at the end of the shift, the shortage of which, in all fairness, came out of Leanna's pocket.

At 4:30, she sat in the restroom, crying softly. Her sniffling echoed in the cold, hard porcelain canyon as she mourned the tragic day.

She had gotten to work almost an hour late and was immediately chewed out by her boss, Leon Reeves. The café was swamped with customers, and poor Julia ran her tail off trying to keep up. When the flow of business finally tapered off to a trickle, Leanna apologized to Julia. Julia had understood oversleeping; that was no big deal. The shame she felt consumed her mind the entire day, not to mention the devastating fear that she really was an alcoholic. What would she do? She couldn't be!

That's all there is to it! She rose from the commode. *I'm not a drunk. I can do without it.* She left the restroom and walked quickly to the kitchen.

Julia was there, out of her apron, waiting by the back door. She saw Leanna's puffy red eyes and knew she had been crying. "Are you going straight home?" she asked.

Leanna looked down. She nodded. "Yeah, I guess."

Julia pulled the door open and started out. "I'm comin' over," she said in a no-nonsense tone. Leanna felt a twinge of panic, but without any more words, they each got into their car and left, Julia following Leanna.

At Leanna's apartment, Julia got an ashtray that she kept for herself in a drawer in the kitchen cabinet. While Leanna changed into blue jeans, Julia dug out an open pack of New Ports from her small leather purse. She struck her lighter to it and sat on the couch, avoiding the nasty stain.

She had never seen any hint of a mess, dirt, or filth of any kind in Leanna's apartment, so the stain was out of place. She could smell the beer. She had seen more than a few beer stains in her twenty-six years. She had also seen Leanna drink a lot of beer. She could put it away pretty well. She could imagine how the stain got there, but she was at a loss as to why it hadn't been cleaned up. She surmised that the reason for that was the same reason that Leanna had been late for work. She had gotten drunk.

Leanna entered the room and sat in the large stuffed chair in front of a curtained window on the wall left of the couch. The room was small, and its only other furniture was a portable TV.

Looking at Leanna, Julia took a deep draw from her cigarette, lifted her face and blew the smoke toward the ceiling.

"So, what happened last night?" she asked.

Leanna shrugged. "Nothing," she said. "I overslept." Her eyes glanced at the dark space on the floor beneath the couch. The beer bottles were not visible. She wondered what Harley had done with the one he had teased her with that morning.

"I've never known you to oversleep. Were you up late?" Leanna leaned back in the easy chair and pulled her feet up under her on the cushion.

She pointed her chin toward the table in the kitchen. "I was working on those forms for the art school, and it got pretty late." Julia gazed at the mess of papers on the kitchen table. The state of their order was no different than it had been last Sunday when she saw it.

"Are you still working on those? They're not that hard to fill out, are they?"

"Not really. It just takes a lot of time, and sometimes I get side-tracked." Julia was silent, smoking her cigarette. She waited impatiently for the opportunity to confront Leanna about her beer drinking. It was a touchy subject that, in her opinion, had needed to be discussed for a long time. Crushing her cigarette into the ashtray, she cautiously eased into the moment of opportunity. She motioned toward the beer stain beside her.

"If you leave that too long, it will be hard to get out." Then, looking at Leanna, she added, "How did that happen? Did you fall asleep?"

Leanna felt a quiver of apprehension in her stomach. Julia was asking some dumb questions. *Probing,* she thought. *She is leading up to what she really wants to talk about.* She hated getting into a position that required her to lie, especially to Julia. That kind of situation had happened, but rarely. She could see a rare lie coming. She would have to lie to hide her secret about how much beer she drank last night. It wasn't really enough to cause a problem, but that was something only she would know. Julia would say it's too much and jump all over her, making it an issue.

Her tone had an edge, a little intentional sarcasm when she answered. "Yeah, I was sitting there drinking a beer and fell asleep."

Julia pushed a little but spoke pleasantly, she thought. "And you just left it there? I'm surprised you didn't clean it up right away before you went to bed."

Well, I'll be! She's gonna keep it up till it pisses me off. "Now, why is a little beer stain so terrible all of a sudden? I'll clean it up sooner or later!"

Julia suddenly realized that she had been too persistent and had made Leanna defensive. "I'm Sorry. I didn't mean anything by it. I'm just surprised because you always keep everything neat and clean."

The innocent statement fell on Leanna like a tree. The insinuation that Julia saw her at that moment as less than Julia expected crushed her. She moaned inside. The loathing of herself that she began to feel suddenly turned to anger, close to rage. She could never keep up. She tried and tried but always came up short of what they wanted of her. Everyone else could do it. Why couldn't she? They know she's not as good as she should be, so why do they expect so much from her? The fire smoldering inside her flashed and burst into flame.

She suddenly erupted from the chair and, in silence, flung herself down on her knees in front of the couch. In a flurry of motion, she bent down and, with her face close to the dark space at the bottom of the couch, jammed her arm under the couch as far as she could. With an animal growl, she swept the four hidden empty beer bottles out onto the floor in front of the couch. The glass bottles clanked and clinked as they bounced against each other on the hardwood floor. Then, each taking a different path, rolled this way and that.

Without any hesitation, she jumped to her feet. Grabbing the bottles, she filled one armpit and both hands, stomped to the trash can in the kitchen, and flung them into it one by one, shattering most of them. She then rushed to the kitchen sink.

Julia sat frozen by sheer astonishment. She had never seen her fly off the handle in the seven years she had known Leanna. She wanted to grab her and hold her cherished friend. But getting near Leanna, flying around like a crazy person, wasn't safe.

She watched in amazement as Leanna dug a pan out from under the sink. She jerked out a box of dishwashing soap and a stiff brush. She slammed the pan into the sink, turning the hot water on full force. The water struck the flat bottom of the pan, splattering everywhere. She shook Tide into the splashing water and filled the pan to half full.

She came toward Julia, who was sitting on the couch, stunned. She set the pan of soapy water on the floor and, using the brush, began to furiously scrub the beer stain on the cushion beside Julia. The soapy water flew.

In fear for her safety, Julia pushed herself from the couch. Struck with disdain, she stood a few feet behind Leanna and watched, "Leanna! You're acting like a mad woman. Good crap! I'm sorry! I didn't mean to make you go crazy!"

Leanna kept right on scrubbing. "Maybe I am crazy, but heaven forbid I have a dirty spot in my house." She bent herself down farther into her work. The sarcasm in her voice got louder and louder.

"Can't have anything like this gigantic beer stain that will surely destroy the world! It may be too late already. It's been here all night and all day, growing bigger and bigger. It has damned near swallowed the whole apartment, and the city is next. Tell the people to run. Leanna Danziger has neglected her housework."

"Housework!" Julia was angry, and her words were loud. "I don't give a tinkers' damn about your housework. I'm worried about your drinking problem! I care about you spending a night by yourself getting drunk!" Leanna twisted around on her knees to face Julia, fire in her eyes.

"Drunk? Now, who's crazy?" They stared at each other, Julia expecting a denial, and Leanna, unable to come up with anything truthful to say, turned back to the stain.

"Are you gonna tell me that you emptied all those bottles, a whole six-pack, and you didn't get drunk?"

Drunk? Yes, I got drunk! That's why she hadn't thought to clean up the spilled beer; it hadn't been important. She threw the brush at the couch. It bounced back, almost hitting her in the face. She screamed at Julia!

"I did not get drunk! But if I did, it would be none of your business! None of your damned business! Now leave me alone!" Julia stood still for a moment, then softly said, "Forget you," and walked out the door. Leanna flung herself into the easy chair and began to cry.

She was still there crying sporadically when evening shadows slipped in and watched the scene with sadness.

CHAPTER 28

The following day was empty of the usual lighthearted teasing and amusing remarks. Leanna and Julia spoke to each other only when necessary. Their eight-year relationship as close friends had taken a devastating hit, and restoration was stubbornly slow to develop.

Upon leaving Leanna's apartment that day, Julia's first impulse had been to seek out Harley. "She's started drinking alone now, Harley," she had told him. "And you know that's a bad sign." Harley had added to their conversation the observations he had made that had gotten him wondering about Leanna. He had promised Julia that he would talk to Leanna as soon as he got the chance. That evening, after work, he had made it a priority and invented a chance.

He pulled in beside her car as she struggled to wrestle two sacks of groceries from the back seat. He parked, exited his new 1964 maroon Chevy, and hollered at her. "Hey! Let me help!" She was head and shoulders into the back seat. She came out and stood up straight, leaving the groceries on the seat. She looked at Harley over the top of her car without expression. Then she bent down, pulled one of the full sacks off the seat, and, without a word, started toward her front door.

Harley became aware of her sad demeanor immediately. Her eyes were red and puffy, and he knew she had been crying. He wondered what he was going to say to her that would ease the emotional pain that she must be feeling from the falling out that she had had with Julia. He had no idea. He was not good with other people's emotions. He thought maybe he should have waited a day or two. Being critical of her, at that point, may do more harm than good. Carrying the other sack of groceries, he followed her into the apartment.

In the kitchen, Leanna was putting away the groceries she had carried in. As Harley approached her, she was at the open refrigerator, making a place to set a six-pack of long-neck Coors beer. He set the sack of groceries on the counter and watched her put the beer away. She closed the refrigerator. She was aware of him but paid no attention to him. He stepped back away from the counter as she began putting away the items from the sack he had just set on the counter. She was silent. He chose to respect her mood even though the sight of the beer had urged him to talk to her. He would wait a moment and then say whatever came out of his concern for her. She emptied the sack, folded it and the other one, and shoved them behind a row of canisters on the counter against the wall. She turned to him and looked him in the face as if to say okay, let's hear what you have to say. He obliged.

"Julia tells me you two had a falling out, and I see you've been crying." His manner was kind. "You wanna talk about it?"

Leanna's expression was blank. "Talk about what? What did the big mouth tell you?"

Harley was surprised at her attitude toward her best friend. "Why would you call her a big mouth? She didn't tell me a big secret, did she?"

Leanna sounded hateful. "She told you I got drunk last night, didn't she?"

Harley nodded. "Yeah, she did! Did you?"

She ducked his question. "Now, how in the world could she know *that*? She wasn't there." Leanna hesitated, wanting desperately to hang onto her secrets, so she chose to lie and spoke in a matter-of-fact manner as if she were insulted.

"No, I didn't get drunk! I was by myself! I had no one to get drunk with!"

Harley persisted. "Julia said there were five empty beer bottles hidden under the couch. If you were alone, you must have drunk all of them. And what about the stain on the couch that I saw this morning? She said it was still there this afternoon when she was here?"

"Well, lordy, lordy, haven't you heard of an accident? Sober people have accidents, too!"

"Yes, but if they're the kind of housekeeper you are, they don't just leave it."

"In the first place, it wasn't a six-pack, and in the second place (she gestured toward the couch), it's all cleaned up! It's not dry yet, but I cleaned it!"

The fact that the spot was not dry told Harley that she had cleaned it recently. Was it just before she went to the grocery store?

He also realized that Leanna was in a defensive posture. Was she hiding something she thought she shouldn't have done, something she was ashamed of? That would probably explain the five empty beer bottles under the couch. He decided not to press her any further on that for now. He wanted her to quit defending herself and hear his concern for her.

"Look, Leanna, I didn't come here to accuse you. I only want to find out if my little sister is okay. And if you're not, I want to know what is wrong. I want to know if I can help you. Now, believe it or not, your friend is very worried about you. She thinks when a person who drinks socially starts getting drunk alone, they're starting down a very dangerous road. That's what alcoholics do. She loves you dearly, I do too, and we don't want you to go off the deep end."

"Alcoholic? I am not a drunk! I drink a beer now and then, for cryin' out loud!" She had become exasperated, leaning her body toward him in her attempt to convince him.

"Harley! Do I look like an alcoholic? Do you know what an alcoholic looks like? They look like death on a stick. They're thin and pale with a rosy nose and bloodshot eyes an, an, an..." She tried exaggeration. "Bleeding sores all over their body. They cough around and pass out in their puke!" She let that soak in. "They don't hold down a job! I go to work every day, and I'm there all day. Do you think old man Reeves would let me in his café, let alone work there if I were an alcoholic?" She felt a strange relief in her own words. Maybe they wouldn't work on Harley, but they sounded good to her.

Harley didn't know what to say. She brought up a good point. Someone on the booze could usually be spotted a block away. Leanna didn't look anywhere near like someone who always got drunk. As a matter of fact, he had never seen her drunk. But he was sure Julia had, and she said Leanna was drinking too much. He was just taking her word for it. Maybe Julia was imagining things. He should avoid drawing conclusions on the strength of someone else's judgment. He shouldn't consider only Julia's words. On the other hand, she was far more familiar with drinkers and booze than he was. He needed first-hand information. He needed the truth from Leanna.

"Okay, I can see you don't look or act like an alcoholic. I'm sure you're not, and I'm not accusing you, but I've noticed some changes in you in the last few months. Just tell me what's going on. You need to tell me about things that might be causing you trouble. I'm the only one you have that you can go to. I am responsible for you. Besides, I promised Mom."

Leanna stood motionless, staring at her brother. His words deeply moved her, bringing a lump to her throat. She swallowed hard and turned her head in case the rising tears slipped out of her control. She wanted to say something. What? She regained her composure and turned her face back to Harley.

" Well, I..." she said in a reassuring, matter-of-fact tone. I'm okay. It took a week for those five bottles to accumulate under the couch," she lied. They stood silent for a while, absorbing the relief of a satisfying conclusion. Then Leanna shifted position and disturbed the comfort.

She changed the subject. "I just miss Mom a lot."

Harley was neither surprised nor moved in any way; he nodded.

"Well, anyone would. You haven't seen her for, what, seven years?"

Lordy, lordy, has it been that long?

She wondered how those seven years had changed her mother. Did she still have those beautiful eyes? Probably not if she is still letting Sam, the man, talk her out of being herself. She imagined herself as the grown-up daughter going home to help her poor, browbeaten mother from the overbearing, wicked father. Harley suddenly broke into her wishful musing.

"I guess I'd better be getting home. I told Linda I wouldn't be long." Arms folded across his chest, his butt against the edge of the counter; he pushed himself away and started for the front door. Halfway there, he turned to Leanna, who was following him.

"Are you gonna patch things up with your best friend, "big mouth?" He grinned.

Leanna gritted her teeth in a grimace. "C'mon Harley, you know I didn't mean that seriously. But I do wish I wouldna said it. It wasn't very nice." Then, finding an excuse, she added, "I was defending myself, and it just came out."

"And another thing," he said, indicating the refrigerator with a jerk of his head. "Am I going to see some of that six-pack in the fridge still there this weekend?"

Leanna felt a small surge of defense in her spirit. "Hey, don't worry about it," she said, wanting to ease his mind with an explanation but holding herself back. If she told him the real reason the beer was there, it would be admitting what she feared about herself and would get him started all over again. He turned toward the door and, walking out, said, "See yuh later."

The door closed, and she was by herself again. She stood still in the middle of the living room, attentive to the sounds outside those four walls. She heard the muffled slam of Harley's car door.

The children who lived three doors down were apparently in the grassy area across the parking lot and sounded excited, calling their dog. Harley's car started and drove away, the sound of its pipes falling away into the distance. Leanna felt terrible, on the edge of the world: so close and yet so far away.

The noisy hum of the old refrigerator starting up suddenly reminded her of the reason she felt so bad. She turned and stared at the fat, bulky box of a machine. Its white enamel was chipped and scared, and the handle, once bright silver chrome, now showed only a hint of its waning splendor. Leaning slightly from its anchor, it barely managed its job. The beer was *in there*.

She felt a dread of its presence. She wondered about her strength. Could she do it? Then, did she have to do it? Was there a cause for her fear? Was she putting herself through this unnecessarily? Did she have to find out if she could leave the beer alone? That's why she had bought the beer.

She felt no desire to walk over there and get one, but this was encouraging, almost soothing. A small sigh escaped her, and she felt some relief, but it was not enough to walk to the refrigerator and dare to open it.

Instead, she went to the table and stared at the scramble of papers awaiting her attention. She sat down at the table and lifted one of the sheets of paper. It was the half-filled-out questionnaire she had been working on the night Julia had accused her of getting drunk.

Good call, Julia, but you'll never know for sure. No one will cuz it will never happen again. She felt good about her conviction. She picked up a pencil and began working on the questionnaire.

That was last week. This week, she and Julia were at least exchanging looks that weren't as deadly as the week before. At the moment, Leanna was just about to get up enough courage to tell Julia she was sorry. It had always been very easy for Leanna to apologize in her mind to just about anyone, for just about anything. But standing before someone and intentionally making the words come out of her mouth was something else. It was sticking herself out as a sacrifice to unforgiving faces with mouths filled with abuse. What if one of those said that what she said was unforgivable, and they didn't care that she was sorry? It was hard for her to take the chance, especially with Julia. Can you imagine the blow? She sat down in the back booth where Julia was having a cup of coffee during a lull in business.

"Hey," she said and then scrambled her mind in search of her next sentence. The five-second silence with Julia looking at her over the coffee cup seemed an eternity. "Can we... talk a minute?" Julia did not answer but began to blow on her hot coffee as if Leanna hadn't said anything. Leanna was startled. Was her worst fear going to really happen? Was her best friend going to swat her down like a pesky fly? She felt the red heat begin to flush her face. Every fiber of her being screamed at her to run before her fear came true.

Julia was not surprised by Leanna's approach. She felt a big sigh of relief but suppressed it. She had been hurt deeply by the girl she considered her sister and had brooded for days. Then she became angry as she concluded that she hadn't done anything wrong. Leanna treated her like a nosey neighbor for being concerned for her welfare. Though she had finally settled into waiting for Leanna to come to her senses and talk to her, she was not over her anger enough to welcome her back with open arms at the first sign of reconciliation. She wanted some compensation. She would make her squirm a little. Then she saw Leanna tense up and knew she was about to bolt.

Julia set her coffee down. "I was wondering when you would talk to me again."

Leanna sighed with relief and relaxed her anxiety. Her expression was honest regret. "I'm sorry I bit your head off. I didn't want you to actually walk off and leave me alone."

Julia nodded and said, "I've never heard you talk to me like that before. I'm sorry, but I was shocked. I guess I overreacted." They were silent for a moment, each basking in the glow of the finally arrived reconciliation.

"Anyway," Leanna said, "I am sorry and appreciate your concern. I don't know how to explain to you well enough to make you believe me about all the beer bottles, but I hope you will believe me when I say I did not get drunk." *Liar, liar,* she thought, feeling awful.

"Okay, but you'll have to admit it seemed a little strange, considering how fussy you are about your housekeeping. I figured you had passed out, which was why you hadn't cleaned up the mess."

Leanna felt guilty, wishing Julia hadn't fallen for the lie. If Julia did not believe her, there was a chance for her to be reprieved. Now, the label was on the jam, and she could not be called a trustworthy friend. It made her sick at heart that she now had become some kind of low-life schemer who took advantage of her best friend's trust. She wanted to run and hide. She glanced around for something to do somewhere else. At that moment, just when she needed it the most, a man came in and headed for a table. She jumped up to wait on him. "There's a customer. Talk to yuh later," she murmured and hurried away.

Julia was pretty sure that she had just been lied to. It wasn't like Leanna. She must have a reason, and Julia was sure she knew what it was. She had lived all of her childhood around an alcoholic, and she knew all the characteristics. But for now, she would give Leanna the benefit of the doubt. She wasn't saying that Leanna was a full-fledged alcoholic, but there were hints of things that were very familiar. She would just watch and be there when.

That evening, Leanna was alone in her apartment, sitting at the table with one leg tucked under her. She felt guilty and useless. After gathering all the application forms that had lain scattered over the table for three weeks, her disappointment crushed her. They now lay in a neat stack in the center of the table. It looked like closure to her. She guessed maybe half of them were filled out.

She had wanted to enroll in the school for weeks. One day, after mentioning it again for about the hundredth time, Julia had taken her by the arm, loaded her into her car, and drove her to the college to get the application. It had been easy to do. She didn't know why she had kept putting it off. The first step to accomplishing her desire had been taken. Now, here was the result of the effort. It just lay there on her kitchen table, disregarded by her as her whole life. There was no reason not to finish it. So why didn't she? Instead, she had just stacked it up out of the way. It was still easy to get to if she took a notion to work on it. And she probably would later.

She rose and went to the refrigerator. What was she worried about? There was no big hurry. Her life didn't depend on it. She yanked the refrigerator door open.

The sight of the six-pack of beer was like a slap in the face. She stared at it, horrified. She realized what she had unconsciously come to the refrigerator to do. She slammed the door shut. It popped back open, and she closed it more carefully this time. She hurried back to the table and sat down, trembling inside. How could that have happened? It's been a whole week! She had been tempted more than once and had stood against it. She had resisted with strength beyond her expectations. She had been proud of herself! Only last night, she had had a talk with herself about the benefits of sobriety outweighing the pleasures of her whims. She had jumped up and stood on the couch. And giving the devil the finger, she shouted, "I am not a drunk! I- do- not- need- it!"

She rose suddenly from the table and shouted, "And I never will!" She stomped to the refrigerator, jerked it open, and, without the slightest hesitation, pulled a bottle from its carton. Determined to prove the strength of her will, she got an opener and popped the lid off the bottle. She set the beer on the counter and stared at it, daring it to entice her. After fifteen or twenty seconds, she stuck out her face at the beer, and like a taunting child, she shouted, "Told ya so! Ha!" She closed the refrigerator, returned to the table, and sat down.

She was excited. She glanced back at the beer bottle and tossed it the finger, triumph lighting up her face. She *knew* she could do it. It felt good to be free of the worry that she could be an alcoholic. She poured the beer down the drain in the sink.

CHAPTER 29

Sunday morning at Harley's house had never been a day of so much exciting anticipation. A special day was in the making. Harley had received word Saturday that his mother, Katy, and her family would be at his house the following Sunday morning. Harley, his wife Linda, and the two kids, Charles, seven, and three-year-old Joanna, had gotten up an hour earlier than usual. After breakfast, Charles watched anxiously through the window above the couch for "Ganma Danzjnger's" arrival.

Leanna had driven up into their driveway about thirty minutes before they had gotten out of bed. She had remained in her car, keeping an eye on the direction from which her mother would be arriving.

She exited the car and, slamming the door behind her, looked up the street; nobody was coming. She walked to the narrow concrete porch and took the two steps onto it as she looked hopefully up the street again. She had thought they would be here by now. She looked at her wristwatch. Almost ten-thirty. Katy had said on the phone that they would leave by five o'clock. She stood on the porch momentarily, watching the spot at the end of the street. She had intended to go into the house but stepped down from the porch to back-track to the curb and again stood watching up the street. *What's keeping them so long?*

She felt the trembling inside and wondered what was causing it this time. Was it her anxious waiting to see her mother, not having eaten breakfast, or... *No! It's not because I haven't had a drink yet! That's ridiculous!* Her last drink was Friday night, and it hadn't bothered her all day Saturday. She'd barely thought of it last night. A glass of wine was the last thing on her mind. *Then why am I worried about it? Okay, I am worried that it might be what is giving me the trembles. But why now? It's been two days. If I was gonna get the shakes, it seems like it wouldn't take two days to happen. Can't be the reason, but what if it is? What if I fall apart when I see her and don't make sense when I say my first words to her? What if I shake so badly, she won't want to hug me? What will I say when she asks me what's wrong?*

She wanted to duck and run. The inclination pulled on her body, and the trembling became uncontrollable. The dread that had caused her, as a child, to hide in strange, unlikely sanctuaries had her suddenly standing by her car without a clue as to how or when she had gotten there.

Her shaking arms made a nonproductive effort to pull open the car door. She pulled again, harder. It flew open, and she threw herself into the seat. She bumped her head hard against the frame of the door opening. It was the assault to the head that brought her back to her senses. She realized she was at the wheel of her car,

She wasted only a moment on the surprise and then started the car. Without closing the door, she backed out of the driveway into the vacant street. When the car leaped forward, the door slammed shut. Leanna shot her car down the street in the opposite direction of the way they would arrive. She cussed herself out.

They arrived at Harley's house ten minutes after Leanna had turned the corner at the opposite end of the block. The kids who had been watching through the living room window saw the dark blue car turn off the street into their driveway and announced it the way excited children announce any highly anticipated happening: Loudly! "They're here, they're here," was the cry as they scrambled from the couch and ran to their parents. Harley rose from the sofa chair and moved quickly to the door. Linda came from the kitchen, and the kids fell in close behind.

Lewis and Katy were out of the car when Harley and his family burst onto the porch. Harley was animated, grinning and waving his arm.

"Hey, look who's here!" he yelled to his long-unseen family, getting out of the car.

Katy's pleasure was plain to see in her broad smile. They started toward each other while Sarah and the kids climbed out of the back seat. Sarah beamed with pleasure, smiling childishly. They all came together on the lawn, shaking hands and slapping backs as comfortably as the strictly taught tradition of physical contact in a Mennonite family allowed.

Linda stood watching her husband's family performing the reunion ritual in their way. It seemed a bit stiff and lukewarm to her. She was accustomed to her family's breath-capturing hugs, smacking cheek-kissing, hand-squeezing, and moist eyes.

She recalled Harley telling her about the Mennonite's practice of a traditional behavior called the "holy kiss." It involved men greeting each other by actually kissing on the lips. It had shocked her and made her skin crawl. Watching the constrained greetings of a family after a long-awaited reunion made her wonder where the logic was of Mennonite men greeting each other with a "holy kiss." Why the kissing of men and not the hugging of family?

A *holy* kiss? Not likely. She wondered where in the bible the Mennonite church found the scripture supporting the practice of that activity. The sight of Sarah turning her eyes to her and walking toward her brought her back to the moment.

She had met Sarah on their visit to Kansas with the new baby. That had been seven years ago. She'd had no contact with her since. She watched her approach and was struck with mild curiosity as to why they had remained complete strangers. She remembered being impressed with Sarah's beauty at their first and only meeting. Even now, despite middle age, black head cover, and the long dark blue homemade dress covering any hint of a human body, her presence spoke of elegant beauty and confident stature. Linda was impressed.

Sarah smiled and held out her slim hand. "Hello Linda, it's good to see you again. It's been a while."

"I know. A long time!"

"Too long."

Sarah's attention fell on Charles and Joanna, who stood beside their mother. They were focused intently on this stranger, their grandmother. The little one clutched her mother's skirt.

"Oh, my goodness, Charles, what a big boy you have grown into." She bent down closer to him and touched his cheek with the palm of her hand. "The last time I saw you, you were a tiny baby." She straightened up and, smiling broadly, said, "From a beautiful baby to a very handsome boy. I can tell who your mother is." Then she squatted down to two-year-old Joanna and spoke softly. "My, my, aren't you a pretty one." She held out her hands. "Will you let me hold you?"

Little Joanna held up her arms to her grandma and nodded shyly. Sarah picked her up carefully and stood up, holding her in the crook of her arm. She gazed at her granddaughter for the first time, letting the tears of joy well up in her admiring eyes. There were no words in her mind to describe her feelings, but her heart was bursting with them.

Linda, watching, imagined that she would like her mother-in-law very much.

Harley started for the house. "Well, c'mon in everyone. Have you guys had breakfast?"

Katy spoke up. "Oh yes, we ate breakfast before we left. And we had coffee and doughnuts on the way."

"Okay! Then we have more time to catch up on what's been happening for the last seven years."

Katy voiced her amazement. "My goodness, has it really been that long?"

Sarah grumbled. "Seems more like seventy. I don't know why you kids stayed away so long." No one had an answer. They went into the house in awkward silence, Sarah taking Joanna with her. The other three children stayed out on the lawn, getting acquainted.

Sarah kissed Joanna on the cheek, stood her on the floor, and then took a seat on the sofa. The others each found a place to sit, and everyone settled in to visit.

Looking at Harley with eyes filled with expectation, Sarah asked the question that had been pestering her since she had climbed out of the car. "Where's Lena and Daniel?"

Harley stared at his mother, puzzled. He surely had misunderstood her. He turned an ear slightly toward her.

"Did you say, Daniel?"

It was Sarah's turn to wonder. Her forehead furrowed deeply, accenting an expression of silent questions. Harley glanced at Katy, whose return look also questioned him. He shook his head. His tone was matter-of-fact.

"Daniel isn't here."

Everyone looked at each other as if they were talking through a wall, and no one could hear the other.

Katy came out of the confusion. "Harley, it's plain he's not here. Is he gonna be here?"

"Is he supposed to be here? Did he come too, ahead of you?"

Sarah had been mute and dumbfounded since Harley's first question. Katy went and sat stiffly on the edge of the couch.

"Yeah, three months ago," she said.

"What? Three months ago?" Harley glanced at Linda and then stared at his mother. He said, "We haven't seen Daniel since we were in Kansas."

Sarah moved toward the couch. Her voice was weak and trembled with emotion.

"He told Katy he was coming here. That was in July."

Her manner was apprehensive, and Harley saw the worry in her soft brown eyes. His imagination slipped grave images of an accident scene into his mind: Daniel's dark Ford wadded up in a weedy ditch. He became alarmed but hid it from his mother. He went to Katy and stood in front of her. "No one's heard from him for three months?" he asked.

No one said anything, which meant the answer to his question was yes.

He thought of Leanna, and a fleeting moment of feeling like a traitor went through him. That name Leanna, in his mind, while in his mother's presence, didn't seem right. Where was she? Did she know Daniel had been here all this time? Why would it be a secret? He turned to Linda.

Didn't Charles say, uh, ... Lena... was parked in the driveway a while ago?"

"Yes, he did."

"So, where'd she go?"

"She probably forgot something and went back to her apartment. She'll be back. Why are you so upset?"

"I can't believe Daniel would come to Colorado and not let any of us know he was here."

Sarah voiced her concern as well. "I think the same thing, and I'm worried."

Suddenly, Harley had a question that had not occurred to him. The answer might shed some light on the mystery, so he spoke directly to his mother.

"Why did Daniel leave Garland in the first place? Did he come here to Colorado Springs to stay?"

"Yes, come to find out, but he told Katy he was coming to see Lena. The next day, Lidia Robins came to the house to tell me he had asked her to tell me his goodbye. He packed all his belongings in a U-Haul trailer and left."

He turned to Katy. "Did he tell anyone why he was leaving?"

"He and Dad had a falling out, and he wanted to save Dad from having to kick him out of church."

"Now that's unbelievable!" His tone had raised a step or two. "Daniel was kicked out of the church. What for?"

Katy was sarcastic. "Dad caught him 'dancing with the devil' to country music on his radio."

Harley stared at Katy in disbelief. Sarah, however, was not silent. Katy's tone angered her.

"Katy! Show some respect for your father! He was hurt terribly by what happened between him and Daniel."

"Sorry, Mom, but a radio is a stupid thing to have your whole life changed over. And I think you think so, too."

"But that's no reason to speak of your father as if he were some kinda monster! He's your father, and he was the one who made sure you kids had food on the table, clothes to wear, and a roof over your heads. He loves you all very much, so much that he wants you to have the benefit of God's love, too. And he does what he thinks is right, always!"

Katy felt smacked down. And she knew she had it coming. "I'm sorry, Mom. I don't think of Dad as a monster; now, as an adult, I know he's always meant well. It's just that it was hard to be what you are when Dad was trying to shape you into what *he* wanted you to be. When I was little, I didn't like what I was because my daddy didn't like me. Then, a little further down the road, I knew my daddy did like me but would like me better if I was a perfect Christian. It took years to realize that he expected the impossible."

Harley listened to Katy's words and felt a bond to her he had never felt before. He hadn't known that he wasn't the only one. "You too? Well, I'll be! It used to be that the only way I could get approval from Dad was to exaggerate and lie. And I always thought I needed to be like Daniel."

Now, it seems Daniel turned out to be just like everyone else. Always has been. His father just now found out. He didn't know whether to feel sorry for Daniel or their father. *No, not Daniel. He's always known who he is. A radio! Whoda thought?* He could see how Daniel might be hiding from them.

He went to the telephone. "I'll call Leanna and ask some questions. I'm not waiting till she gets back." He picked up the phone and dialed.

It sounded strange to Sarah to hear Harley call his sister Leanna. It was like he was talking about someone she'd never met, a friend with no face. She felt like lying down and crying. First, Lena ran away and didn't even want to be Lena, then Harley, and now Daniel, not only gone but hiding. At least she hoped that's why he wasn't there. She watched Harley holding the phone, waiting for Lena to answer. After a few more seconds, he replaced the phone to its cradle.

"She may not have gotten home yet. It's a couple of miles from here. I'll try again in a little bit."

"Do you think she might know where Daniel is?" Sarah asked, voicing her worry.

Well," Harley answered, "if he's in contact with anyone, it would be with Leanna."

Sarah gazed with sad eyes at Harley. "Why is she Leanna now? Does she hate us so much that she couldn't keep the name we gave her?"

After she had been told that Lena had changed her name, she had not mentioned it for several weeks. And when she did, it was to Katy one day when they were alone. Katy had no answer then, and there hadn't been further discussion. Now, the response to her question was the same. Everyone was silent. Harley finally broke the silence.

"She doesn't hate you, Mom. She's told me more than once how much she misses you. I think she's trying to stay away from Dad. I don't know why, but something happened to her in the hayloft that day or night. Remember, she did spend the night by herself up there. When we finally got her out of the barn, and Katy was carrying her to the house, she kicked and screamed bloody murder. She was scared to death."

Sarah was perplexed. "So, if she misses me so much, why isn't she here? She knows her father isn't with us, doesn't she?"

"Yes, she knows, and she was here way early waiting for you. I'm sure she'll be back after a while."

Katy spoke up. "Why don't you give her another call, Harley?"

Harley had not left his place beside the phone. He reached down, picked up the receiver, and dialed Leanna's number again. Everyone watched and waited with high hopes.

The silence in the room seemed at odds with the cheerful sunshine streaming in through the light tan sheers on the windows. You could tell by the muffled sound of the children in the front yard that all was well out there.

Its contrast with the room in which she awaited news of her eldest child's safety gave Sarah a deep sense of regret. Though the room sparkled with sunshine, a gloom hung over her, pressing her spirit.

Harley hung up the phone without a word. Katy was anxious. "No answer? Should she be home by now?"

Harley started for the front door. "Yeah, unless something happened on the way. I'm gonna drive over there and see what's keeping her." He opened the door and realized that Lewis and Katy's car was blocking his car in the driveway. That had also occurred to Lewis, who was coming up behind Harley. "I've gotta move my car out of the way, Harley."

They stepped out onto the porch, and each went to his car. Lewis called to the kids. "Okay, everybody up on the porch out of the way." When he saw all the kids on the porch, he started his car and backed out of the driveway onto the street. He parked against the curb. At this point, Sarah, who had decided at the last moment to go with Harley, burst from the house, calling and waving at him. He had already gotten into his car, and when he saw her hurrying down the porch steps, he rolled down his window to hear what she was saying.

"I'm going with you," she yelled. She went around to the passenger's side and got in.

Harley didn't think it was a good idea but kept it to himself. Leanna would not have left his house before their mother had arrived for no simple reason. He thought it might be because she didn't feel ready to face her mother. Maybe it would be wise to let her have a little more time. He had intended to go to her and talk to her. He could help her become more comfortable meeting her mother face to face. Now, he didn't know what to expect. Leanna had run for who-knows-what-reason. Harley backed out into the street and drove off toward Leanna's apartment.

CHAPTER 30

The phone had finally quit ringing. Leanna sat at her kitchen table, clutching a half-filled glass of red wine. She hung her head and was crying quietly. She knew who was trying to call her: probably Harley.

She had wanted to see her mother for *so long!* And yet here she sat, hiding with her glass of support, rendering its purpose utterly worthless. *Why am I so stupid?*

The words of her mind's accusing voice revved up her anger and gave life to her self-loathing.

Suddenly, in a fury, she slung the glass of wine across the room. The deep red wine flew from the glass, helter-skelter on its way to the white wall. It splattered a large area. The empty glass reached the wall last and shattered into a zillion shards and splinters. She laid her forehead in the crook of her arm on the table and sobbed uncontrollably.

Minutes passed before her wails began to dwindle to humming moans. Then, finally, sniffles were all that could be heard in those sad rooms. Minutes later, her eyes closed, her face buried in her bent arm, she lay as still as a sleeping child.

After a while, she raised her head and surveyed the damage to the kitchen. Crimson splatters and thin, dripping streams of wine defaced a third of the wall. She didn't have the will to move. She stared at the wall. The blood-red splatters were like wounds inflicted by a crazed patient in a nut house who had no idea who or what to attack or even why. She guessed it wasn't the wall she had attacked but the wine. Or maybe herself.

She had switched from beer to wine only weeks before. Beer was a get-drunk drink, and wine was more of a social drink. She knew she wasn't an alcoholic, but she didn't want anyone else to think she was. Hadn't Jesus himself changed water to wine to serve His guests? Nothing wrong with drinking wine.

Unless you're hiding from facing your mother after hurting her! Unless it makes you care less about consequences. Which makes living with yourself easier

With disgust, she pushed herself away from the table. She stood facing the wall, her hands clenched into small tight fists. A strong, familiar impulse to run overwhelmed her. She remembered when she used to obey those impulses. But now, her fear was not of God or her father. She was afraid of what she might become. She could not run and hide; her fear was of the consequences! She was afraid that she was minimizing consequences. She was soaking her brain in wine so the jagged edges of sticks and stones would only wound her and not hurt. She had changed beer to wine, but the reason she was drinking at all was the same as always. That's what she needed to change: the reason. She stared at the blood-like wall, not seeing.

The knocking on the front door cracked the silence and was so loud in the silent house that she gasped and jerked. The rapid pounding of her heart was instantaneous. Her senses snapped back into the moment. The hopelessness stood fixed and grew as the telling wall came back into conscious view. The mess! There was evidence everywhere. The broken glass on the floor! Stricken with panic, she went to her knees and began to pick up the sharp pieces, cutting a finger. She stared at her blood.

This can't be happening! Who's at the door? Someone God sent for her! Right when you least expect it.

What was she doing? *It will take a while to clean this up. Just keep them out of the kitchen.*

She got up, dropping the broken glass, and it clinked and clattered back to the floor. She hurried to the sink, put the bottle on the counter, and ran cold water over the cut on her finger. The blood continued to ooze and drip. The knock on the door came again. She ran to the bathroom and tore a piece of toilet paper from its roll, pressing it to her finger. She happened to glance at the mirror over the sink and was shocked. Her eyes were puffy and red from all the crying before. *Now what!* How would she hide *that*? She dropped the bloody toilet paper. Running cold water, she tried to splash it on her face without getting blood on her. It didn't work. Frustration grabbed at her, shoving and pushing, threatening to make her cry again. She swallowed hard and fought back.

The blood was watered down enough to make it possible to wipe her face dry and clean with a hand towel. She grabbed the discarded toilet paper from the floor and, dripping blood, ran to the front door. When she reached the door, she had the paper pressed into her palm with the bleeding cut on her finger tucked tightly into it. She opened the door.

The first thing she saw was Harley, and she was not surprised. He was probably there to find out what was keeping her. But the next thing she saw was her mother's face peering at her over Harley's shoulder. Her head felt funny, and she was weak in the knees. Her dry mouth would not open. She just stared like a statue in a blizzard.

Then, her mother smiled and moved toward her with open arms.

"Lena!" she cried as those arms engulfed her with a tender force that spoke of eternal captivity. Leanna stood stiffly at first. Then, her arms slowly rose to her mother's back and rested there lightly. She closed her eyes and let the warmth of her mother flood her senses. They stood in the doorway locked together.

At last!

She hadn't known how much she missed her mother until that moment. Could you miss someone so much that seeing them again could take your breath away and bring tears to your eyes?

Yes!

Her mother released her embrace, and she felt a mother's tender kiss on her tear-stained cheek. She opened her eyes, and her mother held her by the shoulders and stood back, holding her at arm's length. Leanna also saw tears in those soft brown eyes.

"Oh, my goodness, Lena! Look at you! Just look at you!" She pulled Leanna to her again, choked back a sob, and hugged her tighter. After a moment, she released herself, took Leanna's fisted hands, and stepped back to get a better look.

"You are a beautiful young woman. I just can't..." She shook her head in awe. "You've changed so much! So grown up! It's been so long!"

Leanna was thrilled. She saw the pleasure in her mother's radiant face, and a smile began to form behind the tears. Her long-awaited meeting with her mother was much easier than she had expected. She should have stuck it out at Harley's and taken her chances.

"Hi Mama," was all her teary voice could muster. The sound of her own emotion contorted her face, and she thought she would burst out bawling, but she held it in. Sarah also could hardly keep from crying out loud.

"Music to my ears," Sarah whispered with quivering lips.

Suddenly, Leanna remembered her cut finger and the wine in the kitchen. Then she remembered the wine she had drank. Panic grabbed her breath. She began to pant, her breath coming in short bursts. She lowered her face from her mother, fearing she would smell the wine on her breath. She stepped out onto the porch, pulling her mother with her and closing the door behind her, keeping them out of the house.

"So, let's go to Harley's where we can all sit and talk," she urged. Holding her mother's hand, she pulled her down the steps toward her car.

Harley saw in Leanna's behavior her anxiety and wondered why she was in a hurry to go. He had seen the sudden change in her demeanor. She closed her front door a little too quickly, he thought. Was there something in her house to hide? Daniel maybe? It didn't seem likely that Daniel would be hiding from them. But if he's been here in the city for three months without getting in touch, that would be hiding, wouldn't it?

He was following Leanna and their mother down the steps when he turned and looked back at the door. He stopped and turned to observe the two women walking arm in arm, absorbed in each other, not paying any attention to him. He took the two steps back up onto the porch, opened the door, and entered the house. Not bothering to close the door behind him, he saw nothing different in the living room. He entered the kitchen and immediately noticed the nearly empty wine bottle on the counter. His insides lurched, and dread wrinkled his brow. Then something crunched underfoot. Looking down, he saw the broken glass and splattered wine. The pattern on the floor that the flung wine had made led his eyes to the splattered wall.

What in the world happened here? He stared at the wall. *This is what she's hiding.* There was wine splattered everywhere! She hadn't come home to take additional time to prepare herself for her mother. She came for a little more courage. *From beer to wine already,* he said to himself. *What's next?* He surveyed the damage to the kitchen. He decided from the looks of things that at least she wasn't very happy with herself. He turned and walked quickly to the open door and left the house, closing the door behind him. He was sure that Daniel wasn't there.

From the porch, he saw Leanna and their mother in Leanna's car, backing out of the parking lot. He reached his car, got in, and followed them. Though he was disturbed by what he had seen at Leanna's apartment, the concern foremost in his mind was Daniel's whereabouts. He had hoped to find him at Leanna's, but now his fear for Daniel's well-being intensified.

Leanna removed the wad of tissue from her palm in her car, exposing her cut finger.

Sarah saw the wound and asked, "What happened to your finger?"

Looking straight ahead through the windshield, she answered in a matter-of-fact tone. "I cut it on some broken glass."

Sarah gazed out through the windshield for a very silent moment before speaking again. "So, if Daniel wasn't at your apartment, where could he be?"

Leanna jerked around to face her mother, confused by her question. "Did you say *my* apartment? How could he be at my apartment if he didn't come with you?" As she returned her eyes to the traffic, she heard her mother's serious tone in a very puzzling question.

"So, you don't know where Daniel is, and he's been here for the past three months?"

Leanna's expression was blank. "Three months? How would I know where he's been for three months?"

Sarah showed her surprise. "So, you haven't seen him?"

"No!" Leanna felt the blood rush to her head, and she became sick to the stomach. The monotonous hum of the car was the only sound for several seconds.

"Not since I left home."

"Well, it looks like Daniel has been hiding from everyone. He left home without telling me or his dad, but he told Katy he was coming to see you and Harley. If you haven't heard from him, then no one has, and no one knows where he is."

Leanna was shocked. "Why would he do a thing like that? I don't mean, why did he leave home?" Sarcasm crept into her tone. "I can think of *one* good reason he left. But why is he hiding?"

Especially from me!

She felt betrayed. Then she quietly asked her mother, "What happened?"

"Katy told me that he left to save your father from having to excommunicate him from church." The inconceivable surprises just kept coming.

"What!" The expression burst from her mouth loudly. "Excommunicate? Daniel? What on earth for?"

"He had a radio in his house, and your father caught him listening to country music."

She couldn't believe her ears. "Daniel had a radio," she exclaimed. This was the surprise of all surprises. She whispered, "Unbelievable."

Wayda go, Daniel. Then, a sarcastic thought crossed her mind.

Why doesn't anyone respect God's little helper? After all he's done for us.

"So, I wonder where he is," she said.

She was sure she could find Daniel if he was here in town. Not today, of course, but sooner or later. There were ways: an ad in the newspaper, the radio. *How ironic would that be?*

But for now, she would keep her mouth shut about that. She concluded that Daniel must have a reason for wanting to be in hiding. She would respect that and not contribute to the others' search for him. She, however, needed to contact him to see if he would be happy to see *her*. She felt frantic desperation for assurance that he still approved of her. She was distraught. If only he had come to her the first day of his arrival. Now, she didn't know *where* she stood with him. He might be avoiding her for hurting their mother. She began to feel awful. She still had the aftertaste of wine in her mouth.

The car continued to hum and bump down the street toward Harley's house. The feeling in the car about Daniel's well-being remained unsettled, but words of it were not spoken. *Those* words lurked about only in their anxious minds.

Sarah sat beside Leanna, almost relaxing, knowing that her grown-up children would do what was necessary to find Daniel. She marveled at the change in them. They all looked so different from the last time she had seen them. Especially Lena. Should she call her Leanna? How could she, after twenty-two years of her being Lena? But she wasn't Lena anymore. The ugly black head cover was gone. It didn't hide her beautiful long hair anymore. However, her tight blue jeans and form-fitting sweater caused Sarah concern. She dressed like the English girls. Did she not feel exposed? No shame? Her eyes turned to Leanna's face, and she examined it with a pleased expression. No makeup. At least she didn't paint her face up like some kind of clown or something. Thank goodness for that. Even so, be it for good or bad, she would call her Leanna. The new name seemed to fit this new person. Lena seemed to be someone else she knew a long time ago. A child lost.

CHAPTER 31

Leanna pulled her car up to a spot along the curb, turned off the engine, and faced her mother.

"I'm sorry, Mom, but there's no way that we can find out today what has happened to Daniel. Harley and I can do something tomorrow; exactly what I don't know." Sarah was greatly disappointed, and her expression showed it.

"But I won't be here *tomorrow*," she said sorrowfully. Leanna didn't know what to say to smooth out her mother's sad frown.

Harley came up the street behind them and pulled into the driveway. He exited the car and waited for Leanna and his mother to do the same. His mother struggled with the depth of the seat to pull herself out of its grasp. She finally stood at the curb, red-faced, visibly irritated. Harley offered her his arm. She took it, and they walked toward the house.

No one spoke, and Leanna followed, examining her cut finger. The bloody paper was a problem. She stuffed it into her back pocket.

Katy came bouncing out of the house and down the porch steps. She moved quickly past Harley and her mother, her gleaming eyes on Leanna. Her bright smile showed her pleasure. She was excited to finally see her little sister. She stopped in front of Leanna just short of hugging.

Leanna also stopped but could not contain the longing that seven years of separation had caused her. She lunged at Katy and wrapped her in a bear hug. Having grown taller than her older sister, she lifted her off the ground. Katy's laughter turned Sarah toward them. She smiled at what she saw despite the Mennonite misbehavior.

Having followed Katy out of the house, Lewis stood on the porch and watched with pleasure. He remembered the little girl who had screamed in terror that day at the foot of his front porch. Seeing her now, grown up and quite normal, made the puzzling incident seem like a weird dream he might have had. He wondered if he would ever know what it had been all about.

Grinning at the obvious joy that his wife and her sister were feeling, he was suddenly caught by Leanna's laughing eyes. He saw her smile fall off her face as if she were suddenly dead. Her eyes left him instantly, and she moved out of Katy's hug to turn away from him. He felt her rejection as if he and she shared some distasteful history: some wrong he had done her never to be forgiven. The scene on his porch that day years ago became more vivid in his mind. What had he done to cause her to react so toward him? Nothing, he knew. But somehow, he felt responsible for her apparent discomfort toward him. As he had on his front porch that day, he quickly turned and took himself back into the house.

Leanna was almost frantic. Knowing his eyes had been on her while she had not been aware of him caused a flush of embarrassment in her to a degree she had never felt before. Even those times when the thought of that day would creep up on her and make her cringe inside were not as regretful as now.

How could she have been so stupid to think that of him? To think he was capable of such a thing was ridiculous. Her shame burned in her.

Katy put an arm around her shoulders and turned her toward the house. "C'mon, let's go in," she said. Leanna stiffened. She could not face him! But when she moved forward, she saw he was no longer on the porch. The relief made her weak. Then, everyone else, talking and laughing at once, slowly made their way into the house.

Harley felt his pleasure settle deep in his bones when Linda came out of the kitchen, absentmindedly wiping her hands on her flowered apron. Her eyes were on him, and she smiled her "look-at-you" smile. He felt her happiness for him. He had it all, and it was all right here.

Leanna sat quietly on the couch, unable to feel at ease. Her finger throbbed and threatened to bleed again, but that was not the source of her discomfort. The old feeling of being detached while in the presence of her family was pressing upon her again, as in the days before she had regained her voice. And yet she felt stuck out, exposed to subtle scrutiny.

The wine she had secretly drunk had her almost relaxed, but it had affected her appearance too, hadn't it? Could her mother see that the smile she showed her was just stuck there, like a muscle cramp? Surely, she could. She knew Harley could see the wine in her demeanor, her awful secret. She was sure he had seen the evidence of her drinking it in her kitchen.

She glanced at him, standing with arms folded across his chest. He seemed pleased, surveying his kingdom. He saw her watching him, and their eyes held each other momentarily before she looked away. She was unable to face the accusation she thought she had seen.

She watched her mother, carrying Joanna on one hip, follow Linda to the kitchen. A brief pang of jealousy toward Linda popped its head up but was quickly dunked back under the surface by guilt. She was sure now that her mother had smelled the wine on her. The way she was acting made Leanna suspect that she knew she was under the influence, and she was going to the kitchen to avoid her. She wished she could run into the kitchen, take her mother by the arm, and lead her away someplace. She wanted to beg her forgiveness, to promise atonement and make her believe it. She wanted to set her mother's mind at ease about her wayward daughter. But the wine had not worked *that* well. It would take something a lot stronger than that to prop her up against the results of telling her mother that she was a... *a... drinker? A drunk. A wino?*

She suddenly wanted to leave. She didn't deserve to be here with these people.

My family!

She felt the wetness of tears suddenly spring into her eyes. She quickly bent her head down so no one might see. When she glanced at Harley, she saw that he had become engaged in conversation with Lewis and appeared oblivious to her presence.

But he knows for sure.

She assumed he was trying to ignore the problem she presented. She wouldn't blame him if he were to tell her to "go home and sober up."

Come back when you're presentable to your family.

The threat of crying was now gone, but her eyes were still moist. She rose from the couch, head down, and made her way down the hallway to the bathroom.

Harley became aware of Leanna rising from the couch and felt some alarm that she might be making a move to leave. When he realized she was headed to the bathroom, he let his attention fall back to Lewis and their conversation. Leanna's presence lingered there in the shadows of his consciousness, waiting for her reappearance.

He had noticed her remote manner was more so than usual and guessed she was uncomfortable among them. He wondered if it was because she felt guilty about the wine he was sure she'd been drinking. Or had she? He really couldn't tell the way he had with the beer. Maybe he had jumped to conclusions. Maybe the wine-splattered kitchen was the result of her resisting temptation. He sure hoped so. It would be a shame if the wine would alter her on this special day for her and her mother. He still worried that if she had been drinking, her regret would chase her away and send her into hiding. He kept a distant attachment to the hallway while he and Lewis talked. He was ready to catch her before she snuck away and broke their mother's heart.

In the kitchen, Sarah tried to pay attention to the little girl she was holding and Linda's attempt to carry on a conversation. Her mind was on Leanna. She barely answered half-heard questions and was aware that Linda saw her preoccupation. Linda was at the sink washing several large white potatoes. She turned the water off, dried her hands on her apron, and walked to the table in the middle of the room.

"Let's sit at the table for a minute so we can talk a little more comfortably," she said. She sat, and Sarah followed. Once seated, little Joanna wanted down off Granma's lap and scampered to the living room. Sarah sat with her forearms resting on the table, as did Linda. Each stared down at the rich walnut tabletop. Sarah was troubled by her worry for Daniel and even more so by her nagging questions about Leanna.

Linda wished she could say something to take the frown off her mother-in-law's worried face. Well," she said, "I think it will be fairly easy to find Daniel. If there's a Mennonite church somewhere around here, he's probably been there."

Sarah, looking up, nodded. "Yes, that's right. I guess I really don't have anything to worry about with Daniel. Harley will get in touch with him somehow and find out what the trouble is." Then, the worried expression on her face grew deeper. "It's Lena…" she shook her head, "or Leanna, I guess, that's really bothering me. She acts like she doesn't want to be here. Like she suddenly doesn't want anything to do with me."

"Oh no, Sarah, that's not true. She is always telling us how much she wishes you would come to see her. I know for a fact that she has missed you very much."

"Then why did she go back home before we got here this morning?"

Linda had a pretty good idea why but felt it was outside her privilege to discuss Harley's family matters. *Harley* needed to talk to his mother about Lena's behavior. She could respond to Sarah's question only as a friend would: with suggestions.

"Given the fact that she ran away from you and her family, maybe she felt insecure with your feelings toward her. She probably became afraid, at the last minute, that you might be unhappy with her and would reject her."

"Oh, my goodness! If that is the trouble, then I can see why she's acting the way she is. That's how *I* feel! I should talk to her." Though aware of using the wrong name, she didn't bother to correct herself. She would become used to the name Leanna sooner or later, she was sure.

She rose from the table. "Let's get dinner over, and then I'll talk with her."

In the bathroom, Leanna found band-aids in the small metal medicine cabinet on the wall above the vanity and wrapped her cut finger. She now stood looking at herself in the mirror of that cabinet. She hated what she saw. This woman in the mirror was not the kind of woman that she respected. But then, no one she knew had any respect for this kind of woman, weak and wishy-washy, unworthy of friends... on God's hit list. The only way this woman could get even close to behaving normally is by plying her with booze and fooling her into thinking that her not being okay is okay. Oh God, she hated that. Only the booze believed she was okay.

She felt the tears burn her eyes and saw this woman's face contort and begin to cry pitifully. It was not this woman for whom she cried. There was no pity for her. She had brought it on herself a long time ago. Even God did not pity her. It was her mother that she cried for, or rather, what this woman had done to her. Her mother was the only person she should *not* have run out on. Now, she couldn't go back. Her mother didn't want the trouble she would bring with her. Who could blame her? She did not deserve it. Why should *her mother* suffer for this woman's falling out with God, this crazy woman in the mirror, a boozer?

You can't go back!

The heart-wrenching words fell on her again. This time, their full impact curled her insides and burned her face. She pressed her sobs into her mouth with a fist so hard against her teeth that the taste of blood was on her tongue. Her very soul cried her anguish, her loss, but the sound of it stuck in her throat, choked her, and brought her to her knees. She sank to the cold tiled floor and let her quaking shoulder press against the face of the vanity counter. She sobbed uncontrollably in silence.

After a while, drained of tears and empty of any desire to save herself, she rose, turned on the cold water, and rinsed the tear stains from her face.

Harley became concerned about the length of time Leanna stayed in the bathroom. He took advantage of an interval of silence in his conversation with Lewis to walk down the hall to the bathroom door. He stood facing it and listened closely to the sound of water running in the lavatory. The water continued to run for what seemed like a long time. Anxious to know if Leanna was planning to leave, he tapped lightly on the door.

"Anyone in there?" he quietly called.

"Yes, wait a minute," Leanna replied, and then the water stopped running. There was a moment of silence, and then the door popped open. He stepped back, and Leanna came out in a rush, keeping her face down. Without looking at Harley, she started toward the living room. Harley was at first startled by her quick movement, then recovered his composure.

"Hey, where are you going so fast? Are you alright?" She replied quietly, without turning or stopping.

"Yeah, fine."

Exasperated, Harley let it show in his voice. "Well, slow down. I want to talk to you for a second." Leanna stopped, heaved a great sigh, and turned to face Harley, who was moving toward her. She waited impatiently for him.

When Harley reached her, he saw in her face that she had been crying. "Are you alright?" She didn't answer. "What's wrong? You've been crying."

She shook her head. "No big deal, Harley, just a little private thing, nothing for you to worry about."

He searched her expression for some truth, and she returned his look with defiance.

Exasperated, she said, "What do you want from me, Harley?"

"Nothing! I feel like something's bothering you. If there is, tell me, and maybe I can help."

She stared at him, and he thought she would say something, but she remained silent, her mind in a fight with itself. She wanted to cry to him. Tell him how awful she was. Explain the wine all over her kitchen and beg him to tell her what was wrong with her. Maybe he would say that there was *nothing* wrong with her. That's what a part of her wanted to hear. But the other part quickly reminded her that she, a convicted felon in God's court, was an utter fool even to imagine that kind of consideration. *Of course,* there was something wrong with her. Always had been. There was no way she would ever get away with what she had done in the barn. Andrew hadn't, had he? God had punished him immediately. He was just taking His time with her. It was at that moment that it occurred to her.

Andrew was the lucky one after all, wasn't he?

She whirled around to continue her walk to the front door. Anticipating that possibility, Harley grabbed her arm before she could take a step and held her in her place.

"Please, Leanna, don't do it. You are needed here."

Needed here? She had never heard *that* before. It charmed her, but that wasn't what held her. It was the pleasure of his strong grip on her arm. It made her think she meant enough to him, her brother, to cause him to force her to stay. The sense of connection made her want to tease him. Say something that would make him laugh, be amiable and sisterly. Her washed-out face showed a pale smile, but the nonchalance that she was trying for came out stiff and bland.

"Okay, you got me," she said, then added, "Needed? for what?"

"You and Mom need to get together and... you know... catch up. Doncha think?"

Leanna stared at him. "Why are you saying that? You know what I am. Mom doesn't want anything to do with a..." She couldn't make it come out of her mouth. The word was bad enough in your mind. But making it a live sound that anyone could hear when describing yourself was like stabbing yourself in the heart.

Harley scowled. "A what? You're her daughter, for cryin' out loud! Anyway, if you asked *her*, that's what she'd say. "Lena Danziger is my youngest child, my beautiful daughter who I miss so much." That's what you are, Leanna. I've heard her say it a hundred times." He saw new tears come to her eyes, and she shook her head.

"No, no, she doesn't know me anymore. I'm not that little girl she loved out on the farm. You know as well as I do." The tears were on her cheeks, but the crying stayed inside.

"What do you mean?" he said. "Of course, you're not a little girl. You're an adult."

"But I'm not the adult she would have wanted for her daughter." She wiped the tears from her cheeks. Harley watched her while trying to puzzle out what she was talking about.

"That's baloney!" he exclaimed. "What makes you say that?" He became exasperated and flung his arms up in a helpless gesture. "What, are you some kinda mass murderer or something?"

His sudden show of losing his patience startled her. It brought her frustration to the surface. Anger shaped the words that burst from her in a harsh, growling whisper.

"Damit, Harley, I'm a drunk, and you know it. So why do you want Mom to know? And she will if I stick around." What possible good could that do?" Her words and manner had the effect of a kick in the stomach, even to Leanna herself. They left her panting and squeezing her nails into her palms.

Harley was astonished. The silence fell like a guillotine between them. They stared at each other.

Then the choking smell of dusty hay and the sound of giant wings fell on Leanna and beat her senseless.

CHAPTER 32

In her next knowing moment, she realized she was driving her car down some street somewhere. She was stunned and had no memory of the trip she had taken. Her eyes darted from one side of the street to the other, searching for some recognition of her surroundings. She was in a neighborhood in which she had never been before.

Frantic, she pulled over to the curb and stopped. Leaving the motor running, she sat clutching the wheel, staring straight ahead, and shaking uncontrollably. It took her ten minutes to stop shaking. She needed to start thinking about finding her way home.

She was in the middle of the block of a residential district. The houses were large and well-kept. It was very different from the neighborhoods she was used to. The street itself was heavily shaded. It was hooded by large, old elms as far down the street as she could see. Suddenly, she realized that the time of day was late afternoon, almost evening. She looked at her watch. It was three-twenty. Talking with Harley in the hallway before dinnertime was her last memory before finding herself here. The hint of panic caused her to swallow hard. *Where exactly is here? And how did I drive here without killing myself... or someone else?*

"Oh no," she said aloud. *"Mom!* She shook her head. *"I did it again. How can she put up with me?* She continued to sit, feeling shame for the way she kept treating her mother. *I could do her a big favor by just getting rid of her heartache... me! God is taking too long.*

Peering straight ahead, she put the car into drive. She pulled into the middle of the street without looking for other traffic.

The squeal of tires and the blare of a horn directly behind her rattled her senses and caused her to jerk the car back toward the curb. She slammed on the brakes and sat panting. The car honked its horn as it shot by her and down the street. She checked the rear-view mirror, looked over her shoulder for a clearer view, and started down the street. When she reached the corner, she read the name on the street sign.

Hogan. She had never heard of it. She began to look for a place to stop and ask for directions to *her* street. After a few minutes, she exited the residential district to a small shopping center and parked in front of Pizza Hut. She got out of her car and went inside.

As she stood at the counter, waiting for a clerk to notice her, a male voice behind her spoke her name. She whirled around and was shocked to see Kyle Brungardt. "Hi, Leanna!" He smiled broadly.

Leanna couldn't believe her eyes. She stood dumbstruck. How could *he* be here, in her dilemma? He is the same as a stranger to her.

The only thing they had in common was the restaurant; he took his coffee break there. She knew his name and how to make him stop flirting with her. He kept asking her out, and she kept slipping away. Exactly why, she didn't know, but that was the extent of the connection between her and this silly man. Why was he allowed to butt in on her private life, her personal disaster?

"What are you doing in this neck of the woods?" he asked. An impish glimmer showed in his bold eyes.

She couldn't take her eyes off him, this mystery; neither could she speak.

His smile got brighter, and his eyebrows lifted. "Looking for me, I hope."

Her defense came up on cue. "Hardly Kyle, I came for something to eat," she lied. Why are you here? Stalking me?"

He laughed. "I live just down the street. I come in here at least once a day."

The clerk was a teenage girl standing close behind the counter, waiting for an opportunity to wait on Leanna. Finally, she asked, "What can I get for you today?"

Leanna turned to her and then looked at the menu on the back wall.

"Well, I haven't had a chance to decide. Could you give me a minute?"

The girl answered, "Sure," and moved away to wait on another customer. Leanna turned back to Kyle, who had moved to a position much closer to her, almost against her. She took a step back.

He said, "Let me buy a large pizza, and we can share it." She became nervous at his offer and began to tremble a little. She hesitated with an answer.

He pushed on. "What kind of pizza do you like, sausage, pepperoni... both?" His eyes were on the menu, and he persisted. "Or how about the works, a supreme?"

She felt overwhelmed. In the restaurant, she had grown to feel comfortable with him. It had taken a while, but there had always been a table or the counter between them then. Now, she felt exposed and vulnerable. At the same time, she was charmed by the effort he was making to be with her. She looked around her. They *were* in a public place. She looked at him; he was waiting for an answer. The trembling revved up a notch. She was going to do it.

"Oh," she said and shrugged as nonchalantly as her trembling would allow. "I don't care. Whatever you want is okay with me." The girl who had tried to wait on Leanna was watching them, and Kyle raised his hand and called to her. "Beverly!" She approached them. "Whatcha need, Kyle?" "We want a large with all the junk on it and two large Pepsis." He looked at Leanna. "Okay?" Leanna nodded.

"One large supreme comin' up," Beverly said, adding, "For here or to go?"

"Here. We'll be back there in the corner." He motioned to Leanna. "Follow me," he said, leading her to a table isolated from the crowd.

During the trip to the table, Leanna wished she had something to support her nerves. She immediately realized it was her first thought of a drink since her talk with Harley in the hallway at his house six or so hours ago.

Where was I all that time?

They took a seat at the table. Leanna trembled at the unknown. It was her first boy-girl experience, and Kyle was chomping at the bit.

"So, how did you end up in this neighborhood?" he asked.

That's the second time.

She would have to tell him something about that, but not the truth.

"Well, there's no particular reason. I'm just out Sunday driving. On my way back, I guess."

Then there was *that* problem. How in the world would she get back home without asking for directions?

"You never have mentioned where you live," he said. "Is it somewhere here in West Springs? Are we neighbors, and I've never known all this time?"

West springs! Wow, that's a long way from my house! Not sure.

She was familiar with the name of the area, and she knew the general direction it was from her neighborhood. Unfortunately, she had no idea how to change her present location to return to her apartment. It would take magic as mystifying as the trick that got her here. She was so taken by her dilemma that her mind became insensible to the task of answering Kyle's question.

After a few moments with no response from Leanna, Kyle snapped his fingers at her and, quietly teasing, called to her.

"Yoohoo! Anybody in there?"

She jerked out of her trance back into the real moment. "What?" Suddenly, there he was again, a foot away, pressing her, piling one problem onto another. She couldn't do this! She had never been programmed to handle "situations" with men in them. This was beyond her. A few drinks would have given her the freedom to operate despite the condition. But here she was. She only stared at Kyle as deceiving as a trapped possum.

What Kyle saw was the same shy girl he had come to admire after several months of trying to get to know her at the restaurant. Running into her this way, in a different environment, seemed a good opportunity to improve his chances with her.

He repeated himself. "I was asking if you live in West Springs or maybe in Manitou."

She shook her head. "No," she said and nothing more. She sure didn't want him to know where she lived. There was no telling what time of night he might show up or what he might do...with her living alone.

The abrupt answer to his searching question left him nothing in the conversation to expand upon. His progress toward communicating with her hit a brick wall, knocking him senseless. His frantic search of the void in his mind for something to say was interrupted by the arrival of the pizza.

"Ah, here we go," he said. The waitress placed the hot pizza on the table and left to get their drinks. "Wow! That's a lot of pizza!" He gave her his best smile. "I hope you like pizza a lot cuz you'll have to eat half of this."

With her eyes on the pizza, she suddenly became aware that she was very hungry. She hadn't eaten since a bowl of cereal for breakfast. "I like it very much," she said quietly.

Kyle took one of the plates left by the waitress and handed it to Leanna.

"Here's your plate," he said. Leanna turned her face to him, took the plate, and set it in front of her. She turned her eyes to the pizza and said nothing. Kyle handed her the spatula and said, "Here yuh go. You first."

Thus, her first date, which accidentally happened to her at the age of twenty-two. The food was good, but the conversation was one-sided, if not absent. The result was a parting of the ways filled with relief for one and disappointment for the other.

He had walked with her to her car, opened the door for her like a gentleman, and sadly watched her slide in behind the wheel.

The door closed, and he asked, "So, where are you headed now?"

During the silent annihilation of the pizza, Leanna was nagged by the problem of finding her way home and finally realized a solution. At the last minute, she would ask Kyle for the quickest way to the restaurant. That time had arrived, and his question allowed her to do just that.

"I have to go to the restaurant for a few minutes," she said. Then, as if the question had just occurred to her, she asked, "Can you tell me the quickest way to get there from here?" He had been more than happy to be of some value to her and wrote down detailed directions, which became her way home. There's something useful, after all, for unrequited love.

CHAPTER 33

She had been on her way home for ten minutes, following Kyle's directions explicitly. Driving on Kerry Street, she became aware of her surroundings and was surprised that she felt she'd been there before. The only explanation, it seemed to her, was that she had come this way in her mindless state.

As she drove, her thoughts turned to her mother. The disappointment of a missed opportunity to be with her ached in her throat, and tears welled up to blur her vision.

When she wiped them away, she saw police cars parked on both sides of the street at the next intersection. The area parallel to the sidewalk on the right was taped off in yellow, and several officers were busy out on the street.

Whatever had happened seemed to be over. Lingering onlookers standing on the sidewalk behind the tape were talking and pointing. As she approached, an officer stood in the middle of the intersection, directing her to turn right onto the adjoining street: Beulah Street.

She did so gladly and, at the same time, felt a twist of insecurity in her stomach for leaving the route on which Kyle had given her. She drove one block down, one block over, and returned to the Kerry Street intersection. She could see the scene more clearly now and saw what seemed to be a crumpled-up bicycle lying in the gutter.

Looks like a kid on a bicycle got hit by a car.

She continued on her way, imagining the child being rushed to the hospital and the pain the parents must be going through. She wondered what her own mother was feeling now as she imagined her disappointment that she had such a daughter. She had to pull over for a few minutes to let the tears have their way without having an accident herself.

Thirty minutes later, she saw the restaurant ahead and recognized where she was. She turned left at the next intersection and drove straight to her apartment.

She parked her car in its usual place and sat there feeling lousy. She was riddled with guilt and regret about her confession to Harley. She should have kept her mouth shut. She didn't even know if it was true, that she was a... drunk. She cringed inside when she imagined Harley making the announcement to the family.

Me and my big mouth! Oh well, no one cares anyway.

What had her mother ever done to deserve a pile of crap for a daughter? *Sam* should've been there. *He* should be the one to feel the hurt. She would have told him to his face, loud and clear.

I'm a drunk, Sam! *Your evil little hayloft rat is also a drunk.*

The words, though only silent shapes in the folds of her brain, rang in her ears like the blare of an oncoming freight train.

Evil little hayloft rat?

She was startled, and the panic attack began to hum and surge in the depths of her spirit. She jerked the door handle, shouldered the stubborn door, and it screeched open. She scrambled from the car. Her scurrying sent her down the walk halfway to the porch before she thought to close the car door. She hurried back to the car and slammed the door to have it bounce from its faulty latch. She slammed it again, and this time, it stuck shut.

She started down the walk with hurried steps. Halfway to the porch, she began to trot as she had on nights going from the barn to the house when she was little. She had been afraid of what might be in the dark coming up behind her to do who knows what to her. She was up the steps, through the door, and inside, with the door slammed shut behind her in seconds.

She stood with her back against the door, looking into the room with wild eyes and panting from the effort of her escape. From what, exactly, she couldn't say. It wasn't dark yet. She stood frozen for a full minute, letting her body tremble away the last effects of the panic attack. Still moving in jerks, she went to the refrigerator and bent down to reach for the wine bottle.

"What the...!" she said aloud. She peered into the depths of the refrigerator. It wasn't there! A hint of panic spun her around to the table behind her. Not there either! Then she turned her head to the counter and saw it against the wall next to the coffee canister. She stood, fists at her sides, staring at it. Then she remembered the mess she had made that morning.

She turned to the wine-splattered wall. There it was, like the blood of a battle she knew she was losing. She looked again at the bottle half filled with wine on the counter. She went quickly to the mess, squatted down, and carefully picked up the broken glass pieces. If she got busy and cleaned up the mess, maybe she wouldn't want a drink by the time she finished.

While she worked, she made her mind move to other parts of the day that had befallen her. The most glaring was the trip her body had taken while leaving her mind behind. She had no idea where she had traveled in her mindless state. How had she kept from having an accident? Apparently, she'd had a sense of awareness to a certain degree, but it was without continuity. One moment disconnected from the next, leaving no memory of it. If something had happened to her or if she had caused something terrible along the way, she would have no memory of it.

As the pictures of the accident shuffled around in her mind, one suddenly came into full view. It jumped out at her. The bicycle! It had been lying far enough away from her that only a glimpse of it was all she had gotten. She hadn't seen that it was blue. But now, in her mind, it was blue, plain as day. The blood went to her head and made her dizzy. She froze in horror. Was the clear picture of the color of the bike a memory of the accident as it was happening? What if she ran over the child on the bicycle?

Oh no! Surely not!

She dropped the wet, soapy sponge to the floor and stood transfixed, staring at the vague picture of the accident scene in her mind. The mangled bicycle glared at her. The feeling that she had been there before grew stronger. She had to know for sure.

Suddenly, an idea occurred to her. Maybe the *car* could tell her what happened. She ran from the room, out the door, and to her car. She stopped in front of it and, focusing on the grill, her eyes examined it closely. She saw nothing telling. Not a dent, mark, or a blemish that hadn't been there when she bought the clunker. The headlights were intact. She looked down at the bumper. It was slightly out of alignment. The left side was hanging a little lower than the right, and she couldn't remember if it had always been that way or not. She squatted down and studied it carefully. She moved her eyes from one end to the other, scrutinizing every scraped and scratched inch.

She came to the passenger's side, and her stomach felt sick at what she saw. On the end of the bumper was a thin streak of blue paint about an inch and a half long. She couldn't believe it! Her spirit crumbled. She would *not* believe it! She got closer and examined it, wishing it to turn to a different color or disappear altogether. It didn't look fresh, but she couldn't be sure. She didn't know anything about paint.

She slowly reached out and ran her index finger over the thin blue stripe. It was rough and brittle. It seemed to her that that's how it would be if it were old. But it looked fairly bright. Was it the same shade of blue as the bicycle?

She stood up straight and found her legs weak and rubbery. She began to shake uncontrollably. She walked carefully to the porch and sat down, her head bobbing and her teeth chattering. Her mind became gorged with words of tragic descriptions, leaving no room for logic. She sat staring into space, a waning figure of hopeless despair.

It was dark when she gained enough presence of mind to rouse herself and move into the apartment. Her demeanor was that of an old soul, tried and convicted by life's trials.

Her despair pulled her spirit down to its knees and dragged her to the bottle of wine on the counter. She filled a glass, hauled her dead body and the bottle to the table, and sat. The first glassful disappeared without delay. Then, the second. After an hour, the empty bottle glared at her. She clung to her conviction that this would be the night she would surely die.

She shuffled to the bedroom on a sagging frame and careless legs. Undressing and leaving her clothes where they fell, she folded into her bed and escaped. She had no idea that it was only seven-thirty.

Fifteen minutes later, she lay staring at the darkness of her bedroom. She became aware of pounding on her front door. For a few seconds, she didn't care. She lay there as if in a tomb, where the response of the residing dead person was not required. The pounding became persistent and relentless; the doorknob rattled. She still didn't care. The pounding stopped, and her awareness of that moment was as vague as the passing of time.

Her next confrontation with her awareness was a loud, desperate voice thundering her name and a tumultuous quaking of her coffin. Her tomb had been burglarized, and her corpse lay at the risk of being exhumed and resurrected. She became desperate and played dead. But death cannot be replicated; her failure caused her to moan.

Harley, up on her bed on his knees, shook her again and hollered her name. "Leanna!" then shook her again harder. "Leanna, answer me!"

She lay on her side with her back to him. Flinging her arm in protest at the fierce tugging at her shoulder, she smacked Harley in the face with the back of her hand. He flinched and dodged, then grabbed her arm and held it to his chest. He bent over her and spoke quietly.

"Lena, it's Harley." He spoke the abandoned name again. "Lena, listen to me. What is wrong? Are you sick...or hurt?" She remained silent, her arm sticking straight up where he held it, her limp hand resting on his head.

"C'mon, Lena, wake up and talk to me."

She had felt the impact of her hand against his face and was immediately regretful. When she heard him say her name, it became clear in her wine-soaked mind that Harley was there looking after her again.

Her words were slurred. "I am *nah'* sleep, an my name *is nah-ta,* Le-na, an nemer as ben. Thas nother one uh Samb's screw-ubss." He let go of her arm, and she rolled over to lie on her back. He crawled backward off the bed and stood studying his drunk little sister, amazed.

Her unfocused eyes tried to find his face in the dim evening light. She sat half-up, flopped back down, then struggled to sit up again. He reached out his hand.

"Here. Take my hand," he said. She came up on one elbow and reached into space. They joined hands. She pulled herself up and swung her legs toward the edge of the bed where he stood. Her feet were on the floor, and she sat on the edge of the bed, hanging her head. Harley now saw that she wore only her bra and panties. Quickly backing away, he turned and headed for the kitchen, saying, "Put your clothes on. I'll be in the kitchen."

"Wade, wade, wade... wadcha say?" She squinted at his retreating back. He stopped and, without turning, answered her.

"You're not wearing any clothes, Leanna. I'll wait for you in the other room."

She squinted at his disappearing figure in the doorway, confused. Then, letting her chin drop to her chest, she saw her close-to-naked condition and said, "Well, lorr-dy, lorr-dy! Ain thad uh shame, me bein a woman an all. Can' help it bro I'uss born niked." She giggled.

Harley was already gone from the room as she lurched to her feet. Talking to herself, she began fumbling with her clothes. "I spose you nemer seen uh a woman bare ass niked. Well, you wouldna seen nothin' your daddy ain seen.

She was silent for a moment, then burst into sobs. The memory of her father trying to spank her ravaged her spirit, even under the soothing power of the wine. She stood in the hollow arms of the darkness in her white underwear, her jeans in her hand hanging at her side. Her contorted face was raised toward the textured sheetrock between her and heaven and quaked and shuddered in utter despair.

After a while, slumped and head hanging, she ran dry of tears. Sitting back on the bed, she unconsciously let the jeans slip from her hand to the floor. She heaved an enormous, shaky sigh and shook her head.

"Sorry, Lews, can' splain my crazy brain. Coun' nen, can' now, probly nemer will. All I un say iss... sorry bout whad I thoughd yuh cuda done. Somethin' yer na cable of." She sat for another minute. With a brain numb with wine, she rose with wobbly effort. Then, leaving her clothes behind, she weaved out of the room.

CHAPTER 34

Harley had stayed in the kitchen and made a pot of strong coffee. He sat at the table waiting for her. He wondered if Leanna would be able to help him find Daniel tomorrow.

Probly won't, he thought. It looked like he would be on his own for that.

When she entered the kitchen, he saw her still in her underwear. He opened his mouth to protest but didn't have the emotional energy to go to the trouble. *Besides, it might turn out to be a problem to get her dressed,* he thought. It really wasn't any different than a swimsuit. So, what the hell? His real concern was to sober her up. He rose and said, "Sit at the table, and I'll get you a cup of coffee."

His words voicing his concern for her well-being made her warm and cozy. The rosy wine and her big protecting brother weren't a bad combination. She made it to the table but nearly missed the chair. She caught her descent and made a three-point landing on the chair. Her mental picture of herself landing on the floor in a mess of arms and legs produced a cute little giggle. Then she sat up straight and rigidly placed her arms out with hands flat on the table. And, like a good little girl, waited to be served. He came carrying two cups of steaming coffee. He set one at his place and reached across the table to put the other in front of her.

Thus, the process began. He asked questions pertinent to the situation at hand. She remained detached from relevant answers, with only her pickled brain to work with. They would slip from her mind's grasp, and she would giggle.

Though Harley understood her behavior, his patience was skimpy. He continually encouraged her to drink her coffee, but she was not easily coerced. This went on for an hour. Then, in the middle of her fourth cup of coffee, he saw fewer giggles and more frowns. He thought it was time to start pushing.

"Seriously, Leanna, why did you get drunk? I'm not leaving until you give me a straight answer." She looked at him for a long moment with unblinking eyes. Indecision shoved her this way and that. Her eyes dropped to her hands, clutching her coffee. "I'm not sure... I can't put it all together."

She hesitated a moment. "I came home and..." Harley interrupted. "Where did you go when you left my house?"

She didn't want to tell him about her mindless trip. "I... went across town to a pizza place."

Harley was skeptical. "What? You stayed all afternoon in a pizza hut?" She didn't expect him to believe her, but she had nothing else she could say without lying. Then she remembered Kyle Brungardt.

"Well, not by myself. I bumped into a guy who often comes into the restaurant, and we talked."

"Did you know Mom and Katy stayed around till almost six, waiting for you to come back? Mom was in tears when they left." Those were a sobering group of words. They were like a sentencing to the gallows.

To be hung by the neck until dead.

It was blood-draining, and her pale face showed it. Guilty again. Who could stay drunk hearing that? She'd felt a lot better drunk. But she *hated* boozers!

Gotta be crazy!

Was it her mind doing this to her and everyone around her? She didn't *want* to hurt her mom. She was sure she was crazy! Sometimes, she felt like she was standing beside someone who was making life miserable for her. She couldn't get away from this other person: *My twin sister.*

Harley was staring smoking holes into her. "Well? Aren't you gonna say something?"

She wanted to punch him in the face! She *longed* to say something, to defend herself. She had yet to remember leaving his house. It wasn't she who was being a shit ass. It was this other woman, the boozer. It was the one who blindfolded her and took her to Hogan Street. And probably ran over some little kid along the way.

Then, recall fell on her, smothering her. The memory of the blue paint on her car bumper quickened her heart. Now, she was sober. *Now,* she was crazy Leanna again. She had her shame, fear, and hate for the kind of person she thought she was becoming. Now she *cared* about all that, and it made her hurt.

"I'm sorry, Harley, but I don't know why I left your house."

He gave no sign that he believed her. Instead, he looked to the ceiling for help and sighed with a heaviness that said, "Here we go again."

He said, "C'mon, Leanna, don't give me that crap! People don't keep running off without asking themselves why at some point. Sooner or later, you gotta come up with an answer, even if it's an educated guess. Give me your best guess why you worried us to death and didn't give a damn."

She sat stunned for a second, and then shame, fear, and hate joined hands and surrounded her. Anger was her only weapon against them. Harley was providing the perfect time to vent.

She leaped from the chair, knocking it over. She put both hands on the table and leaned in toward Harley. Her face was crimson with anger. She also was vaguely aware that she was in her bra and panties.

"Hey!" she shouted, "I don't give a hootna holler if you believe me!" Harley's upper body backed away.

"When I say I don't know why I left the house, it's because I have no memory of it. Everything from when I talked with you in the hall till a couple of hours later is gone. When I found myself in a residential district on Hogan Street, somewhere in West Springs, I had no idea where I was or how I got there. I don't know why that happened, so I don't know why I ran away!"

Harley sat very still, stunned by her outburst. There was wonder in his expression.

Leanna stood up straight. "I know Mom is hurt by me, and it's happened over and over. I know what I cause her and my family. But it's like someone else inside me is doing stuff behind my back."

Harley saw her shaking and realized he had made a mistake. He hadn't believed her, and it set her off. She was losing control. He became concerned about what she might do next. He raised a hand, palm up.

"Whoa, whoa, calm down. I'm sorry," he said kindly. "I was outta line. You need to calm down and tell me what you're talking about. I don't understand."

Then Leanna, remembering she had no clothes on, mumbled, "Good lord!" and ran to the bedroom.

As she dressed, she asked herself how far she could go with an explanation to him without giving herself up. She had already talked more about her craziness than she had intended. She would not tell him about the blue paint on the bumper of her car. She re-entered the kitchen, fully dressed in blue jeans and a shirt. She set the chair back up on its legs and sat in it. She sat with her hands on the table clasped together, looking at them.

"There's not anything else to tell," she said.

"How long has this been happening to you?"

She felt reluctant to answer his questions... "It's happened a coupla times since I've been here in Colorado."

"You mean it was happening back on the farm?"

"When I was little."

Do I really want to do this?

They sat silent. She sensed he was waiting for her to go on.

She shook her head. "I really don't want to talk about it."

Harley had begun to realize that he had learned more about his little sister in the last few minutes than he had all the years past. Maybe this was the time to push her.

But he didn't have to. Suddenly, Leanna wanted to tell someone. She studied her hands clasped together on the table and spoke quietly.

"I used to get upset about something, and I'd get a whiff of dusty hay and start sneezing my head off, then suddenly be in the hayloft. And "Sam the man" would hold my head down for God to chop it off with a big 'ol golden ax. Some little sound of reality would pull me back, and everything would be alright." Harley sat very still, his mouth clamped shut, awestruck.

After a moment, Leanna continued. "It was usually Mom's voice that brought me back. She saved me from God many a time."

Harley hadn't heard her refer to their father as "Sam, the man" for a few years and realized that mentioning the hayloft had something to do with her use of the phrase. And why had she needed to be saved *from* God? What in the world had happened in the hayloft? He had never heard how his little brother had fallen from the loft. What had she done to make her so afraid of God? A horrible thought slipped into his mind like a knife into his stomach. He needed to throw up. He rose abruptly from his chair and looked at the sink, fighting the urge. The immediate danger of that happening subsided after several seconds, and still feeling a little queasy, he turned his attention back to Leanna.

He spoke to her cautiously. "The hayloft. I have never heard what, exactly, happened up there. Do you remember any of it? It *was* a long time ago."

She hadn't thought of it for several years, but as the image of that time filled her memory, every moment lit up clearly in her mind. *Evil little hayloft rat.*

It made her heart start pumping faster. She left the chair and started toward the living room but stopped short. She turned to her brother. "It was long ago, and I don't remember much about it." She wanted him to stop asking about it.

"You surely remember why Andrew fell, don't you?" She shook her head, reluctant to hear a lie that her mouth would have to tell. He pressed her. "A thing like that, and you don't remember how it happened?"

"I didn't see it happen." *That* was not a lie.

Anxiety was creeping up on her, but she wasn't being seized by the usual overwhelming desire to run, which surprised her.

Why was he bringing this up after all these years? What good would it do to hear it all over again? He knows what she did. Everyone knows.

"Even if you didn't see it happen, you were still part of whatever was going on up there before he fell down the ladder. You would remember what you and Andrew were doing before the fall." His manner was loaded with accusation. "And I'd like to know what that was."

The dread of what she might say twisted in his stomach. Though the truth might crush him, his whole life might change if he *didn't* know it.

She couldn't believe her ears! He *knew* what they were doing! Hadn't he heard it from Sam like everyone else? Then, a beam of light broke over the cloudy understanding in her mind and shined into her soul.

Maybe he hadn't heard; maybe no one had. Maybe Sam never told anyone! Has she always just assumed? She sorted through her memory and couldn't find one moment suggesting that she had ever heard someone say it.

She was elated. She grew weak in the knees and a little light-headed. She needed to sit *down!* Did she dare ask Harley? She moved to the table, reset the fallen chair again, and sat. Harley was watching her closely, waiting for her to say something. Now, she knew how to find out if Sam had kept her sin in the hayloft to himself.

"Why don't you ask Sam what you want to know? I'm sure he remembers; he was there too."

"Look, Leanna, I'm trying to help you right now. Who knows when I'll get a chance to talk to Dad again? And besides, he won't talk about that day, never has, and never will. You need help now. You've been drinking a lot, having blackouts, and things you probably haven't told anyone about. Don't you think it would be smart to find out what's bothering you as soon as possible?" He saw what seemed to be delight beam across her face.

She heaved a sigh and felt relief ease her back against the chair. She was now relaxed and completely at ease. She folded her arms across her chest and smiled.

"You really don't know what happened in the hayloft, do you?"

"No, of course not. No one does but you and Dad."

"And God," she added. "And no one else ever will," she said with an air of finality that would put a judge's gavel to shame.

Harley could see that he would get nowhere with her tonight. "Okay, I guess you're not gonna tell me." As he rose, he tried to impress upon her the gravity of her drinking. "But one of these days, you will have to come to know your demons, or they will eat you alive." He walked to the front door, said, "See yuh later," and left.

She stood listening to the darkness outdoors until she heard him start his car and drive away. Then she moved lightly to the couch and flopped down in its sagging lap to revel in her exciting discovery.

Ain't this somethun! Thank you, Harley.

CHAPTER 35

She got up off her knees, lowered the lid on the commode, and flushed it. She turned on the water in the sink and splashed cold water on her face. While drying her face, she examined her reflection in the mirror. *Scary!* She hated throwing up. Her stomach muscles hurt, her throat was sore, and the awful taste... She turned the water back on and, cupping her hands under the stream, rinsed her mouth. This was the second time she had thrown up since she'd gotten to work. She examined herself in the mirror again, ensuring nothing was messy on the front of her uniform. She left the bathroom on shaky legs.

As she merged into her work routine, her step became steady again. She had been throwing up since last night's nightmare had brought her up out of bed, hollering and sweating. The look of the horror on the freckle-faced little boy in her nightmare was devastating. On his blue bicycle, he had disappeared below the hood of her car. The crunching and scraping sound of metal being mangled beneath the floorboard had shaken the sleep out of her for the rest of the night. Even the feeling of the bumps and knocks against her feet on the floorboard had not left her. It had been the worst nightmare she had ever had, but that wasn't what made her sick inside.

It was so real! She was afraid it might not have been a dream. Was it a lingering picture of reality in her memory? Maybe she hadn't dreamed it at all. Maybe it had really happened, and her memory of it came in her sleep. The thought made her sick to her stomach again as she carried a breakfast order to a man waiting in her section.

She set the order in front of the man and asked if he needed anything else. "A little more coffee, please," the man said.

"Sure," she said. "I'll be right back."

Julia met her at the coffee station. "You feelin' any better yet?" she asked.

"No, not a bit." She dropped her hand from the pot of coffee that she had been prepared to lift off the burner and looked pitifully at Julia.

Julia searched her face for a moment. "You look awful. Did you get any sleep at all?"

"Not that I noticed. I was in bad shape all night." She lifted the pot of coffee and started back to her customer. Julia followed for a few steps.

"I know you say it isn't the flu, but maybe it is. Maybe you caught a bug, and you should go home." Leanna shook her head and kept walking. Julia stopped and let her go, watching her, worried.

Bouts of nausea and panic attacks brought her to the end of her shift. Tearful, ashamed, and looking like a corpse, she and Julia walked out the back door and to her car. Julia urged her, all the while, to tell her what was wrong.

"There's nothing wrong that a good night's sleep won't cure," was her only response. She reached out to the car door and jerked on the handle, anticipating its usual reluctance to open easily. It didn't budge. She jerked again, using what she thought was all her strength, and was surprised that nothing had happened. Julia gently took her hand from the door and, grabbing the handle herself, jerked open the stubborn door.

"Leanna, you are totally destroyed. I'm gonna follow you home; make sure you get to bed so you can catch up on your rest."

"I can't go to bed. It's only three o'clock in the afternoon!"

"Sure, you can. If you don't, I know exactly what you'll do. You'll sit on the couch and fall asleep. Then, you'll wake up and go to bed sometime in the middle of the night. That is not the way to get rest."

Leanna got into her car and sat behind the wheel. Looking out at Julia, she tried to devise something to say to convince her to stay away. She was too tired to think. She had decided to go to the police and find out what had happened at the intersection of Kerry and Beulah. She didn't even know *why* she didn't want Julia to know about her problem. Maybe it had something to do with her not wanting her best friend to be associated with a child killer. The words sent a chill up her spine. She shook her head and silently screamed *nooo,* inside. Her head sank to the wheel, resting her forehead on her clutching hands. The tears came, and her shoulders quacked with quiet sobs.

Julia saw her break down and felt heartsick for her, but she had no idea how to comfort someone who wouldn't tell her what was wrong.

"Oh, Leanna, please tell me what you need. You're upset about something. Tell me, I want to help you."

Leanna stopped crying and sat with shaking hands, wiping the tears from her face. Julia watched for a moment, then reached into the car and took hold of her arm.

"C'mon, I think I should take you home and stay with you until you feel better." Leanna did not object this time. Moving like an old woman, Leanna slowly hoisted her body from the driver's seat. Julia guided her into her silver-gray Pontiac. Julia twisted the key in the ignition and saw her hanging her head in her hands, crying again. Something was drastically wrong, and Julia intended to find out what.

The twelve-block trip to Leanna's apartment was as silent as the way of a loaded hearse. There were no questions, no statements, not even a sniffle. To Julia, Leanna seemed completely wiped out under the weight of her distress. Julia parked the car, and after a moment, Leanna pushed the door open and got out. She dragged herself toward her front door. Julia caught up and wrapped an arm around Leanna's shoulders. They ascended the porch and went inside.

Leanna didn't bother to change out of her uniform immediately after entering as she usually did. Instead, she fell onto the couch and sat, oblivious to everything around her. She was completely consumed by the terrible mental vision of the horrible thing she may have done. However, her insides no longer churned and gnawed on itself. She had decided to act on the decision to go to the police, no matter what the outcome. She dreaded the possibility that she would be convicted and sent to prison *(or at least to the insane asylum)* for running over a child.

Julia sat across from her in the easy chair, watching her, worried. She waited for the opportunity to start in on her about what could be so bad that she wouldn't tell her best friend. But the opportunity never came. Leanna didn't move or make a sound. It wasn't going to happen.

"Leanna?" She did not look up or give any sign that she heard. Julia rose and took a seat beside her.

"You're gonna hafta tell me sooner or later what's going on, cuz I'm not going away until you do."

Without looking up, Leanna said, "It's too late. I've already decided what I'm gonna do." She shook her head. "There's no point in you or anybody else getting all worked up and trying to change my mind." She looked up at Julia and gazed at her for a moment. Heaving a big sigh, she said, "But I will tell you what I did or what I think I mighta done." Julia's attention was riveted by Leanna's voice. It was breaking her heart to hear the sadness and see the total defeat on her drawn face. What could this gentle, shy sister have done to cause such hopelessness? Her mind whirled, and her imagination leaped to extreme possibilities. The event of death began to force its way into her dark thoughts. Then fear flushed her face and quickened the rhythm of her heart.

"You're scaring me, Leanna. Tell me it's not *that* bad."

The words came out of Leanna's despair like a proclamation of the end of happiness.

"I killed a little boy on his bicycle, and I'm going to the police to turn myself in."

Julia flinched as if she had been slapped in the face. She stared at Leanna, stunned. No, no, that wasn't right. She misunderstood.

Leanna continued. "At least, I think I did. I'll find out for sure at the police station."

Julia was horrified. That *is* what she said. Now what! Now, what's she doing? She was exasperated! She sprang forward to the edge of the couch.

"What are you doing? Why are you saying that?"

"Believe me, Julia, I'm not having a fit or imagining things. I'll tell you what happened."

Leanna told her everything, from the talk with Harley at his house Sunday noon to her discovery of the blue paint on her car bumper Sunday evening. Her horror story mesmerized Julia as the details revealed Leanna's fears and desperation. Julia understood her decision to talk to the police but cringed at the possible negative results.

They sat quietly, staring at each other, thinking about the worst-case scenarios. Then Julia's arms reached out, and Leanna simultaneously slid closer into the embrace. Julia could not contain the sadness in her spirit and began to cry quietly on Leanna's shoulder.

CHAPTER 36

Waiting three months for the day you will quit missing your family is a long time. Daniel tried but found that all the trying kept them on his mind. He had thought that becoming involved in a new life would soon replace their memory. It had been hard enough to leave them, especially his mother, but staying away was a different ball game. It was one he couldn't play anymore.

Sitting in his car across the street from the café where Lena worked, he waited. He glanced at his watch every few minutes, watching the alley's exit for her car to appear.

After accidentally learning where she worked and a week of surveillance, he knew she got off work at three o'clock. She and Julia got off at the same time, and it was now a few minutes past three. At that moment, Julia's silver-grey Pontiac came out of the alley and turned east away from him. Lena's car should be next. She would come toward him and turn left in front of him. He would follow her to her apartment.

Almost a half hour later, Lena's car had still not come out of the alley. He wondered if she was working over for some reason or if she had come to work at all. He pulled away from his parking spot and turned down into the alley behind the restaurant where she parked her car. It was there. He drove out of the alley, around the front of the restaurant, and parked. He sat for a minute, straining his eyes to see inside the restaurant through the glass front. He could not see her. She had to be there since her car was still parked in the back. He didn't want to go in. He wanted their reunion to be a private occasion. After a few more minutes, he decided he had no choice. He exited the car, walked to the door, and entered the restaurant.

The place was empty of customers with no waitress in sight. He stopped at the counter and waited for someone to see him there. Finally, someone carrying two stacked trays of drinking glasses came out of the kitchen. Daniel waved at him, and the man started toward him. The man set the trays of glasses down and met him in the center of the room.

Is Lena here?" he asked. The man looked puzzled.

"No one by that name here."

"Lena Danziger. She works here, doesn't she?"

"Do you mean *Leanna* Danziger? She works the morning shift."

Then he remembered it wasn't Lena anymore. "Oh yes! Leanna! That's the one. Is she here?"

"No, she and the other waitress left a while ago."

"Okay. Thanks," Daniel said and left. She'd been in the car with Julia when he saw it come out of the alley. He got into his car and sat for a moment, not knowing what to do. He had no way of knowing where they went. They were more likely to go to Julia's or some other place than Leanna's apartment. He couldn't waste time waiting until she returned for her car. He decided to go to her apartment and wait for her there. He started his car and left.

As he approached the parking space in front of her apartment, he was surprised to see Julia's car there. He drove by, turned at the corner, and continued on. He had nowhere to go while he waited for Julia to leave. Now that he had given in to his loneliness and come out of hiding, he was anxious to see Leanna. He had visited only twice since she and Harley had run away to Colorado. The last time was two years ago when she was nineteen and still living with Harley and Linda. It would be good to see her. He didn't know how he would explain that he had been there for three months and had not gotten in touch.

He continued driving around the neighborhood, passing her apartment every ten or fifteen minutes. He expected Julia's car to be gone each time, but it remained. After an hour, he drove back to the restaurant and had a cup of coffee and a piece of apple pie. It was close to five o'clock when he drove back to Leanna's apartment. Julia's car was gone.

He pulled in, got out, and, hesitating, stood there. Then he closed the car door and started up the sidewalk. He reached the door and knocked. Moments passed, which seemed like forever, and nothing happened. He knocked again and waited. Still, there was no response.

He wondered if she had left with Julia to get her car. Was she taking a nap, or was she in the bathroom? He would pound louder. As he raised his fist, he heard the deadbolt click and the safety chain rattle. He dropped his fist, and the door came open.

Her face was washed pale, and her expression conveyed irritation and disgust. He immediately saw that she had been crying. Her first reaction was one of disbelief. Then her eyes widened, her mouth flew open, and for an instant, she froze like that.

"Daniel," came out in a breathless gush. "Oh my…!" She leaped at him, her arms encircling his neck. He caught her in his arms and squeezed with all his might. The joy curled up inside each of them, warm and silent. Then he felt her quake as she began to cry.

At first, he thought these were tears of joy, and he was thrilled. He held her, his mind locked, hearing her tear-soaked words from his shoulder.

"Oh, Daniel… thank… God, you're here! Then he realized something bad must have *happened*.

"Leanna? What's wrong? What has happened?" She couldn't talk for the crying. He pulled her away from his shoulder. "Is everyone okay? Is there someone hurt, or…" She shook her head and tried to stop crying. He watched her wipe tears and waited.

She finally looked up and said, "No… no, there's no one hurt, I'm just…" She pressed herself back against his chest and laid her head on his shoulder. "It is so, so good to see you… so good!" Her tears returned, and this time, he became alarmed. He spoke kindly. "I know there's something wrong, so tell me."

It was hard to understand her quiet words. "I'm in trouble."

"In trouble? What kind of trouble?"

She found some composure. "I don't know for sure." She took his arm and pulled him with her.

"Come in the house, and I'll tell you what I'm talking about."

With him sitting on the couch, she paced the floor and told her dreadful story. After she finished, they were silent for a time. She quit pacing and sat next to him. She had not broken into tears during the telling but had come close. She was now washed out. She spoke without emotion.

"I think I should go to the police and ask them about the accident. What do *you* think?"

He paused for a moment, then heaved a big sigh. "I… think… that would be the right thing to do. But you should be prepared to be kept there because they'll want to know why you're asking. You'll have to tell them, and they'll detain you while they investigate. The good side of that is that you're volunteering to come in. That will be good for you if it turns out that there was a hit-and-run accident."

Hit and run!

The words fell on her like a mountain, crushing the breath out of her. She gasped and sprang from the couch, shaking her head.

Startled, Daniel quickly rose to his feet and reached out for her arm. "Leanna, what's wrong?" Panting, she stared at him with wide eyes.

"It wasn't a hit and run, Daniel! It wasn't ... I didn't see anything! I wouldn't have hit a kid and then snuck off! Why do you call it hit and run?"

"I didn't mean you did that. I was only using the language that the cops will use." He took her in his arms and held her protectively. "I'm sorry. I wasn't thinking." She let him hold her for a moment, then gently pulled away from him. "But it's true, isn't it? That's what the cops will call it because they won't believe how it happened."

"Wait a minute now, don't jump to conclusions. You mean *if* it happened. We don't know yet." She took her hair in her hands and shook her head, growling like a dog.

"I'm going crazy, she cried," and flung her hands into the air, spun around, and flopped back onto the couch. Close to tears again, she peered up at Daniel, and he saw shaky fear in her expression.

"I'm scared, Daniel. What's gonna happen to me?"

He sat down beside her. "You're getting way ahead of yourself, Lena" ... he hesitated, realizing his mistake with her name, but went on. "You're probably getting upset for nothing. Besides, I can't see how you could have run into a bicycle and not have been startled to awareness by the noise. I think you would have known if you ran your car into something." She looked at him desperately, wanting to believe him. and felt some consolation. On the other hand, Daniel asked himself, what if? He was starting to feel some reluctance to surrender her to the police. But he could see no other choice. "When were you planning to go to the police?" he asked.

"As soon as Julia gets here, she's going with me." Then she gave him a pleading look. "Would you go with me, Daniel? I could really use your support."

"Of course, I'm going! You couldn't keep me away."

After that, they sat quietly, each in their own struggle with "what if" and "please not," until Julia pounded on the door.

Leanna answered her knock, and they immediately stepped into a hug, tears coming to Julia's eyes. They broke free, and Julia, holding Leanna's hand, asked, "How are you doing, girl?"

"I don't know."

"I can't believe you gotta go do this."

"Of course, I have to do this. I couldn't live with myself."

"I mean, is this really happening?"

Daniel hadn't seen Julia since she and Leanna had left Garland seven years ago. He saw that she hadn't changed much. She was more mature and a lot closer to Leanna. They acted like sisters rather than just friends.

"Hello Julia," he said. She smiled and nodded at him. He returned the smile. "It's been a long time."

"Yes, it has, hasn't it?" There was an awkward moment of silence, and then Julia added. "I guess the circumstances aren't much for happy reunions. Sorry."

"Hey, c'mon, you guys. You act like it's all been decided, and Leanna's on her way to prison or something. Give the other possibilities some positive consideration. Maybe they already know who the runner is. Has anyone heard anything on the news?" They both shook their heads, and Julia said no. "Okay, then, maybe we're overreacting."

Julia added, "No one's mentioned it at work either."

Then Daniel offered, "So let's think about this a minute." His focus was on Leanna, and he asked, "What was the first thing that made you think it could be you?"

She sent her mind to yesterday, and the telling mark of blue paint on the front bumper of her car loomed like a monster in a nightmare.

"The bumper on the car," she said, heading for the door. "I'll show you." Julia and Daniel followed her out to her car.

She squatted down at the bumper and pointed to the blue mark.

"See this blue paint? I don't know if it was there before or not." Daniel bent down to examine it closer, rubbed the mark with his thumb, examined it again, and then examined his thumb.

"This is an old scar. Some of this paint would have transferred to my thumb if it was a fresh scar." He stood up straight and looked at Leanna, who had stood up as well. "I don't think it came off the blue bicycle you saw yesterday."

"Really?" Hope began to shine on her face. "Do you really think there's a chance I had nothing to do with it at all?"

He nodded. "I think there's a very good chance." He began to walk slowly, carefully examining the entire front of the car.

"There are no dents, fresh scratches, or anything that looks like it was recently bent. I don't see any other signs of a collision."

Julia became excited. "Now, that would be really great. Maybe we shouldn't go to the police just yet." Leanna looked at her in amazement, and one hand went to her mouth. Her Eyes suddenly sparkled with joyful tears, and a distorted smile formed behind her hand. Julia took her into a hug again, this time with gladness.

Daniel said, "Now we have good cause to wait and listen for it in the news. If nothing comes up about it, forget it." Leanna came away from Julia and stood, wiping the tears off her cheeks.

"Are you sure, Daniel? I don't know if I can do that. It's scary not knowing for sure."

"But if there is no news of it, you'll know for sure. That kind of hit-and-run news will be all over TV and the papers. If we *do* hear about it, then we go to the police immediately."

She heaved a shaky sigh. "Okay. Going to the police is the *last* thing I wanna do."

CHAPTER 37

Kyle Brungardt wasn't a bad guy. He just got into things. His aggressive nature had gotten him into his share of trouble, but his fair-mindedness had saved him on more than a few occasions. He wasn't that complicated or that far removed from your average, healthy, twenty-three-year-old male. He had a good job, was good-looking, and had a sociable attitude toward the opposite sex. But the most important thing you should know about Kyle is that he was very attracted to Leanna Danziger.

Given his nature, it didn't take much for him to be moved from attraction to action. Bumping into Leanna and having pizza with her had been enough.

He walked into the restaurant for one reason only: to see her. Having coffee and a cinnamon roll was a cover. His usual routine was to sit at the counter, order his coffee and roll, and give her a hard time as often as the responsibilities of her job would allow. This morning, though, he chose a secluded booth deep into what seemed to be her section. He walked to the booth, sat facing the front of the room, and waited for her to come to take his order, scheming all the while.

Leanna's morning had been difficult so far. There was no TV in the restaurant, and a busy breakfast had made it impossible to hear anything but bits and pieces of the news on the radio. At one short break, she had looked over the newspaper's front page and saw nothing about an accident of any kind. The time to examine the rest of the paper had not been there. She was still in the dark about her future and preoccupied with horrible possibilities.

Leanna saw him come in, and part of her cried oh no and shrunk back in self-defense. The other part wondered what he thought of her. She also wished she didn't have those awful feelings about him. That was the part that had always scared her. It seemed like there might be something evil about her. A trait in her subconscious spirit that had overtaken her in the barn and made her feel what she felt. She reached for a glass to fill with water and knocked it off the counter.

The crash of glass on the tile floor caused Kyle to turn his head and look. He saw her standing there, looking down at the scattered shards of glass on the floor. He thought her lips said dammit, then she grabbed another glass, filled it with water, and went quickly to his booth.

Hi," she said, setting the water on the table. "Coffee and a roll, right?"

"Yeah, please."

"Be right back."

He watched her hurry to the kitchen and disappear through the swinging doors. Seconds later, she came back with a broom and dustpan to sweep up the mess of broken glass. A couple of minutes later, she set his coffee and a roll in front of him.

"There yuh go, anything else?" She had asked him that standard waitress question a thousand times. She knew asking Kyle that question always brought a smart-ass, flirtatious answer. He had chosen to sit in a booth in the corner, so she knew he was up to something. Why had she asked the question? Was there something in her subconscious pushing her to put herself within his reach? Was she making it easy for him? Who knows, but Kyle was never one to ask Santa Claus why.

He smiled. "Yeah, there is something else."

Oh, oh, here we go.

"Would you let me take you to dinner tonight?"

Whoa, he's never asked that one before.

She started to walk away, but something in the simple "please" stopped her. She turned back to him. The sincerity in his expression caught her breath and caused a nervous swallow. Fear punched her in the stomach. He was serious! She felt a panic attack coming.

In her mind, she was in an awful, tragic moment. Her desire, however, ignored the panic. Her panting, trembling body was stuck between her desire and her cowardly mind.

Say something, dummy? Her mind had always been very strong in its cowardice; It won. She turned and walked away, aware of her disappointment in herself. She saw Julia at the coffee maker and reached her just as Julia started walking away with a pot of coffee.

"Julia!"

Julia turned to her, saw her face, and immediate concern wrinkled her forehead. "What's wrong?"

"I'll be in the restroom for a minute."

Julia moved to set the pot of coffee back on the burner but noticed Kyle, so she turned back the way she had started. She then did a round of coffee refills, replaced the almost empty coffee pot, and went to the restroom.

Leanna was leaning against one of the sinks, staring at the tiled floor.

"What's wrong, Leanna? Kyle giving you trouble?"

"He asked me out, and I didn't know what to do. For the first time, I didn't know what to do with him."

"What do you mean you didn't know what to do? You've always discouraged him no matter what he said."

"Exactly! I've always known what to do: say no. But it's different this time."

"So, what did you tell him?"

She looked up at the question and hesitated. "I don't think I said anything. I musta just walked away."

"I know you will say you don't know the answer to this question, but if you can be honest with yourself... I mean, completely honest, you hafta know the answer. The question is, what do you *want* to do?" She looked at Julia as if the question was a revelation. That, coupled with the advice, to be honest, had now turned on a switch in her brain that revealed to her what she wanted. Sure, she wanted it all to go away: the police, Kyle... her father. But what she really wanted was a *drink*!

She was appalled. *A drink? Do you hear me? The drunk wants a drink! I could handle all this crap if I didn't care if I made a mistake. A glass of wine or two will do the trick.* There it was. Be honest; don't hide things from yourself, and you will feel better. She thought she might throw up.

She couldn't deny that she was attracted to him. Would going out with him be a mistake? At the moment, she wanted to show herself that she didn't need the wine to handle a mistake.

"Okay, tell you what, I want to..." She couldn't say it! It was in her to think it, but to say that she wanted to say yes to Kyle would make her commit to testing herself against the wine. What if she failed the test?

She pushed herself away from the sink and walked out of the restroom. Julia followed, and, returning to her work, she watched Leanna go to Kyle's booth.

Kyle had changed places in the booth and now sat facing the back of the room. He saw Leanna emerge from the hallway and walk straight for him.

She approached him, pushing a scared smile before her. When she got there, she did something she had never done before. She sat down in the seat across the table from him. He was exhilarated. This was a good sign; this was halfway to the top of the mountain.

She rose and said, "I'll get you some more coffee."

When she returned and refilled his cup, she set the coffee pot on the table and sat again. He was all smiles. She was all nerves. All she had to do was say yes, be ready when he picked her up, and go with him... wherever. *What's so hard about that? But then what if he starts getting...*

He spoke and interrupted her train of thought. "You didn't answer my question, and I hope you weren't offended by it." He was being very polite, and she appreciated that. But she could only look away and breathe nervously, shaking inside. She could feel his stare as she gazed out into the room. Though her interrupted train of thought did not restart, the warning had been issued. The paranoia was there in her senses, like a tattoo on her brain. Fear washed over her, fear of him... no, no, not just him but of *men*. *Fear of men?* Lewis! He was *harmless!* Yet she had screamed! She had been fooled, fooled by her crazy mind!

"Leanna?" She jerked and found herself staring at him, unseeing, not hearing.

She shook her head. "Sorry, I was... thinking, I guess. What did you say?"

He should have been put off by her inattentiveness toward him, but this was Kyle; he was climbing a mountain. There was no stopping him now. "I was hoping we could go out tonight."

She could see the hope in his face, but it made little difference to her at this point. Her best friend had advised her to do what she wanted, and she wanted Kyle to like her.

"Okay," she said, got up, and hurried away, leaving the coffee pot.

He sat watching her walk to the coffee station. Julia met her there, spoke to her, and pointed at the coffee pot that Leanna had left on his table. She hurried back to retrieve it. When she reached his booth, he said, "I'll pick you up at seven, okay?" She said, "Sure," and hurried away to refill her two customers' coffee.

It was five o'clock, and she was at home, sitting stiffly in front of the little portable TV set she had finally bought at a thrift store two years ago. Most of the time, it worked pretty well. As she waited anxiously for the news to start, she hoped this was one of those times. It wasn't.

Time for the news came and went while she fiddled with knobs. She pushed buttons, loosened and tightened cables, and slapped the sides of the set until her hand hurt. Her frustration brought tears to her eyes. The set had given her only bits and pieces of the news between long minutes of snow, a rolling picture, or garbled audio. She knew no more about the accident than when she got home at three-thirty.

Now, it was nearly six o'clock. She had been home for two and a half hours. Each minute had brought on another anxious thought about her guilt about the accident. The two glasses of wine had not flattened the sharp edge on which her nerves were teetering. Anyway, not that she could tell.

The fact that Kyle would be knocking on her door in about an hour was so far removed from the routine that had shaped her life for the past three days that it was as if he had never been born. A date for this evening or any other evening didn't exist.

However, fear of the unknown did. She sat on the couch in her blue jeans and t-shirt, agonizing over the little boy and blue bicycle. They tumbled over and over in her mind. The horrifying possibilities that threatened her future loomed dark and foreboding. She sipped her wine and slipped farther and farther down the slope toward the lowest possible hope for her future.

The light tapping on the door made her angry. This wasn't the time to waste breath on saving her. She didn't want to be saved tonight by Harley or anyone else. Maybe tomorrow.

Julia, Harley, Daniel, or whoever could waste their time tomorrow. It was *her* night to waste *her* time. She waited for the sound of their persistent intervening.

"Go away," she heard herself whisper to the unknown intruder on her porch.

The second time was a solid knock. She raised the half-empty glass to her lips, stopped, lowered it, and looked down into the wine as if she thought she saw something floating there. She took a swallow, set it on the floor beside the couch out of sight, and went to the door.

The figure standing at her door startled her. "Kyle!" Then came the memory. She stood stunned.

"Hi," he said. He took in the way she was dressed and became confused. But when she gasped and her mouth formed to say, "Oh no," he realized she had forgotten. How was it possible that she could have done that? His smile and frown came together. He said, "Remember me?"

She half turned as if to run the other way, then turned back to face him and whispered, "Lordy, lordy!" Then she turned and moved into the room a few steps. When she turned again to face him, he was still standing on the porch like the last guy in a mile-long line at a hundred-dollar-bill giveaway.

"Come in if you want to. I'm not ready. I uh...I haven't even started yet." The apologetic attempt to smile enforced his suspicion that she had changed her mind. Disappointed and tense, he stepped inside.

"I've got a problem and... I'm sorry, Kyle, but" ... She shook her head. "I wouldn't be much fun."

His deep sigh and look of profound disappointment made her feel terrible. She had to say something positive, at least promising.

"I was looking forward to going out with you. I've wanted to for a long time, and just when I get the nerve to say yes, this happens."

He was shocked. She's wanted to go out with him? She sure had a funny way of showing it.

"So, what happened? What's your problem... if it's any of my business?"

She was stuck. She hadn't expected him to ask that. She said the first thing that popped into her head.

"My TV wouldn't work." *Dumb answer!* "I mean, I needed to see something on the news, and I spent all my time trying to get the stupid TV to work. That's why I'm not dressed to go out."

"Well, whatever you needed to see must be pretty important. The news will come on again at nine, and since your TV won't work, I could take you to a place I know that has a TV going all the time. We could eat and talk, or something, till the news comes on again. Whaddya think?"

A solution! That would fix the whole tragic situation. She was pleased and very impressed with Kyle. Thanks to the blood sacrifice of the grape, she felt as capable as Wonder Woman. She smiled and, putting on false airs, said, "Well, in light of your effort, I could hardly say no to such an ingenious solution to my problem."

He grinned. He didn't know where that speech came from, but there it was in all its strangeness.

"Good! And you don't have to bother dressing up; as usual, you look great."

Strangely, she felt no embarrassment. In fact, the attention to her looks was gratifying. Of course, she looked great and admired him for saying so.

She said, "Thank you!"

Her voice spoke of years of being exposed to many such moments of social exchanges. That, of course, wasn't even close to the truth. Again, she was impressed, but this time with herself. Kyle noticed the change in her, and it touched his curiosity. More than that, he was thrilled by the difference in her demeanor toward him. Surely, he was doing something right, maybe everything.

"I guess we're ready then," he said.

She held up an index finger. "Give me one minute." She moved to the end of the couch and bent down toward the floor. When she stood up, he saw the half glass of red liquid in her hand and watched her walk toward the kitchen counter. Wine? That was a surprise, but not near the surprise as when she reached the counter and raised the glass for one more swallow.

Would wonders never cease? Who was this girl he had never seen before? He didn't know he was looking at the other Leanna who appeared when the Leanna he knew took her medication.

CHAPTER 38

Together in Kyle's Grand Prix, they found conversation around every corner and down every avenue. The rapport was comfortable. Kyle wasted no time in engaging Leanna in light-hearted teasing, which soon turned to friendly banter. Laughter drowned out the noise of the car's revving engine as they accelerated from one stop light to another.

Aware of her departure from her usual behavior, Leanna beamed with the pleasure of feeling normal. She barely gave recognition to its cause.

Kyle was astonished and stood high on the mountain. He was elated and credited his charm, not knowing the real reason his charm was working: the wine.

After thirty minutes of driving in city traffic, Kyle pulled into the small parking lot of a place called The Towers. He parked, and Leanna peered through the windshield at the neon display of the restaurant's name in gigantic letters. They stood between two even larger flashing castle towers. It reminded her of the ritzy Las Vegas resorts she had seen in pictures. She guessed the splendor of the interior was equally classy. She looked at Kyle in his suit coat and tie.

"You don't intend to take me in there in my blue jeans and tee shirt, do you?"

Kyle shrugged. "Sure, why not."

Leanna grinned. "Ah ha, I see what your plan is. You're going for the glory by showing the world what a great guy you are, giving a street orphan a taste of the good life."

Kyle laughed. "Okay, okay, tell you what." He pulled his tie loose, slipped it through its knot, and tossed it into the back seat. Then, squirming out of his suit coat, he said, "I'll take my coat and tie off and dress down to everyday clothes like you. Then we'll go in and order the best plate in the house." She smiled, fixing her eyes on his. He thought he saw admiration in her face and was urged to kiss her right then and there but resisted.

"C'mon Kyle, you don't need to impress me. Now that you're dressed down to real, let's just go have a hamburger and a coke somewhere." *That felt good!*

She felt normal despite being aware of the cloud hanging over her, which had an eighty percent chance of rain. It was almost eight o'clock. In another hour, the news would be on. She would find out then if she would get rained out.

They were in Fat Andy's, sucking on their strawberry shakes after cheeseburgers and fries, when the news came on. They had been lucky enough to get a booth that provided a good view of the TV hanging high in the corner above the doorway to the back room. Leanna sat facing the TV, watching intently while Kyle, on the other side of the booth, had to twist his neck around to see it. Leanna became so focused on the television that she hardly noticed when Kyle rose and moved to her side of the booth. She scooted over to give him a space to sit, never taking her eyes or attention away from the television set and the upcoming news.

It came like a clap of violent, heart-stopping thunder. *Yesterday at 3:27 pm, seven-year-old Lonnie Shaffer lost the fight for his young life at Mercy Hospital. He was the victim of a hit-and-run accident while riding his bicycle on the way to his home. He died of severe head injuries. The accident occurred at the intersection of Kerry and Beulah, and Police report that there were no witnesses to the deadly accident. Currently, there are no leads as to who may have been the vehicle's driver.*

That was all Leanna heard. She felt as though the blood was jet-flushed from her body in a single, instantaneous rush. To blink or scream or even breathe never occurred to her locked mind. She was stuck, pinned against a wall by an attack of stampeding mass panic. Kyle saw her gasp, sit up straight and rigid, and stare blankly at the TV. He was confused at first and didn't know what to think of her sudden behavior. It had been apparent to him that she was reluctant to talk about her interest in the news, so he had not asked. But, by this time, after all the friendly bantering and carefree socializing, he felt closer to her.

Seeing what he thought was a reaction to bad news, he didn't hesitate to ask, "Did you see what you needed to see?" She didn't answer; there was no reaction to his voice. He reached over and laid his hand on her shoulder.

"Are you" ...

The touch of his hand set off an explosion in her that flung her arm out at him, knocking his hand away and inadvertently striking him in the face. He flinched, and his hands came out in front of him in self-defense. Her face was white with fear, and her voice was a low half-growl. "Oh God no!" Her head jerked around to face him and stare, mouth gaping and wild-eyed. He didn't know what to say. He didn't know what had happened. He assumed that the liberty he had taken to come in physical contact with her was being rejected... violently. His lip and cheek stung. He felt put off without cause, and it roused a little anger.

"Well, pardon me! If I'm too concerned about you, just let me know!" Before he could get that, all said, she had turned her attention back to the TV set as if he weren't there. He glanced at the TV, seeing nothing but continuing news.

She dropped her head and closed her eyes as one would do in prayer, and he glanced around at the people in the room. Several had become attentive to him and Leanna, waiting in expectation of a show, it seemed to him. Leanna raised her head and made a move to scoot towards him.

"I need to go," she said quietly.

He got out of the booth and, without a word, went to the counter. She watched him walk away, realizing she had upset him. She scooted out of the booth, walked to a spot beside the glass exit door, and waited for Kyle to pay. When he finally replaced his wallet in his hip pocket and started toward her, she shoved the heavy door open and went out into the parking lot. She walked slowly toward Kyle's car, letting him catch up.

He caught up about halfway to the car, and they walked side by side for a few steps before he spoke. He had composed himself as he walked, and his tone was kind. "I apologize for whatever happened back there."

She was solemn, disconnected, then, "What...? Oh... sorry." A couple of steps later: "It wasn't your fault. You didn't do anything wrong. I hope you'll forgive me. I..." She hesitated. She didn't want him to know how *crazy* she was.

"I can't explain what happened, but I have an excuse for the way I acted. It had nothing to do with you, and I hope you can trust me on that and just let it go."

He was silent as they reached the car and got in. Behind the wheel, he put the key in the ignition but stopped there and faced her. "You know I like you very much, and I care about what is going on in your life. If you're having a problem and I can help, then I want to do that. You are important to me, so I don't want you to wonder if you should ask me for help. Just do it. You'll be doing me a favor." She was amazed. He started the car and pulled onto the street to take her home.

He parked beside her car at her apartment, and before he could reach over to turn off the engine, she opened the door to get out.

"Thank you, Kyle. I know you don't know how much you helped me tonight. But take my word for it. I needed help, and you were there. I am very grateful for that."

He was disappointed that she wasn't going to invite him in, and he could see that she was still very upset.

"You are very welcome," he said. "I'm glad I was there. I hope you can tell me all about it someday."

She looked at him eye to eye and wondered if he meant it. If he did, maybe... well, she could hope. At the moment, though, she had a bigger hope upon which her whole life hung. She got out of the car and closed the door, not thinking to say good night. She walked quickly to the porch, up the steps, and to the door. Her mind was crowded with an anxious intention to get to the phone and call Julia.

When she got to the phone, she had to dial Julia's number twice before she got it right. It rang and rang.

C'mon Julia, answer the phone! Please!

It kept ringing, and now she counted them. *Four, five,* then she heard a breathless, "Hello!"

"Julia?"

"Leanna! I've been trying to call you! I was just walking out the door to come looking for you when the phone rang. Did you see the news?"

"I saw it. Julia, I'm scared!"

"Okay, I'm coming over. I'll be there in five minutes." The phone went dead.

Leanna hung up the phone and stood there for a minute. Then she went to the kitchen, where the wine bottle stood on the counter. She filled the glass she had left there earlier about half full. She took two swallows. It went down easily and hardly distracted her mind from the effects of the tragic turn of her life. She raised the glass again and became aware of it staring her in the face. She quickly poured the remainder of the glass of wine into the sink, turned the tap water on, and rinsed the glass. She laid it in the sink and put the wine bottle in the refrigerator. Then she retrieved the glass from the sink, filled it with water, and rinsed her mouth. The glass went back into the sink. She went into the living room and sat on the couch, very much at loose ends.

A few minutes later, Julia came in without knocking and sat on the couch with Leanna. Their mutual silence paid respect to Leanna's tragic turn of life.

Julia finally broke the silence. She quietly asked, "What are you gonna do?"

Leanna, staring straight ahead, muttered, "It's too awful to think about,"

"Did you see the whole thing on TV," Julia asked.

Leanna shook her head. "No, I... was... too shocked."

"I think I saw your car on TV... at the scene."

Leanna lifted her head and gazed at Julia with only minimal interest. "You probably did. I saw a news van there."

"I saw a car like yours, and a policeman made it turn onto another street. It came from the same direction that the street the announcer said the hit-and-run car came from. Was that you?"

Leanna's interest was suddenly piqued. "Probably; I was going east on Kerry when I came to the accident. The policeman made me turn south on Beulah, and I went around the block and turned east again back on Kerry." They sat looking at each other, wheels in their minds turning gently.

Leanna said, "Did you say the hit-and-run car went through the intersection going east and hit the bicycle?"

"I didn't say that, but that's what the newsman said the police determined."

Leanna became intensely thoughtful, carefully examining the picture of the scene in her mind. Her eyes had never left Julia's, and they held Julia captive, anticipating. Suddenly, Leanna burst up off the couch. She stood facing startled Julia.

"If the bicycle was hit by a car traveling east, it couldn't be me," she exclaimed excitedly. I was going west! I was going *east,* coming *back* from the pizza place after the accident had already happened!"

Julia also became excited. "That's true. There's no way you could have been involved!"

Leanna plopped back down on the couch, all smiles. "I don't think I was there; I couldn't have been!"

She jumped back up from the couch, exuberant. "This calls for a celebration!" She hurried to the kitchen and poured half a glass of wine for each of them.

Julia had followed her into the kitchen and stood beside her, watching her pour the wine. She felt a little let-down. The wine was a negative in the happy event, but she didn't say anything when Leanna handed her one of the glasses of wine.

Leanna raised her glass toward Julia. "A toast," she proclaimed, mimicking some player in some movie she had seen, "To all the bad things that turn out good." Julia half-heartedly raised her glass and clinked it against Leanna's. She watched Leanna take a healthy swallow and winced inside. She wished Leanna had another way to celebrate; there had to be hundreds of different ways. Maybe she could distract her.

"Are you sure you're not celebrating too soon?"

"What do you mean?"

"Well, what if the police are wrong about which direction the car was moving."

Leanna's beaming expression went pale. "Do you think that could happen?"

Julia shrugged. "I guess it could. Anything's possible." Julia set her wine on the counter, hoping to influence Leanna to do the same. It didn't work.

Instead, she went over and sat at the breakfast table and downed another swallow.

Disappointed, Julia gave up trying to get Leanna to quit drinking the wine without actually begging her. Her attempt to do that had, at another time, only made things worse.

Leanna went back to thinking negatively. The situation was right back where it was before. To be sure about anything, they would still have to talk to the police.

Leanna gave her a worried look. "You think I should talk to the police anyway."

"I don't know, Leanna, maybe."

Leanna, first to voice her observation of the dilemma, spoke quietly. "If I talk to the police, they'll want to know why I'm interested and, not having a suspect, they'll make *me* the suspect."

Julia agreed. "And you will go through their process as if you did it. It is conceivable that you may be imprisoned for it whether you did it or not."

Leanna nodded. "It's happened before." Then she felt sick. "What if I did do it?"

Julia shook her head. "You couldn't have Leanna; you just couldn't have!"

"There's gotta be a way to find out what direction the car was going. Then we'll know if I could have done it."

"Only the police know."

Suddenly, there was a knock on the front door. Leanna rose from her chair and moved toward the door. "Who in the world?"

She got to the door, opened it, and there stood Daniel, "Daniel! Am I ever glad to see you!"

He came in and closed the door behind him. "Hey, kiddo, how are you doing?"

Julia came into the room from the kitchen. "Hi, Daniel."

"Hey Julia, I'm glad to see you here with Leanna. How are things?"

"Did you see the nine o'clock news?"

"Yeah, I came over as soon as I could."

He turned his attention to Leanna. "What have you decided to do?"

Letting his question slip by, she said, "Did you see the whole news broadcast?"

"Yes, from beginning to end. Why?"

"What did they say about the hit-and-run car?"

"I don't remember off hand... Oh, they said by all indications, skid marks and position of the bicycle, that the vehicle was eastbound when it came in contact with the bicycle."

"Yes," Julia said, "and Leanna was going east *after* the accident."

"Oh really! That's great," he exclaimed. "Well, there's something else. They also said, judging by the width of the skid marks, they could have been made by a pickup." Everybody was silent for a few seconds.

"Oh wow, that sounds wonderful," Leanna gushed. "I really don't want to go to the police."

Daniel agreed. "I don't think you should, not yet anyway. You could get in trouble unnecessarily. Just keep watching the news and see what develops."

Leanna still held the almost empty wine glass and suddenly became aware of it. She emptied it in one swallow.

CHAPTER 39

Daniel had noticed her holding it when he came in but had imagined it was cool aid or some other cherry drink. Now, after having had it brought to his attention again and getting a better look at the empty glass, he wondered what it really was. At the same time, he was surprised that he wondered. Maybe it was because the red residue reminded him of wine. Is Leanna drinking wine?

Julia noticed Daniel's attention to the empty wine glass. She thought it might be an opportunity to do something that would cause Leanna to stop, at least for the moment. She remembered the glass of wine she had left on the kitchen counter. She moved toward the kitchen, saying, "I left my drink in the kitchen. We were celebrating when you knocked, Daniel. Would you care to join us in a glass of wine?" She reached the counter, picked up the glass of wine, and turned to Daniel and Leanna. Daniel, surprised, looked at Leanna and the wine-stained glass in her hand.

Leanna, having not yet guessed Julia's intentions and wouldn't have cared much if she had, joined Julia at the counter. She poured herself another glass of wine. The fact that Daniel was there to see her and would surely object to her drinking occupied a spot in the back of her mind. She'd had enough wine to make her comfortable with her rebellious activity. She got another glass from the cupboard. She poured it half full and, pointing it toward Daniel, smiled and said, "C'mon, big brother, celebrate my good luck with me. I think everything's gonna be okay, don't you?" She held the glass of wine out to him.

Frowning, he looked into her face. "You know I don't drink alcohol, and I'm surprised you do; very surprised."

She pulled the glass back to her. "No, I *didn't* know that." A little embarrassed, she shrugged. "Now I'm surprised. Doesn't the bible say a little wine now and then is good for you?"

"Yes, it does, but it spoke about medicinal use. It's good for a nervous stomach. And it also was, in those days, better than the water in some areas. So, I think the *reason* you drink it is the determining factor in whether or not it's good for you."

Leanna's stiff smile was no longer needed. It faded into an expression of defiance, but she was silent, staring down her big brother.

Daniel said, "I don't think you should be drinking that stuff. It can sneak up on you and replace you with someone you won't like."

"I doubt that. I've always been someone I don't like... my whole life! Any kind of a change would be an improvement."

"You don't really believe that, do you?"

"Oh boy, do I ever!" She daringly raised the glass again and took a swallow, making it plain that she didn't care what he thought. She would be who or what she wanted to be. She had never had the luxury of making that choice before, and the feeling lifted her to a position ... as an equal. That long-desired feeling was earth-shaking. It wasn't that she felt big enough to do *anything*. It was that the wine reduced the consequences of her behavior to a size small enough for her to handle if she needed to. That was the pleasure that overwhelmed her. That's what made her cling desperately to the feeling that shimmered there in the glass.

Daniel was mesmerized by the strangeness of his sister's behavior. He, or anyone else for that matter, had never seen her act this way, and it made him wonder if it was because of the wine. He looked at Julia as if she would tell him without asking. She stood quietly, holding her wine, peering at Leanna in disbelief. Daniel couldn't just stand there and be quiet about it. "Just how much wine have you had?"

Leanna was defensive, of course. "Just enough. I drink socially." She nodded toward Julia. "Ask Julia. She knows I don't get drunk if that's what you want to know."

"Why do you drink at all?" Daniel asked.

She smiled a warm, cozy smile and shrugged. "Oh, I don't know." The next words came out in a matter-of-fact tone. "It makes me comfortable! What's wrong with that? Why am I under the third degree all of a sudden? You'd think I committed some crime or something."

Julia spoke up. "Well, as far as I'm concerned, drinking booze is a crime against your own body and mind. I've seen it hurt the boozer and everybody around him."

Leanna was offended. "Julia! I am not a boozer! You have never seen me drunk!"

"No, I haven't." She set her glass of wine on the counter. "But let me tell you this. Like Daniel said, if you drink for the wrong reason, it will sneak up on you. Someday, you won't care if your *mother* sees you drunk. I don't want to be around when that day comes." She walked out of the kitchen, through the front door and was gone. Leanna stood looking at the front door, stunned. The silence in the room spoke, loud and clear, of shock and disappointment.

Daniel moved to the breakfast table, pulled out a chair, and sat. He set his hands on the table, fingers interlaced, head bowed as though in prayer. He heard the click of glass against the countertop behind him and felt a surge of thankfulness even though he didn't know if the glass had wine left in it or if she had downed the last couple of swallows. Leanna came to the table and sat stiffly in the chair across from him, her hands in her lap.

The silence lingered for a few moments. Then Daniel, with a kind voice, said, "I thought you two got along better than that." He looked up at her and saw her sad regret.

"Me too," she said

"You know she's concerned about you, don't you?" he said.

"I guess. I didn't intend to make her leave. She's my best friend... my only friend."

"You never were easy to make friends with, and it's only been, what, six, seven years since you came into this world?" Leanna peered at Daniel, puzzled for a moment, and then understood his meaning.

"Since I made the big mistake, you mean."

"Mistake? What mistake was that?"

"When I started talking again."

"So, did you come back into our lives because you started talking again, or did you start talking because you came back?"

Her words were still tainted with disgust. "Good question. All I know is that sometimes I wish I hadn't done whichever one it was that I did first."

Daniel didn't say what was on the tip of his tongue. It occurred to him that since she was talking freely of the past, this would be a good time to get her to talk about the accident in the barn sixteen years ago. They were quiet, and he was hesitant. But learning some secrets about that day might make it possible for him to help her. He needed to push her further.

"I remember you when you wouldn't stop talking. Then the accident happened. It wasn't that you stopped talking. It was like you went away, and somebody who couldn't talk took your place."

Leanna stared at the tabletop, her mind absorbing his words, trying to fit them into the pictures in her memory. No luck. There were things that she knew were there, way back in the dark, but it was the nightmares that she could see clear as day.

She raised her face to Daniel. "You remember?"

He nodded. "Like it was yesterday. Do you?"

She shook her head.

"You don't remember when we found you in the hayloft the next day, and Katy carried you, screaming, to the house?"

She didn't remember that. Her memory was of her and Andrew. Everything else of that day was what she saw in a nightmare.

"I remember the nightmares, is all."

Daniel showed surprise. "I never heard about any nightmares. Can you tell me about them?"

"I still have them now and then. But they're not as bad as they were when I was a little girl. I even had them when I was wide awake back then."

"You mean you imagined things, like in a make-believe daydream."

"No. I could smell the dust, and all of a sudden, I was in the hayloft, and things got...." She stopped. Daniel saw her face turn almost evil, and she sprang from her chair. She stood facing the window for a moment. Then she turned back to her chair and sat down.

He was stunned. He leaned forward in his chair and quietly asked, "Are you alright?"

She was silent for a minute, feeling some anxiety as the awful pictures started popping up. She was surprised that the old familiar impulse to run wasn't very strong. Maybe she could handle this. A question concerning the effects of the wine crossed her mind.

Her smile was pale. "Yes, I'm fine."

"What happened just now?"

"Nothing, really; I was reminded of the hayloft."

His words, "the next day," echoed in her mind, and she was filled with curiosity. "You said you found me in the hayloft the next day?"

"Yeah, and Katy had to carry you out you were so scared.

"I stayed in the hayloft all night and wouldn't come out the next morning?"

"Yes, that's right. I can't imagine how scared you must have been... the whole night."

She tried to do just that: put the night she spent in the barn into her head. It was not there. There was only the glaring nightmare in her head.

"Why were you so afraid to leave the barn after you spent a whole scary night alone? What was outside in the daylight that was worse than the night in the barn?"

"I don't remember any of that, but the nightmare has always been there. It is the reality; what you just now told me is a story.

"Describe the nightmare. Maybe something in it will lead us to something you can remember."

She was sure she could do it, but the thought started a boil of frantic seething in her insides. A dread spread over her that reminded her of the tight space under the porch with her dog Butch dying at her fingertips. Now, she wondered if she could do it. Would a little wine help? She could not see the bottle on the counter without making an obvious effort to look around Daniel. She kept her eyes on his face.

"I have never told anyone this. You are the one and only." She hesitated. "It's not easy to get started."

Daniel was pleased. "It's okay, take your time."

She heaved a heavy, shaky sigh. "What I see in the dream is a giant, ugly old man. He has a long white beard, gold teeth, and a big silver key on a long silver chain around his neck. He has chicken claws, or eagle's feet, that clamp around a sparkling golden axe. He came from far away and is there to chop my head off." She hesitated for a moment. "This is where it gets uncomfortable."

Daniel waited for her to continue, anxious but giving her time to change her mind if that's what she wanted. He saw her eyes glance at the counter behind him. He realized that she was looking toward temptation and resisting it. It suddenly occurred to him that it might not be a bad idea. A couple of swallows of wine would relax her and give the success of his efforts a better chance. He rose from the table and went to the nearly empty bottle of wine. He immediately saw that she had not emptied her previously discarded glass. He picked it and Julia's almost full glass up and took them to the table. He set her glass in front of her and sat down with the other, saying, "A little wine for relaxation never hurt anyone." He took a sip.

Leanna was astonished. She watched him set the glass down, and then, having been given an unbelievable freedom to do so, she took a drink. She held the glass, felt the warm spread of the wine, and stared at Daniel. She began to feel more comfortable almost immediately. Knowing that it would take several minutes for the wine to take effect, she realized it was her brother's unfamiliar behavior that made her feel so good. His coming down to her level is what put her at ease. She continued to describe her nightmare in a more comfortable manner.

"I try to run, but it is impossible to get up. No matter how hard I try, I can't get to my feet. Then, all of a sudden, I see Dad's face." She hesitated at the sound of the word "Dad" coming out of her mouth. It almost got by Daniel, but it raised his eyebrows. She quickly slipped into her next words.

"Sam is over me, looking down at me frowning, shaking his head, and that's when I realize he's holding me down! I can't get up because he's holding me down for the ugly old man, which is now God, to chop my head off!"

Daniel did not respond immediately. He was bound to the story, fascinated by the picture of his father playing such a dark role in the nightmare. When he spoke, his words came limping.

"I can't... imagine Dad... being the bad guy in your nightmare. You must have a... low opinion of our father. Why do you suppose that is?"

Leanna's scowl was dark, her voice hushed and vehement. "I *hate...* Sam!"

Daniel jerked inside, astonished. He sat motionless, his eyes on his little sister. He cherished her without reservation. She had never caused him a bad moment in all his life. But what he saw was menacing. She took a drink. Her motion pulled him back to the moment, this awful phenomenon.

"Leanna!" he rasped, "You don't mean that! You don't hate your father!"

She felt his disapproval but had her own two legs to stand on with the wine. Bursting from the chair, she started pacing. Her tone was defiant.

"Well, I hate somebody!" she cried. "You tell me who it is then. He told me God was gonna kill us! Where is Andrew now? Dead! And who held my head down in the hayloft so God could chop it off? God's little helper, no doubt!" There was the silence of astonishment and final revelation in the room.

Daniel was speechless. He sat processing the inadvertent donation of information. Leanna's outburst was the product of a desperate mind exposing what lay within. It was invaluable to understanding his beloved little sister, Lena. He spoke softly. "Did you hear what you just said?" When she looked at him, he saw tears in her eyes and nothing else. "You just described what Dad did to you in a *dream!* In a... *dream,* Leanna! It didn't happen!"

She stopped pacing and stood transfixed. Now, with sudden access to some memory of that moment in the hayloft and in awe of it, she also spoke quietly. "You're wrong. What he said to me in the hayloft he said before God pushed Andrew off the ladder. And while I hid in the hayloft so God wouldn't come down from the sky and kill me, *your* father had his hands on my neck, holding me down for God's punishment."

Daniel was astonished. "God pushed Andrew off the ladder? God doesn't do that, Leanna! And He doesn't chop off your head either! It was a dream! But you've been living it like it was real."

"I was five years old, Daniel. Of course, it was real! I dreamed what I thought Sam would do if he had to. You know as well as I do that God comes first. Or actually, *good standing* with God comes first, even before his family. As far as I knew, at five years old, he would have obeyed God and helped Him kill me in a second. Wasn't that what he preached: obey your God at all costs? I was five years old. I believed every word my father spoke." Suddenly, the sound of Andrew saying the last thing he had ever said blared in her mind. She gazed at Daniel with the final piece of proof on her tongue.

"Besides, Andrew told me that *Dad* was gonna kill us."

"Why Lena... *why?* What did you and Andrew do that you should be killed for?"

She stared at him. She felt the panic tighten its grip on her senses, and she closed her eyes and gritted her teeth.

It's not real, it's not real, it's not real. It... is... not...REAL!

It didn't help. She was shaking inside. Then she realized she was putting up her resistance against the wrong thing. It wasn't the dream she feared. It was what she and Andrew... But no one knows about that but God... and Sam. Daniel will never know! She began to calm down, feeling a return to sanity.

She gazed at Daniel for the length of time it takes to fabricate "any ol' answer." "It doesn't take much when it's God's rules," she said. "Obey or, oh boy, you're down the drain."

Daniel showed his exasperation. "C'mon, Leanna, it doesn't work that way! He is a forgiving God."

"Sure, but He forgives only those who obey. Isn't that what Sam preaches? And He punishes us poor sinners who slipped up."

"We're all sinners, Leanna, and every one of us slips up, as you put it, every day. Do you see everyone getting punished every day?"

Leanna became still, thoughtful. "Then why did Sam try to make us believe we were doomed if we didn't toe the line every minute?"

Daniel shrugged and shook his head. "I guess that's all he knew. He was raised that way."

"So, what you're saying is that God's little helper is a sinner just like me. And out of ignorance, he shakes his finger at me, no, no, bad girl, God's gonna get you! So where did he get his say-so if he ain't no better than me? Has he told you?"

A simple question, Daniel thought. One he had asked himself. He didn't have the answer for her, but he was pleased to see Leanna responding to his efforts to make her feel better about herself.

"We've never discussed it," he said. "And yes, no one is without sin. That's why we don't have the right to judge others. What I mean by judging is pronouncing sentence. Making them pay. As human beings, we will judge in our minds that a person is either bad or good, and that's not a terrible thing. But we can't punish them for it. Dad didn't have the authority to try to make you believe that God was going to kill you for what you did in the hayloft. And I'm sure he knew that. He was just trying to scare you into never doing it again."

Kill you for what you did in the hayloft! His words caught her off guard. She caught her breath and felt the rise of heat in her face. The shaking inside was immediate.

Daniel saw the wild look come into her eyes and was startled by it. "What's the matter? Are you alright?"

The sound of him there in the room grounded her, and she answered him with a shaky voice. "I'm... I'm okay." She heaved a shaky sigh and relaxed a little.

Daniel watched her closely. Whatever she and Andrew did in the barn was the driving force behind his little sister's misery. He realized then that she hadn't taken another drink of wine since he had started the conversation. He was pleased. He felt like this might be a good time to let her off the hook and save more for another day.

They were silent for a few moments before he rose to his feet. "I guess I better be going. It's getting late, and you need to get up early." He started for the door, saying along the way, "See ya later."

She made no effort to move from her chair. He made it to the door and left. She sat with her thoughts: the reassurances Daniel had planted in her heart. It was not until she had sipped away the rest of the wine in the glass that she went to bed for a sleepful night.

CHAPTER 40

It had been three days. Three torturous days since she had first heard the news report on the hit-and-run accident. She had been on the job all those days, and one customer after another paid the consequences. The first day was the worst until Julia spoke to her again. She had expected Kyle to come in, but that didn't happen, and it was very disappointing.

The news remained the same. *"The Colorado Springs Police have had no further leads as to the identity of the driver of the vehicle that ran over and killed seven-year-old Lonnie Schaffer as he rode his bicycle...."*

Her whole life was up in the air. There didn't seem to be any results of her getting up every morning except to worry and feel guilty. A good night's sleep was almost impossible. Daniel had come over for an hour or so every night to talk to her about her relationship with their father and her God. It usually left her mind spinning with eyes wide open far into the dark morning. And on top of that, her TV finally gave up the ghost.

She'd argued endlessly with herself about whether or not she would go to the police "first thing in the morning." She kept winning the argument, so that particular morning hadn't happened yet. The only thing reliable was the bottle of wine.

The knock on the door startled her and sent her flying off the couch. She ran to the kitchen and hid a half glass of wine in the sink, covering it with a dirty plate. She ran back to the door, thinking it was Daniel, as usual. She pulled the door open to find Kyle standing there, a grin on his face and a wrapped package in his hand.

"Hi, Leanna!" She was stupefied and gawked in amazement.

"Kyle! What on earth are you doing here?" *He's visiting dummy! How rude!* "I mean, I'm surprised to see you! Come in." She stepped aside, doorknob in hand. He stepped in and handed her the package.

"Happy Birthday."

Astonished, she took the package. "How in the world did you know it's my birthday?"

"Julia told me." Oh-oh, there goes the surprise he was supposed to be keeping. She'll want to know why Julia would tell him about her birthday.

Because he asked? Why would he have asked? He knew she was getting ready to ask these questions as he watched her stare at him. He needed a diversion. He nodded at the package. "It's not much. You wanna open it? Go ahead."

She became excited as she tore the wrapping paper and felt the heat of embarrassment creep up to her face. She was compelled to search her mind for something appropriate to say while the paper ripped. But her mind was clogged with her opinion of her social shortcomings. The paper, once removed, revealed a fancy box of chocolates. She was pleased. It was her first gift with romantic intentions and was perfectly traditional. She gave him her very best blushing smile.

"Thank you, Kyle, the perfect gift from you."

There was more awkward silence while he patted himself on the back, and she wondered how she was doing.

She then became aware of the cool air and realized she hadn't closed the door. When she turned her attention to the door, she was struck with another surprise. There were Linda and Harley coming up the porch steps bearing smiles, a big, decorated cake, and a bottle of something... champagne? She burst out laughing. "Lordy, lordy, what are you two up to!"

Kyle felt he didn't belong in this particular gathering. He wanted to get Leanna's attention to tell her he needed to go. But then, on the other hand, he saw her exuberance in the joyful gathering of her family. He set himself aside against the wall, out of the way. And admired the girl he was falling in love with. He could only grin. Leanna saw it and embraced the added thrill as their eyes met.

Harley raised the bottle toward Leanna. "A party, a happy birthday party!"

Linda joined in. "Surprise, surprise! Happy birthday, girl!"

They came inside, and Linda headed for the kitchen with the cake. As Harley reached for the door to close it, someone yelled from the parking lot, "Hey, hold that door!" Everyone looked as Julia reached the walk and hurried to the open door. She entered, and as Harley closed the door, Leanna saw past him out into the black yard as headlights swung in beside Julia's car. It was Daniel.

The excitement was building, and she felt like a child on Christmas day. She fought the impulse to hop up and down and clap her hands. Her bitter day was faded and gone. She reached out to Harley, who was walking away to the kitchen, and tugged on his coat sleeve. "Hey Harley, I've got a surprise for you too."

He stopped and turned to her. Her face was beaming with delight. "A surprise for *me*? What surprise?"

"Daniel's here. He's been here at my house several times the past week, and I just saw him drive up."

Harley was elated. "Are you kidding me? Why didn't you tell me? Oh man, you don't know how great this is. It's perfect timing!"

"What do you mean? Perfect timing for what?"

But Harley was already on his way to the front door, paying little attention to Leanna's question. He jerked it open just as Daniel started up the walk.

"Hey, Daniel," he yelled, hurrying out onto the porch and down the steps. They collided on the sidewalk with a hard gripping handshake and "How yuh doin?" They walked to the door, preoccupied with swapping current information about themselves.

Inside, Leanna waited for their entrance in anticipation of Harley's answer to her ignored question. She had to know what Harley might have going on. It would have to have something to do with Daniel. When they came in, she asked Harley the question again.

"Harley, what is this the perfect time for?"

He reached into his shirt pocket and drew out a slip of folded paper.

"This! I will call this number at exactly eight o'clock, and the three of us will talk to Mom."

The surprise showed on her face, and she brought her hands to her mouth. "Oh wow!" she gushed. "Really? Are you kidding me?"

Harley was grinning. "Not kidding. Happy birthday, Leanna."

She shifted her position so she could see the clock on the end table beside the couch. "What time is it? Seven fifty-five! Five minutes!"

Then she saw Daniel looking at her with a grin that reflected her own excitement. She rushed to him, flung her arms around him, and hugged him as hard as she could. He responded in like manner. Holding to the hug, she called to Harley. "Thank you, Harley! Thank you, thank you *everybody*!" She broke the hug and moved quickly to the phone.

"C'mon, Harley, make the call! It's close enough to eight o'clock."

When he reached her side and unfolded the paper, she asked, "Whose phone number is it?"

"A close friend of Mother's, Lidia Robins." Harley picked up the phone and dialed the number. After a couple of seconds, he said, "Hello! Lidia? Yeah, this is Harley Danziger. Is my mother there?" There was a silent moment, then, "Hi, Mom! It's really good to hear your voice!... I know! How have you been? And Dad? Yes, Lena's here, of course. Hold on, here she is." He handed Leanna the phone. "Here you go... *Lena,*" he whispered.

She took the phone with trembling hands. "Hi, Mom."

The birthday phone call was a glorious success filled with beautiful assurances and sweet relief. Daniel also spoke with his mother, bringing his "lost" status to a close and an answer to his mother's prayers.

After the phone call ended, the party continued. Daniel and Harley caught up. One more little oddity was Julia's attention to Daniel. Only Leanna noticed.

After an hour or so of the usual having of a party and most of a bottle of champagne, two people remained. They sat, comfortable with each other, saying something now and then, using small talk to be together a little longer. Then, at the moment of a perfect exit, Kyle moved to kiss her goodnight. She knew he would do that, hoped he wouldn't, and regretted her impulsive arm against his advances.

Later, in her bed, in the unblinking loneliness of the dark morning hours, she called herself stupid. She lay there burning in her regret that she ruined the opportunity to experience her anxious desire to be normal. Even the two quiet trips to the kitchen and obnoxious bottle of red relief were of little consequence. Gravitating to the wine was just another regret to pile on, adding more reason to stare at the ceiling or keep an eye on the time.

Five o'clock was stealing through the darkness to rattle her alarm clock, ending her fight with another sleepless night. Tomorrow would be a long day working her ten-hour shift at the restaurant.

She couldn't lay there another second. She kicked the covers to the foot of the bed and ran for the shower.

The ten o'clock coffee break came as usual, and groups of men invaded the restaurant. Leanna picked out Kyle as he came through the door, alone and reserved. Had she not been so busy pouring coffee and dishing up cinnamon rolls and doughnuts, she would have felt her heartbeat jerk faster.

Kyle, having always sat on a spinner stool at the counter, chose to find an empty booth in Leanna's section. She saw him settle and, after pouring a couple of refills, carried the pot to his table.

"Hi," she said and filled a cup.

He responded with his own, "Hi, how are you this morning?"

Now, she was aware of her rushing heartbeat. "Pretty good so far," she said. "Whether I make it through the day or not is another question."

He grinned mischievously. "You should have gone to bed earlier. Staying up till all hours of the night with some man is not the way to get your rest."

That startled her. The alarms going off in her defense system switched her demeanor to a posture of retreat. She stared at him red-faced and asked if he wanted anything else. He recognized the sudden change in her, and his teasing expression fell like demolition sheetrock. There was silence between them as she looked around, suddenly concerned with the care of her other customers. He cleared his throat with a nervous grunt and peered down into his coffee. The expression in his voice was one of defeat. "Yeah, I'll take a cinnamon roll."

She whirled around and headed for the kitchen. Her embarrassment was overwhelming, not only because of his insinuation but also because of her reaction. She was giving herself a talking-to before she got halfway to the kitchen.

He was only trying to be funny. A friendly gesture, dummy. You made him feel awful.

She was angry with herself and burst through the kitchen's swinging doors. Julia, on the kitchen side of the doors, had also reached the doors at the same time. There was a near collision.

"Oops! Sorry! My fault," Leanna exclaimed as she bustled by. Julia was mystified and silent.

Leanna quickly dished up the cinnamon roll and hurried back to Kyle, anxious to apologize. She set the roll on his table and wasted no time giving her apology.

"I'm sorry, Kyle. You probably think I'm a pretty awful person. I know you didn't mean anything by what you said, so don't pay any attention to my silly ways. I hope you won't think too badly of me."

His smile beamed with relief. "Hey, no, not at all. I should have been a little more sensitive to what you call your silly ways. There's nothing silly about you at all, Leanna. And I apologize for being so thoughtless. I was only trying to make you laugh."

"I know. I'm sorry."

He took a sip of coffee, and she looked toward the kitchen to see if her boss was watching her. He wasn't, but Julia was.

"I'm too busy to talk 'cause I gotta get back to my customers. Sorry." She moved away, and he called after her.

"May I come over this evening?"

She turned and stared at him for a moment. Then she nodded, fully aware of the furious pounding in her chest.

CHAPTER 41

She had made an effort all day to listen to people in the restaurant for anything that might be said about the accident. She had heard nothing. The radio, too, had reported nothing. The absence of the subject was as aggravating as the other shoe that wouldn't drop. She consoled herself with the notion that if God were going to run over her with a train, He would at least let her hear it coming. She pounded on the hissing snow-filled TV set with her aching fist again. Maybe this would be the one to shake it into action. It wasn't.

She yelled at it. "You crippled creep!" then kicked the stand it sat on in the leg. She picked up an empty glass off the stand and took it to the kitchen sink. She was rinsing the residue of wine from it when the knock on the front door came. It shook her insides and caused her to stand frozen for a moment. First, it was the vision in her mind of policemen standing on her porch, guns drawn, ready to throw her to the ground and handcuff her. Then the probability, nearly as threatening to her emotional comfort, was that Kyle, in all his male presence, was there. He confused her. She wished she hadn't let him come over. Why had she nodded yes? Because she wanted him to, dammit! She liked being with him! The knock came again, louder this time. She moved toward the door, wondering what she would do this time, hoping it would be normal.

Normal? Not a chance. Shaking like this isn't normal!

She opened the door and felt pleased it was him.

"Hey, Kyle." She stood there, not knowing what to do. She wanted him to come in but didn't want to deal with the commotion it would cause in her.

"Hi, Leanna," he said and waited. She stared at him. "May I come in?" he asked. Good manners intervened. She impulsively stepped aside, and he came in smiling all the while.

He bowed slightly. "Good evening, Miss Danziger." He spoke, attempting to mock the tone of highfalutin society as he reached for her hand. "Would you honor me with the pleasure of your company this evening, my dear?" he said as he raised her hand to touch the back of it with his lips. She giggled. She couldn't help herself. He sounded like a drunken English butler. Besides, her high anxiety needed a vent.

His face turned red, and he laughed louder than she. "I never said I was an actor."

She laughed again. He still held her hand, and she made no effort to take it from him. Though the situation felt strange to her, she remained aware of the feel of his warm hand and her desire to keep it. She also smelled dusty hay. To ignore it occurred to her, but the unknown result of that overwhelmed her bravery. She jerked her hand away suddenly as if he had clamped it to hold her captive.

"Oh, sorry," he apologized

She was embarrassed. "S'okay," she said and took a seat on the couch.

He remained standing and became aware of the hissing TV set. "Have you heard any more about the accident?"

She shook her head. "No, not all day, and I can't get the dumb TV to work, of course."

He moved over to the TV and turned it to access the back of it. He bent down to get a better look at the cable connections, then began twisting the nuts to test them for tightness. The reception did not improve. He turned the TV back to its prior position. He fiddled with all the knobs for a few seconds, but the machine showed no sign of recovery.

"No, sir, it's not gonna work." Gazing at it, he added, "You know what?" Then, he turned to Leanna and said, "I could take it with me and drop it off tomorrow at a good repair shop I know to see if it can be fixed."

"That would be great except for one thing. I don't have the money to spend on it."

"Hey, who knows? Your rich uncle might die and leave you all his money before they get it fixed.

She grinned. "Oh, sure. I don't have a rich uncle."

He began looking around for the receptacle it was plugged into, spotted it, and pulled the plug. She was amazed, stood up, and protested.

"What are you doing?"

He lifted it from its perch. "I'm gonna put it in my car so I won't forget it when I leave."

She became slightly alarmed. "I'm serious, Kyle. If you put it in the shop, I won't be able to get it out."

"If it gets left, you won't be losing anything. It's not any good this way. If you *don't* take it to the shop, we know for sure that it won't get fixed... ever, right?" Then, his manner became more gently reassuring. "Trust me. If it gets fixed, it will be gotten out of the shop."

He carried it out the door, saying, "Come and get the car door for me." Mystified, she quietly followed him to his car. As she walked, she gave in to the obvious probability that he intended to pay for the repairs. She felt pleased that he would do that for her, but at the same time, she warned herself.

They loaded the TV in the back seat of his new Chevy Bel Air and then returned to the apartment.

Kyle had always known that Leanna Danziger was cold-shouldered. She was either shy or had something major against men. He didn't know which but figured it wouldn't hurt to find out. He was extremely taken with her. She was beautiful and smart. Someone he could imagine himself with for life, even though she seemed to have no social life whatsoever.

He knew very little about her, at least nothing he could be positive about. The one time he cornered Julia into talking about her, he only learned that she was a farm girl from Kansas who was running away from her Mennonite father. He knew about the Mennonites. He had always heard that they were extremely religious and exceptionally good people.

He was twenty-three years old, had come a long way toward getting his wild oats sown, and was leaning toward settling down. He had a good job selling insurance. He made enough money to get a good start on saving up to buy a house. He thought he and Leanna could make beautiful children together.

He first needed to get to know her and let her get to know him. These were his intentions with Leanna Danziger as they spent the next two and a half hours together talking. They told and asked, confessed, and denied. They shared moments of laughter as well as serious embarrassment. They drank a little wine and endured a little silence. Never once did one feel the need to resist the other as they grew closer and closer.

If there had been a moment that Leanna could have called "anxious," it would have been when they stood at the door to say goodnight. She became nervous about his lingering. She was afraid he might try to force himself on her for a kiss goodnight. She became preoccupied with strategizing a defense as he talked and talked and talked. However, her fears were unfounded. He eventually made a gentleman's exit into the "goodnight" while she stood on the porch and waved the last farewell.

She went back into the apartment. After closing the door, she leaned against it momentarily as if to give the old friendly room a chance to applaud her debut into a whole new world. She felt good about herself. A rare feeling

Her gaze fell on the empty wine-stained glass that sat on the end table by the couch. She picked it up and went to the kitchen sink to rinse it and leave it there. She laid it in the sink and stood looking at it for a moment, acutely aware of the bottle standing on the counter close by.

What harm could it do? Might help me sleep.

She filled the glass half full and took it to bed with her.

After Kyle returned the repaired TV set, they watched both newscasts every night for the entire week. They hoped to finally hear that the police had arrested someone for the crime. But it was like it had never happened. The hit-and-run crime remained unsolved, going cold. The devastated parents would never know. Without closure, their lives would be under a dark cloud from now on, and she was to blame. Kyle talked with her for hours, using every kind of argument known to man, but couldn't pull her out of the pit of guilt into which she had pushed herself. He continued to try, even though the reason seemed to have changed into an excuse to be with her.

They sat in Kyle's car at a Little Davy's drive-in, each sipping a large Pepsi. A trip to Little Davy's had become a pleasant nightly outing. However, that night, the atmosphere was quiet and gloomy. Her Pepsi cup was still half full, and she sat slumped in the seat, knees up against the dash, staring out through the windshield. Kyle was swamped with her depression.

Peering down into the lingering small chunks of ice in his cup, he said, "So, if you go ask the police about the accident, they're gonna wanna know why you're interested. And if you're honest, you will tell them your story. They'll find out you had a blackout, and you will lose your driver's license. And that's even if you haven't done anything wrong at all."

"I know. If I go to the police, the sure thing is that I'll lose my license." They returned to silence for a little while longer. Then Leanna continued.

"But it will be worth finding out if I did it."

"Leanna, you've got to quit basing every conclusion on the assumption that you probably did it. Start thinking you probably *didn't* do it!"

"But what if I did? You know they will find out who ran over that little boy sooner or later. When they come and arrest me, I can tell them I didn't know I did it, but they won't believe me. They'll think I'm the awful person who knew she did it and tried to get away with it.

"But what if you didn't do it?"

"Then I'll celebrate! And I'll go on with my sorry life. At least I'll be able to live with myself knowing I didn't cause that poor family the grief they must be going through."

He heard the crack in her voice and knew that tears would glisten in her eyes if he looked at her. He hated to see her cry. He turned his face to her, and she looked away. "Leanna, I don't want you to take the chance. I don't want to lose you."

What? For a moment, it was as if she were some kind of machine, and he had flipped her off switch. She was so still he couldn't tell if she was breathing. There are times when fifteen seconds is a long time. Then she sat up straight and gave him a long look, tears on her cheeks.

Her voice was very quiet. "I can't believe you said that." At first, he didn't know if that was a negative or positive remark. With her, he never knew for sure. But then her expression, despite the tears, showed that she was pleased. He reached out his hand to her, and she hesitated, staring at it as if she didn't know what to do. Then, she carefully accepted it and looked at him with awe.

"No one's ever said anything like that to me before."

"I meant it. I like you very much." Now, she was embarrassed and, at the same time, thrilled by the actual reality of what had just happened to her.

He was not aware of her emotional state and continued his effort to talk her into staying away from the police. Even so, he was not about to let go of her hand.

"So now you know why I don't want you to go to the police. It's just asking for trouble. I think that you couldn't have been there at that intersection when the accident happened. You were probably with me in the Pizza Hut."

That jerked her insides and locked her attention to him. She was suddenly excited. "Now, that would be really nice to know! So how could we find out the time it happened?" Asking the police for that information would be a good way, but that was exactly what he didn't want her to do.

"Maybe the newspaper would have that information," he offered. Her eyes shone with pleasure as she became aware of his sincere concern for solving her problem. "I could go there tomorrow and try to find out," he added.

"Oh wow, Kyle, that would be great! Do you remember what time we were at the Pizza Hut?"

"Oh yeah, it was almost four o'clock."

"So, if it happened after four, I couldn't have been there!" Then she shook her head in quick jerks. "Oh, wait a minute! I just remembered something! It was twenty after three when I was at Hogan Street before I got to the Pizza Hut, so any time after that, I'm safe!"

"So, three-twenty is the time we're talking about..."

He held her hand as she nodded, and they got quiet.

After a moment longer, she gently removed her hand and said, "I guess I better get back home. I need to get up early."

"Sure," he said, straightened up behind the wheel, and started the car. He backed out from under the canopy and drove into the street. Leanna, still excited, broke the silence.

"So, when will you go to the newspaper office tomorrow?"

"First thing. I'll tell you what I find out when I come to the restaurant for coffee."

"Perfect," she said. "If you don't see me there, I'll probably have died from a nervous breakdown."

He smiled. "I don't think you need to worry."

Regardless of her revved-up emotions, Leanna kept a tight restraint on her tendency to jabber. That and the mulling over tomorrow's possibilities produced silence as they drove to Leanna's apartment. Kyle wondered about his chances of getting a kiss at her front door or even an invitation. He was hopeful, and she was oblivious.

As they turned onto the street to the apartment, Leanna saw a car up ahead back out of the parking lot and drive down the street away from them.

Leanna became excited. "Hey, isn't that Daniel's car?"

Kyle peered intently into the darkness at the taillights moving ahead of them. "I can't tell," he said. "Could be." The car moved on and approached the intersection. Leanna saw a side view of the car as it turned onto the crossing street. She was pretty sure it was Daniel. She wondered why he had been to her house.

Kyle parked and turned off the engine. At first, it surprised Leanna, but then she realized he intended to get out of the car with her and walk her to her door. She turned to face him and gave him a look as if he had just told her some shocking news. Without returning her look, he opened his door and climbed out of the car.

Focused on his obvious intentions, she sat motionless, staring at what she could see of him in the open door frame. She didn't know what to do to discourage him. She wasn't sure she wanted to, and the guilt overwhelmed her. She got out of the car and started up the sidewalk, her eyes straight ahead and her legs shaky. He walked beside her.

Now, what do I do?

She was acutely aware of him close beside her. She didn't react to the contact when his arm brushed hers but anticipated his next move with dread. If he does what is usually done under this kind of boy-girl circumstance, he will take her hand. If she does what is normal, she will let him. She, however, was not normal. She wanted to be normal! All she had to do was to resist jumping out of her skin when he took her hand.

Don't jerk or gasp or stop. Just take it all in like it's the millionth time a man has walked hand in hand with you.

And that is exactly what she did when his hand slipped into hers. She did not flinch outwardly, but her insides were in a frenzy. She was taken in by the pleasant feel of his warm hand. At the same time, she felt an overwhelming impulse to jerk away and run. Reaching the porch steps and engaging her mind to step up restarted her, and she exhaled. She hoped he hadn't noticed. They were on the porch and at the door when he let go of her hand. She dug her cluster of keys out of her pocket and, after isolating the door key, started to poke it into the lock. He covered that hand with his, and she looked up at his face. His expression was one of hope, but what Leanna saw rose from deep in her mind, and the ghost of her hay loft monster nodded to her father to hold her head down.

The dusty hay made her sneeze, then sneeze again… and again. Kyle stepped back, and the door keys fell with a dull jingle on the concrete porch. As Leanna bent forward, her hands covering her face, she sneezed three more times. Kyle was taken aback and thought it unusual that she sneezed so much. Then, he became a little alarmed. He started reaching out to her to help somehow, but she ran off the porch toward the parking lot. Kyle was astonished. He called after her. "Leanna? What's wrong?"

She was out into the street, oblivious to his calling and the danger of possible traffic. She was across the street and into the trees of the vacant wooded area in what seemed to him an instant. She disappeared, and he began to run with more urgency. He had no idea what happened. Had he scared her? Where was she going? Did she know what lay in the dark, hiding in those woods? He couldn't see her in the darkness but could only run blindly in the direction she had gone.

CHAPTER 42

She'd been standing at the door bent over, sneezing from the dusty hay in the loft. The next thing she knew, a loud, blaring car horn startled her. Looking up, she found herself partway out into the street, obstructing traffic. She was stunned!

She didn't know where she was! Blinding lights coming at her! Another car! She scrambled back to the curb, stumbled over it, and landed on her hands and knees in weeds filled with stickers. She got to her feet, ready to run into the trees in front of her. The streetlights glanced off the trunks and branches, showing her the outline of this place she suddenly recognized. She realized that she somehow came to be on the other side of the wooded lot across the street from her apartment. She stopped.

Oh no! No, no, no! Not again!

She'd had another episode. That's the second one lately. It had been years, and she had hoped the one she had last week was a straggler, the final heartbeat of a dying monster. What was worse was that Kyle had seen this one.

She peered intently into the darkness of the woods for a sign of him looking for her. She saw nothing but the vague shapes of the trees that seemed to be standing patiently, waiting for her to do something. She forced her eyes to look deeper into the black woods and listened intently for crackling footsteps that would tell her of Kyle's approach.

She finally saw a blotted form coming out of the woods, moving toward the street fifty or sixty yards to her right. There weren't many lights along the street, and she couldn't tell if it was Kyle, but who else would it be?

She quickly hunkered down and twisted on the balls of her feet to examine the dark woods to her left. She saw very little detail, but she had walked around these woods many times, using up Sunday afternoons to explore out of curiosity. It really didn't matter what was there anyway. She had to go in. She stayed down, duck-walking in the knee-high weeds, keeping an eye on the spot at the edge of the woods where she had seen the figure that she assumed was Kyle.

She couldn't let him see her. How could she face him after showing him how crazy she is? She couldn't handle the disapproval that she knew would be there in his manner. His judgment would crush her. She saw him walk out to the street as she went back into the cover of the trees, nearly vanishing. She rose to stand up straight and quickly and quietly headed for the apartment.

Kyle came out of the woods in a rush, stopping at the street's curb. He was shocked at the emptiness of the space. He had expected to see Leanna standing there, having nowhere else to go, preparing to go back. He looked anxiously up and down the dim street. Houses lined the other side of the street for blocks in either direction with a sidewalk in front of them. The sidewalk was empty, tapering off into the night and disappearing both ways. There was no telling where she had gone. He stood perplexed, like a traveler in a strange land waiting for a bus that had already been there and gone.

He felt awful. He didn't know what he had done to cause her to run away, but he felt responsible for her being out in the dark alone and vulnerable. A zap of panic struck him. Who knows what might happen to her? He had to find her!

He started at a trot, running to the street with no plan of action. Not knowing which direction she had taken, he just ran, searching the darkness ahead with his eyes. He moved with blind hope that she would, somehow, magically appear. After a hundred yards or so, he turned around and went back the way he had come. He continued running in that direction for another hundred yards.

He stopped, and as he stood bent over to catch his breath, he came to a more reasonable train of thought. This was crazy: Running around in the dark in circles like a windup monkey with a broken leg. He would never find her this way. She won't go far. She has to go back to her apartment, and she will.

He started walking back to the edge of the woods. She'll be okay. She's probably already on her way back home. After a few minutes, he entered the woods and started back to the apartment, feeling guilty about abandoning a friend. More than a friend in this case. He could only hope she would be there when he got there... or soon after.

Upon seeing Kyle's car still parked in front of the apartment, she stopped before stepping out into the open. She examined the scene before her very closely, hoping to see him but at the same time dreading the results. What would she say to explain her running away? What would *he* do? She couldn't see him anywhere, not on the porch, not in his car... nowhere. Had he actually gone after her? Couldn't have.

He doesn't care that *much!*

She turned her head to look back into the woods behind her and listened intently. She saw and heard nothing but the silent, knowing darkness. She turned and examined her front yard more thoroughly and again saw no sign of life. She stepped out guardedly and stopped.

What if he's someplace where I can't see him?

She quickly stepped back into the woods, indecisive and angry with herself.

Girl, what're you gonna do, wear a hole in the world walking back and forth?

She stood a few seconds longer, clinging desperately to the safe feeling of the dark woods. She turned, stepped back to a large elm, and squatted in the crisp leaves at its feet. She could clearly see the area in front of her apartment; she watched for Kyle.

Kyle came to the edge of the trees, and just before he stepped out into the open, he saw her move back into the trees' cover. He was elated. There she was! He stopped, took a few steps in her direction, and then stopped again.

A dawning came over him, causing him to stare at her activity and frown. She seemed to be hiding. He glanced over at the apartment. There was no one there from which to hide. His car was there. It would be obvious to her that he was still around somewhere. He turned his attention back to her but lost sight of her. She was hiding from *him*, his return! Was she? He imagined himself calling her name but didn't dare. The risk of her ducking and running at the sound of his voice was too great. He wouldn't be able to handle it the second time.

He felt some panic begin to stir his insides. He was going to lose her! He had thought she had feelings for him. How could he have been so fooled? One minute, she had made him feel close and cozy, and the next minute, she was running from him like he had attacked her. He had only taken her hand to touch her skin, to feel something of her. He had gone too far, in a hurry, too anxious to give her something of himself. Apparently, way too much. She was... what, complicated? Probably not. He stood staring at the spot in the woods where she had disappeared.

She just doesn't like me! Not enough, anyway.

He had no idea what to do! This was a feeling unfamiliar to him, Kyle Brungardt. The guy who always knew which button to push or at least the one that wouldn't kill him if he did. Now, the mistake he'd made hurt like hell. Well, there was one thing he knew for sure. He wasn't going to make the same mistake twice. The pain was more than he wanted.

He walked out into the open ground, keeping his eyes on his car, and crossed the street. He reached his car and turned to gaze for a moment at the spot in the woods where he had last seen her. He got into his car, backed into the street, and drove away.

Leanna had felt relieved when she saw him come out of the woods. She no longer had to wonder what to do. She also felt her attraction to him raise a couple of notches. He had actually gone after her and tried to find her. That was amazing to her. As she watched him walk across the street, she wanted to call his name and reward his effort. She was hesitant, and he had reached his car by the time she had talked herself into it. When he turned and looked straight at her, then got into his car, she was jolted as if struck by lightning. He knew she was there and was leaving!

She stood motionless, absorbing the shock. She watched the taillights of his car disappear into the dark street. She wanted to cry.

She slowly regained awareness of where she was and what she was doing. There was a slight breeze whispering its presence in the woods behind her, and the lights went out in the house next door to her apartment. A car horn honked over by the playground at the far end of the block. There were several seconds of silence before its doors were slammed, and its engine was revved into motion. Someone other than her was on the planet, but it didn't feel like it.

She walked to the apartment and spotted her cluster of keys lying on the porch where she had dropped them. She picked them up, unlocked the door, and went inside. Leaning her back against the closed door, she closed her eyes and listened to the sound that lived with her. There was more silence than outside, more darkness, more hiding. *There's Only one to defend, only one to kill: easier for the attacker, more dangerous for the victim.*

She slid her hand on the wall, found the light switch, and flipped it. The transition to reality was startling. The light revealed everything in the room around her. Wood and plastic, flesh and bone, glared at her. That reality was a result of the light, but the dark revealed what was inside *her*; that's what she needed to see. She stood momentarily, her finger still on the light switch, and flipped it off again. There she was! As always, she was worthless, weak, and crazy, and condemned to Hell. She was at the end of the line, waiting her turn.

My turn may be a while. Could get boring. Maybe I could help it along and speed things up a little bit.

She easily navigated the dark, familiar room, walking on shaky legs.

Hope the world made enough wine.

She reached out with a trembling hand to the refrigerator, pulled it open, and drew the nearly full bottle of wine to her breast. She embraced its offering, looking forward to her rebirth as another drunkard.

CHAPTER 43

Half an hour passed by in the night unnoticed before the knock on the door.

Kyle? Probably not. A sexual predator with a chainsaw? Who cares?

She turned the knob and pulled the unlocked door open.

"Hey! You *are* home!" Daniel's shadowed face wore a barely visible pale smile. "I thought I saw a light come on when I drove by a while ago."

Leanna stepped back without speaking, making room for Daniel to enter. Half in, half out, he tried to see her expression in the dark, sensing a darkness in her mood. He attempted some light-heartedness.

"Whatsa matter, didn't you pay your light bill?"

Her response was a let-down, a quiet "Hi Daniel." Head-bowed, she retreated to the kitchen table, not bothering to flip the light on. He stepped into the room, closed the door, and just as he flipped the light on, he saw her raise the wine bottle to her lips. The light did not distract her. He watched her take a swallow, then lower the bottle to the table and gaze at him from what seemed to him an expression of total defeat. Not an ounce of defiance.

He felt alarm rise inside him as he would if he saw a child wander too close to the edge. But she was not a child, not his little sister anymore. Her wanderings were those of an adult who was as aware of the edge as he was and seemed unconcerned. He mustn't jump on her; he had to respect her judgment. Maybe ask why. He went to the table and took the chair across from her. She was nonresponsive to his activity, as if she were too busy to notice him. It made him feel intrusive. At the same time, he was under the impression that she couldn't care less.

He searched for words, but a single question glared from his worry. "What are you doing, Leanna?"

She lifted the wine again and tipped another swallow into her brain.

Her speech had not yet been affected by the wine. "If youda held that question just a bit longer, I wouldna had the brains to answer it, then everything woulda been just fine." She frowned at him. "But ya didn't, didja?" She shook her head. "I used to wish Ida never started talkin' again,

274

but it doesn't matter anymore. I ain't got nothun to say anyway. So, if you wanna know what I'm doin' you'll just have to watch me to find out." Holding the bottle by the neck, she took another swig and lowered it. She tilted the top away from her to examine the contents. It was still half full, or maybe half empty.

What's the difference?

She took another swig.

Daniel burned with anger. He wanted to swat the bottle out of her hand, take her by the shoulders, and shake her. But he just sat across the table from her, his hands knotted into fists on top of the table. He watched his beloved sister hate herself beyond reason. Why was he just sitting there?

He spoke in an even, controlled tone. "So why *did* you start talking again?"

The bottle came down from her mouth. She hesitated for a moment, and then she popped it against the tabletop. Daniel was surprised that it didn't shatter. She stared at him intensely. Nobody but she had ever asked her that question.

Without moving anything but her mouth, she spoke. "Now, there's a question worth talking about."

She pulled on her memory, trying to extract from it some event of that day that would give her a hint of the answer to his very unfamiliar question. What had been so important to cause her, on that day, to make a noise that would draw God's attention to her? She'd been hiding from Him all that time. Was it the dog? No, not the dog. The dog had died because she spoke, not the other way around. It was before Butch got run over on the highway. She had been pissed at Sam because he hadn't given her a chance to tell him that she was not quitting school.

"It was school," she said. "I needed to talk to Sam to tell him that I was going to school whether he liked it or not." She blinked at Daniel, waiting for his response. None came. She was disappointed. *Guess he doesn't care that much... or believe me.*

To tell the truth, she didn't either, but it wouldn't hurt to have one last talk. Besides, it seemed like the wine made it easy.

"I never got the chance to tell him. But Mom and I talked a lot that day... and Katy too. They made me see that I wasn't gonna get around Sam to go to school."

She remembered the new feeling that talking with her mother had brought her. The wonderful feeling was that she belonged and was a valuable family member. That was the moment she had committed to joining her life with theirs. Letting herself be pulled down the road with them to wherever. Starting to talk again had made that wonderful miracle happen.

So, what did she do? She messed it up, hurting them as she messed up along the way. She took another drink of the wine. Forgetting Daniel for the moment, she remembered what she had just done to Kyle... to herself. Now, who was killing her? It looks like God would let her take over and do it herself.

Daniel sat still, hoping she would let the mystery of the barn slip from her wine-careless mind and tell him what happened. He was sure it was the root of her problem, the reason she was so miserable. She was silent. He wondered what was going on in her head at the moment. Were there pictures of what happened in the barn flashing in her mind? Was she talking to herself about how she had to keep the secret? Or maybe she was on the brink of telling everything about what she and Andrew were doing. He could help her make the leap.

"I remember Andrew like a picture hanging on the walls of my mind. He was a mischievous little guy. He was a lot like Harley, always cooking up something and getting into trouble all the time. Do you remember?"

Of course, she didn't remember. How could he think she would remember? And at the moment, she didn't want to try to remember. She had other disasters to think about.

He just wants to get me started talking about what we did in the hayloft. Ain't gonna happen. Sam knows, and that's enough. More than enough!

She was beginning to feel the effects of the alcohol in her system, and she was becoming a blob on the kitchen chair. Her head was hanging; it was difficult to keep it balanced. She lifted a heavy hand to the bottle on the table, got hold of it, and let her arm hang there. She closed her eyes. Might as well, she couldn't see anyway: too much spinning.

She heard Daniel stand up. There was silence; then she heard his footsteps leaving the room. They got to the door, and she heard it open and close. He wasn't, she decided, gonna waste any more time on the drunk. She didn't care. She just... didn't... care. *Who cares? Good for you Danny boy.*

Her two-ton head was now resting on the arm that hung from the neck of the bottle, and she *did not* begin to cry. She did not cry for Kyle. She did not cry for Andrew. She did not cry for herself. She did not cry for her mother or the little boy on the bike. There were no tears, but there was plenty of wine. Before passing out at the kitchen table, the last thing on her mind was that she could at least do something about the little boy... first thing in the morning.

CHAPTER 44

The "first thing in the morning" didn't come until two o'clock in the afternoon. When she opened her eyes, she was confused by the bright light of day. The time of morning that she usually woke offered only the dim sunrays of dawn. Then, realization punched her in the stomach. The time to go to work was long gone. She jerked to a sitting position and was shocked to find herself on the couch, fully dressed.

What time is it? She couldn't see the clock on the kitchen wall. Last night popped into her memory, her head roaring its protest of her upright position.

Oh no! She grabbed her head with both hands and squeezed her eyes shut. Her Job! She had just lost her job!

No, no, no! Don't let this happen! Damit! Damit! Damit!

She sprang from the couch, hungover and all, and stumbled to the phone. She got a look at the clock on the way. *Five after two? In the afternoon?*

She quickly dialed the restaurant, praying Julia would answer. She waited anxiously while the ringtone buzzed four times. She heard Julia's voice: "Hello, Reeves restaurant. How may I help...?"

"Julia! Am I fired?"

Julia was silent for a moment. "Well, I'll be darned you are still alive. I've been trying to call you all day."

"What did Mr. Reeves say?"

"He was not a happy camper. What's goin' on? Where are you?"

"I'm home! Will it do me any good to go to work in the morning?"

"Of course. He's not gonna fire you if you have a good reason for not showing up."

"Then I might as well start looking for another job. I don't have a good reason."

Julia's heart skipped a beat, afraid she knew the reason. "What did you do, Leanna?"

Leanna felt the regret beginning to creep into her insides. Another lie was about to slip from her lips. "I was up most of the night... sick. The strength of her lie was pale, invalid. Julia heard the quiet weakness but didn't challenge it. Not in a direct way, at least. She was sarcastic again.

"With what? The flu or something, I'll bet."

"I don't know. I'm okay now... except for a headache. I just now woke up."

"Well, that sounds like a good reason to me, so what are you worried about? Show up tomorrow and see what happens."

"Yeah, I guess so. See yuh, bye." She heard Julia's "bye" and hung up. She was sure Julia had not believed her and thought she had probably gotten drunk.

As she got into some fresh clothes, she suddenly remembered what she had decided to do first thing this morning: the police! She needed to talk to the police. She finished dressing, did her makeup, and left the apartment, ignoring the hangover.

In her car, she became nervous, and the squeezing in her stomach made her nauseous. She fought to appease it, but that only made it worse. By the time she parked across the street from the police station, she was sick. She wanted to go back home.

Twenty minutes later, she was still in her car, feeling a little better. Good enough to go in and face whatever the police would do. She exited the car, slammed the door, and leaned against it.

The building she faced was a giant two-story gray stone monster. No windows made it a blind monster that could not distinguish the innocent from the guilty. Its double glass doors swallowed you whole and gobbled you up into the innards of law enforcement without prejudice or favoritism. She thought she knew what a lamb-to-the-slaughter felt like.

She stood, mentally clinging to the car in case she was just having a nightmare and would need time to wake up before the monster grabbed her.

She finally started across the street and was startled by the blast of a car horn. Her wide eyes saw the car, and she jumped back, slamming her back against her car.

Good lord, watch where you're going... Leanna!

She carefully looked down the street both ways, then trotted safely across.

She reached the glass doors, jerked one open, and disappeared into the monster's belly.

In front of her was a counter. A slender, dark-haired woman in her fifties, wearing a police uniform, stood behind the counter staring at her. The words INFORMATION DESK were painted black on a board above the counter. She walked to the counter. The woman's hard stare was locked on Leanna all the way.

There was a hint of annoyance in the woman's voice, a blank expression on her face.

"May I help you?"

Leanna was hesitant. "I... uh... don't know."

Nothing about the woman changed. It was like the film in an old home movie projector getting stuck. She stared patiently at Leanna, making her even more uncomfortable. She wanted to turn and run... and run and run. She turned from the woman but did not take a step. She squeezed her eyes shut, and her hands became bone-hard fists. She forced herself to stay put.

The woman couldn't see the fierce private battle in which Leanna was engaged. She only saw this young woman in front of her who seemed frightened, confused, and desperate.

"Miss, are you alright?" That did it. The voice infused reality into Leanna. A few more seconds, and she would have run.

"Miss?"

Leanna turned back to the woman and nodded. "Yes, I'm just nervous."

"Did something happen to you? Someone hurt you?"

"No, I guess... I need to talk to someone... about the accident."

The woman became very attentive. "Which accident would that be?"

At that point, a uniformed officer came into view behind the woman. She turned her face toward him. "Leo, would you come here a minute?"

The officer stopped walking and turned his attention to the woman. He started toward her. "Sure. What's up?"

With a sideways motion of her head, she indicated Leanna. "This young lady wants to speak to someone, an officer, about an accident."

The officer came to stand beside the woman, his eyes on Leanna, "Did you have an accident?"

Leanna opened her mouth to speak but realized that what she was about to give for an answer would sound ridiculous. Her mind scrambled around for a sane answer but failed. There was no other way to say it.

"I don't know," she said quietly.

The cop's expression was blank. "I'm sorry. Did you say you don't know?"

"What I mean is... I'm not sure." She swallowed the lump in her throat. The cop continued to study her. Leanna glanced at the woman. She looked puzzled also.

The cop persisted, "Do you mean you're not sure there was an accident, or you're not sure you were involved in one?"

Her scalp tingled with goosebumps. *Involved!* It sounded official, so matter of fact. Like they had stamped it on her forehead, that way, there would be no mistake when they sorted her out to be put where she belonged. INVOLVED. She was feeling light-headed and weak in her knees. Panic began to swell around her mind, squeezing the oxygen out of her. She had to pant! She could not hear the words "RUN, RUN," but they were in her bones and muscles, pushing and pulling.

She suddenly found herself running. As she approached her car, she caught herself from slamming into it with the palms of her hands. She was stunned to the same degree as always when returning to reality. She spun around to look behind her at the traffic in the street she had just unconsciously crossed. There was only one car... and the policeman on the other side waiting for it to pass.

He yelled at her, "Hey, stay right there!" She stood there and waited for him to reach her. He came trotting up to her and grabbed her arm.

He spoke with a tone of warning. "What do you think you're doing? If you have information concerning an accident, you are obligated under law to tell me."

She felt the intimidation that he had intended. "I'm sorry. I didn't mean to run. It just happened."

"Please come with me back to the station." Still holding her by the arm, he took her back across the street and into the police station.

He led her to a room deeper into the building and sat her at a table. She had seen this on TV before; nothing *good* ever happened in that room.

The officer sat across the table. He took a small hand-sized notepad and a pen from his shirt pocket. "What is your name?"

"Leanna Danziger." He wrote in his pad: her name, she assumed.

"Now, Leanna, do you want to tell me about your accident?"

"That's what I came here to find out. I'm not sure I was in an accident."

"Explain yourself."

Leanna heaved a shaky sigh. "There was a little boy, Lonnie Schaffer, who was run over on his bicycle, and I'm worried that I may have been the one who did it."

"Are you telling me you might have but don't know? How is that possible?"

Leanna's hands were on the table, clenched in tight fists. Her voice trembled. "On the day it happened, I had a spell where I blacked out, and when I woke up, I was driving my car in the neighborhood where it happened."

The policeman sat silent momentarily, studying her, looking for signs of lying. He saw nothing in her body language or facial expression that indicated that she was straining under the burden of deception.

"I see that you are telling the truth, and you really believe that you may have been involved. What kind of vehicle were you driving?" A pickup? Car? What?"

"Car. A green, 49 Plymouth."

The policeman leaned back in his chair and smiled. "You can relax," he said softly. The vehicle that ran over the Schaffer boy was a pickup or a small truck. "But...," he said hesitatingly. Then, leaning forward, he continued, "I need to ask you some questions."

Leanna jerked inside with elation at his first words: "A pickup or truck..." Then the "But..." froze her rise to joy and made her swallow hard. She locked her gaze on his face and waited for a punch. It came, but it was only a glancing bump in the pit of her stomach.

Questions about what?

"You said you blacked out. What did you mean by that?"

She suddenly remembered the possibility of losing her driver's license. Her mind spun around in a rising panic, unable to manufacture words for her mouth. All she could think was, *they're gonna find out, and I'm gonna lose my license.* Those were not words for her mouth. She couldn't say *that.* She opened her mouth, but for a moment, there was nothing in there.

She stammered. "Uh... I... I... I uh...!" She shook her head and heaved a sigh in surrender. "You're gonna take my driver's license away, aren't you?"

Observing in this girl what he thought was guilt, the cop said, "Now, why would I do that? Did you break the law? Did you do something you're not telling me?" She was silent, thinking now. Her brain had rebooted itself. She had just transformed from fugitive to defendant. "No, not really."

"Had you been drinking? Were you drunk? Is that why you blacked out?"

"No! I wasn't drunk! I just... lost track of time, that's all." She could see he wasn't going to believe her. The cop stared accusation at her, smothering her. She shifted uneasily in her chair and watched her shaky hands. She knew she wasn't going to get away with this. And whatever else was going to happen, she did not want the cop to think she was a drunk.

Without looking up, she said, "I've had this condition lately, and I find myself in a place where I don't know how I got there. But it's never caused me any trouble."

The cop spoke kindly. "I see. Are you under a doctor's care?"

"No."

"You know, of course, that you can't be allowed to drive under those conditions. It's very dangerous. By your own account, you could kill someone and be aware of it only after the fact. You'll need to give me your driver's license." Then she realized that she had left her purse in the car, which was an irritating thing she often did.

"It's in my car," she said.

The cop let his exasperation show. "You left it in your car? Is it in your purse?"

"Yes."

"And you left your purse in your car? Is your car locked?"

"No. The locks don't work."

"Do you think it will still be there?"

She started to rise from her chair. "I'll go get it."

The cop raised his hand at her. "No, you won't. I'll get it. You stay put." He rose and left the room, shaking his head.

She felt utterly defeated. She sat waiting, and what she waited for was the coming moment when she would be cut off. The cop would bring her purse to her, and she would give her driver's license over to him. She would become stripped of her independence. Her license would go into the shredder, and her freedom with it.

How will I get to work? Looking up from her trembling hands, she asked herself an even more pressing question: *How will I get home? Will I have to Walk? It's gotta be miles!*

While she waited, she began to imagine her options, preparing herself for her meager future. After pondering what to do next, she realized she had been waiting a long time.

Where in the world did he go? She left her chair and began pacing the tiny room. The soft, squeaky sound of the rubber soles of her tennis shoes against the grey tile floor was the only sign of life. She could easily imagine she was the only life on the whole earth.

Wouldn't that be something? I walk out of here to an empty world. The idea was not scary, not even regrettable.

Suddenly, the door opened, startling her as though the wall had caved in. The cop entered, holding her small leather purse. He stared at her for a second, then, with the purse, pointed at the empty chair in which she had been sitting.

"Sit," he ordered. She did so without hesitation. He moved to his chair and sat as well, tossing her purse onto the table in front of her. He also tossed her keys onto the table.

"You left your keys in the ignition. You're lucky some lowlife didn't take you up on your invitation to steal your car." He held out his hand to her. "Let me see your driver's license."

She unzipped her purse, slipped her driver's license from it, and handed it to the cop. He took it and examined it for a few seconds. He raised his face to her, looking her in the eye.

"You said your name is Leanna. Your driver's license says Lena. Explain that to me."

Feeling a sense of being on the wrong side of the law, Leanna was startled for a moment, then regained her composure. "Oh, yes. When I left home and came to Colorado, I started calling myself Leanna. Everyone knows me by *that* name. Is there something wrong with that?"

"Under these circumstances, no. But if you were pulled over by a policeman for a traffic violation, and the discrepancy came into play, you would be cited for obstruction. In other words, causing difficulty to the due process of law is illegal. I would advise you to do what you have to keep the use of your name as simple as possible. You could change your name legally or go back to using the name Lena. You'd be doing yourself a favor if you did one or the other." He stared into Leanna's eyes for a moment, then continued.

"So, you say you have blackouts, and when you become conscious again, you have no memory of how you got to where you are. And this happens while you're driving?"

"Just this once; it's never happened in my car before."

He looked at her accusingly again. "You do see how dangerous that is, don't you?"

"Yes, I do!"

"I can't let you have your license back. You will have to appear in court to get a judge's ruling on how you will be dealt with concerning driving while in the condition you described. Do you understand?"

She nodded, "Yes."

"Good. I'm going to write you a ticket for that. You will comply with the instructions on the ticket and appear in court on the date and time the ticket says. Understood?"

"Yes." He wrote the ticket and handed it to her. "Any questions?"

"No.

He stood. "We're through here. You may go."

She rose from her chair and left the room.

Out on the sidewalk, she read the ticket as if it were her obituary. Without a car, she might as well be dead. She had no idea how she was going to get home. Looking at her car parked across the street, she wondered what would happen to *it*. Was there anything in it that she needed to take with her? She couldn't think of anything, and after a moment, she stuck the ticket in her purse and started walking toward her apartment. Hanging her head, she felt beaten down by the pounding her life was giving her. That she was giving herself.

The choices she made were causing her grief beyond reason. Why was she doing this to herself? She should have ignored the responsibility that she had felt for the accident, shouldn't she? *No!* That she couldn't have done. The guilt would have destroyed her. She surely did the right thing. She had, all her life, tried to do the right thing. Except once, when she left home and came here to Colorado. And yet, that was the best thing she had ever done. She did that for herself. She got her high school diploma, didn't she? *So what?* What has that gotten her? The same job she had when she enrolled in high school. Getting an education was the right thing to do. Didn't matter! No matter what she did, she always came up short of having a positive outcome. It was like she was being set up all the time. Something would happen to her. She would do something about it, which would cause something worse or at least unexpected. She remembered when she was a teenager. She had thought that God was always setting her up for the day he would chop her head off. Now she knew that way of thinking was the hayloft messing with her mind.

And who caused the hayloft? Her father, of course. *God's little helper,* she used to call him. He's why she's made her choices. He gave her the kind of mind with which to work her life: examine, evaluate, consider, qualify, and decide which move to make in which situation. Isn't that the way she did things? Isn't that the result of what he said to her in the hayloft?

Doing this to myself? I don't think so! And even if she was, it was because of him... what he made her. She was what *he* made her! She didn't have anything to do with it. What happened in the loft was caused by her father, Sam Danziger. And her becoming Leanna Danziger is the result of what happened in the hayloft. How could she reverse that? She couldn't go back to being Lena again, no matter how messed up Leanna was.

She continued to walk toward her apartment, knowing it was a long way. Consumed by the busy workings of her mind, the city blocks slipped easily beneath her feet, almost unnoticed. She had new situations to weigh and sort. And because of the loss of her driver's license, she had hard days to face.

The two hours it took her to get home gave her time to think and finally convince herself that she couldn't do it. She moped and cried and hated herself for her way of living. After much arguing with herself, she gave up to a friend who made her struggle unnecessary. A friend she could depend on, easy to pour, easy to swallow.

Part 3

CHAPTER 45

Leanna was fifty-three years old when the seed for murder was planted in her mind. She was a recovering alcoholic, had a police record, had been "sweet sixteen and never been kissed" for thirty-seven years now, and blamed it all on Sam.

She felt old for her years. She blamed that on Sam, too. Her hair was grayer than her *mother's!* And her sister Katy, still beautiful and slender, with her long dark hair, looked ten years younger than she did. At least she had at Leanna's fiftieth birthday party.

The chair she'd been sitting in for the past hour was beginning to take its toll on her back and butt. Hospital chairs were not known for comfort, but she didn't think she should feel this bad at fifty-three.

All the years of hardship she endured because of the incident in the hayloft deeply affected her. The drunkenness for weeks at a time and the unspeakable shame in police custody for driving under the influence and without a license. These had significantly contributed to her present low self-esteem.

The pain, as she had foolishly made her long blacklist of regrets, was what had made her old before her time. The worst regret that sat on her chest and tore at her heart in the bleak, lonely nights was her running from the only man she would ever love, Kyle Brunghardt. It was all Sam's doing. It was he who made her what she is: an old maid with a record and a life so full of regret she had once tried suicide for penance. It hadn't worked. She was sure God had prevented it. Out of greed, she supposed. He would not be deprived of the pleasure of punishing her.

And Sam? God's little helper? *He has done his part well. I need to drag his wrinkled old ass up to the hayloft and chop his head off.* The thought was appalling! Now, what kind of sorry person would *think* such a thing about their *father?*

Rehab had twisted and squeezed her out through the neck of the bottle and showed her how to pour temptation down the drain. However, her opinion of Leanna Danziger remained undaunted. She could not escape her conviction. As long as she could not forgive Sam Danziger, she would always be guilty as charged and un-forgiven.

She sat in the dim light of her mother's hospital room, watching the woman she adored struggling for every breath God would hand her. *Pneumonia.*

Her mother had been sick for a week before Katy and Lewis had returned from Oklahoma to learn of it. Not realizing how bad she was and operating with an eighty-two-year-old brain, Sam had chosen to wait until Katy returned to do something about it. Leanna suspected he hadn't cared enough to take her to a doctor.

Leanna, irritated by the thought, shifted in the hard hospital chair. Maybe at eighty-two, he hadn't realized the seriousness of her condition. But even if he had, he still wouldn't have telephoned Katy or anyone else to let them know. You sure wouldn't catch Sam Danziger using an "instrument of the devil's making," no matter who was dying. Even himself... *or* his wife. And, of course, he wouldn't have contacted Leanna if they were next-door neighbors. Ever!

The brain-washed old sack, uh...! Be nice, Leanna, for your mother!

Mom's flat on her back fightin' for her life because he was more concerned about his relationship with his God. Well, he better be worried about what I'll do to him if Mom...

She couldn't say it, not even to herself. The possibility of her mother dying was unthinkable. If her mom didn't get well... it wasn't only God that Sam needed to worry about. *He will have to answer to me.*

Her back ached. She had come into the room around three-thirty in the morning and found her mother asleep, getting her oxygen from a tank. She had pulled a chair closer to the bed and had been sitting there ever since. The sight of her mother lying there in the kind of stillness where the sick lay praying for relief, and the dying waited their turn to go had made her heart ache. Her precious mother did not fit in that kind of scene. She choked back the sound of her emotion, fearing her mother might hear.

Now, she rose from the chair and stood with her lap against the bed, peering into her mother's face. The oxygen tube in her nose and the hesitant heaving of her chest caused a sob to creep from the bleak depths of her being. She swallowed hard, but she couldn't keep it in this time. Her despair moaned softly in the dim light.

"Oh, Mom, please!"

Suddenly, she thought she saw her mother move her head. Then her mouth moved to speak.

Her voice came in a weak whisper. "Katy?"

Leanna's heart thumped furiously. She spoke softly. "No, Mom, it's... Lena."

Her mother turned her face toward Leanna and opened her eyes. Expressionless and silent, she lay still, staring into Leanna's face as if unsure she had heard right. "Lena?"

"Yes, Mom, Lena. How are you feeling?"

She smiled, barely making it stretch her lips. Her eyes became instantly moist. She ignored the question.

"Lena, it's really you?"

Leanna could hardly hear her and bent closer. "Yes, Mom, it's me."

"You stayed away so long. I missed you terribly!"

Leanna looked for her mother's hand among the bed sheets. Finding it, she took it into both of her hands and squeezed it gently.

"I'm sorry. I missed you too." She felt her mother squeeze back.

"Are you going to stay this time?"

Leanna's voice was stuck in her throat, and Sarah, aware of the hesitation, responded by pleading. "At least... for a little while?"

Leanna's answer came out shaky. "Yes, Mom, I'll still be here when you get out of the hospital." She felt the squeeze of her mother's hand again.

"Thank God," Sarah whispered. Then, frowning, "I'm so tired. Why am I so tired?"

Leanna could not speak. She just stood there, bent over the one she loved the most, bowed to the ache in her heart, and let the tears distort her face and blur her vision.

Sarah spoke again softly. "I want to stay awake to visit with you. We haven't talked for such a long time." She drifted off.

That was the last thing her mother ever said. She never regained consciousness. She died later that afternoon in the somber presence of her husband and children. Leanna had not moved from that spot beside her mother until Daniel and Harley gently pulled her away. The sound of her grief filled the hallways and caused people to pause. Sam could not be consoled and was taken back to the farm by Katy, who negotiated the highway sobbing pitifully.

Harley stood at the third-story hospital window, looking into the blue spring morning sky. He felt like he had as a little kid watching his mommy and daddy in their old black Ford heading toward town. As he had then, he wished his mother was coming home instead of fading away down the highway.

He hadn't seen much of her during the past several years. Knowing that she would never be in another tomorrow for him to visit, he knew he would miss her beyond belief.

Daniel, his arm around Leanna to support her, had led her to an elevator. He took her down to the ground floor and out onto the grassy hospital grounds to calm her down. They sat on a concrete bench there in the clear, cool May morning and cried together.

They didn't see the hearse come to the rear of the building where the deceased were collected and taken to the morgue. That was a good thing. Leanna would not have survived seeing her mother being loaded up like a broken-down appliance and hauled off to the junkyard. She would have wound up in the hospital herself.

After a while, they walked back to the hospital entrance. There, they met Harley, who came out to tell them that their mother had been taken from the room. Daniel helped Leanna into his car and drove out of the hospital parking lot, leaving Leanna's car where she had parked it in the wee hours of the morning. Harley followed in his car.

Daniel and Leanna reached the bridge south of town before any words were spoken. It was Daniel who broke the silence. "I'll see to the funeral arrangements tomorrow." They were silent for another mile or two. "What are we gonna do with Dad?" he asked, not taking his eyes off the highway. Leanna showed no signs of hearing. She couldn't have been less responsive if nothing had been said.

They reached the farm a few minutes later. Katy's car was not there; she had not stayed long with her dad. Daniel got out. Leanna remained seated; the dread of her father's presence in the house pushed her back in her seat. She had barely been aware of him in the hospital room as her grief had consumed her. So, figuratively speaking, she hadn't laid eyes on him since she had left home thirty-eight years ago. She would rather keep it that way. Or would she? He had gotten away with his attitude toward his family all these years, especially to her. Now, it felt like he had the same as let her mother die. Maybe she would change his attitude a little bit, make him answer for what he had done to her mother.

Wasn't any different than if he'd locked her in the closet till she quit breathing. Unshed tears glistened in her eyes. *She's gone!* The reality kept sinking deeper and deeper into her spirit. It hurt so much! She *could* make him pay for *that*.

Harley pulled up next to her in his car. She watched him climb out and noticed how much older he appeared to her. It wasn't as if she hadn't seen him in years. He lived just across town from her. She called up her memory of him in his thirties, and the difference was considerable. He still had a full head of hair, but mostly gray, no longer lean and wiry, a paunch, but not disgraceful. Time had snuck up on her and changed things. Now that she thought about it, she, too, looked different than she did when Kyle Brunghardt had eyes for her. *A hundred years ago!*

He wouldn't be interested in an old lady. She wondered how *he* looked now. He also still lived in the Springs with his family, but their paths hadn't crossed over the years.

Fresh tears glistened in her eyes. The devastation of the day's events seemed to have stirred up all kinds of heartbreaking sorrows. Death always made you aware of the years gone... good and bad.

She exited her car, and she and Harley caught up with Daniel. The three of them walked slowly toward the front door, heads hanging, spirits low, each in their own world of pain and sorrow.

Without looking up, Leanna, in a bitter tone, said, "I'll just chop his head off and be done with it. We won't have to figure it out." Daniel knew her sarcasm was her answer to the question he had asked out on the highway. He made no comment. Harley didn't need to guess to what or whom she was referring. Leanna was being Leanna about her father. Her feelings toward him were no secret.

CHAPTER 46

They entered the house at the living room door to find that their father was nowhere to be seen. Leanna was relieved. The last thing she wanted was to be in the same room with him. However, she would have to stay at the house with him until after the funeral, as would Harley and Daniel. She was sure they were both dreading their stay as much as she was. Or almost as much. She wasn't sure about the other two, but she knew she would be gone, on her way back to Colorado Springs when the funeral was over. It was going to be a rotten two or three days on the farm with him. It was time she dreaded but couldn't escape.

She became focused on her surroundings and realized that Daniel hadn't moved from where he had stopped behind her a few steps inside the door. Harley had gone upstairs to his old room. He was busy, she imagined, establishing his place to stay during the few days he would be there. Leanna turned to Daniel. He was gazing around the room. This was the childhood home he had left as a young man, to which he had not returned until now.

The moment gave Leanna a shock of realization. Sam had lived the last forty-five years without seeing or speaking to his favorite son. For him, it must have been as if Daniel had died. She felt some sympathy despite her opinion of her father. But then she would have given any stranger the same respect under the same circumstances. And what about Daniel? How has he felt about his separation from his father all these years? She couldn't remember ever having heard him mention it.

She spoke to him. "It's been a while, hasn't it," she said.

He turned to face her. "Longer than that," he answered. "It's like I had this dream when I was a kid, and it has now come true. I feel like I've never been here before except in that dream."

Leanna likened it to a nightmare but kept it to herself. Instead, she said, "Why did *you* stay away, Daniel? Why did you never come back home?"

He didn't answer but walked into the kitchen. She watched him disappear through the doorway and then followed. He was at the kitchen sink running a glass of water when she entered and sat down at the table, one she'd never seen before. She could say the same for the living room furniture.

"The furniture is all different."

It's been thirty-eight years. Stuff wears out."

"Guess you're right. Even this new stuff looks old." Then she shrugged. "But not too bad, I guess."

"Like you said, it's been a while."

He pulled up a chair and sat across the table from her. Leanna and Harley were the only members of the family that had been a part of his life since he had left Garland.

Neither of them was hardly in a position to ask why he stayed away from their parents.

The three or four times that he had taken part in Katy's visits to Harley and his family the question had never come up.

"And why do *you* think I left home and never came back," he asked.

"I have an idea, but I would only be guessing; why don't you *tell* me?"

"It's no big secret; I just never felt comfortable around Dad after the radio incident. I wanted to avoid any bad moments with him. And knowing Dad, there woulda been a struggle with him every time we came face to face." I chose the lesser of two evils. There was less hurt in being gone than fighting."

"I wonder where Dad went." The voice coming from the doorway was Harley. The two at the table were startled and jerked their heads to face him.

Leanna spoke quickly in her surprise. "Well, I spose he's in his bedroom."

"Nooo, I was just there, and he wasn't." He went to the window above the sink and stretched to look out toward the barn, hoping he might see his father there. He then came to join them at the table. "It might be a good idea to go look for him. He can't get around very well anymore, and if he should fall, he probably couldn't get back up without help."

Although Daniel dreaded a deliberate face-to-face encounter with his father, he was as concerned as Harley. "That's probably a good idea," he said and got up. Looking at Leanna, he asked, "You coming with us?"

Well for... Leanna suddenly felt betrayed. *Who cares about the old...?* It was their *mother* who had died. She wasn't mourning Sam Danziger! He was still here as inconsiderate as he ever was. Her mother was gone!

Shoulda been him instead of her.

Tears came to her eyes, and she lowered her face into her hands. She began to weep pitifully. The two men were moved and didn't know what to say or do. Their eyes grew moist as well, and Daniel moved to Leanna's side, putting his hand on her shoulder.

She wept and moaned, making her words scarcely audible. "Why didn't he take her to the doctor? What is wrong with him? He ruined my whole life, and now he let my mother die!" She laid her face in the crook of her arm on the table and sobbed without restraint.

Daniel softly rubbed her back. "Please, Leanna, don't cry so. I'm sure *Mom's* not sad."

Harley stood silent, his arms across his chest. His face was distorted by his stubborn effort to keep from crying out loud. After a minute or so, Leanna grew quiet, only sniffling.

Harley wiped his tears with a white hanky from his back pocket, and Daniel withdrew his hand and moved toward the back door. Harley followed, and the brothers left the house to look for their father.

Outside, Daniel stopped after a few steps and gazed toward the barn. Harley reached his side and also stopped. "You think he might be in the barn?" he asked.

"I don't know. I was thinking about what Leanna said: That he ruined her life and let Mom die." He kept his eyes on the barn, drawing Harley's attention to it. He said, "Man, I wish I knew what happened to her in there and what Dad had to do with it. Then we'd know why she hates him so."

"Yeah, I know what you mean." They were silent for a moment, each bouncing their thoughts off the big red hulk that had always been in the picture of their lives. Over the years, when discussing their sister Leanna's troubled life, it was "where it happened," the thing that was the cause.

Daniel was thoughtful. "But you know what," he said. "I'm sure it was something he said to her, not something he did. Knowing Dad, he probably said something to Leanna to make her obey."

"You mean like he said something that scared the wits out of her."

"Yeah, exactly. I remember she once told me that Dad had told her that God was gonna kill her. She was left up there all night alone with that fear. She came out of the barn a different person than when she went in."

Daniel started toward the barn. "Let's go look; he might be in there."

They walked to the barn and entered through the walk-in door. They stood for a moment, leaving the door open to help see in the dimness of the windowless room. Daniel gazed around at the interior, seeing changes time had made. He knew that Lewis had taken over the farm nine years ago. He was sure Lewis and Katy were doing things their way and had made changes that worked for them.

The appearance of Katy in his thoughts reminded him that his father had left the hospital with her. It suddenly occurred to him that their father was probably at Katy's house.

Before he could speak, Harley hollered out into the barn's shadowed nooks and crannies. "Dad, are you in here?"

Daniel let the silence speak the answer, then spoke himself. "I just realized he's probably at Katy's since she took him with her from the hospital."

"You're right," Harley agreed, then moved toward the door. But rather than leave it at that and go back to the house, he turned around to Daniel. "I'm gonna take a quick walk around the yard," he said, "just in case he's here somewhere."

Daniel followed. "I'll take the north side, and you take the south," he suggested.

They left the barn and began their search, calling out to their father. Daniel walked to the tool shed while Harley went among the machinery that stood parked behind the barn. He even went out toward the pasture a ways to the stand of cottonwoods, calling and searching with his eyes. He saw nothing but the usual discard of farm maintenance lying around. The old Model T was gone.

As he approached the far side of the barn, he saw an empty five-gallon tar bucket on its side and a stack of asphalt shingles. An extension ladder rested against the eve of the barn. As he walked along the side of the barn, he wondered what repair work Lewis had been working on in preparation for re-shingling the roof. It was odd that he had left the ladder out in the weather. He would put it away later.

He rounded the corner of the barn and, turning toward the house, saw Daniel enter through the kitchen door. The search had been nonproductive. He was sure their father was at Katy's, and she would bring him home sometime before dinner.

CHAPTER 47

It was almost one-thirty when Katy's car came down the driveway. Leanna had made hamburgers and fries for herself and her brothers for lunch. Now, they sat quietly in the living room, too mournful to be of good company to each other. They all heard the car drive up, and Harley stood to look through the window to see who had driven up. He saw Lewis and Katy in the car's front seat, but the back seat was empty. The sight was startling. He jerked to his feet, making a sound of surprise, and moved to the window.

"It's Lewis and Katy, but Dad's not with them!"

Daniel rushed to the door and opened it to stare at the couple in the car. Harley left the window to stand behind him, puzzled as well.

Too grief-stricken over her mother to stir, Leanna remained lying on the couch, unconcerned about the turn of events taking place.

Harley shouted to the couple as they got out of the car, "Where's Dad?"

Katy stopped in her tracks. "Isn't he here with you?"

"No! We looked for him but didn't find him. We thought he was with you!"

Katy came rushing closer. Her face was ashen, her eyes wide with alarm. "You look everywhere?"

"Everywhere," Harley said.

Katy started for the house. "Well, I let him off and watched him enter the house."

Everyone was silent, wondering where he could be, until Katy reached the door. She spoke as she entered. "Did you look upstairs?"

Harley answered as he and the others followed her into the house. "He's not in my old room, but I didn't look into any of the other rooms."

At this point, Leanna became aware of the tone of concern and sat up. "What's going on?"

Katy's worried answer came from the bottom of the stairs as she started the climb up to search the upper floor. "Nobody knows where Dad is."

As Leanna watched Katy ascend the stairs and disappear at the top, she felt a small tremor of anxiety. However, it didn't last long enough to cause surprise or curiosity. She didn't wonder why Sam was suddenly someone to care about. But on the other hand, that could be why she rose quickly from the couch and went outside to stand on the porch. She scanned the yard's perimeters with intense concentration.

She wondered where he could be and then re-entered the house. Harley, Daniel, and Lewis had all followed her outside and now walked out toward the highway to check out the ditch. They would look everywhere this time.

Inside, Katy came down the stairs. "He's not up there," she said to Leanna. Then asked, "Can you think of someplace he might have gone?"

Leanna saw the worry in her sister's face and wanted to help ease her mind. Besides, what if something bad *had* happened to Sam, and he was lying unconscious somewhere. That would be awful. Even *he* didn't deserve that. "C'mon," she said kindly, "Let's go look for him." They hurried out the door.

Half an hour later, Leanna separated herself from all the others. After exhausting all the possibilities of places Sam could have gone, she walked to the house where the other four had convened to discuss the next plan of action. She had hollered herself hoarse, calling his name. The reality of the dire situation had slowly sunk in. She was now fully emotionally engaged in the search for Sam, her father. Even the mourning of her mother's death had taken second place to finding him alive and well. She couldn't remember ever feeling all this concern for her father. It felt strange to see her father in the same picture with illness or injury. But after Katy had brought her up to date on his physical health and his diminished mental capacity, there he was in her mind, old, decrepit, and pitiful. She also had the feeling that she was running out on someone. *Her mother?*

She walked briskly toward the house, becoming increasingly connected to her father. There was even some anxiety stirring in her.

Suddenly, the barn behind her jerked her around to stare at it. It stood before her, its faded red hulk towering against the clear-blue, May afternoon sky. Her eyes went up to the loft door, tucked under the peak of the eve. To her, its cold wooden face seemed to be a one-eyed monster waiting patiently for something to pass by, close enough to snatch it away and gobble it up.

Could he have gone up into the loft for some reason? She began walking faster toward the barn. She felt the "trembles" coming on as she approached the patient monster. She hadn't been up there since that day... the accident!

When she entered the dim light, it occurred to her that she may be unable to make herself go to that dark corner of her childhood horror. She felt flushed and became aware of the coolness of the damp cloth in her underarms. She was shaky inside.

She walked in little jerks as she entered the barn and approached the ladder to the loft. She stopped and looked up at the hole in the loft's floor. It was the opening through which her brother Andrew had left this earth. Once as threatening to her as the end of the world, the hole was now the way to the possible discovery of her lost father. All she had to do to find out was climb up through it.

Her hand reached for a rung on the ladder, gripped it, and froze. Was it still up there?

What's wrong with you? There's nothing up there! Never was! You were just a scared little girl. It was all in your imagination. Get over it!

But what if it all came back? What if it was still in *her*, waiting for an encouraging push at the right time? She hadn't had an episode for years and years.

She mentally examined her physical feelings and realized she was panting. Her heart was racing, and panic was pressing to break out. It felt too familiar. She dropped her hand from the ladder and stepped back, looking up at the opening.

"Sam?" she hollered and felt silly. If he had been up there and could answer, he would have been able to call for help or come down on his own. *Wouldn't he?* She visualized him lying paralyzed from a stroke, unable to speak or move. Trapped in his own body with only his mind working, telling him the inescapable trouble he was in. That would be pure torture! She moved to the ladder again and did not stop to wonder what might happen to her. She stepped around some broken shingles and old tar paper lying on the floor at its foot. She climbed the ladder as quickly as a fifty-three-year-old woman could.

She poked herself up to her shoulders through the square hole and looked around as far to the right as her neck and waist allowed. She then did the same to the left. All she saw was a few bales of hay stacked haphazardly along the north wall. Fine powdered dust lay everywhere. A shoe, its lace still tied in a bow, lay on its side on the floor. The question of how it came to be there was barely a flash in the far corners of her mind. A guess at how long it had lain there also popped out of her imagination.

Her eyes went to a corner of the room, and her mind returned to that night she had spent in her nightmare. She shuddered. She recognized the smell of the dusty hay in the air and was surprised it didn't affect her except a tickle in her throat. Being there head and shoulders in the loft didn't cause her to go crazy as she had feared it would. The relief she felt was a rising joy in her chest, and the room became a place to look for Sam.

Her eyes fell on the odd black shoe lying out of place there on the dust-covered floor. The scrambled pattern of marks in the dust around it told of its crash landing.

She looked up into the rafters and was amazed to see a jagged splotch of blue sky through a hole in the roof, a hole large enough to accommodate the shoe. Could the shoe have fallen into the loft through that hole? She remembered the stack of shingles she had seen on the west side of the barn and realized that they were meant for the roof she was looking at. She guessed the roof must be rotten, and Lewis was about to repair it.

Her attention went back to the shoe. She couldn't see it that clearly from where she stood on the ladder. She climbed through the rest of the way and went to the shoe. She bent down and picked it up. She was shocked by its appearance. It was shiny black, almost like new. An oxford; the shoe worn to church by the Mennonites, the old men... like her father. Was it her father's shoe? She bent her head back, looking straight up at the hole in the roof. He could have stepped on a rotten spot and fallen through with one foot, then jerked his foot out, pulling his shoe off.

So why would he be on the roof? No telling. She remembered seeing the ladder leaning against the eaves. *He could have gone up and still be up there!*

She kept the shoe and moved to the access opening. She started down the ladder, realized it was difficult to safely hang on to it with the shoe in her hand, and dropped it to the concrete floor below. She descended the ladder slowly and carefully, her legs shaking all the way. She reached the last rung, stepped down, and moved quickly away. She felt the same panic she had always felt as a child out on a dark night, running for the back door, escaping whatever might be chasing her. Goosebumps danced on her scalp.

Outside, while walking west along the front of the barn, she looked back toward the house, hoping to see at least one of the others. Rounding the corner north, she looked again over her shoulder and saw no one at the house. She reached the ladder and climbed as fast as she could to the roof, a slight breeze flapping the hem of her skirt.

As her eyes came up over the eaves, she saw him halfway up the pitch of the roof, a shoe missing and lying on his back. She rose higher on the ladder and transferred from the ladder to the roof, knees shaking all the while.

Out of the corner of her eye, she noticed a lightning rod set on the peak near the end of the roof. As that unfamiliar observation became clear in her mind, she heard the most unlikely sound she could ever have imagined hearing on a rooftop. Her surprise was stunning. She was surely mistaken. She remained motionless and listened. There it was again!

He's snoring! Snoring? Was he just lying up there on the roof, sleeping? She had not moved for several seconds, then finally regained her presence of mind. She moved carefully across the roof and sank to her bare knees beside him. There was dried blood on his cheek and forehead, but not much, just from scraped skin. Was he unconscious? She reached out to his shoulder and then drew her hand back. She felt intrusive, daring to touch this man. What help did she have to offer this symbol of unapproachable authority that had dictated the terms of her life ever since she could remember?

Then she saw a frail, fallen figure, wounded and lying at the edge of his grave. Once strong and vibrant, a rock now turned to skin and bone. A victim of all that rose against him.

Her heart leaned toward him and extended its compassion. Her hand went to his shoulder, shook it, and called to him. "Hey, can you hear me?" There was no response. She shook him again, a little more demanding this time. "Wake up!" Still nothing. She needed to get the others. As she put her hands against the shingled surface to stand, she felt the give of soft, rotted wood beneath her. She quickly sank back down to hands and knees and remained motionless for a moment. She sat back on her heels, feeling the rough surface of the wooden shingles scraping the skin of her knees.

She had forgotten the precarious condition of the roof and was now afraid to move. She stared at her father, not knowing what to do. Then she realized that he had stopped snoring. Her attention flew to his chest. It still heaved gently. He was still breathing. Maybe her attempts to rouse him had drawn him partially out of his sleep if that's what it was...

She called to him again. "Sam, are you awake? It's Le..." She caught herself. "Leanna" would not do. "It's Lena," she said. "You gotta wake up." Still nothing.

She twisted around to look back and locate the ladder sticking up above the roof's edge. It was only a matter of several feet, but, fearing the dangerous condition of the roof, it seemed like a mile. Then, on the other hand, she had walked on that same part of the roof only minutes before without trouble. She felt frustrated with herself, sitting there like a frightened child, unable to make a decision.

Her attention was drawn again to the strange lightning rod. She stared at it hard. She remembered hearing years ago of a conflict within the church regarding the use of lightning rods on Mennonite buildings. It was a practice that involved her father's fervent opposition. He had argued that lightning was an act of God and should not be resisted or deterred. "It was God's will!" His argument against using lightning rods became a rule of the Mennonite church.

A man named Jason Becker, who had broken the rule, faced the excommunication panel. He defended himself with the argument that "rain and snow and wind and hail were also acts of God. And yet, we build houses, sheds, and structures to protect ourselves from those acts of God. So, why was the line drawn at the use of a lightning rod?"

She had heard that the battle between common sense and religious idealism was fierce. Common sense had prevailed, and the church had abolished Sam Danziger's rule against the lightning rod. She had heard that even her mother had stood against Sam.

For a time, they had created their own lightning between them. He had eventually given in to the lightning rod. Its presence there on the roof of his barn was proof of that *unless the rod being up there was Lewis's doing.*

Then she began to shout. "Daaaniel... Harrrley... somebody hellllp!" They were in the house on the other side of the barn, and she didn't know if they could hear her. She hollered again as loud as she could. "Heyyyy, I found him! I'm up on the barrrn!" She went silent, listening. The sound of a car out on the highway coming from the north hummed its way past and soon far south out of hearing. She shouted again, cupping her hands around her mouth. "Heyyyy! Somebody help!"

Suddenly, her attention was drawn to what she thought was movement in her father's still body. She stared intently at him. She could have sworn he moved the limp arm across his chest. His breathing rate increased, and a moan escaped his closed mouth. Leanna became excited, hoping he was waking up.

"Hey? Can you hear me? Please wake up," she pleaded. She shook his shoulder. His reaction was to jerk himself away from her touch, make a sound of alarm, and open his eyes wide with fear.

It startled Leanna. "It's okay! It's Lena!" His wild eyes stared at her without recognition. She spoke again, touching his withdrawn shoulder, trying to soothe him. "It's Lena. Everything's gonna be okay." His expression began to soften, and she saw that he knew who she was. His arm relaxed, and his shoulder fell back against the roof. He looked away from her face at the blue sky. Suddenly, his face contorted, and tears filled his eyes. His voice cracked and was distorted with grief.

"She's gone, he began to sob, and I didn't do anything, I didn't know... How could she be so sick? I didn't know. What have I done?" His sobbing overran his words, and Leanna was swallowing back the tears. She had a hard time understanding his crying words but was sure of his anguish.

She was also taken with what seemed to her an absurdity: Sam Danziger, the rock, had been reduced to a sobbing grown man. The pitiful picture shocked her sense of order. She felt out of place. Now, she was moved to comfort him.

"Please, Dad, you can't blame yourself." She couldn't believe she had just said that. "Just calm yourself and listen to me." She became aware of her calling him dad and was mildly regretful. "We have to get you down off this roof and see how badly you're hurt."

His crying stopped, and he blinked several times. He turned his face toward her and raised his head to look.

"Roof, did you say roof?" He peered past his feet at the ladder and stared at it as if trying to focus on it, then let his head lay back on the roof.

"You're on the roof of the barn," Leanna said. He did not respond but lay still, gazing at the sky. Leanna wondered why he was up there, and she thought he might be asking himself the same question from the looks of him. But she would tend to that question later. She needed to get him down and go to the hospital for now.

"Where are you hurt?" she asked. Again, he was slow to respond. As Leanna waited, she suspected he was preoccupied with trying to remember what had happened.

Finally, he answered. "I was after the lightning rod, and my foot went through. I think I bashed my face against the roof." He reached up and touched the wound on his forehead.

"How about your foot or your leg? Are they hurt?" He started to bend the leg with the shoeless foot but got it up only a couple of inches before crying out in pain.

Leann was immediately alarmed. "What is it, what's wrong?"

Sam's face was twisted in pain, and he squeezed his eyes shut. He grunted his answer. "My hip!" Sweat had broken out on his forehead. Now, what were they going to do? There was no way that he would be able to climb down the ladder. He won't even be able to walk down the incline of the roof to get to the ladder. She felt a little panic rising "Daniel! Harley," she yelled. "Heyyyyy! Help! Hellllp!

She listened for a sound. Then the kitchen screen door slamming announced that someone had come out. She rose up on her knees, cupped her hands around her mouth, and directed her face toward the roof's peak, she yelled. "Hey, I found him! We're up on toppa the barn!" There was only silence down there where someone should be. Had she imagined the slamming of the screen door?

"Is anyone down there?" she hollered.

"Leanna?"

It was Harley! *About time!* "Come to the west side of the barn. There's a ladder!"

His voice floated over the roof to her as he moved to get to the ladder. "What in the world are you doing on top of the barn?"

"I found Dad up here, and he's hurt!"

Until then, Sam had not been aware that Lena had been calling him Dad. His eighty-two-year-old brain had not processed that portion of the incoming information being sent to it. This time, he heard it, and it soaked in. Its importance, however, was fleeting, chased away by his grief for Sarah. He could say that he couldn't believe how he had missed the severity of her illness. But, considering his forgetfulness and his inability to think things through gave him cause to believe it. More tears sprang to his eyes, and the clear blue sky grew blurry, just like his life. Nothing but a day-to-day blur! *My God, my God, what have I done?* He closed his eyes, and his body quacked with silent sobbing.

The hard surface he lay on was painful pressure on his back. He raised his head, getting ready to put his hands down beside him and push himself up. The movement agitated the injury to his hip, and the pain washed over him in a consuming wave of nausea, causing him to cry out and fall back flat.

Leanna, her attention on the ladder as she waited for Harley's appearance, turned to her father, startled. "Dad? Are you alright, what's wrong?"

It took a moment for him to answer. "My hip is really bad!"

"Well, just lay *still!* We'll get you down from here and find out what's wrong with it."

Harley started climbing over the roof's edge, but Leanna warned him of its dangerous condition.

"The roof is really rotten where I'm sitting, so be careful where you walk." She pointed to the hole and said, "Dad went through there and hurt his hip. We need to get him to the hospital to have him looked at."

Harley stood up on the roof and assessed the situation. "Can he walk to the ladder?"

"No, he can hardly move."

"Then we've got problems. How are we gonna get him down off of here?"

Their father lay still, his eyes closed, paying little attention to the discussion. Harley guessed he was probably praying.

Answering his own question, he said, *"We* aren't. I think we have to call the fire department. *They'll* have a way to get him down."

"There's no phone here. You'll have to drive to town to get them to come out here."

"Doesn't Katy have a phone at her house?"

Harley remounted the ladder and started down. "I'll get Katy to go to her house and call." He disappeared from Leanna's sight.

She sat there in her safe spot on the rotting boards, knowing she would eventually have to move. She would have to carefully test the other spots on her way to safe ground one at a time. A fact as inevitable as the "tomorrow" in her life. She felt a slight breeze pass over her, and she envisioned the wisp of a friendly ghost. It brought to her attention the inescapable probabilities that go along with progressing to the future. She became drawn back to being aware of her father there with her: another rotten spot to tread carefully on her way to the rest of her life. How had she gotten here in this moment? Here she was, in the clutches of this red, wooden monster, while saving the man who had held her down with his foot on her neck all her life.

CHAPTER 48

It took nearly half an hour for a fire truck to come from Garland and get Sam off the roof of the barn. He was loaded into an ambulance and taken to the nearest hospital in Cagle City, twenty miles west of Garland. Besides the skinned patches on his cheek and forehead, he had a dislocated hip and a minor concussion. The bruising that covered most of his left leg and hip was extensive and ugly to see. After the doctor told them he would keep Sam in the hospital overnight for observation, everyone returned to the farm.

Supper was hardly considered by anyone, their appetites quashed by the weight of their grief. They moped around the deathly silent house until it sunk into the shadowy dusk. The clock ticked loudly, and someone finally turned on a light in the kitchen.

Eventually, a spattering of short, quiet sentences, an attempt at conversation, grew in the dim silence. The question, "Why did Dad go up on the roof?" was asked, and Lewis explained that he had talked Sam into putting a lightning rod on the barn in the nineteen eighties. Leanna added that Sam had told her he was up there to get the lightning rod down. The hand tools it would take to do that were found in the back pocket of his overalls. Why he chose that particular time to do so was anybody's guess. Maybe his age had something to do with it, his mind, Harley guessed. He had been doing some strange things lately, was Katy's contribution. His reasoning probably made sense to only him and only in the time it took him to do the deed.

Leanna knew Sam's reason for wanting to remove the lightning rod had to do with his wife being taken from him. It was an effort to make amends with his God. She kept *that* opinion to herself.

Katy and Lewis mentioned the chores at their house needed to be done. They quietly left in the dark. The purr of their car's engine and the scrunch of gravel in the driveway were the only sounds heard in the house. They were hardly noticed as they drove away.

All the Danzigers suffered a long sleepless night, and the next morning at their house wasn't good for anything but reliving it. The death of their beloved mother and then their father being taken to the hospital all on the same day was tragedy doing its best work. It was the second worst day of their lives. Having left Lewis to do what needed to be done at their house, Katy pulled up at the Danziger house early. Leanna had been dressed and waiting for nearly an hour. Daniel and Harley were just finishing their breakfast. They were both ready to go before Katy got into the house. Leanna met Katy on the porch, and they walked immediately to the car with the two men close behind. The twenty-minute ride to the hospital exemplified the invention of silence.

Katy parked beside Leanna's car, which she had left there the day before, and they went directly to their father's room. Leanna entered first and realized immediately that he was asleep. She turned to the others and held her finger to her lips.

They returned to the hallway and stood together, not knowing exactly what to do. Leanna suggested they go to the nurses' station and find out when their father would be released.

The nurse told them that after the doctor examined Sam during his morning rounds, he would tell them when Sam could go home. She assured them the doctor would get to Sam's room within the hour. However, it being seven-twenty, she was also sure that a nurse would be in that room shortly to wake Sam for breakfast. It would be alright if they woke him now instead. They went back to the room and found their father already awake. He lay flat on his back, the adjustable bed cranked flat, his head nearly swallowed by the puffy pillow. His face was pointed at the white ceiling, and he barely turned to them as they walked into the room. He then turned his face away.

Katy went around to the other side of the bed and stood before his face, cheerful. "Good morning, Dad. How are you feeling?" His woeful eyes peered at her as if he were trying to figure out who she was, and the look startled her. She became afraid he might be showing signs of dementia. But then his response eased her mind.

"I don't feel very good," he half whispered. He cleared his throat and tried again. This time, he was clear. "To tell you the truth, I feel awful." He turned his face to the others on the other side of the bed.

Daniel and Harley spoke almost in unison. "Hi, Dad." He didn't look at Leanna, and she didn't speak but watched him intently.

Katy spoke. "The doctor will be here in a minute to check you over, and if everything's alright, we can take you home."

"Home?" He pointed his face at the ceiling and, with a bitter tone, exclaimed, "There will be no *home* without your mother!"

Lena was surprised by the bitterness in his voice. It was almost as if he were on the verge of whimpering over some wrong done to him. She had never heard Sam Danziger with such a feeling-sorry-for-myself tone. Whatever struggle or trial in his life that had ever befallen him was of his God's doing and, therefore, divine intervention. It was a gift of instruction to him to do God's will; certainly nothing to be sorry about, but rather something for which to be thankful. Now, it looked like he was refusing to go farther. No one said anything. They were silenced by the unfamiliar sound of surrender in their father's words.

Suddenly, a cheerful voice from the doorway behind them caught their attention. They turned to see a smiling, young, blond nurse. "Hello, Mr. Danziger. It's time for breakfast," she said. Everyone got out of the way as she pushed the food cart to the foot of the bed and adjusted the head of the bed to a sitting position. After arranging the pillows, the nurse left the cart and cheerfully promised to return shortly.

Leanna quietly watched the others try to talk their father into eating. Finally, she told them she would drive her car out to the farm and see them there.

She drove as far south as she dared, looking at the dangerously blurry traffic through streaming tears of grief for her mother.

Finally, turning off onto the sandy shoulder, she laid her forehead against her hands on the steering wheel and sobbed uncontrollably. The pain she felt for her loss was far worse than any she had known in all the fifty-three years of her tragic life. The memory of her first official heartbreak came to her at this unlikely moment and consumed her mind.

She was fourteen years old, sitting on her folded legs in the weeds at the foot of that giant cottonwood. She held the heavy, limp body of her dead dog. Hidden from Harley and his misguided sympathy, she had cried her eyes out, then her heart. She had killed her dog that day, her best friend. That was her first physical proof of the evil that lurked within her. There was something in her that crackled out from her and struck the ones she loved. It had called to Butch and had pulled him out in front of that car.

How ridiculous, she thought. But what other explanation was there?

And poor Kyle. How could she have hidden in the dark trees from the only man she ever loved until he ran from her, never to return? It was a misunderstanding, sure, but what was in her that had not let her go to him and explain the mistake? Surly something evil, or at least stupid!

And my mother! Oh God, oh God, she sobbed. *How could I have left her with him?*

Would she be dead now if she had been there instead of him to take care of her?

Didn't he know? She lifted her head as if she had heard something and, with teary eyes, stared out through the windshield. *Or is it the evil thing in me that let my mother die? My punishment.*

Her fists came off the steering wheel, and she beat the wheel and wept. "Kill *me,* she cried, not her!"

Nearly an hour later, the others were in Katy's car, with Harley driving, on their way home from the hospital. They came upon Leanna's car, which was still parked on the shoulder of the highway. Harley pulled over.

The engine in Leanna's car was still running, and she sat at the wheel, staring out through the windshield. "Just having a good cry and giving myself a talking to," she had said.

Feeling uncomfortable with his father in such close quarters, Daniel got into the car with Leanna. Ten minutes later, they were all in the house, each privately dealing with their grief. The old house was silent. Sarah no longer lived there, and Sam, who had gone to his bedroom, seemed to be equally absent,

That was on Tuesday. The funeral was on the following Friday. The turnout was enormous, attesting to Sarah's high standing in the Mennonite community. The grave site service in the large cemetery behind the church was well-occupied. Seeing the respectful throng might make one wonder how they had all gotten into the small church building at the same time.

After the service, Katy helped their father into the car. Leanna stood sadly by, and Harley shook hands with curious people he didn't know. Daniel, trying to avoid the trial Harley was going through, drifted to the outer fringes of the crowd to wait.

After a few minutes, he saw his family across the way getting into the car to go home. He moved quickly down a path between rows of headstones to join them.

As he approached, he saw Katy and Leanna in the back seat with their father and Harley behind the wheel. He heard the car start and hurried to climb into the passenger seat, mentally thanking Leanna for taking the seat beside their father. The seven-mile trip home was filled with the silence of the mournful and the engine's hum of indifference.

Leanna sat next to Sam, careful not to make the slightest contact with him so as not to make him uncomfortable. She knew he detested her and would rather not be reminded she was there.

She represented to him almost everything to which his God objected. From the makeup and clothing she wore to her independent way of life. She had no children and, at fifty-three, was still unmarried. She had not produced a family, as was her purpose. But even worse than all of that was what she meant to his relationship with God. She was his punishment, his cross to bear for his failure to perform, to the letter, God's commandments.

She did not think that he believed he could be perfect. There was only one who had achieved perfection. But she had heard him, all her life, preach that "we must all, each in our way, bear responsibility to God for that failure. We will all pay the price we owe... in one way or another."

He had cherished her. She was God's gift to him. Then it happened. Like a thief in the night, God had snuck up on him, taken his youngest son, and snatched away his gift. She was lost to him, never to be recovered. Remembering the child was all he had of her.

The grown woman who had replaced the gift now sat squeezed into a spot on the back seat beside him. She was literally folded in on herself to avoid touching him. He wondered what, if anything, he could do to ease the disgust she must feel for him. He wanted to comfort her and cool the hatred that God had allowed Satan to burn into her heart.

Foolish old man, he thought as Harley turned into the driveway. *Probly too late. Besides, God has His reasons, and they're always good ones.*

CHAPTER 49

That afternoon, Harley left for home, which was still in Colorado Springs. His oldest grandchild, James, would graduate from high school the next day, and Harley wanted to be sure to be there to attend the ceremony.

After he had gone, Sam voiced his disappointment. "He and Linda hardly ever come to see us anymore. When they do, it's just overnight, so they're sleeping most of the time they're here and hardly have anything to say. He could have stayed till tomorrow."

Leanna spoke up in Harley's defense. "Well, he can come visit you anytime, but a grandchild graduating from high school only happens once." An uncomfortable silence fell on the room, but only for a moment. She couldn't resist a sarcastic follow-up. "But then you wouldn't know about that, would you." Ducking the retaliation that might be coming her way, she quickly turned from him and entered the kitchen.

Sam watched her walk away. The look on his face told of the pain he felt. The fact was, he had been struck dead center, straight in the heart.

Daniel was sitting on the couch and saw his father's reaction to Leanna's bitter remark. He couldn't see his wound, and because of his blank stare, he could only make an educated guess about how Leanna's words made him feel. He was sure they must have hurt. He was equally sure that Leanna had fled at the realization that she had thoughtlessly made a regretful mistake. He rose from the couch and followed her to the kitchen.

She stood at the sink, looking out the window through the stand of cottonwoods and the thicket of sand-hill-plum bushes. They had grown wild where the clothesline had once been years ago. The highway to town could hardly be seen anymore through the tangle of budding growth.

Like the road my life is on, has always been on, she thought, *hard to see.* She remembered the battle she had waged against Sam as a teenager. The war that should have made it possible to ride the bus down that road to school. But it had put her on another road to another life away from her home, her childhood, and, more sadly, her mother. She had been cut off from the one person who had made a place for her in that empty world she had lived in, her mother. She was now gone... *forever. But Sam, sure as hell, is still here!* Why was the one who had put her in that awful world and her mother in her grave still here?

Suddenly, she felt someone behind her. Daniel was in the room. "Hey, you alright?"

"Sure. But shouldn't you be asking Sam that question? He's the one that needs to be watching his back."

Daniel frowned. "What do you mean? What did he do?"

"He same as killed my mother, and I could just..." Her hands came out in front of her, shaped as if she were squeezing someone's neck. Her face contorted, and gritting her teeth, she growled. Daniel was taken aback. Leanna was staring at him with defiance in her manner, and he saw the bitterness that made her so.

"What are you talking about? He had nothing to do with..."

Leanna broke in before he could finish. "Well, he sure as hell didn't have anything to do with her living, that's for sure! He's deprived her of most of what she deserved, what any woman deserves... all her life." She continued to gaze out the window, then added, "Pure ignorance, that's what turns his crank, and that same ignorance is what killed her too.

The room became as still as pulling the plug on a radio. The whole house hissed with the silence that followed. Daniel moved to the counter, turned, and rested against its edge. Leanna, beside him, stared out the window. Her lip began to tremble, and she tucked it in and bit down on it. Tears came to her eyes. Her vision blurred, and her facial muscles squeezed against themselves as she tried to speak. Daniel could barely distinguish her words.

"I shouldn't have left her with him. I should have kidnapped her or some such damn thing a long time ago." She squeezed her eyes shut for an instant to rearrange the tears, then wiped them with the heels of her hands. She left her hands pressed against her wet eyes and held back the sobs.

"Oh, Daniel, I feel like I never had a mother when she was here. Now she's gone, and the hope I've hung onto all this time will never happen. What will I do? What have I got left?" Daniel felt her anguish but could say nothing; he swallowed hard. His throat ached with emotion.

Suddenly, Leanna emitted a desperate whimper, whirled around, and rushed toward the doorway to the living room. Startled but aware of what she was on her way to do, he called to her in a hushed tone.

"Leanna, don't! He's your father no matter what you..." She was through the doorway out of reach.

As she charged across the living room toward Sam in the recliner, he appeared to be sleeping. She slowed her charge and approached him in a less forceful manner. His head hung low enough to allow his grey whiskers to brush the bib of his overalls, and a gentle snore buzzed in rhythm with the rise and fall of his chest. She stood before him, fists clenched, anxiety clamping her jaw. His frailty enticed her. Not to save him this time but to pound him violently. She felt the shaking begin, and her legs grew weak.

Sleeping! He's sleeping! She had no desire to beat on a defenseless man in his sleep, but she had been ready to do what she had imagined more than once. Her anguish had given her permission and made it the logical thing to do, but not dishonorably. She wanted justice, not revenge.

She felt a hand on her arm. *Daniel!* Does he know? Can he guess what she was about to do? She looked into his face and raised a finger to her lips. "Ssh, he's asleep," she whispered and walked to the stairs and up to her old room.

After kicking off her shoes, she lay on her bed, fully clothed, talking to herself. She almost convinced herself that had he been awake, she would have attacked him only with words and would not have actually hit him. But he hadn't been awake, had he? So how could she know for sure?

Daniel surely saw what must have been in my eyes: the hate coming through. She wondered again, as she had all her life, what kind of person she was. Tears threatened her eyes again, and the sobbing that followed contributed nothing to an answer.

CHAPTER 50

The early morning popped Daniel's eyes open from what seemed like a night of naps. He lifted his stiff, tired upper body to a sitting position and threw his legs over the edge of the bed. He remained that way for at least a minute. The day before still buzzed and bumped around in his mind as it had all night.

He peered at the dim morning light that filled the window and wondered where his wristwatch was. It had to be getting late. The sun was almost up, and he had to get home. It was a good six-hour trip. He finally rose and slipped into his jeans, listening for sounds of life downstairs. Hearing nothing but a semi out on the highway, he wondered if anyone was awake. He wondered if Lena and their father had gotten into it yet.

He quickly finished dressing and found his watch, seeing that it was after six. He attacked the stairs, aware of the silence except for his shoes tapping on the squeaky steps in a quick rhythm. He could see that the living room and kitchen were empty even in the dim, dawning light that sliced its way through the window drapery. No evidence of breakfast littered the counter, stove, or table.

Nobody's up yet... or Leanna's already gone! She wouldn't do that! Would she? He moved to the living room's front window and peered at the driveway. Her car was gone!

"Well, I'll be..." he muttered, peering further down the driveway as if the power of his will might make her car appear. He went back toward the kitchen, stopping to gaze down the dark hallway, and listened for any sound of activity from his father's bedroom. He felt dread creep into his spirit, imagining his father coming from the bedroom and being in the house alone with him.

Not a word had passed between them all the time he'd been there. Those few discontented days were now compacting the air into something impossible to breathe. Brought together by circumstances beyond his control, there would be nothing he could do about the close proximity. Sooner or later, they would have to say things to each other. The discomfort would be nerve-racking. But he couldn't just ignore him and walk out as

Leanna had done. He continued to the kitchen and went to the refrigerator to see what he could scrounge up for breakfast.

After deciding on a bowl of Cheerios, he ate and then rinsed the bowl under the faucet. He turned to see his father in the doorway, leaning on his cane and watching him. He pulled a dishtowel off the rack and dried the bowl. Putting it in the cupboard, he heard his father shuffle to the table behind him. Grunting and plopping into a squeaky chair, he dropped his cane. Daniel became alarmed at the sound of what may have happened and turned quickly.

"Are you alright?" he asked. He immediately saw that his father, though panting heavily, sat back in the chair. He didn't answer but only looked at Daniel thoughtfully. Daniel moved to pick up the cane and laid it on the table. He felt his father's eyes on him but did not meet them. Instead, he started for the doorway to leave the kitchen.

His father's voice was crackly and small. "I wish you would stay and talk?"

Daniel stopped and turned in surprise. His father was gazing through the window across the room, letting Daniel leave without interference. Daniel came back and sat at the table. His father continued gazing through the window, allowing Daniel to speak first.

Daniel's tone was quiet. "I didn't know if you wanted to talk to me or not."

His father looked at him. "What you did was a long time ago. It's done, and the outcome is a reality. It's part of what made you who you are. It is God's privilege to deny forgiveness, not mine."

Daniel was shocked. Or maybe amazed would be a better word, but it was easy to keep it hidden. This type of rationalization coming from his father, this old Mennonite, should not have surprised him. It should have offended him, but it didn't. It struck him as slightly amusing instead. He also kept that to himself.

He spoke kindly. "So, who *have* I become that makes you think I need forgiveness? For what, exactly, did *you* forgive me?"

Daniel felt anxious to hear what his father had held against him all these years. His father shrugged in a slow, careless manner. "God commands that we forgive those who trespass against us. You've never done anything to *me*. Whatever you've done to cause God to deprive you of His church is between you and God. I am only your earthly father who suffers a broken heart over the loss of his son. All I long for is your return to God's will, for you to repent and ask your heavenly father for forgiveness. To turn away from your sin and return to the church."

Daniel nodded, "You sound like a man who has no sin in his life."

His father looked at him thoughtfully and patiently. It was as if he were trying to decide how to respond to an innocent child in the most helpful way.

Daniel waited only a moment for a response, then asked, "Is that how you think of yourself, as being without sin?"

Sam shook his head in pity and said, "Of course not. We are all under sin."

"So, what do you do about it when *you* commit sin?" Sam's face flushed angry-red, and he stared at Daniel with disgust showing in his expression. "Why are you talking to me this way? You know how I have lived my life: in God's will, always."

"I *don't* know that any more than you know how I live *my* life in relationship with God. But you didn't answer my question. You say that you, and everyone else, sin. So, I'll ask again, what do you do to repent?"

Sam's tone came out angry and loud. "Well, ask for forgiveness, of course!"

Now Daniel leaned forward in his chair, poking himself at his father in defiance. "Well, I do the same thing, so what makes me different from you? Why do you think you are in a position to judge that I need to return to God's will? What makes you holier than me?"

Sam stared at his son. *So much disrespect!* His defense came up in his voice.

"Are you accusing me of being holier than thou?"

"No, of course not. I'm just wondering what you say to yourself that justifies your telling me how to conduct my spiritual life. What are the words you use to permit yourself to criticize me for being guilty of sin when you, by your own words, are just as guilty as I am? Does God give you the words?" He hesitated. Sam stared at him, ready to burst but silent. "Or is it the church?" Daniel finished.

He saw a change come into his father's expression, a realization maybe, but it didn't stay long enough to tell for sure. Then, an air of surrender came over his dad, and he knew what his next words would be. The old man huffed and looked away at the window. "You tell me," He muttered, grabbing the cane from the table to rise. "You seem to have all the answers."

Ah, yes, the patented Mennonite answer to the unexpected question.

The old man began to get up from his chair, but his injuries caused him to cry out and plop back into the chair immediately. Daniel jumped up from his chair and reached for his father. "What's wrong?"

Obviously in pain, his face twisted into a pale contortion. Through gritted teeth, he moaned, "I moved too fast." He closed his eyes and held his breath. "Give me a minute, and I'll be okay!"

Daniel was near panic. He could hardly understand the words from that straining, thin, crackly voice. "What can I do? Can I do something to help? Do you need something?" His father made no sound or movement. Daniel bent down closer, alarm in his voice. "Dad?"

The old man opened his eyes and heaved a shaky sigh. "It's okay," he half whispered. Daniel stood up straight. "I think we need to get you to your bed where you can rest. Whadya say?"

"And just how'er you gonna do that? I don't think I can walk right now."

Daniel was aware of some disgust in his father's tone. He didn't know if it was for him or the handicap he was enduring, but dealing with his dad's discomfort in mind, he ignored the sarcasm.

"Now would be a good time for a wheelchair," Daniel said, trying to think of a way to get his father to his bed. Though the old man was frail and lightweight, he was sure trying to carry him wouldn't be a good idea. *The chair! Just leave him in the chair and drag it. A wheelchair with no wheels!* He moved around behind his father.

"I think we can leave you in the chair, tip it back on its back legs, and I can pull you down the hall on the carpet to your room. Whadya think?"

Now, the old man was irate. "You'll break the chair down," he squawked. "Or tear the carpet! Just leave me be!"

Daniel felt fallen upon. He was accustomed to the infirm and negative response to a helping hand. Over the years of employment in the nursing home, of which he was now director, he had developed an emotional immunity to their lack of appreciation. But this was his father. The rejection of a loved one that he had tried to please all his life was hurtful. He stood behind the chair, looking at the top of his father's nearly bald head for a moment. Then he walked toward the living room, saying, "I've gotta go so I can be home by this evening."

He went upstairs and gathered up his overnight belongings. Ten minutes later, without hearing a sound from his father, he was gone from the farm.

After a few moments on the highway and some time to recover from the pain of his father's rejection, he saw Katy's corner up ahead. He then realized he needed to tell Katy the old man was alone. He turned up the road to her house and was soon surprised to see Leanna's car in the driveway. He pulled up and parked behind Leanna's car, got out, climbed the front porch steps, and knocked on the screen door. A moment later, the door came open, and Leanna stood before him.

"Hey, Daniel." She stepped back, and Daniel entered.

"I thought you went back to Colorado," he said.

"No, I came to visit with Katy for a while before I went home. But now it looks like I won't be going home for a while." She peered around him through the doorway of his car. She saw that Sam was not there. "You left Sam home by himself?"

He glanced into her face, looked away, and shook his head. "I had to. There's no talking with that old man. He told me to leave him alone." Then he saw Katy looking at him from the couch. "Hi, Katy! What are you guys doin'?"

"Oh, just cussin' and discussin'. So, you're headed home?"

"Yeah. I've got some new residents coming in tomorrow, and there's lots of paperwork to get done before they arrive." He joined her on the couch. Leanna sat in the big sofa chair across from them.

Daniel directed his attention to her. "What did you mean you won't be going home for a while?"

"Katy needs me to stay with Sam for a while, so I guess you'll have to do without me till I get there. Daniel showed his surprise.

"Really! Are you sure you and Dad living under the same roof is possible?"

"Lordy, I don't want to, but Katy needs to help Lewis with some stuff, and you can operate the nursing home without me being in the office for a little while."

"Sure, that's no problem." He stared at her for a moment; she stared back. "You never know," he said, "something good may come of it."

Leanna frowned. Her doubt made her sound sarcastic. "Like what?"

"You and Dad being together might get some things ironed out."

"Oh sure, it will never happen, Daniel. How is anyone gonna change his mind about me? He believes God set me against him way back when. According to him, it's what I was born for. I *know* that's what he believes! Ever since the day in the hayloft, he's been enduring my existence like an ugly birthmark. I am Sam Danziger's punishment for something he didn't do right for his God!" Katy and Daniel were both silent, taken aback by their sister's revealing of her analysis of her and their father's decayed relationship.

Wearing a sad expression, Katy shook her head. "You don't believe that. Dad loves you dearly! You were always his favorite. And he doesn't think God is some kind of monster or something."

"Oh, *Katy*, you've been out of the Mennonite church too long. You've forgotten how they use the threat of God's wrath to control their members. And you know Sam has always tried to scare Hell out of us and Heaven into us." She didn't get an argument from either one of them. She went on. "But it's more than that in my case. In his brainwashed mind, God gave me away to the devil that day up in the hayloft. He's been praying that God forgive him of his debt and write off what he still owes. Which would be whatever's left of me, his once favorite child."

Katy and everyone she knew had wondered all their lives what terrible thing, if any, had happened in the hayloft. They speculated about what might have caused Andrew to fall to his death and Lena to become a psychotic wreck.

"So, you think Dad sees you as his punishment for some sin he committed, but what about Andrew? If there were a price to pay, you would think that it would be the death of his son that he considered was the price."

Suddenly filled with astonishment, Leanna was void of useful thought. She felt a hot flush burn her face, and her stomach squirmed with nerves. She could hardly breathe, let alone answer Katy's question.

Katy and Daniel both saw how Katy's words affected their sister. She seemed surprised and embarrassed, like someone who had assumed some importance to themselves and then realized their mistake. Katy wondered if Leanna had been a victim of her own misunderstanding all these years. Did she think their dad had been affected by his loss of only her? She thought this would be the time to ask. She turned her face to Leanna, was hesitant, and then asked, "Can I ask you something?"

Leanna felt a strange sense of crushing guilt, and a long-forgotten frantic urge to run and hide came over her. Not waiting for Katy's question, she scrambled to her feet and made for the front door. Katy and Daniel sat stunned and wide-eyed as they watched her jerk the door open and slammed through the screen door. They were bewildered, not knowing if she was stomping off in anger, which she was known to do, or had a sudden relapse into her childhood behavior.

She reached her car and stopped as if she had been instantly frozen. Her eyes were fixed on the glass of the door window, which she did not see, but she saw only what was happening in her mind. She was fully aware of every second and step she had taken to get to where she was, standing beside her car. She was able to ask herself, *what am I running from? There is nothing here to harm me!* She moved her eyes to the house. *They must think I'm off my rocker!*

She returned to the house, imagining what she would say to Katy and Daniel to explain her behavior. She reached the porch steps as Daniel stepped out onto the porch.

"You alright?" he asked with genuine concern. Head down, she climbed the three steps and stood beside him as Katy appeared at the door.

Leanna heaved a shaky sigh. "Yes, I'm okay," she said in a matter-of-fact tone. "I just got beside myself for a minute."

Katy came over next to her and put her hand on her arm. "I'm sorry I upset you," she said.

Leanna shook her head, disgusted. "It wasn't you. I upset myself." Then, giving up on an explanation, she descended the steps, saying, "I'm going back to the house. I'll talk to you later, Katy." She turned to Daniel. "I'll see you in Colorado when I get there," and she went to her car, got in, and backed out of the driveway. They watched her drive away, a cloud of dust whirling behind like a baby tornado scampering to keep up with its mother.

Daniel asked no one in particular, "Wonder what that was all about?"

Katy answered, "I think it just dawned on her that she's not the only one who got hurt in the hayloft."

CHAPTER 51

As she approached the house, she was aware of changes to the place that the last thirty years had made inevitable. The cottonwoods and elms around the house were a little bigger. She would have thought some of them would have to have been cut down by now.

The house was still white and as pristine as she had always known it, its green trim as fresh as a new-cut lawn. The roof, which was once wooden shingles, was now light grey asphalt and looked even better than before. Her eyes fell on the back of the house, which could be seen from the highway, and she realized something was missing. The double row of clotheslines was gone!

She saw in her mind her mother there at the clotheslines, the ever-present black Mennonite scarf tied with a small knot under her chin. The white, frayed, homemade cotton clothespin bag hung from her shoulder, across her chest to her hip. Her arms reached up to the line, pinning the shoulders of Sam's white Sunday shirt.

Her foot came off the gas pedal and pressed the brake, slowing the car as she pulled off the pavement and stopped. She peered at the place where the clotheslines once were. Staring at the picture in her mind, she felt overwhelming regret for the way she had treated her mother. Tears began to fill her eyes, blurring the picture by the clotheslines. How could she, who had needed all the love she could get, be so selfish? She had removed herself from the life of the person who loved her the most, disappearing for years. She had been a weakling against Sam's intimidation. Why had she found avoiding Sam an acceptable trade-off at the cost of her mother's happiness? She was too wrapped up in her own feelings to consider her mother's. *That's why!*

But then, why had she needed to make a choice in the first place? What caused *that* condition? The anger that suddenly attacked her brought a quick hand to her face to roughly smear away the wetness on her cheeks.

Sam! That's what! When the world turns over on me, it's always Sam at the crank! Doing God's work, no doubt!

The barn was also in the picture she viewed from where she sat at the side of the highway. She hadn't been consciously aware of it until it reached out and grabbed her attention. Its east side was stuck flat against the western sky, as threatening as a big red warning sign.

The big red monster, she mocked herself. *It had Sam for a little bit. I should've just left him up there. Let somebody else take the blame for putting him back in the system.*

She listened to what she had just said to herself and frowned as if she had heard someone else say it. She shook her head. *You should be ashamed of yourself, Leanna Danziger,* she scolded. *Mom loved him.* Then, a thought sailed across her mind like a taunting ghost.

Or did she? She began to argue with herself. *She stuck by him, didn't she? Well, yeah, she had to! But love isn't the only tie that binds. Loyalty, stubborn commitment, and even fear or ignorance can hold one to another.*

But then, how could she know? She'd never had a man hold her to him for any reason. She realized that she, in all her life, had never seen her parents hug or touch each other in even the most innocent way.

Lordy, lordy, she exclaimed to herself. *Do the Mennonites even believe in love...? I mean, romantic love? Surely, they do; they have children, so they have...* She couldn't say the word, not even in the privacy of her own mind. She felt the heat of embarrassment rise to her face. There was the memory of how she had felt toward Kyle those years so long ago, and the embarrassment still overwhelmed her. Even now, at the age of fifty-three. She began to shake inside, and as usual, it was difficult to form a thought.

Operating without the benefit of forethought or reasoning, she pulled off the shoulder and out onto the highway. Suddenly, she slammed on the brakes. "Damn, damn, damn," she swore aloud. "What is wrong with me?" She had almost pulled out into possible on-coming traffic without looking. Where was her head? She looked at her shaking hands and felt the sting of tears. Then, she carefully examined the highway behind her. "Well, you can't just sit here stuck halfway out on the highway." The way was clear. She carefully pulled out into her lane and drove the rest of the way home, crying all the way.

She pulled up to the house, turned the car off, and sat there trying to maintain some composure. It didn't come easy. The tears finally quit, and the ache in her throat eased up. She got a hanky from the glove compartment, wiped her cheeks dry, and blew her nose. She continued sitting there, staring at the front of the house, dreading to go in, knowing what awaited her inside.

She couldn't let Sam see that she'd been crying. Showing him any sign of weakness made her cringe inside. He'd like nothing better than to latch on to an opportunity to lecture her on her lost soul. If he thought she was having a problem with anything, that would be all he would need. She heaved a heavy sigh, reached up, and turned the rearview mirror so she could examine her face. She saw red, puffy eyes and a pale complexion without make-up.

Oh well! Nothing I can do about it now.

She climbed out of the car and walked to the house, consoling herself as she walked. *Maybe he's asleep.* She crept into the house.

The living room was vacant, and there was dead silence. She stepped as quietly as possible to the stairs. She knew the squeaks in the loose boards when she climbed them would reveal her attempt to sneak into her room. Then, an aggravating question occurred to her. What good is sneaking into the house going to do her? She stopped at the foot of the stairs. It's not like if she makes it to her room undetected by him, he will no longer exist. She will still have to put up with him sometime sooner or later. She turned back and went to the kitchen, glancing down the hall to his bedroom as she passed the hall's entryway. As she approached the kitchen doorway, the sound of his voice, thin and alarmed, came from in the kitchen, near pleading. "Katy? Is that you?"

She ignored his error in assuming who she was, entered the kitchen, and saw no one at first. Then, to her left, next to the doorway, lying on his back, was Sam. His head was raised, looking over the toes of his black high-top lace-up shoes to see who was there. He saw her and laid his head back on the floor, his face pointed at the ceiling. A chair lay on its side five or six inches from his head. Nothing was said.

There was only enough room between the wall and the table for him and the chair. This made it necessary for Leanna to walk around the table and put the chair back on its legs. She retraced her steps around the table and stood at his feet, hesitant to do what she must.

She felt anger rise in her that flashed a vision of her just leaving him lying there and going home. She didn't know how he had wound up helpless on the floor, but she was sure it was something stupid he had tried to do. He must have been sitting in the chair.

So why didn't he just stay in the chair till somebody was here to help in case he couldn't get up by himself? Now, she would have to get him back into the chair. Not that she couldn't do that; she had gotten plenty of experience dealing with the infirm in the twenty-five years she had worked in Daniel's nursing home. Though she hadn't worked on the floor for the last three years, her position in the administrative office had not diminished her capabilities as a nurse. What made her want to call someone for help was the prospect that she would have to make physical contact with him. She would have to get her forearms under his arms from behind and pull him up, practically hugging him all the while.

As she stood over him, getting up the emotional strength to do what she must, a flash of hellish memory jerked her mind and flushed her face. It was here in this very spot that he had tried to spank her at the age of fourteen.

She, again, felt the cool air on her bare legs and exposed panty-clad behind and jumped back from him, being as alarmed as she had that day. She reacted as she had then and kicked out at him, striking him in the foot. His response was to raise his head, frown at her, then lay his head down again. He was not surprised by that kind of treatment from her. But he did wonder at seeing her standing wide-eyed with her hands over her mouth, staring at him in disbelief.

She spun around and ran from the room, then through the living room and from the house, leaving the far-flung door gawking at her as if in astonishment. She nearly stumbled on the porch steps but caught herself and ran to her car. She scrambled in, slammed the door shut, then sat there behind the wheel, panting. Her wild eyes were fixed on the gawking front door. What had she just done? She couldn't believe it!

What am I doing here? Maybe I should get out of here before I kill the poor guy! She reached for the key in the ignition and got hold of it but stopped there. She couldn't just leave him lying on the floor. She let her hand drop from the key and remained still, her mind rushing about, looking for the thing to do.

Just sit here for a minute and get hold of yourself. Good lord, what did I just do? Kicked my old defenseless father! What kind of person was she? Then, the memory of what she had felt at the moment of her rash behavior rushed in on her. Now, she was on an emotional roller coaster, descending and rising from one feeling to another.

If he'd been standing, I woulda slapped him silly.

"What kind of person is *he?*" she asked aloud. Disgusted again, she let that emotion move her out of the car and stomped back into the house. She entered the kitchen and stood over him at his feet in full defensive mode. He lay there as she had left him moments ago.

C'mon," she said, impatiently, and bent down, reaching toward him. "Give me your hands. We have to get you up on your feet." He didn't respond immediately, and it added to Leanna's irritation. Her tone was stern. "C'mon Sam, the longer you lay there on that hard floor, the more you're gonna hurt." At the sound of her calling him by name, he raised his head and looked at her. A disapproving frown clouded his face. He rested his head again on the floor, tucked his hands into his armpits, and stared at the ceiling. Leanna, reminded of a stubborn little boy, straightened up and looked down at him.

"Good lord, you're acting like a spoiled brat! But if you want to lay there on the kitchen floor like a dead tree, go ahead." She started on her way to the refrigerator. "I've got other things to do besides babysit you." Her watch showed eight-thirty, and she needed breakfast.

She examined the interior of the refrigerator and retrieved eggs and sausage from its stock. She felt satisfied with her response to Sam's behavior. She had never imagined that she would be so bold when she and her father finally got into it. If he should retaliate, that would suit her just fine. In fact, she looked forward to it. She kept him in the background of her attention as she prepared breakfast.

"How do you find being disrespectful to me, okay?" came his thin, shaky voice from behind her as she worked at the cook stove.

Without turning in his direction, she said, "I hardly know you now. Back when I was a child, my respect for you was in the making, and what you did or said as my father formed my opinion of you. I saw and heard nothing but negative reasons to obey, and every one of those reasons was a threat or a warning. You never had one good word for me, or Harley, for that matter. You were an obstacle we had to get around before we could gain any ground toward anything we needed to do to be happy. You were a painful sore that wouldn't heal. No one looks up to a sore. I don't know you any other way. As far as I'm concerned, all I have to go by now is what you showed me then."

She fell silent, flipping the sausage patties. Then she turned toward where he lay behind the table unseen by her and spoke as if it were to the table.

"Now let me ask you, why haven't you ever had any respect for me... or any of your children, not to mention mom?" She turned back to the stove and, after a moment, spoke again. There was quiet disgust in her tone.

"I wonder if you have any respect for anyone or if you even know what respect is."

"My being your father should be enough to get your respect," he retorted

Now, she moved quickly away from the stove to stand at his feet again. Perplexed, her high-pitched voice conveyed her annoyance.

"Are you kidding? Do you think that your children automatically come fitted with respect for you, like a belly button or a nose? You *don't* know what respect is! Respect is learned by the giver and earned by the receiver. It's what happens when you make people feel good about you! It's admiration you get for the way you say and do things in life. It's a result of your actions. It's not stamped into your children's DNA."

Now Sam was as animated as she. His voice came out as pronounced as eighty-two years of wear and tear on vocal cords allowed.

"Well then, what have *you* done to earn *my* respect?"

"Hey, you were here first. I was five years old, and you were my parent, my caretaker. It was your God-given responsibility to show me how to respect you. I never had a chance to learn anything from you! One of the first things you did was tell me, that day in the hayloft, that God was going to kill me. Then you held my head down on the chopping block for Him to chop my head off. I never had a chance to do anything to earn your respect! I was too busy ducking you and hiding from your God, waiting for him to strike me dead! Do you notice any hint of respect, either learned or earned, in there?" There was a moment of silence as she stood over him, fist clenched and jaws setting her teeth in a painful grip.

She became aware of the sound of the sausage sizzling on the stove and went back to looking after breakfast. When she spoke again, it was done calmly and quietly.

"I was in my twenties before I realized you lied to me. God was not going to kill me. He was not that kind of God. You don't tell your child that God is going to kill her just to make her behave. And I still, to this day, fight the childhood habit of reacting to certain natural human feelings with panic. That's why I could never marry and have children. That's why I have a criminal record haunting me every day. That's why I feared sharing my mother's life. All because of *you*. You and your ignorant church believe that all you have to do is show God respect, and then everything will be alright. Well, you are wrong! It's not only God. It's your children too!

Sam lay on the floor, trampled by her accusing rant and crushed by the weight of her words. He was quiet. Her words lit up his mind, shining light into every corner and showing him a way of things he had never seen. His face toward the ceiling, he could only let the silent tears run across his cheekbones into his ears.

After a while, the house was steeped in silence. Leanna set breakfast for both of them on the table and, without a word between the two, wrestled her father into the chair. Having dumped on him some of the things she had wanted to say to him for years, she didn't bother to take any notice of his physical presence any further. Determined to ignore him, she was oblivious to his grief, tears and all.

CHAPTER 52

That was on Monday, which came and went without further incident. Tuesday, he moved about the house on crutches as best he could without her help. His greatest pain was that she avoided him. Now, knowing why made it worse than before.

She busied herself in and out of the house, examining the change in things. Searching for good memories, she lingered on things of her mother's, letting the occasional tears come as they may. She even took some comfort in them. She had been such an awful daughter. At least she had the decency to cry over her mother's death.

The rest of the week was Monday over and over as he hobbled about in the house. She stayed away from him, wandering around the yard. There were occasions when she wished desperately for a telephone. She needed to call Daniel to hear how he was getting along with the office work without her. She also wanted to stay in touch with Julia in case she needed help with something at the apartment they shared. She supposed that she could use Katy's phone, but she didn't know what the long-distance charges would be so she could pay them.

Mostly, the "change in things" around the farm was close to a complete makeover. New locations and arrangements of sheds and buildings had made it necessary to rearrange roads and pathways. And though unfamiliar, the new look was just as pleasant as those pictures that stood vividly in her memory. Excluding the barn, of course.

It stood off to one side of her no matter where she walked like a truant officer, arms folded, waiting patiently for someone to make a mistake. It nagged at her, always over there watching.

Two weeks passed while she waited for the day he would become healed, or Katy would be finished helping Lewis. She wanted to go home.

The days were uneventful except for when she went to town and arranged to have a telephone installed in Sam's house. The following morning, when the Bell Telephone truck pulled up in the yard, Sam was the first to be aware of it. He suggested to Leanna, who was preoccupied with making his bed that she tell the man he was at the wrong house.

"He is at the right house," she said with little expression.

Sam stood at his bedroom doorway, leaning on his cane. Puzzled, he peered at her. "What do you mean," he asked.

She continued to be busy at the bed as if she hadn't heard him. Then, after pounding a pillow, she turned her face to him. In a matter-of-fact tone, she said, "I don't intend to stay here another day without a phone, so just get used to it."

She put the pillow in its place, squeezing past him in the doorway, and left the room. Sam, seething inside, grumbled quietly. Carefully turning on his cane, he went into his bedroom, where he remained the rest of the day. That communication arrangement between the two of them was just fine with Leanna.

After the telephone was installed, she satisfied her sense of responsibility for her job and made her phone calls to Daniel and Julia,

However, *care* for Sam was only an occasional blip in her sense of responsibility. Once, as she waited for the evening and the opportunity to visit Katy's, she wondered if he would come out of his bedroom. That was the total brainpower she spent on him that day.

She had been spending almost every evening at Katy's house. Sometimes, they talked until late in the night, reliving those years in their lives that Leanna had skipped. They learned things about each other as if they were not sisters but recently found friends with much to confess.

So it was that on one of those nights, Leanna, Katy, and Lewis sat lazily talking in Katy's living room. Leanna was prompted to finally explain why she got off the school bus and the strange behavior that Lewis had witnessed. Unable to say the word that would explain her fear of Lewis that day, she stammered her description of what she had thought could happen to her. Lewis, hearing her confession, was flabbergasted. Leanna was beside herself apologizing. Katy was dumbstruck, speechless. The fears of her fourteen-year-old sister must have been monstrous. How had her little sister become a victim of ignorance and so much misunderstanding?

After a moment of uncomfortable silence between the three, Katy quietly asked Leanna, "Did you really think Lewis might rape you?" There was torture in Leanna's eyes, and Katy immediately regretted the question. She backed off.

"I'm sorry, I shouldn't ask that. You don't have to answer."

Leanna's eyes moved to the floor, and she shook her head. "No... no, I want to answer you. I'm a grown woman; there are things I need to get over that embarrass children to talk about, not adults." Then her gaze fell on Lewis. He sat forward in his chair, hands clasped between his knees, looking at the floor.

"Ask Lewis if I acted like I believed it," she said.

Katy's attention turned to her husband. He nodded and said without looking up, "She was scared to death! She screamed and fell down, running away a couple of times." He looked up at Leanna, who was staring at him. "You were definitely in a panic."

"I don't know why Lewis. I only know that just the thought of... s - e - x..." She hesitated, raised her face toward the ceiling, and shook her head violently. "I can't say the word even now!' She sprang to her feet and began to move around the room nervously. Alarmed, Katy and Lewis watched her. It was obvious that she was struggling with something.

"It's ridiculous," she exclaimed in disgust. "I am a mature adult. It's a normal, natural human function designed by our maker to keep the human race going. Yet, the mere mention of it or even the thought of it coming into my head is startling. It's like getting pushed off the Gano Grain Elevator or being tied to the railroad tracks!"

She couldn't stop pacing and began to shake, muttering to herself. "It's as common as sleeping, and I can say *sleeping!* Lifting her face toward the ceiling, flinging her arms up, and shaking her fists, she hollered as if to someone on the roof, "So why can't I say *seeex!*"

At that outburst, she crumbled to the floor on her knees and began to sob pitifully. Lewis stood perplexed, and Katy jumped to Leanna's side. She stood there for a moment, taken by Leanna's sobbing, not knowing what to do. She sank down beside her and put an arm around her shoulders. "Please, Leanna," she said softly. Then, "It's okay, just let it out."

Moments later, Leanna quit crying and got to her feet. "I'm sorry," she said, wiping her eyes. "I didn't mean to make a spectacle of myself. I'm always alone when this happens." Then, on reflection, she added, "But that is the first time I have ever been able to say it."

Katy was astonished. "You mean the word... sex?"

Leanna lowered her face and clapped her hands over her ears. "Yes, that word!"

Katy was taken aback. Lewis, who had been watching in awe, sat back down in his chair, keeping silent, intensely engrossed.

Katy spoke in alarm. "Leanna? Are you alright?"

Leanna remained head-bowed, hands over her ears. "Yes," she panted. "It's just a panic attack. Give me a minute, and I'll be okay." Katy moved back to the couch and sat down, wondering *what in the world could have caused that in her sister.*

A moment later, Leanna dropped her hands away from her ears. She sat up straight and, with a pale face, apologized again, then fell silent, as did Katy and Lewis.

A long moment passed as the silence gave anyone the chance to say what they were thinking.

Katy broke in, speaking to Leanna. "Do you have any idea what caused this to happen to you? I mean, what's so terrible about..." She avoided the word for Leanna's sake. "That word?"

Leanna felt the inevitable, raising its ugly head, getting ready to stand up and expose her shame. Her heart rate quickened, the muscles in her jaw tightened, and she swallowed hard.

"I... I'll tell you." She stammered. It was difficult to make it come out of her mouth. "I'm surprised Sam hasn't ever talked about it!" Then, on second thought, she said, "I guess it's too shameful."

Katy was fully absorbed, mesmerized. She spoke as if in a daze. "I can't imagine what..."

Leanna was suddenly adamant, as though Katy had just started an argument. "Oh, you don't know what kind of a person you *have* for a sister!" Then sarcasm pitched the tone of her voice and chose her words. "Why, ... I started young. By the time I was five years old, I was on God's "MOST WANTED" list and barely escaped the death penalty. At least according to "Sam's Word." She hesitated, then spoke in a quieter voice. "But Andrew didn't escape." She heaved a heavy, shaky sigh. Her manner had turned somber. "Our loving father told his five-year-old daughter that God was going to kill us for what we did..., Andrew and me."

She felt strange saying it out loud like that. Keeping the secret had been a part of her existence. Like the brown spot next to her belly button.

And now that I've told you it's there, everyone will want to see it.

But if that's what it will take to be able to live with it, then that's what she would have to do. She'd show Katy and Lewis what kind of "sweet, little girl" she had really been and what she and Andrew had done.

"And when I saw Andrew lying on the barn floor, I knew God had killed him, and He was going to kill me next. Just like our daddy said He would. That whole night alone in the barn hiding from God, and even ten years later, I had terrible dreams of my daddy holding my head down so God could chop it off." She fell silent, aware of Katy and Lewis like statues sitting in the park, watching the worst accident in history take place.

She raised her face toward the picture window and stared, seeing only the terror of that night. When she returned to the moment, she spoke quietly, her tone stone-cold and bitter.

"Do you know how that feels knowing that the one person you trusted the most was helping the enemy to try and kill you?" She raised a hand, palm forward, and tilted her head. "I know... I know. God doesn't work that way, and he's not the enemy. But remember, I was five years old, and the one I trusted the most taught me otherwise. All I knew was that the sin I committed was so bad that the God of everything had killed my brother for it, and my dear daddy was gonna help Him kill *me* too."

She got that far in the telling of her secret with only a few weak tremors of anxiety that had churned in her stomach. But now, at this point, when it was time to tell on herself, the strong flow of words froze in her throat.

Katy watched her sister go still, which made her begin to think she wasn't going to go on. But that wasn't enough. What did all that she'd told them have to do with why she reacted so badly to the word sex? What else had happened in the hayloft? What was the sin she and Andrew had committed?

Good lord, five years old, and she committed some sexual sin? Or any sin! Not likely.

Her manner became aggressive. "C'mon, Leanna, tell me. What did you do in the hayloft that was so terrible?" Leanna did not respond. "It couldn't have been that bad, and if it was, I can understand how hard it

would be to tell about. It might do you good to get it out of your system."
Leanna only stared. She was aware of panic setting out on its second attack.
She was sure Katy was right and wanted to finally tell the secret that had
been on the tip of her tongue for years, especially to her mother. Her chance
to spit it out was here. She had already come this far; it should be easy to
just say it. But to imagine saying it felt scary, like the child's first step who
couldn't let go of the finger. Then she saw the hope in Katy's face, and she
wanted to tell her every bit as much as she had wanted to tell her mother.
She could think that her mother would hear it, too. A calm comfort came
over her. She closed her eyes and quietly let go.

Almost inaudibly, she said, "Andrew and I were playing a game he
called... naked Indians."

There it is! Her heart thumped rapidly in her heaving chest. So
suddenly! It was hard to breathe. *Heart attack!* Could she be having a heart
attack? *Of course not! It's panic, a panic attack!* She felt sick to her stomach.

The exposure she felt was overwhelming. She scrunched up inside like
a child, hugging herself. She suddenly unfolded from her position on the
couch and hurried to the bathroom.

Katy and Lewis sat stunned into motionless silence as they heard the
bathroom door slam shut. A tight frown on Katy's face was all that was
left of her persistent probing into Leanna's secret. Had she gone too far?
She had seen the shame on Leanna's face. Feeling regretful, she rose, walked
quickly to the bathroom door, and stood listening for any sound behind it.
Then she heard the retching sound of vomiting. *I knew I shoulda kept my
mouth shut!* She waited a moment longer, then knocked on the door.

"Leanna, are you alright?" She heard only silence, which prompted a
pang of alarm. She called out a little louder. "Leanna?"

Inside the bathroom, Leanna sat on the floor in front of the commode,
red-faced from the exertion of throwing up. She waited to make sure there
wasn't anymore. As she heard Katy's voice calling to her, she felt another
upheaval coming to the surface. She rose to her knees, putting her face over
the commode. Nothing happened. She heard Katy call to her again. This
time, she was able to answer.

"I'm okay!" *Just stupid, is all!*

The door popped open, and Katy entered, stopping behind her. "I'm sorry; I didn't mean to upset you."

Leanna raised her face to her sister.

You're sorry? I'm the one who's sorry! I shouldn't have told you.

She didn't want her in there to see her like that. A wicked, sorry heap of crap on the floor in front of the crapper, unable to get herself into the pot where she belonged.

She got up, speaking kindly. "Quit, Katy. You don't need to try to make me feel better." She flushed the commode. "It's not what you think. It has nothing to do with you. I shouldn't have brought it up."

"But I poked my nose in where it didn't belong, and I am so sorry. I hope we can just forget it and ... It won't happen again."

Leanna felt the panic begin to squeeze her insides. She was surprised at Katy's reaction. Now that her sister knew what she had done and how awful it was, she wanted to forget it, pretend it didn't happen.

Oh my God! What have I done? She felt as if she had just slipped at the edge of a very high cliff.

She told one of the people who had always shown her devoted love and support exactly what a demented freak she really was and always had been. She was sure that now Katy knew her sister Leanna wasn't what she always thought she was.

Katy saw Leanna staring at her, an expression of wide-eyed horror changing her face into a stranger. She reached out to reassure her, but Leanna burst from the bathroom, moaning. She ran down the hall and out of the house as if she were running from a monster. Katy was struck numb and stood frozen until it was too late to catch her.

Leanna jammed herself into her car and careened out onto the dirt road that ended the dark, frantic night.

CHAPTER 53

The violent bouncing of the car brought her back to sanity. She had been aware of everything around her during the trip down the gravel road to the highway. The fact that she had approached the stop sign at the highway at fifty miles an hour had been, for her at the time, no reason for concern. What kept her foot pressed on the accelerator was that she was gaining distance between herself and Katy's house. Her mind's total focus was on the regret of her shameful confession. That mistake was back there behind her, chasing her.

The stop sign up ahead was not in her way. It had always been there and would always be there. So, what? She had no objection. What she wanted was to be in a comfortable spot somewhere way up ahead beyond the stop sign. She could hide there in the dark at the end of the headlights. She could be far away from the spot where she had made a fool of herself in front of her beloved sister.

The stop sign whizzed by without arousing one ounce of concern for her safety. The rise in the road at the highway's side bounced the car aloft for an instant and awakened her sense of self-defense. Then, the obtrusive landing in the middle of the highway abruptly re-bounced her into reality. The headlights showed her the weeds in the ditch, then shot their beam into black outer space. The posts in a barbed wire fence became visible at the bottom of the bounce when her foot jerked toward the brake pedal. Her body tensely reared back against the seat in recoil of mighty harm. Her eyes were wide with alarm, and she pushed the steering wheel out in front of her as if to put the car between her and a crash. She heard the screeching of barbed wire scratching metal and the thumping of wooden posts flailing their self-defense against the sides of the car and undercarriage. Momentum carried the car several more yards into the wheat field before it slid sideways to a stop.

She sat in shock, looking wildly at the bright wedge of green that the headlights had created in the total darkness surrounding her. She trembled uncontrollably.

It was not seconds or minutes but quarters of the hour that the car idled in the quiet night, patiently waiting. Bold crickets back at the ditch restarted their concert one at a time.

The slice of the new moon, a little east of straight up, paid no attention to Leanna. Gripping the top of the steering wheel with both hands and laying her head on top of her clenched fists, she wept for a long time.

Finally, Leanna's shaking hand on the ignition key turned the engine off, and the crickets, sensitive to the sudden change, stopped their monotonous chirping to listen suspiciously. The silence in the dark wheat field was final. Only the headlight's beam that stretched across the field's emerald flooring connected her to reality. She imagined that if she turned them off, she would disappear as surely as the green earth before her. Her hand went to the headlight button and pushed it.

The blackness was startling. She peered through the door window into the near-zero vision outside the car. Oddly, she felt some comfort in the emptiness.

The idea of removing herself from it all was very appealing. She could not ignore it. It was not a new idea. It had occurred to her many times, especially upon waking in the morning with only her self-loathing shame to remind her of the drunken night before.

Now, here in this silent, dark, "end-of-the-road," she wondered why suicide was a real consideration in her life's struggle. Why was *she* one of those poor demented souls she would hear about and used to feel sorry for? How had she come to common ground with the insane?

Sam, the father of the century, that's how.

Well, there was nothing that she could do about Sam. Like the oldest shoe cobbler in the village, he had cobbled up his last soul. Now, considering the condition of her soul, all she could do was get rid of the shoe. She exited the car and tried to see where she intended to walk. She reached back into the car and turned the headlights back on.

There was a gentle breeze in the spring atmosphere. She became aware of it and realized the smell of rain was on it. She looked up at the night sky. There were no stars, and that skinny new moon was gone from sight. Clouds, no doubt. She felt sure that a storm would be upon her before she could walk to the house. Her safety didn't matter. She had nothing to save. A good ferocious lightning storm might be the answer to her problem.

She started plodding across the wheat field. The stiff, whiskered heads on the pale green half-ripe wheat stalks slapped and scrapped the legs of her jeans. She walked on the loose, furrowed surface of the field toward the house, which stood a mile south. She felt fortunate that she might not have to be bothered with the solution to her problem. Maybe God would just go ahead and finally do it and quit waiting for the right moment to surprise her. *A healthy bolt of lightning would do the trick.* If it happened in mid-stride, that would be great. She wouldn't know what hit her. It dawned on her that dying was not an experience. *You were, and then you weren't... period.* The thought offered her some comfort.

She had trudged along for about half a mile, struggling with her footing every foot of the way. Huffing and puffing, she raised her flushed face to the dark, flashing sky. Suddenly, a hole in the ground gave her foot nothing to tread against, and she plunged face-first down into the stiff stalks of young wheat. She cried out into the empty dark, flinging her hands out before her. She felt the scratchy wheat stalks on her bare arms and face. She lay there for a moment, afraid to move in case she had broken something. She mentally felt herself all over but had no pain severe enough to suggest anything broken or sprained. Bruised, maybe, but still intact.

Rolling over onto her back, face to face, now with the black heavens, she saw bursts of lightning illuminate mountains of clouds. Then ferocious claps of thunder, in quick succession, shook the earth. It vibrated her body clear to her soul. Silence, then just a wink of lightning, and she was reminded of God being up there, perhaps toying with her. He now had her where He wanted her. She lay like that for a while, feeling sacrificial. She gave little concern for her safety or welfare, consciously doing what she imagined someone in a suicidal state of mind would do. It then occurred to her that she may be acting silly. People who are actually prepared to commit suicide are not in a devil-may-care mood as she seemed to be. But then, even the notion that she was making a mistake and might back out at the last moment made no difference to her whatsoever. Even her earlier hope that God would pop her out of existence like a short circuit socket had lost its punch. She giggled out loud at the words in her thoughts.

Short circuit socket, short circuit socket, say that three times fast.

How could she be so silly at a time like this? Suicide was, after all, a serious matter.

For the ones left behind, maybe. All the shock and embarrassment. The show of sorrow by relatives and the hidden whispering by the neighbors...

That would be their problem. She just didn't care.

The lightning flashed brighter, and the thunder cracked louder this time.

She sat up. Looking south toward the farm, she saw a blinding jagged wire of lightning flash above where she estimated the farm might be. A giant whip-crack of thunder split the thick black air. She got to her feet and continued in that direction, wading through the knee-high growth.

As she carefully made her way in the dark, with only flashes of lightning to show her where to step, her journey was akin to a walk of the blind. God occasionally flashed a light along the way, but she walked in pitch-black darkness between flashes.

Like in a tomb. A preview of her immediate future.

She turned her eyes toward the highway that lay to her left, wishing for the headlights of a passing vehicle. Nothing! There was more to see in her mind than in her surroundings.

Kyle Brunghardt was there as usual. Sometimes, she was amazed at how he remained so fresh in her memory. It had been twenty-five years since she last saw him.

Seems like yesterday.

Nothing of him had escaped her senses then. All these years of having him there over and over in her mind had molded it to her as certainly as her skin. You would think his being with her in memory, almost constantly, would be a pleasure. But who could think with joy about her greatest failure, the loss of her only love? He would always be her only experience in romance, but hardly an experience at all. A hint, maybe. More regret than anything. And it was her own doing in a roundabout way. Sure, Sam made her what she was, but she'd had a choice... or did she? Who knows? Who cares? Who wants to care? Not her, not anymore. Another good reason to fall into the arms of the lightning. She couldn't kill *Sam*. So, getting rid of the other part of the problem, which was herself, was the logical solution.

She stopped long enough to take her eyes off the unpredictable ground before her. In an attempt to see something of the farm, she tried, with her eyes, to pierce the blank darkness. She saw nothing and continued on.

She was getting tired. The muscles that had carried her around for fifty-three years were not as durable as they once were. She was not accustomed to the kind of walking surface on which wheat fields were made. If she were still waiting tables, she would be conditioned and have a better chance against the struggle. But she hadn't walked any significant distance since she went to work for Daniel doing his office work eight years ago.

She hated that it would be hard for Daniel to find a new office manager. And what about Julia? She won't be able to keep the apartment. Her check by itself wouldn't pay the rent. She had sworn off men fifteen years ago when her husband took off with another woman. So, she'll have to find a cheaper place to live.

She is going to be maaad Boy, is she ever Oh well. It wouldn't be the first time she's cussed me out. She mulled over that thought for a few seconds, feeling the emotion toward Julia that had developed between them. They had stayed closely connected for more than thirty-five years. She was sure that she had always been a burden for Julia, being the runaway, then the drunk, and finally now a *suicidal maniac!* Julia had saved her more than once.

But not this time, girlfriend. Only God can save me now! With a glaring eye, perfect aim, and a flick of the wrist, He's gonna blow me outta this hell on earth! Suddenly, she was jerked back into the present state of circumstances. A long air-buffeting rumble of thunder vibrated her insides.

The light from another long, brilliant vertical line of jagged lightning stabbed the ground. It showed her what she thought might be the barn way off in the distance. If she remembered the lay of the land, there was a small gully about fifty yards before you reached the tree line behind the house and the barn. The wheat field ended at that gully, but she couldn't tell how far she was from the gully.

She adjusted the direction of her footsteps to head for the place where she thought she had seen the barn. The flashes of lightning and deafening claps of thunder were getting closer together. The thunder was almost a constant rumble now. It *was* the barn that she saw glaring in the flashing storm.

She was sure she was seeing God's discontent. He had always been discontented with her, and she had always known that He had good reason. Her fall from His grace had started in the barn, up there in the hayloft, playing "naked Indians."

Nasty little girl, nasty little boy! Andrew was the lucky one. He didn't have to go through the torture. God didn't make him grow up to cause his family any trouble. Andrew hadn't caused his mother to mourn for him for the rest of her life. God had made him pay immediately and left *her* here to mess things up. Well, she was about to fix that if He didn't beat her to it. She hoped He would. She couldn't be more exposed to His wrath than she was right now, *stuck in this half-square mile wheat field like a lightning rod on an outhouse.*

Five or six more minutes of trudging along took her closer to where the ending started. That is what her whole life had been: *One long ending.* The barn seemed an appropriate place to get it over with.

The brightest and most violent lightning strike yet split the sky, letting the light of heaven out to turn night into day for a split second. The thunder roared and rumbled on and on.

She stopped at the edge of the shallow gully and raised her face to the violent heavens. If He was going to reach down and strike her dead, right now was a perfect time. Another strike stabbed into the earth somewhere close, she thought. She was sure she felt the fringes of the electrical charge brush against her. She ducked her head and squeezed her eyes shut. She stood like that for several seconds.

A puff of wind came up and tossed her long, grey-streaked, blond hair to one side. Then, a stronger gust pushed on her body, causing her to adjust her footing to catch herself and brace against its shoving persistence. She could have sworn she was being pushed toward the barn.

With her eyes closed, arms straight at her sides, and face straight ahead, she stood as if at attention, waiting. The wind became more and more powerful, pushing and tugging at her. She stood in the black storm, fearing life more than death, waiting for the lightning's embrace, God's wrath. The seconds came and went like passers-by peering at this strange figure standing stupidly on a stormy ledge at the end of the world. Nothing happened. Maybe it was all too obvious. He couldn't surprise her the way He'd rather.

She opened her eyes and bowed her head in disappointment, but she remained standing in the lightning like a sacrificial offering.

Maybe I'm too impatient. Maybe I need to wait and give in to His say-so. He is God, you know. And what are you, Lena Danziger? He can do whatever He wants with you... whenever He wants. Lena... Where had that come from? She couldn't recall when she had last called herself Lena. She guessed her life had come full circle and was back where it started. A good place to end it. The last thing to keep her here, her mother, was as gone as all the other reasons to stay.

The dream of becoming someone had been the first to go. She had thought an education would be the cure for her miserable life. Going to college and getting into journalism was what she had wanted. The possibility of becoming an alcoholic had never entered her mind. But that's what washed her dream down the drain. One day, she was drinking a beer or two, and the next day, she didn't remember the night before or having had a dream of being someone. She remembered the night in the hayloft, though... over and over and over. That was all she'd had to remember in her wine-induced stupors.

But now, after being sober for twenty years, her memory was full to running over with every stupid thing she had done. Sometimes, she remembered so well it made her sick, and she would go for days and nights without sleep or any other form of relief from the regret. But she hadn't gone back to the bottle.

Suddenly, she jerked her face to the flashing, rumbling night sky and yelled as loud as she could. "God, you know I don't! You know I would never do that again!" The dark heavens crackled and rumbled. She bowed her head again and spoke softly. "At least I did that right. You gotta give me that." She fell silent and let the wind push her around until she sank to the ground on her knees. It didn't occur to her that it wasn't God who was *not* going to "give her that." "But then I shouldn't have started drinking in the first place, should I?" she said out loud. "To have to right *that* wrong shoulda never existed. I guess I've never done anything right after all."

She sank lower, her spirit first, then her shoulders until only her tear-streaked face and long, wind-worried hair shown above the young stalks of wheat. All she wanted to do was to wait for God to strike her dead.

Poor Kyle, he never had a chance. I nipped him in the bud but quick. The evening she'd done that was the regret that ground her insides the most. Some nights, even now thirty years later, she filled her lonely bedroom with hours of sobbing and whispering her remorse. And though she did well hiding her grief, Julia knew.

"Oh yeah, Julia knows everything, almost everything." If it wasn't for Julia, she'd have done God a favor and killed herself a long time ago. What she had put Julia through all those years was inhuman. All the rescues from drunken trouble, getting her into rehab, and hauling her around after losing her driver's license. She was one grief after another for Julia. So why did she allow her beloved friend... no, *soul mate*, to suffer for a worthless ingrate such as Lena Danziger? *Because Lena Danziger is a weak, selfish mistake.*

She raised her teary face toward God again. "You made a mistake," she hollered. "C'mon, admit it! I shoulda never been born! Why did you take the good one and leave me here?" She wailed in the wind, covered her weeping face with her hands, and lowered it to her lap. With the ferociousness of the insane, she beat her fists against the wheat field and yelled, "It's my fault Andrew died! You should have chopped my head off when you had the chance. While you had Sam to hold me down!" Her ranting went unheard in the din of God's thunder.

After fifteen or twenty minutes of quietly waiting for the busy lightning to find her on the planet, she reasoned that God was ignoring her. As usual, she would take it on her chin, shrug it off, and do it herself. She should go the same way as Andrew did. It's only fair.

She rose, walked down the slope into the gully, up the other side, and pushed herself against the strong wind. She headed for the barn as the flashing lightning showed her the way.

CHAPTER 54

Sam stood at the window over the kitchen sink, trying to see what he could of the storm. What he saw between flashes of lightning were quick snapshots of whatever lay in the spot in the dark that his eyes happened to be aimed at. The short stretch of visible highway behind the cottonwoods was caught in a flash. The John Deere combine parked in the clearing beside the barn was caught in another. The barn itself loomed, at moments, against instant bright night skies again and again.

Earlier, he had wandered around the house, hobbling on crutches from room to room and window to window. He tried to get a sense of the strength and character of the storm, and he decided it was the worst lightning storm he had seen yet.

He had been concerned about Lena being away from the house, not knowing where she had gone. From all his years living in Southwestern Kansas, he knew the deadly danger in one of these lightning storms. During the past hour, he had managed to make himself sick with worry for Lena. The telephone had rung on two separate occasions. Since no one else knew about the phone but Katy, he knew it was her. He hadn't answered it. For all his years, he had managed pretty well without the devil's instrument. He was not about to start lowering himself to Satan's methods now.

He knew Lena might have gone to Katy's. The phone calls were probably Katy, telling him not to worry about Lena. But he could not bring himself to pick it up and say hello. Relief from his worry may have been only a hello away, but too close to the fire pits of hell to take the chance.

Two quick flashes of lightning lit up the entire farm, followed by an immediate double blast of window-rattling thunder. The time between the flashes and the blasts of thunder was nearly nonexistent. The strike was very close. The storm flashed and clapped again; in that flash, he thought he had seen movement along the side of the barn! Surely not!

He focused his old bleary eyes on the spot in the dark where the barn had shown up when the lightning flashed. He could see absolutely nothing. He lifted his hands off the support of the crutches, placed them on the countertop, and leaned in closer toward the windowpane. As if in compliance with his efforts, three more quick flashes gave him plenty of light to see Lena enter the barn. The following claps of thunder were as one long solid explosion. He stood transfixed, astonished by what he had seen.

Why in the world was she wandering around in such a storm? She had come from behind the barn, of all places. What was she doing behind the barn at a time like this? Why didn't she come to the house? Why was she in the barn, a place she had to be forced to go? It didn't make sense. With the trouble he'd been having with his eyes, he was beginning to wonder if it was Lena or anybody at all that he had seen.

He focused on the bright snapshots of the barn's walk-in door, hoping to see her come out. At that moment, the phone rang again.

The inside of the barn was like being submerged in a can of black paint. Leanna stood inside the door, unable to move. Smothered by her anxiety, she gasped for breath. She pushed her face forward and, with straining eyes, tried to pierce the blank darkness in front of her.

It had been only weeks since the last time she'd been in the barn, but she had paid attention to only the loft. She knew where the ladder up to the loft was. She turned her head in that direction, in a way that a blind person would, and examined the floor. There may have been something lying there to stumble over, but the darkness prevented her from seeing even a hint of anything in her way.

She took a few cautious steps and then waited for a flash of lightning to show her the way. Surprisingly, none came. She slowly slid a foot forward along the concrete floor and brought her other foot to it. She continued this slow, cautious method of negotiating the invisible floor toward the general area of the ladder.

She stopped at about where she thought the ladder should be and reached out a hand to sweep it from side to side through the air. There was nothing there. Unknown to her, her hand had come within inches of bumping the ladder. Her feet rested just a step from a small amount of debris that Lewis had swept from the loft's floor when he had repaired the damaged roof. Part of that wood trash in her path was a small piece of shingle with a nail protruding point up.

She slid her foot forward, followed by the step of the other foot. When it came down on the point of the nail, it punctured the sole of her shoe and drove deep into the ball of her foot... dead center. She cried out and bent down, pitching forward into the unseen ladder. She struck her forehead and, falling unconscious, struck the side of her head again. This time against the concrete floor. She lay at the foot of the ladder on the hard, dusty floor, as lifeless as Andrew had that day long ago, in exactly the same place.

Sam stood leaning on his crutches, staring down at the nagging phone. Could he use it for just a moment and still avoid the devil's evil reach for his soul? Just long enough to ask Katy to come to the house? Surely, he could! God would surely help him! He reached for it, and it rang again. He held his hand until it quit, then carefully picked it up and slowly raised it to his ear. Listening intently to the silence, he held it for a moment.

"Hello, Katy?" he finally said.

Katy's loud, excited voice came over the phone. "Dad? Is that you?" Before he got his answer out, a blinding flash and simultaneous deafening crack compacted the atmosphere. It rattled the house, causing Sam to duck and squeeze his eyes shut. Then the lights went out.

Wow, that was close!

He quickly set the phone back in its cradle and leaned into his crutches, motionless. *What have I done? I knew I shouldn't have.* He stared at the phone in fear. *God has spoken!* He spun around and moved to the other side of the room, shaking his head.

He needed to get to the barn, to Lena. He was sure there was something wrong. He couldn't imagine why she was in the barn, not the house. Where had she come from?

He pivoted on one foot and, in slow, short hops through the dark house, got to the front door window. He peered out into the black yard but could not see the driveway. He would have to wait for a flash of lightning.

As he waited, he realized the wind had quit. Finally, a burst of light showed him that Lena's car was not there.

How in the world...? She walked! That's why he had seen her come from behind the barn. *Something happened to her car, and she walked across the wheat field!*

He went back into the kitchen to the window above the sink.

As he approached the window, he noticed a hint of weird light playing on the windowpane. It was a reflection of light coming through from outside. It was dim and moving, like somebody walking with a flashlight.

He reached the kitchen sink and peered out the window toward the barn. What he saw struck him full-on. Like a bolt of lightning, He sucked in his breath and stared hard. His first impulse was to wait a moment for his old eyes to quit tricking him, but it was no trick. The reality was plain to see. The barn was on fire. Small, visible flames with an orange glow showed through the cracks and loose joints by the back peak of the roof. A straggling flash of lightning snapped a picture of a column of silvery smoke boiling into the night sky.

He yelled at the window, "Lena, get out of there!" Then, turning on his crutches, he hopped for the door, yelling again, "Lena!"

The lights came back on at that moment, and the kitchen table was suddenly partway in his path. But the light had not shown it to him in time. The left foot of his crutch hooked a table leg. Off balance, he lurched forward and to his right, which smacked him into a chair. Both hands grabbed for the chair to catch himself, letting the crutches clatter to the floor. About to fall, he clung to the chair and brought himself upright to stand, shaking and holding on. Breathing heavily, he stared at the crutches on the floor, wondering how to reach them to pick them up. He turned to look behind him at the window above the sink. The glow from the flames in the barn was brighter and more active. The fire was growing fast. He clung to the chair, panic-stricken, utterly helpless.

"Oh God! Oh God help me," he cried! "Leee-naaa," he wailed as he let go of the chair and fell to the floor on his knees.

The pain in his injured hip brought a gasp and nausea. He doubled over, pressing his hands to his mouth. A few seconds passed, and when he raised his face, it glistened pale with sweat. He located one of the crutches, reached for it, stretched, and got hold of it. The other crutch was too far away, so he used the one in his hand as a hook and pulled it to him. He had both crutches now and sat momentarily to figure out how to get back up on them.

The pain was there in his hip, but it held second place in his consciousness. He was consumed with only one thought. Lena was in the burning barn and, for some reason, had not come out. Maybe she had already been overcome by the smoke. He needed to get out there!

He jerked the crutches up one at a time with shaky, hurried hands. He leaned them against the table's edge, then got hold of the chair, pulled it closer, and used it for support. He began to pull himself up onto his feet. The pain made him cry out and halted him for a second. The possibility that it might prevent him made him try even harder. He finally was able to cock his good leg and plant that foot flat on the floor. His hands were on the top edge of the chair back, and he pulled himself with all his strength, but it would not be *that* easy. He pulled the chair over backward on top of himself. He again was lying on the floor on his side, this time excruciating pain contorting his face into a pale, hideous mask.

He began to struggle to rise again, ignoring the pain and nausea. He pushed the chair off himself and struggled to stand it on its legs.

He regained the position he'd been in with one foot and one knee on the floor. This time, he used the chair's seat to support his struggle to stand, and this time, the chair stood solid. He quickly reached for the crutches, got them into his armpits, giving nothing to the dreadful pain, and vaulted himself to the door and out.

The sight of the barn in its entirety, with flames dancing on the roof, was horrifying. Almost the entire back half of the roof was engulfed in flame. It hurled dense clouds of silver smoke skyward and spit sparks of cindered pine into the night like daredevil fireflies. However, only small puffs of smoke came from the cracks and seams in the front of the building.

As he sent himself along by the high output of adrenalin, he carelessly stabbed the crutches into the rough barnyard ground. He imagined Lena inside, lying unconscious and inhaling gulps of smoke into her lungs. Had she gone to the hayloft just to prove something to herself and had fallen trying to get down?

Not again! Dear God, not again!

He was sure the tremendous crack of thunder that had occurred earlier was a lightning strike. Had she gone up into the loft and was struck too? Staring wide-eyed at the terrible scene, he could only think the worst. Only one purpose drove him recklessly toward the walk-in door. It made him disregard the dimly lit path he was on. Though it was as familiar as the cover of his bible, he lost his crippled footing and fell once again. This time, face first into the barnyard dirt. He lay stunned for a moment, then rolled to his back but remained lying there. He summoned the strength to rise. He could feel the heat of the burning barn, and its menace pulled him up to a sitting position.

The door stood only a few yards from him, the smoke streaming steadily from the crack around it. His crutches were barely seen in the dancing light of the fire. He could reach them, but how could he get them into his armpits and stand up? He *could* just *crawl* the rest of the way. He didn't hesitate to try it.

When he shifted his posture to hands and knees, the weight on the leg in recovery sent a searing electric shock of pain through his thigh to his groin. It took his breath and sent a thin cry from his tightly stretched lips. On hands and knees, his head hung like a whipped dog. He waited for the pain to come to a manageable level. Then, he began to crawl to the walk-in door. He could only drag the bad leg along with him and balance gingerly against it. He slowly made his way, though desperately hurrying every inch.

When he finally reached the door, he found that he could not reach the latch from his hands and knees. He would need to raise his upper body up and straighten it to its full length from his knees. He pushed the door open. The pain in his hip was even worse than he had guessed.

The smoke puffed out through the door in a large cloud, choking him and making his eyes sting. He stood on his knees coughing, peering into the dim, fire-lit, smoky room. His watery eyes searched the floor below where he thought the ladder should be. There she was, lying on her side, her back to him.

"Lena," he yelled, his high-pitched, quivering voice, thin with eighty-two years of wear and tear, not making much sound. "Lena," he yelled again, trying to be louder. He then dropped his hands to the floor and began crawling toward her. Frantic, he pushed and pulled himself across the rough concrete floor, giving no thought to how he would get her out of the burning barn.

He finally reached her and put a hand on her shoulder. Shaking her, he called her name.

"Lena... Lena, we gotta get out of here!"

There was no response. He pulled on her shoulder and turned her upper body toward him, enough to see her face. Her eyes were closed, and there was blood from a two-inch gash on her forehead, but she was breathing. Now, the question of how he would get her out jolted him and churned in his stomach. The helplessness he felt was overwhelming.

Suddenly, there was a loud crash above. The building shook all around him, and red glowing cinders fell from above through the cracks in the loft floor. The part of the roof that had first caught fire had collapsed into the loft. It would be only a matter of minutes until the ceiling, which was the loft's floor, would come down on top of them. Now, the smoke in a great dense cloud boiled down from the hole through which the ladder protruded into the loft.

The absence of a large portion of the roof and the door being open caused a draft. It sucked the smoke that had been sailing into the night sky down into the lower interior. It consumed Sam like Jona's whale.

Suddenly, he was being smothered. Black, thick smoke was pulled into his lungs with each breath. His eyes stung, and his chest began to burn as if he were on fire inside. He began to cough, and he coughed to the end of his breath only to inhale great gulps of more smoke.

Holding his breath, he grabbed one of her arms at the elbow and began to back toward the door on his knees. He backed up as far as he could without letting go of her, then pulled her to him on the rough concrete floor. He repeated this maneuver, stopping to cover his mouth and nose long enough to take a new breath.

The pain in his hip was excruciating. His bony knees scraped against the rough concrete floor, scratching the old thin skin. His eyes were running with tears, as much from crying as from the smoke. Each time he pulled Lena across the hard rough floor, he knew he was probably tearing the tender skin on her back and butt. He agonized over it, but there was no other way. He had to get her out!

After four or five minutes of tugging with all his strength and going through lung-wrenching bouts of coughing, he managed to drag Lena to the door. The smoke was not as heavy there, and after stopping to take a new gulp of air, polluted though it was, he sat there staring at Lena. He looked for a sign of her breathing, but he couldn't tell, under the shroud of smoke, whether her chest was active with life or not. It caused him even more alarm and gave him excess to some unknown strength to pull even harder.

He finally pulled Lena through the door and out into the night air. He continued to drag her away from the smoke pouring out through the door. After a couple of minutes and gaining a few more yards of distance from the fire and into fresher air, he stopped. He sat on his knees, coughing mercilessly, gagging, and swooning with dizziness. He was completely useless to help Lena, but he could see her chest heaving with breath. He studied the bloody gash on her forehead, and he supposed she had a concussion. She needed to be taken to the hospital. He needed help desperately. He turned his face to the driveway where the pickup was parked. He needed to get to it, get Lena inside it, and drive to Katy's.

Then, out of nowhere, he remembered the telephone in the house. He began to crawl toward the house but suddenly stopped. He remembered how God had previously taken the use of the phone from him. *He could not* use the phone.

The dizziness immediately worsened. The coughing was still there and taking control of his breathing. He stopped crawling as the ceaseless hacking took his strength, and he began to crumble. The night darkness became a void, and he fell into it with his face against the barnyard.

CHAPTER 55

Half an hour after Leanna had bolted from Katy's house, Katy called the new number at her father's house every ten minutes. There was no answer and knowing that her father would have nothing to do with the phone, she guessed Leanna had not gone home.

The storm had appeared out of nowhere, and when it escalated, she became concerned about Leanna being out in it. She was surprised when her father answered the phone and greatly disappointed when it disconnected before she could tell her father to have Leanna call her when she got home. The electricity had gone off, and she called again when it came back on. No answer. She was back to square one.

She began to think about getting into the pickup and going to the house. Maybe her father knew where Leanna was. After a few more minutes watching the storm, through the windows, it became worse. She and Lewis decided to go to the house to see if Leanna was there. They braved the ferocious wind and lightning and ran for their pickup.

As they drove toward the highway, they saw car lights ahead that seemed to be beyond the stop sign.

Katy pointed at the strange scene. "Well, would you look at that! It looks like someone is out in Dad's wheat!"

"Sure does!" Lewis was astonished. "What do you suppose is going on?" They approached the stop sign staring at the headlight beam skimming out across the top of the carpet of wheat.

Katy gasped, "That's Leanna's car, isn't it?"

Lewis stopped the pickup at the stop sign and stared at the white Chevy Malibu, its passenger door stuck out like the one good wing of a plane crash.

"Looks like her car," he said.

He drove across the highway down into the ditch, then turned south and parked. They both got out and trotted anxiously through the torn-down barbwire fence and through the wheat to Leanna's car. The ding, ding, ding of the door alarm sounded strange there, mixed in with the wind rustling the wheat stalks in the dark country.

They peered inside, expecting to find Leanna frightened and shaken up or even worse. She was not there. Her being somewhere out in the dark storm on foot, perhaps injured, increased their anxiety.

Lewis called out into the black wind and thunder as loud as he could. "Leanna! Leanna, where are you?" They listened intently, spearing their sense of hearing deep into the darkness, trying to pierce the noisy storm. There was no human sound. Katy shouted her name, but it went nowhere against the wind and was made mute by the cracking thunder, even to Lewis who was standing beside her. They began to walk around the car, looking out through the depths of the wheat. They eventually widened the search perimeter to forty-five or fifty yards around the car.

Finally, Katy suggested they drive to the house; if she wasn't there, they would come back to search the field all the way to the house if needed. Looking toward the farm as she spoke, Lewis drew her gaze in that direction. There was a dim glow toward the south about where the farm might be.

"What *is* that?" she asked.

Lewis started toward the pickup. "I don't know," he said. "But the lightning's been striking toward the ground, and that could be a fire at your dad's place. Let's go!" Alarmed, they jumped in the pickup and were speeding down the highway on their way to the farm within seconds.

Leanna was aware of her body feeling like it was on fire! Her back and shoulders seemed to pulsate with searing pain like glowing hundred-watt light bulbs. What was wrong? She moved herself to rise, but she was much too heavy. Then she tried just her head. The pain in her head made her moan, and she laid it back down carefully.

She looked up into the night sky and searched her frenzied mind for some memory of why she was there and what she was doing. Then she noticed the space around her was aglow. She tried to raise her head again to look past her feet to see where the light was coming from. This time, she managed it and was shocked at what she saw. The barn was on fire. She held her head up and stared despite the pain. Then it all popped into the vision of her memory like a flash bulb, and what it showed her made her gasp.

Now, she found the strength to rise up on her elbows. She gazed at the fire, seeing herself in there, trying to find the ladder. She shuddered! She could have been one with the ladder in there right now... roasting.

Then, a mind-blowing question fell on her. How in the world had she wound up out there in the yard? She struggled to rise into a sitting position. Her back and shoulders were still on fire, and now her butt also as it became the sole support of her weight. Sitting up, she looked around her, turning her aching head in search of someone who must be there with her.

When she first saw the unfamiliar mound lying on the path to the house, her eyes skimmed over it. Then, wondering, she returned her attention to it and focused on it at the dim edge of the firelight. As her persistent eyes examined it to find some resemblance to something, she wondered where her father was. *In the barn!* She turned back to the fire. *No, surely not!* She had been in there by herself. She looked hard at the something lying in the path. *That must be him! He must have been trying to get to the house.*

She turned onto one hip, got her hands on the ground, and gained a position on her hands and knees. She was vaguely aware of a pain in her right foot. She raised her left foot and planted it on the ground under her, steadied herself with both hands on her bent knee, and rose. When she caught her balance by planting her right foot, the pain took her breath away. She looked down and saw she was standing on a piece of something. It stuck out from under her shoe. She lifted her foot off it, but it came with her shoe. It was stuck to her.

She carefully sat back down and examined her shoe. A piece of shingle was stuck to the sole. She looked over at the form lying on the path. It remained the same. She got her thumb under the edge of the shingle and pushed at it. "Oooh," she cried out. The pain brought tears to her eyes. She realized that the shingle was nailed to the sole of her foot.

She sat still for a moment, gritting her teeth against the pain, waiting for it to subside. She considered what she could do to remove the nail. She decided the puncture wouldn't bleed with the nail removed, so she could just jerk it out. She got hold of the piece of shingle, gritted her teeth, and gave it a sudden jerk. It came out easier than she had thought, and the pain wasn't any worse than before. She sat still for a moment, eyes closed, and again, waited for relief.

When the wound felt better, she placed her attention again on the heap in the pathway. It had not changed. If it was her father, she thought he must be passed out. She again went through the pain it took to get to her feet and limped toward the form lying in the path.

As she drew near, she could see that it was indeed her father lying motionless on his side. She got to him as quickly as her injury allowed and went to her knees beside him. Her alarm heightened when she could not tell if he was breathing in the darkness. Her anxiety was in her voice and in the hand that shook him by the shoulder. She fairly shouted.

"Dad? Dad, can you hear me?" There was no response. She tugged on him to turn him on his back. He was limp. She felt for a pulse at his throat. *THERE IS NONE!* "Oh, God no," she cried! She became frantic and searched more carefully for a pulse. *Is that it...? Maybe...! I don't know!* She bent down, putting her ear close to his mouth. As she straightened up, she yelled at him. "Daddy, don't you do it," and began CPR on him.

To her amazement, he responded very quickly. His sudden burst of coughing caught her by surprise, and she was astonished at her success. She had feared only a few seconds ago that he was beyond death's door. She took his arm and lifted his upper body to help him turn to one side so the coughing was easier. The coughing subsided, and he lay back down on the ground.

"How do you feel," she asked. "Do you hurt anywhere?" He tried to say his throat was sore and his chest ached. After repeating it a couple of times, Leanna finally understood.

"Did you go into the barn and breathe a lot of that smoke?" He nodded, then had another spell of coughing.

He pulled me out! How did he do that? He could barely hobble along, let alone drag me all that way! She gazed back where she'd been when she regained consciousness. It was quite a way from the fire, even for a healthy man. Could she say that his recovery was miraculous?

He quit coughing and struggled to sit up. He saw that Lena had turned her attention to the burning barn, now fully consumed by the flames.

He was drawn to the spectacle as well, and they watched. However, his mind was filled with how he had felt when he came to. Why had he been overwhelmed with a feeling of warmth toward Lena, the feeling that everything was very good between them? He looked at her as she stared at the fire. He wanted her to turn her face to him so he could see if she looked at him in a different way than she used to.

Though her eyes were on the fire, Leanna's mind was also preoccupied with the events surrounding her father's recovery from his unconscious state. She was aware that she had called him Daddy. Maybe his sudden burst of coughing that came immediately after she had inadvertently called him Daddy was just a coincidence.

She remembered something Daniel had once said. He said, "Among all the great acts of God, one of the greatest is coincidence." At the time, it was one of those things Daniel said now and then, and you took it for what it was worth. Now, it made her wonder. Had Sam, in his unconsciousness, heard her call him Daddy? She had been near panic when the word came. She had barely been aware of it herself, there in the background of her stricken mind.

Now, in the calm of the storms passing and the gentle crackling of fire, the May night felt normal again. Her reluctance to call "Sam the man" Dad, or even worse, Daddy, returned. Her regret that she had called him Daddy rose in her and burned there, reminding her of her vow to never forgive him.

The distant remembered words from Daniel made her feel something. Hope... for some reason. What better antidote for suicide than hope, even a reluctant subconscious glimmer?

The pain in his hip and groin was still tormenting him, of course, and Leanna had a killer headache. But there they were and had been for the past few minutes, out of reach of the monster barn. They calmly watched it burn to the ground, sitting side by side like buddies at a wiener roast. She mused that the monster was quickly going to hell, screeching and moaning with each cave-in. It warmed her heart.

She turned her face from the fire and studied her father. He would need to be taken to the hospital. She needed to be examined for a concussion. Her head was killing her. She needed to call an ambulance for her father.

Considering how bad she felt, the telephone in the house seemed like it might as well be a mile away. For the moment, she was putting off that trip. She was sure suicide would not have been nearly as painful.

Sam spoke without taking his eyes off the fire. "Why didn't you come to the house instead of the barn?"

Leanna was silent for a moment, carefully constructing her answer. The truth was unspeakable.

"Maybe it's a good thing I didn't. If Ida came to the house, *it* would be on fire now."

Sam gave her a scornful look. "What do you mean? Are you saying the lightning was *after you*?" He paused, then added, "I hope you know how ridiculous that sounds."

"Is it?" Though her remark was not serious, she felt angry at his response. She wanted to push him back away from her, like a kid on the playground looking to start an argument.

"You mean as ridiculous as what you said to me in the hayloft that day?"

She surprised herself. She hadn't intended to jump on him like that. It just came out of her like a cuss word popping up at a stressful moment during a day of aggravation. But why not? The scary barn was going to hell, and her suicide was on the back burner; she was on a roll. Now would be a good time to come out of hiding and tell him what she thought.

His expression was one of startled curiosity. He assumed that she was referring to the accident. He had no idea what he had said to her that would cause her to be upset with him this many years later. He didn't answer her immediately, and their silence was uncomfortable. He could see that she was angry.

"I don't remember what I...

"Oh, c'mon," she broke in. "Don't try to make me believe you don't remember!"

That offended him. "And just what are you accusing me of? Do you think I'm lying? I *said* I don't remember!"

"How could you possibly forget something you did that ruined your child's life," she ranted.

Her words were like a slap in the face. The first assault in the war that she would launch. But knowing that she was about to reveal what she had held against him for forty-eight years was worth the pain.

Joining the fray, he retaliated. "What did I do to you, Lena, that you can't forget? Our God tells us to forgive so we can be forgiven."

"Forgive! Sure, that would make it easy for you, wouldn't it? I forgive, and you're home free with a pat on the back from your God... and what did I get? A life so screwed up I'm going around hiding from Him so that he won't kill me, then finally begging Him to kill me! You want *me* to forgive? What are you gonna do to make up for what *you* did?"

She saw his blank expression. It was a look you would see on the face of a foreigner who didn't understand English. "Or do you have to run to the church to ask what to do? Can they tell you how to erase the years of fear you caused me?"

He was perplexed. "What are you talking about? What did I do to you in the hayloft? I only tried to discipline two of my children as a father should. But I didn't even get the chance to do that, so how did I hurt you? God took it out of my hands and did what *He* thought was necessary."

She clamored to her feet, too mad to acknowledge the sickening pain in her head and the dizziness.

Standing before him, she looked down on him sitting in the barnyard dirt and dried-out cow manure, looking up at her. She towered over him, the anger squeezing her face into an ugly mask of hate. In the dancing dim light of the burning barn, she saw a shriveled-up old man. His sunken cheeks bore the grey hew of the smothering smoke.

Her first impulse was to kick him like debris blocking her way. She raged instead. "So now you're gonna blame it on God! Why, you holier-than-thou ignorant old Mennonite! You really do believe what you told me in the hayloft! You talk about *me* sounding ridiculous!"

Now, he was enraged. The way she talked to him made his insides curl. He wanted to slap her like a spoiled brat. "What did I say to you, Lena?" he yelled in a puny voice.

She yelled back. "You said you didn't have to kill me and Andrew because God was going to! I was five... years... old, in total submission to my hero, my father. You were second only to God. I believed every word you spoke as fanatically as you believe your God. When Andrew fell dead on the barn floor, I knew God had killed him just like you said He would. I knew that you were going to let God kill me, too."

She fell silent, panting from the effort of her outburst. She bent down toward him and, in a half-whisper, continued with bitter calm.

"Do you know what that did to the little five-year-old girl who worshiped her father? The father who turned out to be the man who was going to help God kill her. It destroyed her. What was left of her spent the night alone in the barn in a nightmare where you held me down, waiting for God to chop my head off. Do you know how scared I was to come out of the barn the next morning? Right out in plain sight where all God had to do is reach down and strike me dead?"

Her voice soaked into the night and left total silence but for the fire. The barn crackled and popped behind her, uttering its last sound as it slowly evaporated into thin air.

Sam came alive first, quietly. "I don't remember ever saying that... to you or anyone in my life." Leanna did not respond. He went on. "Why would I say such a thing?"

"Because you didn't know any better," she said with bitterness in her tone. "The church has kept you tucked away, out of touch with the rest of the world for so long you're ignorant. All you know is that fear is a damned good way to control your children. So, instead of leading them to heaven with encouragement, you try to push them away from hell with fear. It's been your way of discipline for so many generations that it's second nature. You never give it a thought; it's just automatic."

"Well, that's the way I was raised. *I* didn't run away from home, and I don't cuss. I've never yelled at my parents with disrespect, and I've never been drunk or thrown in jail. Can you say the same for yourself?"

She felt like her breath had been knocked out of her. She suddenly became intensely aware of her throbbing head. The pain in her foot went clear to her knee. She gasped for air as she sank to her knees and sat on her legs, her hands clasped together in her lap.

She stared at Sam, catching her breath, letting her spirit absorb the blow her father had just landed. It wasn't easy. She had always been the one to proclaim her dishonor. She thought it and said it. It coming from her own mouth was no more threatening than the thought. Hearing it from another person, especially her father, was devastating. The words constructed by another mind gave it substance, a life of sorts, and it was ugly.

So here she was, exactly what she had always claimed to be. It was terrible. Again, she was sure dying was her best option. She turned her face toward the burning barn behind her and imagined the inferno engulfing her. She shivered.

After a minute or so, she heaved a shaky sigh and spoke. "No, I can't say that for myself, but I can say that growing up was hell for me! I spent hours hiding from you and God. I was afraid every minute that I would be struck by lightning. Or a tornado would grab me and tear my arms and head off. I hoped that God would forget about me if I didn't make any more noise than I had to." She hesitated momentarily, then added sarcastically, "That's how *I* was raised. Can you say the same for yourself?"

He was indignant. Her attitude toward him disgusted him. "And you're blaming me for not raising you right. I didn't raise you, period. You wouldn't listen to me or even come near me."

"Well, now you know why!" she retorted. "Any attention from you could have been the moment that God told you to catch me and hold me down a minute."

Sam stared at her in disbelief. Sad dismay wrinkled his brow. He shook his head. "Why Lena... why? I am your father! How could I hurt you? You say I said a terrible thing to you in the hayloft, but what made me say that to you? Why was I scolding you? Do you remember *that?*"

She felt the heat of embarrassment on her face, and her heartbeat quickened. The shame she felt was overwhelming. Panic began to swell in her, and she wanted to run. She jumped to her feet, feeling the pain, and whirled around toward the fire. It was going out. There were more black ashes and smoke than flames now; soon, the monster would be gone. She stood looking at the burned-out remains, thinking maybe she should have gone with it. Sam's voice behind her brought her thinking back to reality.

"Do you, Lena? Do you remember what you and Andrew were doing in the loft when I scolded you with those words?"

Remember it? It's been killing me for years!

It had been a stone around her neck all her life. Sometimes, she thought she might have been born with it. It's what she was. It's why God punished her and had her marked for hell. Suddenly, she felt an old, almost forgotten tremor in her body. It made her gasp in surprise. As she inhaled the smoky night, it was not the smell of smoke that filled her senses. The dusty hay in her nose tickling her throat began to wrestle her from reality.

No! No! She would not be dragged into the hayloft! *Not this time!* She cried out, grabbing with her voice some thread of connection to hold her to reality.

She reached out and grabbed Sam's shirt sleeve, twisting it in her tight fist. She screamed at him. "We were just playing a game! I knew we weren't supposed to be doing it, but I didn't know it was a deadly sin! Andrew said *you* were going to kill us, but I knew you wouldn't really. He was just saying that, but then you said *God* was going to kill us. *GOD...* not just anybody! You knew God. He always talked with you, told you things, ordered you to do this, and ordered you to do that. You helped Him all the time. Then He killed Andrew, and when you grabbed me, I knew you were going to help Him kill *me*!"

Sam was horrified! Lena's screaming in his face, ranting, spit flying, with tears on her cheeks, shook Sam Danziger to his soul. When she began to beat his chest and shoulders with her fists, he had not the presence of mind to defend himself.

Punctuating each word with a beat of both fists against his chest, she screamed, WHY - DID - YOU - DO - THAT!" A wailing sob burst from her mouth. "We were playing a game!" She raised her fists and struck him again, once. Sam didn't even flinch. "Andrew said it was naked Indians, a game; we didn't know it was a death penalty!" Her sobs were as intense as her flying fists. Then she quit beating on him and fell to her knees. Wadded up into a shaking heap, she bowed her face into her hands and wept. The sound blotted out the distant thunder as it mumbled its lingering departure into the eastern night.

CHAPTER 56

Sam was stunned. To believe that only a thoughtless few words of discipline spoken fifty years ago would cause an adult woman to beat up her father was ridiculous. That wasn't all there was to it. Something else was behind all this, Sam was sure. He was also sure he had been right to investigate the disturbance in the loft that day. He had stopped them from doing... who knows what. Or had he? Has God, through Lena's shame, been punishing her all these years for doing what he had been too late to prevent? He watched her crying, wanting to put his arm around her shoulders and say something to console her. Instead, he waited for her to get hold of herself. After a minute or so, she grew quiet and still.

Suddenly, the ground in front and around them was flooded with light, flashing out the dimming firelight. Behind them, the sound of a rushing engine came up and slid to a stop. Katy was out of the pickup at the exact moment it came to a stop, hitting the ground running and yelling with alarm.

"Dad?" She saw him sitting, his butt on the ground, his legs straight out in front of him. Then she saw Leanna raise her head and face her.

"Leanna? Are you guys alright?" Reaching her father first, she dropped to her knees beside him. "Dad?" He turned his soot-smeared face to her. "I'm okay," he said, then barked a fit of coughing.

Leanna was getting to her feet, pulling Katy's attention from her father.

"Leanna, are you okay?" she asked, franticly.

Leanna said nothing as she turned and started limping toward the pile of burned lumber. Behind the mask of soot, her expression was dark and brooding.

Katy was puzzled. "Leanna, where are you going?"

Not answering, she continued forward. Her injured foot barely cleared the ground with each painful step. Katy watched, expecting an answer at any moment, but realized that she wouldn't get one.

She called out to her again. "Leanna?" Nothing: as if she was deaf. She turned to her father. A questioning expression clouded her face. He only returned her look. She turned back to Leanna's departing figure. *She's just walking away*. It upset Katy. *What is wrong with that woman?* She quickly caught up with Leanna and stopped her by taking her arm.

"Hey, I asked you where you're going. Did you not hear me?" Leanna's face was expressionless, her answer flat.

"I heard you." Her demeanor surprised Katy, leaving her with nothing to respond to. Then Leanna frowned and looked at her almost pleadingly.

"Please, Katy, let me go. Your father needs help, I don't. He inhaled a lot of smoke, enough to make him pass out. You need to take him to a hospital and have him checked out." Katy caught the "your father" in reference to *their* father, and it caused her to frown more. What was going on?

"Well, what about *your* father, Leanna? Does he not need help?"

Leanna pulled her arm away and continued to limp toward the dying fire, murmuring under her breath: "I don't have a father." Katy heard the bitter remark. She quickly came up beside Leanna again and walked beside her.

"Stop talking like that," she scolded. "You weren't hatched. Of course, you have a father, and he... Leanna interrupted her, speaking with disgust.

"You're right, I wasn't hatched. I was salvaged out of broken little girl spare parts twisted together with baling wire, then thrown in the junk box so *your* half-assed father wouldn't have to mess with it. That's where I've been all my life. In the junk box, and everybody wonders why I act like junk! You get treated like junk long enough, and you're gonna be junk!"

Katy was exasperated. "Who treats you like junk? Where in the world did you get an idea like that?"

Leanna stopped dead in her tracks, showing astonishment. "Are you kidding me? Don't you remember our childhood? Why did you get married at sixteen? Why did Harley go away and stay away? How come Daniel, a man of God and a born preacher, isn't preaching? Who made me a runaway rather than a college graduate? Who stopped us all in our tracks because he was afraid his kids would cause him to lose favor with his God? We all shamed him in the eyes of God. He needed proof that he was worthy of God's grace and his children were gonna be it. Never mind *our* relationship with *our* God. Never mind *our* happiness as long as he was sure of his good standing with God... or was it the church?" She fell silent. Her breath came in short, agitated huffs. She stared at Katy. Katy, overwhelmed by the deluge of words, stood silent as well.

Leanna spoke again, still in a rage but a little more gently. "You damn right I don't have a father. I've had an uncertain little man, made afraid of God by a church just as scared as he is. A father protects his children from their fears and lack of understanding about the mysteries of heaven and hell. I never had one of those, and neither have you." She looked back at Sam, sitting on the ground, closely watching them. She wasn't sure if he was able to hear what was being said or not. She didn't care.

"So, you can call him father if you want to. I can't!" She started limping away again.

"Where are you going," Katy demanded again.

"To get my car," she answered without looking back.

Katy had not moved and had to raise her voice to span the growing distance between them.

"That's ridiculous, you know! You left the lights on; the battery's gotta be dead by now."

Leanna stopped and turned to Katy. She stood there for a moment, undecided about what to do.

"Lewis can get it in the morning," Katy called to her. She hesitated, then started back toward Katy, and Katy waited for her. But instead of moving to Katy, Leanna aimed herself for the house. As she limped along, she looked over her shoulder back at the smoldering remains of the barn to take one last satisfied look at the destruction of the object of her childhood fears. Katy came up beside her and walked with her for a few steps.

"Yes, I remember our childhood," she said, "but that's what it was. It's gone, Leanna. It doesn't exist anymore. So why are you still living in it? Why do you still react to situations in your adult life the same way you did back then as a child?" Leanna's limping stride slowed considerably at Katy's words as if she had suddenly lost her concentration, distracted by a new thought. She sank deeper into thoughtful silence.

Katy took it for stubbornness. "Okay," she said, "I'll *tell* you why. It's just a dumb habit. You spent your whole childhood basing your every decision on that moment when your father threatened you with God's wrath. You never got past that way of doing things. Even after you realized, as an adult, that what he said couldn't be true, you kept reacting to it the same way you did that day in the loft. It became a habit. Well, the threat is gone, Leanna. You don't have to pay attention to it anymore. Did it ever occur to you that those words Dad said to you did not change a thing? If he hadn't said them, the reason Andrew fell down the ladder would still be there. The fact that you were forgotten in the excitement and left in the barn by yourself all night would have still happened. The difference the words *did* make happened in *you*. And the only reason it happened in you was that you misunderstood with your child's mind."

Leanna stopped and stared at her sister. First, she was amazed at how much sense that made. She became pleased with the revelation. But the old habit was stubborn. As always, she was hesitant about the accuracy of what her sister said.

She spoke accusingly. "Are you saying that my miserable life is my fault?"

Katy quickly shook her head and took Leanna's hand. "No, no," she said gently. "I'm saying there has never been a reason to have a miserable life, Leanna.

Leanna took her hand away from Katy and stared at her in disbelief.

"Think about it," said Katy. "What happened in the hayloft? A couple of little kids were caught doing something their father disapproved of. While one of them tried to run from the punishment he knew he was gonna get, he fell from a ladder and was killed. It was a tragic accident, Leanna. Nothing more."

Leanna was perplexed. "Of course, *that* was an accident, but that isn't what caused my miserable life!" "Then what did?" Katy asks.

The words hung between them as if even the night around them couldn't believe what it had just heard. Leanna stared at Katy, who was wide-eyed and silent. The expression on Leanna's face seized Katy's total attention. She had always thought that her sister's problem was that she blamed herself or her father for Andrew's death. Now, she thought maybe not, and Leanna appeared as surprised as she was. Had she just had a startling realization about herself?

Leanna's mind was in a frenzy, wondering this, denying that, grasping at explanations. Katy's words about there never being a reason for her miserable life began to display themselves as a noisy parade marching through her mind. Was it true; was the suffering in her life a misunderstanding? If what she had just realized moments ago was true, then... She felt the blood drain from her face and a sick feeling tumbling in her stomach.

Katy saw Leanna's hands go to her face and her mouth open to gasp for air. As she watched, mesmerized, Leanna spun around to run to the house, stepped down on her forgotten nail-punctured foot, and, with a cry, fell to the ground. She lay on her side and began to cry. Katy went to her quickly and knelt beside her.

There was alarm in her voice. "Leanna! Are you alright? Did you hurt yourself more?" Leanna moaned and let her crying fill the night stillness. Katy, beside herself, didn't know what to do. "Leanna, talk to me," she pleaded. "Can you stand up?" There was still no answer from Leanna. She was unable to talk coherently over her crying. Katy turned and let her worried gaze fall on Lewis and her father, who were twenty or twenty-five yards away. With one arm around Sam's shoulders in a supportive position, Lewis was staring back at her. Sam looked like he was leaning sideways against Lewis. "Lewis, is Dad alright?"

"No," he yelled back. "I think he's about to pass out on us."

"Oh lord," Katy moaned. "Leanna, tell me now if you are hurt and need help because I've got to get Dad to the emergency room!"

Through her tears, Leanna finally managed to say she was all right. Katy whirled on her knees, rose to her feet, and moved quickly to her father. Leanna, in the meantime, became concerned for her father as well but, upon standing, quickly realized that, in her condition, she could not be of any help. She tried to hobble to them while she watched Katy and Lewis put Sam in the pickup but could not reach them before they drove away toward Garland. As she watched the roaring pickup bounce urgently down the driveway and leap out onto the highway, she relived, for a moment, the abandonment that had seized her young heart alone in the loft that terrible day. But she was no longer that little girl, and the old woman the years had made of her understood.

Leanna gazed at the smoldering remains of the barn. There was very little left that resembled a structure of any kind. The concrete slab that had been the barn's floor could be seen in its entirety. It lay like a huge, flat, cluttered tabletop in the place it had always occupied but now free of walls and doorways. By their locations, she recognized certain charred objects now crumbled to ashes or partial remains of things that had been useful only two hours ago. They stood as worthless junk in the clouds of lingering smoke. She could only make a wild guess as to where the ladder from the disintegrated loft had set on the floor. Only things made of metal that were objects of a barn remained whole. It made her imagine iron and stainless-steel memories that could withstand anything.

She felt very old. It seemed so long ago that the elements of human behavior had shaped her existence, making her what she was. She was a sad old woman, addicted to regret and non-responsive to hope. She felt like a pair of old shoes needing polishing but with a sole too worn to waste the polish.

Favoring her injured foot, she hobbled closer to the ruins. She approached a large, jagged hunk of concrete that had lain outside the barn for years. She sat on it and cried. Bowing at the feet of the dead monster, she mourned the absence of her life, a life that was never born. She wondered if reclaiming her given name would make a difference. Would Lena have done things differently?

The emergency room didn't keep Sam long. The doctor put him in a room on the second floor, gave him medication to help clear his lungs, and put him on oxygen. He was there all that day and the following night.

Leanna finally got into the house that morning and treated her foot to prevent infection. Her headache hung on all that day, but by the time Sam was released, she rose without it, and despite a nearly sleepless night, she felt physically better. Emotionally, not so much.

She had spent the day arguing with herself, insisting that she had been an abused child and, as an adult, had suffered the results of her abuse. Though try as she might, in all honesty, she could not argue a case that could hold her totally unaccountable.

By noon, she was devastated. The possibility that Katy was right, that most of her life was a misunderstanding, had viciously stabbed into her gut over and over. There were tears... more than tears, there was agony. Moments of wailing face down on her bed and beating her fists into the bedding alarmed the stillness of the whole house. Suicide? It nagged at her, argued its point of view, and assured her of a total cure. Had it not churned in the pit of her to the point of giving her dry heaves and the shakes, she might have given more consideration to its promise.

Evening came upon the house, putting a hush on echoing cries of despair and the clang of steel cusswords. She had become silent an hour ago. The walls embraced the rooms in which she had ranted. They now remained still as if afraid they might stir up another tantrum.

Then, as the house faded into the darkness of the evening, she, as Leanna, became obscure and made a resolution to push her "other self," Lena, forward into a new dawn. She suspected there were not enough years left for her to do that. Even so, if just one day was the total of her experience as an ordinary woman, she could count herself a winner. It is not always at the finish line that the race is won, she happily told herself.

Friday, just an hour after supper, Katy and Lewis arrived with Sam; he was wheelchair-bound but alert and amiable. When Leanna saw him, she wondered if he would be as pleased about her reclaiming the name he had given her as she thought he would. She was sure he had never thought of her with any other name but Lena. She decided telling him would not be necessary.

As she took control of the wheelchair, she saw a frail, helpless old man, not the tyrant her childhood had fashioned out of fear and misunderstanding. She had anticipated his return from the hospital with fear that he would dwell on her assault on him. She half expected to be plunged back into hours of more weeping. She was greatly relieved when he smiled at her pale greeting.

After realizing he harbored no hostility toward her, she felt protective of him and was pleasantly surprised by her feelings. The pleasure she felt was proof that she was a good person after all, the Lena she had abandoned. It made her qualified to look after his well-being. To Katy's and Lewis's surprise, Lena, still Leanna to them, met her father with timid respect, almost doting on him. "Would wonders never cease?" Sam felt good, but not because he would recover without side effects. He was pleased that Lena had chosen to stay and take care of him until he was back on his feet.

The next day was spent dealing with the results of the dreadful night the barn burned down. Lewis and Katy jump-started Lena's car and brought it to the house, where Lewis hooked the battery to a charger to restore its power. He then returned to the torn-down fence to repair it.

Meanwhile, Lena had called Daniel to tell him about the barn and their father's resulting stay at the hospital. Daniel was shocked, and his voice expressed his alarm.

"Is he gonna be alright? What did the doctor say?"

"He is okay. There are no lasting effects. He has to stay in bed for the time being, though."

"How long will he have to stay off his feet?"

"A few days."

"Do you think you should stay with him for a while yet?"

"Yes, I was going to tell you to plan on me being gone from the office for a week or so longer. Will you be able to handle that?"

"Sure! Julia is doing a great job! Everything is going as smoothly as if you were here. I'm glad she's here... to fill in for you."

"Yeah, I knew she would be good at it. So, I'll see you when I get there, okay?"

"Take your time. We have it under control, Leanna."

"Okay. Oh, by the way," she added, the name is Lena." She hung up. She stood looking at the phone for a moment, examining her thoughts. It sounded like Daniel really didn't need her there. If Julia could be talked into taking her place permanently, she might do well by moving back to the farm.

Epilogue

Lena was fifty-three years old when she reclaimed her given name, put her childhood back in the past where it belonged, and started over. Of course, everyone should be so lucky to start life with fifty-three years of maturity in their starter kit. But then, considering the tempest in which she had gained her maturity, she wasn't as lucky as it might seem. She had more bad habits to forget than good ones to keep.

Her decision to return to the farm and take care of her father in his final years was met with approval on all fronts. Julia was more than happy to take Lena's place beside Daniel at the Home. Julia was also happy for Lena, as she had finally found peace with her father. In Julia's view, Lena, the girl she had discovered many years ago, tended to run off and hide and had come out of hiding for the last time. Lena had returned, and Leanna was gone. She was looking forward to getting to know Lena. She was sure she would love her even more than the sister Leanna had become...if possible.

Katy's prayers had been answered. All except one. It was that her mother would have been there to see Lena finally at home and on good terms with her father. Everything would have been perfect if she had lived just a few weeks longer. It was heartbreaking that her mother had to die to bring Lena home. The irony was obscene.

Monday morning, Lena rose early. A crew of Mennonite members and Lewis would be there to start cleaning up the barn's charred remains. They would bring trucks and a front-end loader to load the rubble and haul it off. She knew her father would want to be out there to watch, and she would be there to push him around in his wheelchair. She also wanted to be there to revel in the closing of the lid on her cremated monster.

She had to finish breakfast before the crew arrived. She dressed in her blue jeans and one of her dad's work shirts that had been hanging in his closet for years. It was a little large but fit well enough for the occasion. She went downstairs and down the hallway to her dad's bedroom and knocked loudly on the door.

"Dad, are you awake yet? I'm starting breakfast." She walked away toward the kitchen without waiting for an answer. She knew that he was probably awake. He had become able to dress himself the day before. When she entered the kitchen, she was surprised to see him sitting in a chair by the table, his cane lying across his lap.

"Oh! There you are! I see you're up and at it this morning. How are you feeling?"

He peered at her as if wondering what she had said, then spoke quietly. "Pretty good," he said. Nothing more was said while she fixed bacon and eggs for breakfast. They ate quietly.

Lena washed up the dishes, and soon, they were out at the piles of burnt black lumber and charred objects that had been "the barn" for seventy years or more. The crew hadn't gotten there yet, and father and daughter moved about, making slight comments about this object or that damage. They looked at the destroyed barn differently, Sam with his loss and Lena with her gain.

Suddenly, Lena saw something straight and slender sticking up out of a portion of the barn's roof that lay lopsided on the ground.

The blackened object protruded from the roof's peak, spearing the air like the useless blade of a dropped weapon in battle. It was the lightning rod still bolted in its place, holding its position with inept, obnoxious bravery. Lena pointed to it and exclaimed, "Look, Dad, the lightning rod is still there!" Surprised, he looked where she was pointing but didn't see it, "Where? I don't see it." She pushed the wheelchair around some charred debris and got in closer. His old eyes finally caught sight of it, and he stared momentarily, then said, "It didn't work!" Lena thought she heard a triumphant tone in his crackly, old voice.

"No, it sure didn't," she said, then added, "I'm surprised to see it there in place. I thought Lewis took it down when he was working on the roof.

"I thought so, too."

"But it was there during the storm," she said, "and lightning struck anyway." They turned to each other with questioning looks on their faces.

"So," Sam said quietly, "the All-mighty lightning rod is worthless after all." They were silent, each in their own thoughts, quietly applying explanations to the surprising revelation. Sam couldn't find any that fit. Lena was struck with awe at the implication.

"You can't say it's totally worthless," she offered.

Sam was skeptical and prone to stand by his assessment. "You can't say it's worth anything either. There's no way of knowing if it has saved anything from the lightning. But... " he added, gesturing toward the burned-down barn with a wide sweep of his arm, "Here is proof that it *didn't* save something." Lena agreed, and the strange irony brought goosebumps to her arms. Did the lightning rod have anything to do with anything? Sticking its puny defense in God's face, daring Him to perform His will over all of creation? Lena doubted that God even noticed it while He was busy saving her from herself.

About the Author

Richard Koehn was born in the small farming community of Cimarron, Kansas, and raised with five younger siblings. Despite the church's excommunication of his father (at the age of twelve), the author was shaped by the influence of the Mennonites.

The Characters' deep-rooted attitudes and activities in this fictitious story directly result from Richard Koehn's unique perspective on life. His observations of the world around him as he grew into adulthood and his eventual departure from the Mennonite church contributed to his intriguing and diverse experiences.

He is a former Nashville songwriter with three songs published, recorded, and released. He wrote for the Dodge City Daily Globe, and at 73, this was his first attempt at his life-long desire to write a novel.

Made in United States
Troutdale, OR
02/12/2025